Sonya had changed quite a bit after her most recent resurrection in Colmo.

Every time the Lady brought her back, she was a little more beast, a little less human, both inside and out.

"In all likelihood," said Sebastian, "it's some poor recluse who's as frightened of us as we are of them."

"I'm not frightened," objected Sonya.

"Wary, then," amended Sebastian. "Regardless, we're not enemies, so we should be able to pass by peacefully with no harm done on either side."

"I suppose," said Sonya.

She should have known better. She should have remembered that Sebastian possessed the survival instincts of a week-old puppy, and that in the wilderness, one did not need to be an enemy to become prey.

By Jon Skovron

THE GODDESS WAR

The Ranger of Marzanna

The Queen of Izmoroz

The Wizard of Eventide

THE EMPIRE OF STORMS

Hope and Red

Bane and Shadow

Blood and Tempest

THE
WIZARD
OF
EVENTIDE

JON SKOVRON

THE GODDESS WAR: BOOK THREE

orbitbooks.net

Copyright © 2022 by Jon Skovron
Excerpt from *The Bladed Faith* copyright © 2022 by David Dalglish
Excerpt from *Engines of Empire* copyright © 2022 by R. S. Ford

Cover design by Lisa Marie Pompilio
Cover illustration by Magali Villeneuve
Cover copyright © 2022 by Hachette Book Group, Inc.
Map by Tim Paul
Author photograph by Ryan Benyi

Orbit
Hachette Book Group
1290 Avenue of the Americas
New York, NY 10104
orbitbooks.net

First Edition: July 2022
Simultaneously published in Great Britain by Orbit

Orbit is an imprint of Hachette Book Group.
The Orbit name and logo are trademarks of Little, Brown Book Group Limited.

The publisher is not responsible for websites (or their content) that are not owned by the publisher.

The Hachette Speakers Bureau provides a wide range of authors for speaking events. To find out more, go to www.hachettespeakersbureau.com or call (866) 376-6591.

Library of Congress Cataloging-in-Publication Data
Names: Skovron, Jon, author.
Title: The wizard of Eventide / Jon Skovron.
Description: First edition. | New York, NY : Orbit, 2022. | Series: The Goddess War ; book 3
Identifiers: LCCN 2021053108 | ISBN 9780316454681 (trade paperback) |
    ISBN 9780316454667 (ebook) | ISBN 9780316454698
Subjects: CYAC: Fantasy. | Goddesses—Fiction. | War—Fiction. |
    Brothers and sisters—Fiction. | Magic—Fiction. | LCGFT: Novels. | Fantasy fiction.
Classification: LCC PZ7.S628393 Wi 2022 | DDC [Fic]—dc23
LC record available at https://lccn.loc.gov/2021053108

ISBNs: 9780316454681 (trade paperback), 9780316454667 (ebook)

Printed in the United States of America

LSC-C

Printing 1, 2022

In memory of Cheryl Benyi: adventurer, warrior, and mother.

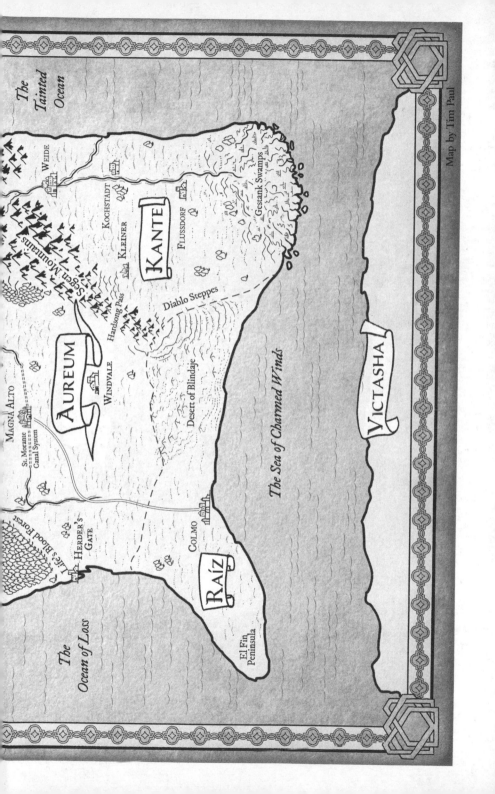

PROLOGUE

It was said that Lady Marzanna, Goddess of Winter, Change, and Death, was heedless of suffering. But this was not so. Marzanna knew suffering intimately. After all, suffering chased after death like a loyal puppy, and it was often both prologue and epilogue to change. Every action she took was in some way rooted in suffering, and she was always aware of that fact.

It *was* true, however, that Marzanna did not consider suffering something to avoid. Rather, she viewed it as the surest way to forge the tools that she required. If it at times seemed she delighted in the suffering of her servants, her pleasure came not from their pain, but from the anticipation of what they would become after.

Some might suggest that this did not necessarily discount sadism as a character trait, but she was not troubled by such paltry concerns.

The Eventide was an empty space in the truest sense. There was nothing there. Not even the laws that governed existence. So *anything* might be there. Perhaps a tower so vast it could look out over all the world at once. And it was from this tower that Marzanna cast her gaze upon her mother's creation.

Ah, there were those funny little islanders with their life-twisters and swordmasters. Someday they might do great things, though not anytime soon. And directly above them was the vast and varied landmass of those who looked ever outward, seeking mysteries elsewhere that they had squelched within themselves so long ago they no longer remembered ever having them.

But those places were not Marzanna's present concern. Instead, she looked to the other side of the world. To the land of Rangers and travelers, of death and iron. A place that held its breath, tense and straining with the swell of impending convulsive change. It was like the surface of a bubble, at once delicate and surprisingly resilient. If the wind blew a bubble, it merely bobbed away, still intact. To pop it required more focused pressure, either internal or external.

Marzanna's gaunt hand stretched out above this bubble. Her sharp bone finger hovered over the glistening surface of the world. It would be so easy to burst...

But no. Not this time. This time was special. This time, change would consume all, without exception. And to make certain of that, it had to come from within.

All she could do, then, was wait and trust that the suffering she had wrought would bear fruit.

Part One

What Lies Beneath
Every Thing

"There have always been tales of twin deities who meddle in the affairs of mortals: one who forever seeks change, the other who refutes it. I, for one, have never believed in such nonsense."

—General Matteo Fontanelli,
Memoirs of a Humble Servant to the Empire, Vol. 5

I

Sonya Turgenev Portinari thought she'd understood summer. But she'd been wrong.

Summer in Izmoroz was a gentle kiss—an all too brief period of golden sunlight and soft breezes. The ferocity of spring had settled down and the sharp brittle fingers of fall did not yet grip the land. Game was plentiful, crops flourished, and people seemed a little more at ease. The days felt blessed, and the nights cozy and sweet. That was summer in her homeland, and she had never considered that it might be quite different elsewhere.

But in the Blindaje Desert, which stretched across the easternmost part of Raíz, summer was as hard and mean as any Izmorozian winter. The sun penetrated everything with unrelenting brutality. The air was similar to the inside of an oven, so that Sonya's lungs felt like they were baking with every breath she drew. Yet she didn't sweat. Or rather, she did, but it evaporated the moment it appeared on her skin. Everything felt dry. Desiccated. Like the long-dead flesh of a sluagh gorta.

The evenings offered relief from the heat, but brought such a sudden surprising cold that some nights Sonya had to don her fur-lined Ranger coat. More than anything, it was this violent shift between these two climates that made the environment such a trial.

Sonya had always thought the Great Western Tundra of Izmoroz to be both the harshest and the most beautiful place in the world. But now she wondered if this desert might claim that title. After all, there was a beauty to it as well. The clear blue sky somehow seemed more vast than it did up north, and every sunset was a work of art to rival the greatest Viajero painters. But along with that beauty came an austere severity that brooked no weakness. How could life persist in such an inhospitable land?

Yet it most certainly did. Lizards and snakes lay in the shade of the scraggly acacia trees and shrubs that dotted the dusty landscape. Buzzards occasionally flew overhead, perhaps hoping Sonya and her brother would succumb to the heat. And sometimes she could hear the scrabble of small mammals beneath the ground.

Life was tenacious, and it persisted no matter the challenge. This, Sonya knew, was what kept the balance between Lady Marzanna and her sister, Lady Zivena. Implacable death and intractable life. Mikhail had taught her that the balance was necessary. Otherwise, Mokosh, the Damp Mother Earth, would wipe it all away.

As Sonya guided Peppercorn across the craggy landscape, she wondered how much of that legend was true. How much *any of it* was true. After all, Mikhail had told her she must always treat the Lady Marzanna with reverence. He'd warned that any hint of disrespect would be met by instant punishment. Yet the last time Sonya and the goddess had spoken, after she'd been stabbed to death by Rykov, Sonya had been downright belligerent, and Lady Marzanna hadn't even seemed to notice. Was it possible that the Rangers didn't understand the Lady as well as they thought they did? Perhaps they had gotten much of their religion wrong, and the Lady was simply too preoccupied with other things to correct them. If that was the case, then everything must be reevaluated. Including herself.

Will I still be me? Sonya had asked just before the Lady brought her back from the dead in Colmo.

The Lady had answered with a question of her own: *What is "me," I wonder?*

At the time it had felt like mockery. But now Sonya asked herself if the goddess had been trying to teach her something. To reveal some deep truth of the world...

Or maybe this desert sun was starting to addle her brains.

The surrounding air rippled with heat, and at times she was certain she could feel her skin actually cooking. She'd inherited her mother's fair Izmorozian skin, and much of it was now an angry, painful red. Her brother, damn his luck, had inherited their father's olive complexion, which had turned a rich, appealing bronze.

She glanced over at him now, still amazed at how much her little brother had changed during these last few months. Once they'd left Colmo, he'd removed his imperial officer uniform and dressed in the light airy fabrics favored by Raízians. Though his blond hair was shot through with gray, and the creases in his face were deeper than those of a man twice his age, he actually looked healthier and happier than Sonya had ever seen him. Well, perhaps not happy. He smiled and laughed more, but there was also a haunted look behind his eyes that would occasionally manifest into anguished guilt. He carried his burdens openly, with an unapologetic earnestness that perhaps only he could muster.

She was surprised to find that she was actually impressed with the spoiled brat. At least a little.

Then Sonya's pointed ears picked up the faint trill of a flute. Her golden fox eyes swept the area, but all she saw was more scrub brush and rocks wavering in the heat.

Wavering perhaps a bit too much.

Sonya was no stranger to the illusions that could be cast by Viajero music, and Jorge had warned her that there might be Viajero hermits living out here in the desert. Potentially hostile ones.

And then she caught it. A flash of the distinct scent of sweat-evaporated skin. It was better hidden than Lucia's illusion back in Colmo, which meant this Viajero was potentially more powerful. Or at least more clever. But it still wasn't enough to hide completely from Sonya's enhanced senses.

She kept Peppercorn on his slow trod, but her lip curled up over her fangs. "We're not alone."

"Oh?" Sebastian squinted as he looked around. His eyesight had gotten so bad, Sonya doubted he could see anything farther than thirty feet away with any clarity. "What should we do?"

"Nothing yet," said Sonya. "It could be they're just hiding themselves because they want to be left alone."

"And if not?"

"Then they're trying to ambush us. But that's already failed. So either way, we have the upper hand."

"Unless there's a third possibility," said Sebastian.

"What third possibility?" she demanded.

He shrugged. "How would I know? But nobody can think of every eventuality. Not even you, Yasha."

She sniffed. "Yeah, well, for now, we should hold off on attacking."

"Who said anything about attacking?"

"Nobody," she said quickly.

Sonya had changed quite a bit after her most recent resurrection in Colmo. Every time the Lady brought her back, she was a little more beast, a little less human, both inside and out. This time, her long black hair had changed to fluffy white fur. She didn't mind that so much. But she'd revived amid the blood and carnage wrought by the imperial attack on the city, and the sights and smells had nearly driven her into a bestial frenzy. While those heightened feral instincts had calmed considerably once they'd gotten away from the chaos of the city, they hadn't left completely. Instead they had settled into a constant low buzz in the back of her mind that eagerly looked out for any opportunity to hunt. And she could not deny that the feeling was at times rather pleasurable.

"In all likelihood," said Sebastian, "it's some poor recluse who's as frightened of us as we are of them."

"I'm not frightened," objected Sonya.

"Wary, then," amended Sebastian. "Regardless, we're not enemies, so we should be able to pass by peacefully with no harm done on either side."

"I suppose," said Sonya.

She should have known better. She should have remembered that Sebastian possessed the survival instincts of a week-old puppy, and that in the wilderness, one did not need to be an enemy to become prey.

2

Jorge Elhuyar liked to believe that nothing was truly unfixable—
that every problem had a solution. But when he looked out at the
sheer scope of devastation wrought on his beloved Colmo by the
recent imperial attack, he struggled to hold on to that belief.

He stood on the observation platform that had been constructed on
the roof of the Anxeles Escuros guild headquarters with his brother,
Hugo; his sister, Maria; her semi-secret lover, the Viajero Lucia
Velazquez; and the guild chief, Javier Arzak. They all gazed silently at
the city's uneven skyline under the midday sun. It should have been
a hazy summer paradise, resplendent with brightly colored buildings
and gleaming tile roofs. But instead, a large section of it was charred
and broken, as though it had been smashed by a great flaming fist.

"It has a certain beauty," murmured Lucia as she leaned against the
ramparts.

Jorge looked sharply at her. "I beg your pardon."

"Yes, I'm inclined to agree with my brother," chimed in Hugo.
"All I see is a travesty."

Lucia gave her habitual cavalier shrug, which always felt somehow
judgmental to Jorge. As though other people's concerns were foolish
or trivial.

"A Viajero sees beauty in everything," she told them, her eyes still
fixed on the rubble below. "Even terrible things."

"When I was young, I remember feeling something similar on the battlefield," Javier said in his deep, rusty voice. The old mercenary was resting on a stool after their steep climb to the platform, his bad leg propped up. "For some there is a . . . *thrill* in witnessing chaos."

"But you don't feel that anymore?" asked Maria, who stood beside Lucia at the ramparts.

Javier looked at her with his heavy-lidded eyes. "A person grows weary of such things, until finally there is no thrill to be found at all on the battlefield."

"Yet you fought anyway," pointed out Jorge.

A tired smile broke out on the guild master's bearded face. "Battle may no longer excite me, but the potential for real and lasting change? That gets even my sluggish old blood pumping."

Hugo's expression grew tense. "I suppose . . . it is easy for one to forget that change is even possible."

"For those who live comfortably, yes," Lucia said, still not bothering to look back at them. "For the rest of us, it is all that keeps us going."

"Now see here," objected Hugo, taking a step toward Lucia. "If you're just going to—"

"Stop it, you two," chided Maria as she stepped between them. "Lucia, don't bait people. Hugo, don't fuss over minor disagreements. We must all work together if we are to move forward."

"Move forward?" asked Hugo. "Toward what exactly?"

"Toward what?" Lucia turned and squared herself up to Hugo, her pointed chin thrust out pugnaciously as though already anticipating a fight. "Building a free and independent Raíz, of course."

Hugo seemed dumbfounded. "Building an independent . . . *Are you kidding me?*" He gestured to the broken skyline. "Let's take a step back and first ask how we're going to repair what we already *have* without imperial funds or supplies. No, let's take a step *further* back and ask how we'll stop the empire when they inevitably return with an even larger force than before. After losing Izmoroz, they surely can't afford to lose us, too."

"We will beat them back just like we did last time," declared Lucia.

"We beat back nothing," said Hugo. "According to my brother, they would have *decimated* us if they hadn't been forced to call off the battle and return to Magna Alto."

Lucia turned on Jorge, her expression offended. "Is *that* what you think?"

"W-well, I mean…" Jorge held up his hands placatingly as he backed up to where Javier sat. "It's just that I had a good vantage of the entire battle and it did seem to me that once they brought the siege engines to bear, they had us at a serious disadvantage."

"We would have rallied," snapped Lucia.

Jorge doubted that but kept silent. Why was he so intimidated by her? Sure, she was a renowned Viajero singer with great artistic and magical ability. But he'd encountered more intimidating people in the past and been far less cowed by them. Not even the presence of the fearsome Uaine warlord Elgin Mordha had prevented him from speaking his mind. So why did he continue to hold his tongue against this tiny diva?

"What interests me most," said Javier, "is the reason behind the imperial army's sudden departure. Señor, you said there may have been a coup at Magna Alto?"

"According to Sonya and Sebastian," said Jorge. "Although that was just secondhand information they received from an enemy, so it's impossible to say if it's true."

"Oh, it's true all right," said Lucia.

"How would *you* know?" demanded Hugo.

An odd moment of panic flashed across Lucia's face, but it was so fleeting, Jorge couldn't even be sure he saw it. Then she gave a dismissive wave and turned her gaze back to the skyline. "The Viajero have ways of knowing things."

But it appeared Javier had also seen the brief hesitation, and would not be put off so easily.

"Lucia, the Viajero have many astonishing abilities, but in all my years, I've never known omniscience to be among them."

"Yes, well…"

She kept her eyes fixed outward, not looking at the old mercenary. Was it wrong that Jorge felt some pleasure at seeing Lucia squirm beneath the steely gaze of the Xefe?

But after a moment, her expression firmed into defiance.

"I happen to know someone who was at the palace and escaped just before the coup took place."

Javier's eyes narrowed. "Friends at the imperial palace? I was not aware that you kept such...*illustrious* company, Lucia."

Her face creased into a scowl. "There is a lot about me you don't know, Xefe."

"This seems to be true." Javier did not speak loudly or with much emphasis, yet there was a weight to his words. "And I hope, most honored Viajero, you will forgive my bluntness when I say that is not acceptable. If you expect the mercenary guilds to continue an alliance with you, we must know what other alliances you already have."

It hung there for several seconds.

"I don't like being pressed, Xefe," Lucia said ominously.

"And I don't like being kept in the dark," Javier said lightly.

After another tense moment, Maria put her hand on Lucia's shoulder. "Please, darling. Just tell them. They'll need to know eventually."

"*You* know who it is?" Hugo asked in amazement.

Jorge was fairly certain his brother still didn't realize that Lucia and Maria were lovers. Despite his savvy when it came to business, Hugo could be astoundingly clueless about other aspects of life.

Maria gave Hugo a weary look. "Of course I do." Then she gazed expectantly at Lucia.

Lucia groaned. "Fine." She turned to Javier, though she still couldn't quite seem to meet his eyes. "My friend is Ambassador Ceren Boz of Victasha."

Javier let out a low whistle.

"You've been colluding with a *foreign power*?" asked Hugo.

Lucia did her shrug again, but this time it didn't have the same conviction as before. "The enemy of my enemy is my friend." Then she turned to Javier with a surprisingly anxious look. "Isn't that right, Xefe?"

Javier thoughtfully pursed his lips within his dense, braided beard. "Only sometimes, Lucinita."

"Well...what about this time?" Jorge asked.

"That, Señor, is what we must now determine."

3

Galina Odoyevtseva Prozorova stood on the outer wall of ancient Gogoleth, her hands clasped behind her back. The gentle Izmorozian summer breeze tugged at her golden hair and pale blue gown as she gazed down at the people gathered in the yard below.

"Well, Andrushka, I do believe they're starting to look like soldiers."

"Indeed, Your Majesty," rumbled the hulking Ranger Andre beside her. His small bear eyes blinked slowly beneath the afternoon sun.

The old imperial garrison had been repurposed as a training and education center for the recently formed Izmorozian militia. Galina watched as young men and women who hailed from all over the country were drilled on simple strength and endurance training exercises in the central yard. The intention of such activity was to temper their bodies as well as acclimate them to working together as a unified group. In the first few weeks, their efforts would have been laughable if the continued freedom of Izmoroz had not rested, in part, upon their success. But now they moved as one unit, fluid and confident. It was time for them to begin weapons training, which would be led by Andre. His clawed hands might prevent him from holding a sword or bow now, but he had a lifetime of experience and skill in weaponry and had survived the Winter War. If he could impart even a portion of his knowledge on her new militia, they would be in respectable shape.

But combat training was not the only pursuit of the Izmorozian militia. The younger boys and girls were gathered in one wing of the officers' quarters where they were taught to read and write, for they would be the message runners of the militia. Galina had been reading extensively on military strategy, and it was evident to her that swift and precise communication between various units within an army was essential.

Then there were the adults that Galina deemed too frail for combat, who were being trained in administrative tasks. She hoped that at least some of them would show an aptitude for strategy, planning, and leadership so that they might assist with some of the more mundane aspects of running the militia. Galina could not be everywhere at once, after all.

"Let us offer our congratulations to the latest batch of countrymen and women ready to defend their homeland, Andrushka."

"As you wish, Your Majesty."

Galina had seen no reason to reinvent the wheel, when so much of the garrison remained intact. That included the wooden scaffolding lashed to the outer wall of Gogoleth, which had allowed soldiers to easily ascend the wall for guard duty. Galina was astounded they had not been torn down during preparation for the battle with the Uaine, but she supposed it was just one more indication of Franko Vittorio's grotesque arrogance. An arrogance that now seemed poised to engulf the entire continent.

"I have been thinking about a comment you made the other day," Galina told the Ranger as they made their way down the zigzagging wooden scaffold steps. "About Vittorio possibly benefiting from supernatural aid."

"Yes, Your Majesty?"

Andre rarely offered anything in the way of useful ideas. Galina knew that this was because he had sacrificed so much of himself to the Lady Marzanna that he was barely human anymore. As such, he sometimes struggled with even the most basic intellectual pursuits. But he was a wonderful listener, and very occasionally, his simple, magic-driven view of the world shone a light on ideas that she herself would never have considered.

"If we are to believe Ambassador Boz's account, Vittorio was successfully executed in Magna Alto, yet returned to life shortly after. I have heard the Lady Marzanna is capable of bringing people back to life."

"She is, Your Majesty," agreed Andre. "In fact, to be considered a Ranger, one must first slay a polar bear with only a knife. Then one must wrap themselves in its skin and kill themselves in order to seek audience with the goddess."

"What a grotesque initiation," said Galina. "But is she the only supernatural entity who can bring someone back from the dead?"

"No, Your Majesty. Her sister would also be capable of such miracles."

"The Lady Zivena, Goddess of Spring."

"Yes."

"In all the poems, Zivena is described as kind and beautiful, but possessing a ferocious temper," Galina said. "Have you ever met her?"

"I have not had the honor."

Galina glanced at the stoic Ranger but could not determine what opinion he might have of his sworn goddess's sibling and rival.

"Well, we should keep her in mind as a possible...adversary in the future. I suppose if we have Lady Marzanna on our side, it's only fair for Vittorio to have Lady Zivena."

"The two must always balance each other," he said. "Or else the world will be unmade."

"That sounds foreboding. But I'm generally not inclined to put much stock in prophecy."

"It isn't prophecy, Your Majesty. It is a promise."

"I see..."

Galina still struggled with the supernatural aspects of her alliance with the Rangers. Supposedly the Lady Marzanna was their ally, yet Galina had no idea what the deity's larger plans or ultimate goals were. Goddesses, she decided, made for good poetry but lousy comrades.

Galina and Andre reached the bottom of the scaffold and headed toward the soldiers-in-training, but they were intercepted halfway across the yard by a very irate-looking Lord Konstantin Belousov Levenchik.

Levenchik had not made a favorable impression the first time Galina met him, what with trying to use his influence among the other nobility to pressure her into sex. And he had done little to improve upon that impression since. But at least he was fully clothed and no longer attempting to "seduce" her. In fact, in the month since Galina had taken power, his behavior had become increasingly antagonistic. It turned out that his famously affable demeanor evaporated once he no longer had the money to indulge in his many vices.

"Galina, I say!" Levenchik stalked toward them, his perfect curls bouncing. "This is a—*ghuuck!*"

Andre calmly grabbed him by the throat and lifted him into the air.

Galina watched the noble squirm and writhe for a moment. She did not savor it, exactly. But perhaps it was not so disagreeable to see the man who had once put her in an uncomfortable situation now in one of his own.

"I'm sorry, Lord Levenchik," she said cheerfully, "but I must insist on a certain level of decorum, which includes a use of proper titles. Flap your hands a bit if you understand."

He gave up his futile struggle to free his neck from Andre's grip and waved his hands with a desperate energy that suggested he might soon faint.

"Wonderful. Andre, you may let him go."

Andre took that command quite literally, and Levenchik dropped onto the grass with an audible thud.

Galina beamed down at him. "Now, my lord, how may I be of service to you?"

"Gali…" He glanced at Andre as he struggled to his feet. "Your Majesty. I wish to lodge a complaint."

"Oh?"

"It was bad enough that you recruited so many of our servants for your army that we can hardly run our households anymore." Levenchik brushed dirt off his satin trousers as he spoke.

"Izmoroz appreciates your sacrifice, my lord," Galina replied.

"That's just it! We have *already* sacrificed, and now you've begun diverting our tithes as well? How on earth will we afford to restock our pantries and cellars?"

Galina looked thoughtfully up at her Ranger's large, impassive face. "I believe seeking employment is the traditional means of attaining money, is it not, Andre Medved?"

"It is, Your Majesty."

Levenchik gaped at her, his face shifting slowly from pale to flush. His eyes were so wide it looked uncomfortable. "Are you suggesting that I, Lord Konstantin Belousov Levenchik, get a *job*?"

She smiled. "I'm so glad we understand each other, my lord. As your queen, I strive constantly to be in open communication with my subjects."

"But that's...it's..."

"I realize seeking employment can be a daunting task, so perhaps I should help get you started. Your interest in food and drink is legendary, my lord, so you may find cooking here in the mess hall for our brave soldiers a satisfying vocation. We do have a great many mouths to feed, and I know they would be ever so grateful to have someone with your refined palate seeing to their needs."

For a moment, it seemed language had left Levenchik entirely. He sputtered, growled, and grunted like a cat being forcibly bathed. Galina observed it all with a calm, slightly concerned expression.

But then he rallied and drew himself up to his full height, which admittedly was not much higher than Galina herself. "This is untenable! I will not stand for it! *We* will not stand for it! Do you hear me, Galina Odoyevtseva Prozorova? You have made enemies this day!"

Then he spun on his heel, slipped slightly in the dirt, and hurried back across the yard. As he entered the city gates, he passed Masha coming from the opposite direction. She glanced at him with a worried look, then continued over to Galina and Andre.

"Your Majesty." Masha curtsied.

"Ah, Masha," Galina said. "How are things at Roskosh Manor?"

"Tense, Your Majesty. I'm afraid your mother is still struggling to adapt to the new Izmoroz." She glanced back in the direction Levenchik had gone. "Another complaint from the nobility, Your Majesty?"

"I'm afraid so," said Galina. "I had hoped my father would be able to keep the peace, but since he couldn't unify the nobility before, I suppose it was wrong of me to think he might be able to do so now."

Andre cleared his throat with a low rumble. "These *complaints* of theirs sound more like threats each day."

"Yes," agreed Galina. "I fear we will need to do something about that sooner rather than later."

4

As a parent, Lady Irina Turgenev Portinari had never seen much value in punishing or even reprimanding her children. Why should she be cruel and discouraging when the world was more than willing to fill that role? She had always advised her children on the proper course of action, of course, but ultimately allowed them to make their own decisions. She would then follow that up by allowing them to suffer the consequences of their choices.

To some, this "hands off" method of child-rearing might have seemed at odds with her paramount goal of protecting the surviving members of her family. But to her mind, such people failed to understand that one of the foremost things a child must be protected from was their own parents.

She also resented the implication some people made that her parenting method was somehow easier than constantly meddling in the lives of her children. Beneath her stern Izmorozian beauty and sharp retorts, she still worried about them constantly. And quite frankly, it was exhausting.

Irina felt particularly strained at present. As a prisoner of the emperor regent, she had been given no information regarding the current fate of either of her children. Her son had been ordered by the now dead empress to go and kill her daughter, something he had assured Irina he would not do under any circumstance. But once he and the rest of the imperial army had left to put down the insurrection in Colmo,

Vittorio had seized power. He had then revealed to Irina that Sebastian's longtime comrade, Sasha Rykov, was a servant of Vittorio's and under strict orders to slip a knife into Sebastian's ribs the moment he stepped out of line. In all likelihood, either Sebastian had been forced to kill Sonya, or he had been killed himself for refusing to do so.

Unless...

No, it was probably foolish to even consider the idea. She had prayed to the Lady Marzanna and offered herself, body and soul, if her children would be saved. And there had been a moment when she had wondered if her prayers had been answered. The awkward but gifted Kantesian, Friedrich Cloos, had presented her with a plan that would theoretically allow her to not only escape the palace but also save her children. He was in the midst of constructing a metal golem fashioned in her likeness—beautiful in its own way, but frightening and more than a little uncanny. He said that once it was complete, he could transfer her consciousness into the thing, after which she would be ageless, powerful, and practically indestructible. Of course, she would have to give up her mortal body in the process. In the hours following Vittorio's violent and bloody coup, the suggestion had almost seemed... *reasonable*. But now, the idea struck her as a fate only slightly preferable to death. The fact that she had not dismissed it entirely only showed just how desperate things had gotten.

Oddly enough, her only real comfort during this trying time came from two of the Uaine barbarians who had aided Vittorio in overthrowing the capital.

First there was the young necromancer woman who had saved her life during the invasion. Irina had been injured and left stranded in the middle of a road awash with undead. One of the loathsome things had its hand around her neck when the necromancer had come along and inexplicably commanded the creature to spare Irina's life. Then, without another word, the woman had left.

A few days after Vittorio had taken power, Irina was in the imperial garden with Friedrich Cloos and another foreigner, Mosi Aguta, the marooned sea captain from distant Aukbontar. The necromancer drifted toward them across the sunlit garden like some sort of *poludnitsa*, or noonwraith, a spectral creature said to haunt crop fields at midday in Izmoroz. The woman did not even seem to notice Cloos or Aguta and instead fixed Irina with her colorless eyes as she drew near.

"You are the mother of Sonya Turgenev Portinari?"

Given her daughter's previous alliance with the Uaine, Irina had anticipated that at least some of them would be acquainted with Sonya. But since she didn't know on what terms her volatile daughter had parted with them, she had been reluctant to volunteer her connection. Now she answered with some unease.

"I am."

"Then I am glad that I stopped my sluagh gorta from killing ye. I am Bhuidseach Rowena Viridomarus, and I was once an ally o' your daughter. Though it be true our parting were not happy, I still consider her an honorable warrior."

"I'm glad she managed to not completely alienate the Uaine."

"On the contrary," said Rowena. "Many among the Uaine, including the mighty Tighearna himself, still hold a fondness for her in their hearts. I found her to be impulsive and headstrong, but always with good intentions."

Irina chuckled. "That about sums her up."

Rowena paused for a moment, as though considering something. "Should ye ever need anything, feel free to speak with me about et. As Bhuidseach, my word holds much sway among my people."

"That is most kind. I don't suppose you happen to know what has become of her, do you?"

Rowena shook her head. "I have not seen or heard from her since she left Izmoroz."

It was possible, then, that Irina knew more than the necromancer did. She almost asked if the woman knew anything about Sebastian, but stopped herself. They might not even know he was her son. Even if the Uaine were fond of Sonya, it would be unwise to consider them friendly. They had invaded Magna Alto, killed many of its citizens, and helped Vittorio murder the empress and usurp power.

So instead, she asked, "Do you know what has happened in Colmo? The imperial army was sent there to put down the unrest."

"We have received word that they are on their way back here."

"I see. And what will...Emperor Domenico do when the army arrives?"

She was of course asking what *Vittorio* would do, not his eight-year-old puppet, but she hoped Irina would understand that.

A brief flicker of a smile crossed her lips. "Ah yes. The child emperor. Unfortunately, I have not been told anything as yet."

Irina wondered what Rowena *had* been told. She was unclear about the nature of the continued alliance between Vittorio and the Uaine. Did they act as a peacekeeping force for him? If so, what did they gain from this arrangement? She supposed they could simply be mercenaries for hire, but she didn't get that sense from Rowena.

"Let us hope their return doesn't result in bloodshed," she said.

"Oh?" Rowena appeared surprised.

It seemed an odd response. After all, it remained to be seen whether the returning imperial army would recognize Vittorio's authority as regent to the child of the late Empress Caterina Morante. Particularly considering Vittorio had murdered her other children in front of a number of witnesses, then gave the "honor" of killing the empress herself to Mordha, the Uaine warlord. It was almost as though Rowena welcomed the potential coming conflict. But to what end? Were they so barbaric that they craved battle for its own sake? Or was it some other reason? Irina was about to probe further, but before she could say anything more, Rowena turned abruptly without another word and drifted back the way she'd come, leaving Irina and her two companions staring after her.

"Well," Aguta said after a moment. "That was...interesting."

"In what way?" asked Irina.

"I'm surprised they still feel some loyalty to a former ally like your daughter."

"It's not that surprising if you know Sonya. She can be as beguiling as she is infuriating. I expect her rustic Izmorozian charms went over rather well with a bunch of necromancer barbarians."

A few days later, she understood just how well those charms had worked when she was accosted by another Uaine as she walked through the hall.

"Lady Portinari!"

Irina paused to watch a young man jog toward her. He was hairy and not particularly clean, but he possessed an engaging combination of rugged handsomeness and boyish appeal.

"Yes?"

"Apologies for interrupting you. I am Blaine Ruairc, captain of Clan Dílis. It is a pleasure to meet you."

His command of the imperial tongue was easily the best she'd heard from any of them, and it seemed he was taking great care with his speech. Then he bowed stiffly, as though it was something he'd only recently learned. It was apparent that he wished to make a favorable impression on her, and she wondered why.

"Nice to meet you, Captain," she said.

"I would be honored if you called me Blaine."

"Very well, Blaine."

"I would like to say," he told her in his carefully enunciated speech, "how sorry I am that you must suffer imprisonment like this."

"It's rather luxurious as far as prisons go," said Irina. "But I appreciate the sentiment nonetheless."

He stared at her as though struggling to work out what she was saying. Bless his soul, he was rather pretty for a barbarian, but not particularly bright.

"Thank you," she supplied.

His face brightened. "You are most welcome." Then he glanced around uneasily, and in a quieter voice asked, "Have you heard from Sonya? Do you know where she is?"

She wondered if this young man had enjoyed a *special* relationship with her free-spirited daughter. He had that sort of nervous "meeting the mother" energy about him.

"The last I heard she was in Colmo," Irina said.

"With Jorge?"

"The Elhuyar boy?" she asked. "Do you know him as well?"

Blaine's face flushed bright red at the question. "Oh, uh, aye..."

By the Lady, what sort of hijinks had Sonya been up to? A love triangle with two foreigners? Really, was it too much to ask the daughter of a noblewoman to have at least *some* propriety? Or at least *discretion*?

But then she looked at this poor, concerned soul and realized that oddly enough she might have found someone she could commiserate with. And if she also learned the motives of the Uaine in the process, so much the better. Rowena might have been a bit inscrutable, but she suspected this sweet boy would be far easier to read.

So she smiled at him. "Would you like to join me for tea, Blaine? I am also deeply anxious about my daughter, and hearing some of the adventures that the two of you shared would greatly ease my mind."

He grinned, and his careful speech evaporated with some relief. "Aye, my lady, 'twould be a pleasure."

5

Sebastian didn't know what woke him. But it saved his life.

He had been curled up on the dusty ground near the embers of their meager cooking fire. The moon was only a sliver, but out in the desert the stars were plentiful and bright.

Then he heard a strange growl, followed by the hiss of a knife leaving its scabbard.

He opened his eyes just as Sonya leapt over the fire, knife in hand. As always, she was stunningly fast, and Sebastian only had enough time to roll onto his back before she was on top of him. He grabbed her wrist with both hands to stop her from stabbing him, but the point hovered dangerously over his chest.

"Sonya, what are you doing!" he shouted.

She only growled and bared her fangs as she pressed down, her knife blade nearing his chest. Her golden eyes were glazed over, as though she was drugged, or not in her right mind.

He strained his hearing over his sister's snarls and his own labored breathing and could just make out the trill of a flute.

The Viajero. Of course. Sonya had warned him and he'd disregarded her vast experience and assured her that as long as they didn't act aggressively, the person would leave them alone. He was an idiot, as usual.

If only he still had his gem, he could have ended the Viajero's song with a sudden burst of cold just like he had stopped Captain Reyes and his men back in Kante. But no, since he didn't know exactly where this Viajero was, it would have to be a wide area attack, which could harm Sonya as well.

Except Sonya was immune to his magic, wasn't she? She'd proven that back in Gogoleth. He'd been furious about it then, but now he was grateful.

As his sister pushed the knife closer to his chest, he looked desperately around for some metal to use as a conduit for his magic. But there was nothing within reach. Except...

He stared for a moment at the gleaming knife that hovered an inch from his chest. His sister had always been devilishly strong for her size, and in this possessed state she was more ferocious than ever. His arms were already shaking with fatigue. He wouldn't be able to hold out more than a few seconds longer.

It was either his hand or his heart.

Still holding her wrist with one hand, he grabbed the blade with the other. He tried to avoid the edge, but as they struggled, he felt a hot white stab as it sliced into his palm. Blood ran down the knife, but he forced himself to think through the searing pain and focus on his intention. Since he was using an inferior material, he couldn't do anything fancy or refined. It would just have to be a raw burst of power.

A shock wave of cold traveled out in all directions like an explosion, snuffing out the fire and freezing the rocky ground all around them so abruptly that cracks formed in the frosty surface. At the same time, Sonya's knife crumbled to rusty flakes on his bloody palm.

The sound of the flute cut off abruptly.

A moment later, Sonya's eyes fluttered. She looked down at Sebastian, whom she still had pinned to the ground beneath her. Horror stretched across her face when she saw his injured hand.

"Wh-what..."

"Quickly, Yasha! The Viajero!"

Her eyes narrowed to slits and her lip curled up to show her fangs. "Got it."

In one smooth motion, she pushed off from him, pivoted, then launched herself at a prone and shivering form that was now visible on the icy ground nearby. She landed on top of the cloaked figure and there was an audible grunt. Then she grabbed the person by the collar and lifted them up to her snarling face.

"You think it's funny to make me attack my brother? I'll rip out your throat!"

The person's hood fell back to reveal an elderly Raízian man. His gaunt face plainly showed his terror, but he shouted back at Sonya.

"Do your worst, monster! Better that I die now than face what comes."

"Fine by me."

"Sonya, wait!"

Sebastian watched Sonya's face contort as she struggled to rein in her killer instincts. She had admitted to him when they first set out from Colmo that with each piece of humanity she lost, it became harder to control her animal aspect. Sebastian knew all too well the danger of harming people accidentally, and the terrible remorse that came after. He had promised he would help her.

"Remember who you are, Yasha!" He struggled to his feet, clutching at his bleeding hand.

She snapped her head around to look at him and snarled, "*What is 'me,' I wonder!*"

The sudden fury that poured out of her made Sebastian step back involuntarily. But seeing his fear seemed to finally snap her out of her animal rage. She sucked in a slow, hissing breath through clenched fangs and closed her eyes. Then she nodded.

"Okay. I'm okay."

Sebastian pulled his old imperial uniform shirt from his bag and wrapped it around his bleeding hand, then he staggered over to where she held the Viajero down.

"Why did you attack us? We meant you no harm."

The old man glared up at him, his yellowed eyes bulging. "You can't fool me! You're the Armonia!"

"The Armonia?" Sebastian looked at his sister. "Do *you* know what that is?"

She shook her head.

"You are the servant of Mokosh who will wipe out all existence!"

Sebastian felt a chill. "Mokosh the Damp Mother Earth?"

"*You* know of her?" Sonya asked.

"Just from old legends, mostly. Don't you remember those stories Mother would tell us at bedtime?"

Sonya looked surprised. "You stayed awake for those? I rarely made it past 'Listen and I will tell you a story from when the world was young.'"

"Well, I don't remember a lot," admitted Sebastian. "Mostly that Mokosh was big and scary and wanted to eat the world."

"Mikhail taught me that she's the source of all existence," said Sonya. "The story goes that her daughters, Lady Marzanna and Lady Zivena, struggle eternally with each other for dominance. That's why there's so much conflict in the world. But if one of them ever truly won out over the other, there wouldn't be peace. Instead, there would be a terrible imbalance. The only way to correct that imbalance would be if Mokosh wiped everything clean and started again."

"Meaning kill everyone?"

"Not just the living. Everything. All of existence. Gone. Like it never happened."

"I see...," said Sebastian. "But she's not evil, per se?"

"Good and evil don't really mean anything to gods."

"Does this Mokosh have any servants? You know, like how you used to serve Lady Marzanna?"

Sonya's eyes narrowed. "Why?"

Sebastian had known he'd need to talk to his sister about this at some point, and it seemed unwise to put it off any longer. "Well... there might be something to what this old man is saying. When I killed Rykov, I was sort of...raving. Just a little. And for some reason I started talking about Mokosh. I'm sure it's nothing."

He hoped it was nothing. But he could still remember that darkness invading him and that sense of not quite being himself.

"Yeah..." Sonya didn't look convinced either, but rather than push him further, she nodded to their captive. "So what are we going to do with this guy? He seems pretty crazy. If we let him go, he might try something like this again. Maybe I should break his hands, so he can't play his flute anymore."

"Or," suggested Sebastian, "you could just break his flute."

Sonya turned back to the old man and glared at him. "After what he did to us, I'd rather break his hands."

"Out here in the desert with no one to help him, you'd basically be sentencing him to death," Sebastian pointed out.

Sonya sighed. "I suppose you're right. Fine, I'll settle for breaking his flute instead."

She let him drop back into the dirt and picked up his fallen flute. She held it out in front of him to make sure she had his attention. Then she broke it over her knee.

The old man tried to hide how much that upset him, but his lip quivered so badly he bit down on it. Sonya smirked when she saw that and dropped the pieces of the flute on the ground in front of him.

"I don't think I can get back to sleep after all this excitement," she said. "You want to get an early start? Might be nice to travel while it's cold like this."

"I suppose so," said Sebastian.

"Let's get you stitched and bandaged first, though." Then she patted the empty sheath at her waist and looked around. "Have you seen my knife?"

"Oh, er..." Sebastian gave her a pained smile. "About that..."

6

The last time Jorge walked through the Viajero Quarter had been to check on Sonya. He'd felt out of place then, and this time he felt even more self-conscious because instead of one lone family guard, he was accompanied by both siblings, the famous El Xefe, and a troop of Anxeles Escuros.

"Did we really need the entourage, Xefe?" he asked plaintively as they marched loudly and ostentatiously through the winding streets of the quarter, eliciting stares ranging from curious to unfriendly.

"You will forgive me if I am overly cautious about protecting the offspring of Señor Elhuyar," he said unapologetically. "Sadly, in times of great upheaval, there are always those who take advantage of the situation for their own personal gain. Besides, we have the illustrious diva Lucia Velazquez leading us, which automatically indicates our status as allies instead of outsiders."

"She doesn't look particularly thrilled to play this role."

Lucia walked at the head of their little company beside Jorge's sister. Despite Maria's cheerful chatter and attempts to engage her in conversation, Lucia's expression remained sour. Almost pouting.

"I'm sure she enjoyed feeling special as the sole contact between Raíz and Victasha," said Javier. "But even she must accept that it would be the grossest indulgence of ego to keep this resource to herself any longer."

"Do you think we can trust the Victashians?" asked Jorge. "The last time Sonya and I put our trust in foreign allies, it did not turn out well."

"Trust between nations is always a tenuous affair," said Javier. "The trick is to trust motives rather than people."

"I suppose that was our mistake. We put our faith in specific individuals, thinking they would never betray us. But in the end, we put them in the difficult situation of choosing between friend and country."

Jorge felt a pang of guilt as he realized how painful that decision might have been, particularly for Blaine. It could very well be something that haunted him even now. Perhaps Jorge should be mad at Blaine, but every time he tried to summon up some self-righteous indignation, he remembered the suffering on his friend's tear-streaked face as he silently turned his back on Sonya and Jorge back at the Uaine camp in Gogoleth, and any anger Jorge might have felt dissipated. He simply couldn't stay mad at Blaine.

"A wise and compassionate perspective, Señor," said Javier. "It's easy to view adversaries as evil or malicious, but rarely are things so simple. Everyone wants something, and often that goal requires others to lose something. It's the way of the world. So, the important thing is to understand a potential ally's goals and be certain they don't conflict with yours."

"That makes a great deal of sense."

"Although even then, it's best to plan ahead for the day when your ally's goals might change. A few safeguards never hurt."

Jorge smiled at the limping elder mercenary. "We're lucky to have you on our side, Xefe."

"That you are," he agreed.

They followed the disgruntled Lucia through the Viajero Quarter until they came to a small café. Then she turned and glared at Javier.

"Do you mind leaving your muscle outside?"

"I suppose," said Javier. "As long as you're willing to vouch for everyone inside."

"I am."

"Very well then." He turned to his mercenaries. "Adolfo and Tomás, take up post here. Isaac and Fermina, take the back entrance.

On the off chance that something *does* happen, I don't want any escapees."

All four saluted. "Yes, Xefe!"

Lucia scowled at the two mercenaries who hurried around to guard the back entrance, then turned to Javier.

"Was that absolutely necessary? I feel like you don't trust me."

"Good," Javier said cheerfully. "Then you are starting to recognize the cost of making secret alliances with foreign powers."

Lucia did not seem to appreciate this nugget of wisdom, and only said, "Come on, then," and entered the café. The rest of them filed in after her.

The inside of the café was open and airy, with cheerful yellow walls and clean wooden floors. A waiter stood behind the counter, polishing glasses. He glanced at the strange group for a moment, his eyebrows raised, then went back to his work.

The only two customers sat at a table near the back playing dominoes. One was an older Raízian man with long gray braids and a carefully trimmed beard. He was thin, almost gaunt, but there was a languid ease to his movements that immediately drew the eye. Almost in counterpoint, the eyes beneath the wide brim of his hat burned with a dark intensity.

"Is that Pedro Molina?" Jorge whispered to his sister.

"Of course," she said in surprise. "I know it's been a few years since you've seen him, but surely you remember our family's most cherished Viajero."

In truth, Jorge hadn't really paid much attention to the various renowned Viajero who had visited Cassa Estío throughout his childhood. In fact, Molina might be the only one he could pick out of a crowd, and then probably only because meeting him had been the first time he'd felt attraction toward another man.

The one playing dominoes with Molina was striking in an altogether different way. His hair was cropped short and he was clean-shaven. Instead of a tunic or vest, he wore a long silk robe. Jewelry glittered from his ears, wrists, neck, and even his nose.

Molina was the first to notice the new arrivals. He looked up at them with his piercing eyes and raised one thick, wiry brow. But all he said was, "My, my."

"Sorry to disturb you both," said Lucia with a great deal more respect than Jorge had ever seen her display before. "But it is time to discuss the future of Raíz."

"Ah." The Victashian man eyed Jorge and the others. "I see. You have told them, then?"

"I insisted," said the Xefe. "I like to know who I'm allied with before I actually agree to the alliance."

The man inclined his head. "Perfectly reasonable. I am called Onat Duman and I am at your service. Please." He gestured to the empty tables and chairs surrounding them. "Make yourselves comfortable." Then he turned to Molina. "My friend, you may leave or stay as you wish, I have nothing to hide from you."

Molina's dark eyes swept the group. "If it's all the same, I think I'd like to stay." Then a smile broke out suddenly on his long face. "If for no other reason than to drink in the dazzling beauty of Señorita Elhuyar a little longer."

Maria laughed. "Flatterer!"

He inclined his head as though it were a compliment.

They all took seats, Javier with evident relief. Jorge realized the long walk may have been a challenge for the hobbled old man and felt a pang of remorse for not anticipating it.

"I mean no disrespect, Onat Duman," said Javier once he was settled. "But Lucia said that an Ambassador Ceren Boz was her contact at the palace, not you."

Onat nodded. "Very true. I am merely the ambassador's emissary. She anticipated that this conversation would need to happen eventually and has already given me instructions for when the time came. And it seems that time is now."

"Indeed," said Javier. "I am curious as to why the Victashians have taken such an interest in our continent."

"An understandable concern," replied Onat. "Their Majesties were only just beginning to make headway in establishing mutually beneficial treaties with Empress Caterina when this current unrest broke out. They found Her Majesty a fair and reasonable ruler and were quite taken aback by her murder. They would like to resume treaty negotiations, but not with someone as volatile and unpredictable as Franko Vittorio in such a position of power. To that end, we have been given permission to provide supplemental aid to various factions on the continent who would see Vittorio removed and order restored."

There was, Jorge decided, something unnervingly smooth about this Onat Duman. He seemed surprised by nothing, and his responses were so tempered and sure as to feel almost rehearsed. Perhaps, if the ambassador had truly anticipated this conversation, they were.

"What do you mean by *supplemental* aid?" asked Javier.

"Their Majesties have not authorized the use of the Victashian military, so I'm afraid we can offer little in the way of direct martial support."

Javier nodded. "I can hardly blame Their Majesties for wanting to keep their troops close to home. Should we fail in ousting Vittorio, it's entirely possible he might be reckless enough to cross the Sea of Charmed Winds."

"Just so," agreed Onat. "But Victasha is renowned for more than just our military, as you of all people know, Xefe."

Javier laughed. "So you've heard of me?"

"The name Javier Arzak is used throughout northern Victasha to frighten children into good behavior." He smiled playfully. "Though I confess I am disappointed that you haven't bitten the head off a single puppy since you arrived. And where are your horns?"

"Ah." Javier grinned, showing his teeth within his thick gray beard. "It's a comfort to an old man to know his name will live on, even if it's in infamy." He leaned back and gazed at the ceiling a moment. "So you are offering the assistance of the famed Victashian Intelligence Bureau."

"Correct," said Onat.

Then Javier looked back at him, his eyes sharp. "And what do you want in return?"

"A promise in good faith that treaty talks will resume once order is restored."

"That's it?" Javier seemed skeptical.

"Their Majesties live in hope that true peace will come to this part of the world within their lifetime."

"And?" pressed Javier.

Onat's smile was a little pained now. "And there is some small concern regarding the possibility of potentially hostile forces crossing the Tainted Ocean. If such a thing were to come about, a preexisting treaty with nations on your continent would prove useful."

Jorge had been trying to keep quiet so that the far more experienced Javier could handle this sensitive discussion, but he couldn't hold back any longer.

"Forgive my interruption. Did you say an invasion from across the Tainted Ocean?"

"*Potential*," said Onat. "As of now, there have been no overt signs of hostility. Only what we suspect might have been a scouting and reconnaissance party."

"From whom?" demanded Jorge. "As far as I'm aware, no one has ever crossed the Tainted Ocean."

"No one has ever successfully crossed *east*. But a year ago, a man named Mosi Aguta washed ashore in southern Kante claiming to be from a country called Aukbontar that lies on the other side of the Tainted Ocean. He was picked up by an imperial ship that had been attempting to find a way to attack Kante from the coast. They had little luck in that regard, as the coastline is composed almost entirely of jagged rocks that would make a sizable landing party impossible. But they discovered this man barely alive in the wreckage of a most unusual-looking ship. The small imperial scout ship didn't have the means of salvaging the wreck, but they brought the man back to Magna Alto."

"This doesn't sound particularly worrisome," pointed out Javier.

"We have examined the wreckage of the ship, and even severely damaged, the vessel suggests a sophisticated level of engineering far beyond our own. What's more, the Aukbontaren is now a prisoner of Vittorio, and no doubt getting a very poor impression of us all. He claims he is unable to return home or contact his people in any way. If that is true, and it must be pointed out we have no assurance that it is, it may forestall an international incident for now. But the likeli-hood of future encounters with this Aukbontar is high. We must all be ready for the worst, should it come to pass."

"I'd be curious to see the remains of this Aukbontaren ship," said Javier.

"They are currently in Victasha undergoing careful study." Onat smiled blandly. "Should agreeable treaties be established between Victasha and Raíz, we would be happy to share our findings."

"Ah yes, I suppose I can't fault you there." Javier turned to Jorge. "Well, I'm satisfied for the moment. What about you?"

Jorge was startled that Javier had singled him out, but when he looked around, no one else seemed to object.

"Well, first things first," he said, as much to collect his thoughts as anything else. "You claim that Vittorio staged a coup in Magna Alto. Do you know how he accomplished it?"

"I'm sad to say that it was with the aid of your former allies the Uaine, Señor Elhuyar."

"You know me as well?" That startled him.

"I should hope so," said Onat.

"Why do you say that?"

"One does not take an important role in two seemingly unre-lated revolutions in completely separate countries within six months without gaining the attention of the Victashian Intelligence Bureau, Señor."

"Ah." Jorge didn't feel particularly thrilled by his newfound noto-riety, but there were more important concerns. "So the Uaine allied themselves with Vittorio to sack Magna Alto?"

"Not sack, actually. The Uaine remain in the capital and there appears to be some sort of ongoing cooperation with Vittorio."

That was surprising. Jorge had been led to believe that the Uaine had come all this way to plunder the unequaled riches of Magna Alto. But when he actually thought about it, the Uaine did not strike him as people who were particularly interested in riches. So what *was* their goal? Perhaps he had never known their true motives. As Javier sug-gested earlier, no wonder their alliance had faltered.

"What about the imperial army that attacked us?" asked Maria. "Where are they now?"

"They should reach Magna Alto within the next few days, Señorita."

"What will happen when they arrive?" asked Jorge.

"Yes, well..." Onat smoothed out his silk robes, looking genuinely enthusiastic for the first time. "It will be interesting to find out, won't it?"

7

It was an exquisitely painful experience for Irina to learn so much about her daughter from a barbarian she had just met.

She had no illusions regarding her tendency to favor Sebastian over Sonya. Unlike many parents, she did not subscribe to some sham pantomime of impartiality when it came to her offspring. Sebastian was considerate, soft-spoken, and well-behaved, while Sonya was wild, unpredictable, and often belligerent. When interacting with people outside her family, Irina preferred the former, so why not inside her family as well? She still loved Sonya, of course, and would give up her own life for her without a moment's hesitation. But when it came to parenting her daughter, it had seemed both pragmatic and significantly less troublesome to defer to Giovanni, who in his youth had apparently also been wild, unpredictable, and belligerent.

Only now did she understand just how much this choice had cost her, and how little she truly knew her own daughter.

She sat in her apartments, tea in hand, and listened to Blaine talk about Sonya almost as if it were someone she had never met. To hear him tell it, her daughter was recklessly kind to anyone she met and ferociously protective of those who needed help. She had bold ideas, unshakable resolve, and a boisterous laugh that raised the spirits of everyone around her. She held deep personal convictions, but they never prevented her from learning and appreciating other beliefs and cultures. She was a stalwart comrade, a loyal friend, and an attentive lover.

Irina had to admit she was curious whether the Elhuyar boy had also been their lover, like something out of a romance novel. But she decided it would be best for her own peace of mind to leave the door to her daughter's carnal activities firmly closed. In fact, she was surprised and somewhat taken aback that Blaine was so candid about their relationship. At first, she ascribed it to the fact that the Uaine were clearly a more permissive culture regarding such things. But perhaps he was not quite as thick as he initially seemed because it turned out he was working toward something. He suspected, correctly, that Irina had not yet been aware that Sonya could not bear children.

"She's certain?" Irina asked more sharply than she'd intended.

"Aye," Blaine said quietly. "'Twas the first thing Lady Marzanna took from her. No Ranger in service to the Goddess of Death may create new life. That was the rule, she said."

"I see..."

Irina had frequently expressed her low expectations for Sonya to give her grandchildren, but she had always harbored a sliver of hope that perhaps one day...

"She's not sad about it," Blaine said. "We've talked about it a few times, and she said she never wanted to have children anyway."

Irina nodded, wondering if that was true. Perhaps so. Sonya was not a typical noblewoman of Izmoroz, so it would merely be one more in a long list of unconventional and controversial opinions. But Irina could not help wondering if there might have been a period of grief over the loss of that potential. And who could have possibly consoled her during such a moment? Surely not men like Giovanni or her mentor, Mikhail. It should have been her mother.

As Irina sat in her luxurious imperial prison, she felt something she had not experienced in a very long time. Shame.

She had failed her daughter.

A loud knock at the door jarred her from her thoughts.

"Y-yes?" she asked, struggling to regain her composure.

One of the palace servants opened the door, looked surprised for a moment to see Irina sitting with Blaine, then said, "His Excellency, Regent Vittorio, commands that all guests present themselves in the palace courtyard, suitably attired, to greet the officers of the returning imperial army in one hour."

"Understood."

Irina's heart was suddenly racing. Would Sebastian be arriving with the rest of the army? Would General Barone challenge Vittorio's authority? With Sebastian at his side, he could surely level the palace if he wanted. Unless of course Vittorio's lackey had fulfilled his mandate to stab her son in the back the moment he stepped out of line...

"My lady, are ye well?" Blaine tentatively placed a hand on her arm, looking concerned.

She smiled faintly. "You are such a dear boy. I can see why Sonya likes you."

He flinched at that. He hadn't brought it up, but most likely his relationship with Sonya had taken a fatal blow when the Uaine broke off the alliance. She suspected that he harbored some guilt about it, and that his current solicitude toward Irina was an attempt, conscious or otherwise, to make amends. Well, in such dire and uncertain times, she would gladly accept help of any kind. And despite his background, his company was not altogether disagreeable.

"I suppose you will need to prepare as well," she told him.

"Aye." He stood, then looked back at her. "Can we...speak again?"

"I would be delighted."

He gave her a charmingly boyish grin, nodded, and left. Irina decided he was quite adorable, and all things considered, she could not fault her daughter's choice.

But now she must put thoughts of that aside for the time being, and brace herself for news of Sebastian. She didn't really need to change gowns or touch up her hair and makeup, but she did anyway. Once she was satisfied, she made her way through the twisting corridors of the palace to the courtyard. People were already gathering, either in anticipation or dread. She spotted Aguta and Cloos deep in animated conversation, and joined them.

"Really, Mosi, I thought you more open-minded than this," Cloos was saying, looking offended.

Aguta, on the other hand, looked furious. "Open-minded is one thing. But what you suggest is—" He spotted Irina drawing near and relief flashed across his face. "My lady, Friedrich has suggested the most preposterous thing! That you have volunteered for his horrific 'golem' experiment!"

Irina regarded him coolly. Although she was fond of Aguta, she found him to be the sort of man who presumed a great deal when it came to women, not unlike many Izmorozian men. In this respect, he differed drastically from her Giovanni, and it made him less appealing in her eyes.

"Preposterous, is it, Captain? I would call this entire situation that we find ourselves in preposterous. I trust, therefore, you will forgive me if I begin to contemplate measures that I might have otherwise considered too extreme."

His eyes widened. "So you *are* doing it?"

"I view it as more of a fallback plan, should the worst come to pass. A concern I hope will be made obsolete when my son arrives with the rest of the imperial officers in a very short time."

"But surely you don't think—" began Aguta.

"Do not presume to know what I should think," she said.

That brought him up short. "I'm sorry, my lady. I…have overstepped."

"You have," she agreed. "And I accept your apology."

They were silent for a moment, until Cloos cleared his throat and said, "So what do you think will happen here, my lady?"

"It will all come down to whether the man leading the imperial army, General Barone, decides to accept Domenico as emperor, and Vittorio as his regent. Judging by the spectacle of bringing us all out here to greet him, I suspect that we are to be hostages of a sort. An implied threat to Barone when he arrives."

She glanced around at the nervously chatting guests and Aureumian nobility, most of them retired military or wealthy merchants. Until recently, they had all probably thought that the palace was the safest place in the world.

One of the sentries at the top of the wall gave a little yelp, hurried over to another soldier, and spoke quietly but anxiously to him. That soldier, now also looking quite concerned, hurried down from the ramparts and into the palace.

"It seems there may be some sort of surprise in store," mused Irina. She turned to Aguta. "I detest surprises, but I doubt they would let a lady up on the ramparts. Perhaps a salty old sailor might go in my stead?"

He grinned. "A chance to redeem myself so soon, my lady. I thank you."

He ascended the steps to the ramparts with that brawny confidence of his that she still really did find quite appealing, despite his other faults. He chatted with the soldiers, patting one on the back and laughing, among other chummy activities, even as his eyes swept over the parapet to the town below. His expression did not change, but he soon said farewell and made his way casually back down to where Irina and Cloos waited.

"They were unwilling to discuss the matter, of course," he said calmly, "but it was easy enough to see. Barone isn't arriving with just his captains. He's currently marching his entire army through the Silver Ring on Ascendant Way."

"It seems Vittorio is not the only one familiar with implied threats," said Irina. "This could become even more unpleasant than anticipated."

A short time later, imperial soldiers began to spill out of the palace. They corralled the noncombatants to either side of the gate, creating a path to the palace doors lined with people unable to defend themselves, including Irina, Aguta, and Cloos. Then the soldiers formed up behind them. More surreptitiously, the Uaine also emerged from the palace and moved to take the rear behind the soldiers.

"This is horrifying," whispered Cloos as he glanced back nervously at the grim, well-armed soldiers who had in effect trapped them on the front lines of a potential battle.

"At least they didn't bring any undead up from the city," said Irina. "The stench of those creatures is appalling."

Shortly after, the palace doors opened again to reveal young Emperor Domenico looking small and very frightened in his golden

imperial robes. He was flanked on one side by the scarred and towering Uaine leader Tighearna Elgin Mordha, and on the other by the
sharp-eyed and smirking Vittorio. Irina had not been fond of the previous blowhard or fawning versions of Vittorio, but she found this
newest iteration significantly more disconcerting. It felt as though he
radiated pure malice.

The three stood and waited in the palace doorway, while on the
other end of the people-corridor, the soldiers opened the main gate
with a loud, wincing clang.

Everything was silent except the occasional clank of armor or
weaponry. Then, gradually, the sound of marching became apparent.
The regular rhythm of boots striking the road grew in an ominous
crescendo, until General Barone crossed the threshold. At his back
was a line of soldiers that stretched far out of view.

As impressive as the soldiers were, Irina thought they also looked
exhausted. It was no wonder. These poor men had marched to the
rival nation of Kante to reinforce the imperial army that had been
attempting to seize the resource-rich land there. The Kantesians
had then deployed a giant metal monster, a golem similar to the one
Cloos was creating for Irina, but much larger. The golem had inflicted
heavy damage on Barone's army and utterly destroyed the military
outpost they had been constructing. Meanwhile, on the other side of
the continent, the Raízians declared independence from the empire.
Still stinging from their defeat at the hands of the Kantesian golem,
Barone's troops received orders from the empress to take the company of Raízian troops within their own ranks into custody. They
were then told to march back to the capital with all possible haste,
where they were to imprison the Raízian captain, Ernesto Reyes, and
his men. Men who, as far as Irina knew, were *still* imprisoned in the
brig without trial or promise of release. After such morale-crushing
events, Barone and his men had certainly deserved some respite. But
only days later, they were ordered to march on Colmo, capital of
Raíz, to put down the unrest there. After another long march and
presumably a great deal of combat against the Raízian rebels, Barone's
army had somehow learned of Vittorio's coup, broken off from battle,

and hurried back on yet another long march to the capital. And now they must contemplate assaulting their own palace?

But no. Irina could tell the moment Barone's eyes fell on the young emperor that the battle was over before it had begun. Perhaps if Vittorio had tried to usurp power directly, things would have gone differently. But this loyal servant of the empire would never raise a hand against its only surviving heir. He was cut from the same cloth as heroic soldiers of old and, to Irina's mind, just as foolish.

Barone called his army to a halt once he had reached the courtyard. The sound of marching boots had become so loud that the sudden silence that followed was jarring. Everyone seemed to hold their breath while Barone stared at the three people gathered at the entrance to the palace.

Vittorio nudged the young emperor, and his shrill, pipping voice barely carried across the courtyard.

"Welcome home, General Barone. I thank you once again for your loyal service to the empire. Much has happened since your departed—"

Vittorio nudged him and whispered something under his breath.

A moment later, the emperor resumed. "Since *you* departed. Once you have dismissed your troops, join me in the throne room, where we may discuss the state—"

Another nudge and whisper from Vittorio.

"Discuss matters of state."

It hung there for a moment. Barone's face was expressionless, but there was such weariness in his eyes. Irina wondered if the man had any fight left in him at all.

At last, in a voice heavy with emotion, he said, "As Your Majesty commands."

He dismissed his infantry back to the barracks. Then he and his officers followed the emperor and his retinue into the palace.

Irina scanned the small group of officers, looking for her son's blond head, but didn't see it. What did that mean? She could not say, but she hoped against all odds that it meant he had found his sister and deserted.

Once everything had been settled, both the palace soldiers and the Uaine dispersed, leaving the guests and nobles shaky and unsure of where to go or what to do.

Irina gazed thoughtfully at the open gate that led out of the palace and into the city. If Sebastian was not coming back, there was no reason for her to be here. Now, with everything else going on, it might be her best chance of escape. She had no idea where she would go or what she would do, but it had to be better than living at the whims of a madman.

She began to walk with a deliberately casual air toward the open gate, as though merely out for a stroll. But her pulse quickened with each step toward freedom. Perhaps she would return to Izmoroz. She might have offended some people, but surely she would smooth that over in time. Or she could begin to search for Sonya and Sebastian. Hire a mercenary to assist her, perhaps. Someone versed in tracking people down. She had a few promising places to start after all. It might even be as simple as a trip to Colmo and she could be reunited with both of her children. And if Sonya was still friendly with the Elhuyars, they might live quite comfortably there. If only—

"Lady Portinari!"

She heard a young man call out in a voice she didn't recognize. Her pulse sped up even faster, but she continued walking toward her escape as if she hadn't heard.

"Lady Portinari!"

This time the voice was right behind her. And then, a moment later, a hand grasped her shoulder. She stopped, and slowly turned her head with the iciest stare she could muster. It must have been cold indeed because the man flinched and released her.

"A-apologies, my lady," he stammered. "We've never met, but my name is Marcello Oreste and I'm friends with your son, Sebastian."

That stopped her.

"Do you know where he is?" she demanded.

He glanced around nervously. "Not exactly."

"But he is alive?"

He winced at the question. "Thanks to your daughter."

"You saw Sonya as well?"

"Yes..." He looked even more uncomfortable now. "Perhaps we should discuss this back in your apartments, or somewhere you'd be more comfortable."

"Tell me now."

"Very well." His face screwed up as though he was in physical pain. "I'm sad to say that your daughter, Sonya Portinari, died while courageously saving her brother's life."

"Ah," said Irina.

As she stood there in the courtyard reeling from the news, she heard the gate to freedom slam shut behind her.

8

Galina liked to think of herself as a cultured woman of the world. But the fact was, she'd never left Izmoroz. She had met only one Raízian, a couple of Uaine that she had mixed feelings about, and a handful of Aureumians that she flat-out despised. Most of what made her feel sophisticated came from books. And for whatever reason, she had never been able to obtain a book that went into satisfying depth about Victasha.

So Sezai Bey, the poor beleaguered envoy of Ambassador Boz, had to weather a daily barrage of questions from Her Majesty on the topic of his homeland. Fortunately, the man seemed to have an unlimited reserve of patience. Even when she approached an area of Victasha's political landscape or culture he did not wish to elaborate upon, he avoided doing so with the utmost charm.

"Dual monarchs?" she asked, leaning forward in her chair. "How does it work in practice?"

He smiled serenely, the flickers from the fireplace playing off his smooth brown cheek. "With the grace and beauty that Their Majesties always exhibit."

She gave him a skeptical look. "State secret then?"

He gave a light chuckle. "If you like, Your Majesty."

"I do appreciate you putting up with my endless, and possibly at times impertinent, inquiries," she said.

"If it helps to bridge the chasm in understanding between our two peoples, I am only too happy to oblige," he said.

"And I'm certain that you still hope to get some sort of response from me regarding the ambassador's request."

He inclined his head. "That is my primary purpose here."

"I'm afraid I must beg your patience a little longer on the matter," said Galina. "Although I certainly appreciate the ambassador's generous offer of assistance in brokering an alliance between Izmoroz and Raíz, I felt it best to explore some potential resources of my own first."

She did not elaborate that the "potential resources" relied entirely on the hope that Jorge Elhuyar, a man she knew only passingly well, and who might be rather cross with her for her part in ousting Sonya from Izmoroz last spring, had the pragmatism to look past their tenuous relationship, and the willingness to use the clout of his family name to broker an alliance between Izmoroz and Raíz. If Bey could be evasive, then so could she.

"A wise plan, Your Majesty," said Bey. "Rest assured that while Ambassador Boz is anxious to resolve the current unrest on your continent, *I* am here completely at your disposal for so long as you require."

"I do appreciate that," said Galina.

There was a quiet knock on the door.

"Yes?" called Galina.

Masha peeked her head in and nodded.

"Thank you, Masha." Galina turned back to Sezai Bey. "If you will excuse me, there are some other matters that need my attention."

"Of course, Your Majesty. Please don't let me keep you."

"Until tomorrow, then."

"I look forward to it."

Galina wondered if he truly did, but supposed that as far as jobs went, his was not too onerous. She made sure he was always well taken care of, with comfortable rooms at Roskosh Manor and a seat at her table for every meal. This was, after all, the first direct diplomatic contact between Izmoroz and Victasha in history, and she had no intention of bungling it.

She met with Masha out in the hallway, but motioned them to walk some distance from the door before they began talking. The

Victashians were wise to keep their internal affairs private, and Galina intended to do the same.

Once they were comfortably out of earshot, Galina asked, "My father has returned, then?"

"Yes, Your Majesty."

"And his mood?"

"Distressed."

"Hardly promising."

"No, Your Majesty," agreed Masha.

"Very well. Let's get this sorted out so that we can focus on the things that actually deserve our attention."

"Yes, Your Majesty."

Galina made her way to her father's study and knocked on his door. Technically, as queen of Izmoroz, she didn't need to. But until she had a palace of her own, Roskosh Manor was the finest home in the country and if she were to remain living here for the time being, she felt that some level of thoughtful courtesy was necessary to maintain a semblance of domestic tranquility.

"Who is it?"

Her father sounded peevish. Galina also noted that he no longer recognized her knock. Was he slipping? Distracted? Or had she changed so much that even such minor actions were altered?

"It's your queen and daughter," she said. "May I come in?"

There was a heavy sigh. "Of course, Your Majesty."

She opened the door and stepped into his study, with all its gently nostalgic smells of old paper and fresh ink. Her father was slumped into a leather chair, looking despondent.

"Hello, Papa. I trust you know why I'm here."

"I had hoped to have a bit more time to collect my thoughts before we had this conversation, but as always you move with extreme haste."

"I think you mean decisiveness," she suggested.

A bitter smile flickered across his face. "Perhaps I do."

"And I judge by your demeanor that your conversations with the other nobles did not go well."

"Can you blame them for being upset, Galina?" he asked

plaintively. "Their servants, their tithes...what's next? You take and take, and what do you give them in return?"

"What do I give them?" she asked. "Why, a better Izmoroz, of course. A *stronger* Izmoroz. One that will stand up against the growing number of threats to our recently won sovereignty."

He dropped his face into his hands and groaned. "Yes, yes. Your mighty new Izmoroz. Hail to the motherland, may the Lady bless us all with her strength and ferocity. I have heard your speeches, and it's all well and good for the peasantry. But what about *us*? What does the nobility get out of this? Surely we deserve some consideration for all we've given to your cause."

She gazed sadly at her father for a moment. It wasn't that she was surprised, exactly. She'd given up her idealized version of her father a while ago. But still, she thought he of all people would have been able to grasp what she was trying to achieve.

"The fact that you still express it as *my* cause rather than *our* cause illustrates just how myopic the nobles remain, Papa. I suppose I can't fault them for it. After all, most people who have been conditioned for generations to think only of themselves would struggle to accept a greater good. Still, it is disappointing that *none* of you are willing to step outside your small world, see the larger picture, and concede that there may be a better way."

"The nobility only see it as *your* way, Galina. And I must say, this patronizing, high-handed attitude of yours is not helping to defuse the situation."

"I do not wish to defuse the situation," said Galina. "In fact, if some sort of confrontation is inevitable, I would prefer to hurry it along so that these internal struggles can be resolved before Vittorio begins his inevitable march north to retake Izmoroz."

"Galina, as your father, I urge you to take this more seriously. Right now the only thing that's stopping them from becoming completely unhinged is the fact that you're one of us. And you need to remember that you *are* one of us. After all, where would you be without the nobility?"

Her eyes narrowed. "At present, I would be dealing with one less obstacle to the betterment of Izmoroz. Please tell your beloved nobility *they* should remember that their elevated status exists entirely at my pleasure, and it could be taken away at any time, should they prove too great a hindrance."

He crossed his arms and gave her an almost childish look of belligerence. "I most certainly will not tell them that."

"No?" She considered a moment. "Perhaps it was a mistake to make you my liaison with the nobility. I'm starting to wonder if you have been softening my messages all along to placate your fellows and lessen their ire."

His face paled, but after a moment his defiance returned. "W–well, I had to do something to keep them from complete mutiny. You have no idea what they're capable of if pushed too far."

"On the contrary," she said coldly. "As someone formerly betrothed to the Turgenev family, I know *exactly* what they're capable of. Sebastian had no clue, as usual, but since I am the curious sort, it did not take me long to discover the reprehensible actions that the nobility took against his mother, Lady Turgenev. Because she had the gall to marry an imperial soldier rather than an Izmorozian noble, they burned her family's country home to the ground, with her parents and younger sister still trapped inside."

"Then surely you understa—"

"But what the nobility fail to realize," Galina cut him off, "is that they have no idea what *I* am capable of."

She probably should have abolished the nobility the moment she took power. But the people had still held some regard for them, and their familiar presence had been comforting during the tumultuous transition period that followed.

Well, it wasn't too late. She just needed a *reason* to get rid of the nobility, so as not to seem like an utter tyrant. And since they all seemed intent on acting like spoiled, unruly children, she did not doubt that an opportunity would arise sooner rather than later.

9

Apparently, Sonya's brother had gotten better at lying. At least when it came to his own well-being, anyway. Although she should have been paying better attention.

After their encounter with the crazed elderly Viajero who somehow thought Sebastian might bring about the end of the world, the desert began to transform. Each day, while Sebastian continued east at an even pace, Sonya ranged out in all directions to replenish their meager supplies. She found a stream with fresh water, and herds of what appeared to be some sort of miniature deer. The temperature had eased off, and the sun didn't feel quite so much like a bludgeon on her head. In fact, since the landscape had ceased to be an endless trial, she started enjoying her wanderings and only caught up with Sebastian around sunset. Then she would chat about all she had seen and done that day while she cleaned and cooked their meal. She should have noticed that his involvement in the conversation lessened each night. But sometimes her enthusiasm got the better of her.

It wasn't until they arrived at the Kantesian border that Sebastian's condition became too obvious to ignore.

They had reached the edge of a sharp drop and reined in their mounts to take in the lush valley below. Directly before them, the land descended in a series of short plateaus that almost looked like a giant staircase. At the bottom, the terrain was densely packed with a type of tree that was unfamiliar to Sonya.

"Wow," said Sonya. "I can't wait to see what kind of game is down there. And maybe great cats, like leopards or something? Or even monkeys! What do you think?"

She turned to her brother just as he slid sideways out of his saddle. She leapt from Peppercorn and vaulted over his horse so that she caught him just before he hit the ground.

"Sebastian, what's wrong?"

But when she looked into his sweating, flushed face, she already knew. This close she could smell the infection. She gently laid him down, then checked his hand. Sure enough, it was red and puffy. How long had it been infected?

"You brat," she grumbled at her brother. "I asked you so many times how your hand was and you said fine."

"Nggg..." His eyelids fluttered for a moment.

If that was the most rise she could get out of him after such an unfair remark, he was definitely not doing well. Mikhail had taught her how to make some basic poultices that helped with infection, but those depended upon ingredients that could be found in Izmorozian forests, not these dry southern grasslands. She had no idea what around them, if anything, might work.

Perhaps there were ingredients she recognized down in the forest. She could descend the series of plateaus and forage for ingredients...

But no. It would take at least an hour to get down there, and a few hours to climb all the way back up, with who knew how much time in between for the actual foraging. She'd be leaving him utterly helpless that whole time. What if that crazy old Viajero had followed their trail? He wouldn't need magic with Sebastian in this condition. A foot on the throat would work just fine. And even if the flautist hadn't followed them, she had no idea what sort of predators lurked in this area. Sebastian stank of weakness and infection. Plumb pickings for a hungry wolf pack.

"Okay, little brother. Down we go."

Of course the tricky part would be coaxing two horses down a series of steep slopes, and that proved more of a challenge than she expected. Peppercorn eventually—*reluctantly*—allowed himself to be guided down one level. But Sonya didn't know the other horse at all and it seemed not to have the slightest grasp or willingness to attempt what she wanted. After an hour, with her patience running thin and Sebastian's forehead burning with fever, she gave up.

"Fine! I guess it's either you or my brother, so you're just going to have to go your own way!" She unfastened the saddle and bridle. "Enjoy being a free horse. Hopefully you're smart enough to survive here on your own. Plenty of grass to eat, at least."

The horse watched her with an oddly offended look as she slung her brother over her shoulder and edged her way down to the lower level where Peppercorn waited. As she began the entire process over again to the next plateau, the freed horse continued to watch them, as if unsure what to do. But by the step after that, it began to lose interest and started to graze. After a few more levels, she looked up and saw the horse was beginning to wander off. She hoped it would be okay, but if she could barely coax Peppercorn, whom she'd raised from a colt, down this precarious terrain, there'd probably been little chance she could have coaxed the other.

Progress was slow. Painfully, exhaustingly slow. Sebastian's condition continued to grow worse, but rushing Peppercorn was out of the question. One slip and he could easily break a leg. So she laid her brother on the ground, then carefully guided her horse down the next steep slope with soothing words and gentle touches. Once Peppercorn had reached the lower plateau, she climbed back up, slung her brother over her shoulders, and hauled him down. Then the process began all over again for the next plateau.

Sonya found herself missing Jorge. Not for the first time, of course. While it was true that they'd grown apart somewhat while she was in the Anxeles Escuros, there had always been some comfort in knowing he was nearby. And while she was happy to be back with her brother, it just wasn't the same thing. Also, it sure would have helped to have his potion-making skills right about then. She felt a sharp pang of resentment, which she knew was unfair. It was perfectly understandable that he had chosen to remain with his family, who clearly needed him. But still, she missed him and it was hard not to be upset about it.

As they got closer to the bottom, Sonya saw that it was not a forest, but a swamp. Dense and humid, coated in moss and lichen, and seething with bugs. Mushrooms and ferns abounded, but nothing she recognized. Any real hope of locating familiar ingredients for the remedies she knew began to fade.

When they reached the bottom, she discovered another problem. The ground was thick with mud and at times completely submersed in a brown stew. Peppercorn did not look happy about it.

"I know, *Perchinka*, I know..." She patted his nose as he slowly lifted one hoof, then the next, his ears twitching with distaste.

Sonya was weary from hauling Sebastian and had been looking forward to slinging her brother across Peppercorn's saddle once they reached the bottom. But with footing this unsure, she decided it was too risky. So she continued to lug him on her back while patiently but insistently guiding her horse through the shin-high muck.

The swamp held a very different heat than the desert. Not a harsh hammer blow but a wet blanket that laid upon her so heavily that it felt as if she were swimming through the air. There was also an entirely new lexicon of smells for her heightened senses to assimilate. Heavy, dank odors lingered in the air, blending into each other, and further contributing to the feeling of being underwater. Her sweat clung to her rather than evaporating, chaffing her joints raw as she trudged along. It was far too hot to wear anything except her sleeveless undershirt and trousers, but insects swarmed around her bare arms, shoulders, and neck in a gluttonous frenzy.

Time blurred as murkily as the air while she slogged through the swamps with Sebastian on her back and Peppercorn at her side. The sunlight that filtered wanly through the trees eventually disappeared altogether, so she began looking for a place for them to camp. But she couldn't find a single dry spot where she might lay her brother down. So she kept going, even slower now, so she could watch for tree roots that Peppercorn might stumble over in the dark.

She was tired and hungry and did not know how long she had been lugging her brother through the swamps. But she still had not seen any dry land. Were these swamps endless? How much farther could she go before she collapsed?

But then she caught the scent of roasting fish, and the animal instinct buzz at the back of her mind grew stronger, giving her a boost of energy as she pulled Peppercorn toward the smell.

At last she emerged into a clearing where a lump of land rose from the swamp like a boil. It was ringed with small wooden huts set on stilts. At the very center of the clearing was a large, joyfully crackling fire. Fish were impaled on a row of sticks that leaned toward the fire to cook. A man stood nearby carefully turning the sticks so that they roasted evenly on all sides. He was dressed in a patchwork of hide and cloth, and had long, pale blond hair.

As Sonya splashed through ankle-deep water toward the spit of land, the man turned with a start. He watched her, his fair brow knit together in concern, though for her or for himself, she couldn't tell.

"Please…" Sonya stumbled onto dry land. She dropped to her knees and laid Sebastian on the solid ground with less gentleness than she would have liked. Then she looked up at the man. "Can you help my brother?"

The man looked down at her gravely and spoke in a language she did not understand.

"Of course," she muttered. "Well, at least we made it to Kante."

Then she dropped down beside her brother. The soft, springy moss felt wonderful beneath her cheek and she quickly drifted into unconsciousness.

10

Jorge found it both comforting and troubling that no matter how much Colmo had changed, Cassa Estío remained the same.

Daily life there went on much as it had before the empire marched in, killed hundreds of people, and razed a huge portion of the city's marketplace. The Elhuyars continued their leisurely breakfasts, quiet reading in the library, strolls in the garden, gentle naps, and expansive evening meals. Even the daily concerts continued, despite the fact that so many of their previous musicians had died in the battle. There was always another hungry artist ready to take their place in the good graces of the Elhuyar family.

That, of course, was the troubling part. That Jorge's family was so powerful they could afford to continue on with their lives as usual while the surrounding city struggled like a great wounded animal. He wanted to use his family's vast resources to help people. The question was how.

Javier and Lucia had agreed to work together to prepare the surviving Viajero and Anxeles Escuros for the inevitable return of imperial forces. If Onat Duman's latest information was correct, and Jorge had little reason to doubt it, Vittorio had gained command of the full imperial army. Now it was only a matter of time before they returned.

But Jorge wasn't much for military tactics. So rather than get in their way, he decided to utilize the knowledge he'd gained from Anton Velikhov, the foremost apothecary of healing potions in the world, and opened a clinic in Sonya's old apartment in the Viajero Quarter.

With so many wounded Viajero, the clinic was immediately popular. But he discovered that Viajero could be challenging patients. Some, like the woman who moaned about her lungs being scorched from smoke inhalation, were so dramatic that he couldn't get a sense of how bad the injury actually was. Others, like the man who had to return three times to get his broken leg set because he refused to stop dancing, clung to some fanciful notion that if they could only *wish* hard enough, their injuries would heal instantly.

The saddest were those with injuries that would have a lifelong impact on their art. The guitarist with the shattered hand, the singer with a punctured throat, the painter who had been blinded by pitch. They each came to him seeking hope yet knowing there was probably none to be found. Jorge tried to break the news as gently as he could. The guitarist's hand might one day hold a fork, but it would never again dance upon the fretboard. The singer might eventually be able to speak, but would never again find those haunting upper registers. The painter might one day be able to discern shadows or even shapes, but never again tell the difference between the face of a loved one and a stranger.

However, there were moments of joy as well. A dancer with a dislocated hip who was nearly back to normal in minutes. A flautist who only needed his sinuses flushed with warm salt water to get his hearing restored. For these patients, the look of dread transforming to relief was worth more than any amount of money.

"I have to hand it to you, little brother," said Maria as she helped Jorge wash up after dismissing a patient. "You might be the most useful Elhuyar."

"Not to me," called Lucia from across the room where she was boiling strips of cloth to be used as bandages.

"Thank you, beloved," Maria called back.

"When Sonya and I were traveling through the poorest parts of Izmoroz, I did something similar," said Jorge as he dried off his hands. "I couldn't sit around Cassa Estío doing nothing. Even so, I worry it's not enough."

"I'd say you're doing plenty," said Lucia. "Getting as many Viajero back on their feet as possible is the best way to prepare ourselves for another attack from the empire."

"But I can't help thinking that if Sonya were here, she'd have some bold, possibly crazy idea by now," said Jorge. "She'd be out doing things. Taking the fight to them."

"We can't even get all of Raíz together yet," pointed out Maria. "We're not ready to take the fight *anywhere*."

Although the Great Families had pitched in to fend off the earlier imperial assault, that had been mostly panicked self-preservation. Now that they had some time to think, many had become more evasive concerning their support for a free Raíz. Some had even hinted at looking into the idea of rejoining the empire. Jorge couldn't really blame them. Regardless of what Lucia might think, it was unlikely that the Viajero would have rallied during the last battle. And if they hadn't been able to turn back the army on their own before, how could they do it the next time with not merely imperial soldiers but possibly the Uaine as well?

Thinking of the Uaine brought up a host of more personal concerns for Jorge that he hadn't yet shared with anyone. Would he have to fight against Blaine and Rowena? Even after they had both turned their backs on him, he wasn't sure he could…

"Excuse me, Señor." Ignacio, one of his family's private guards, entered the apartment. He had been standing out front acting as crowd control for the patients, and was accustomed to looking aloof and unimpressed by whatever he saw. Yet now he looked a little wild around the eyes.

"Is something wrong?" asked Jorge.

"There is a…person here to see you. At least I think it's a person. How should I say this…She looks like your friend Sonya but…more so? She has asked to see 'the lemming called Jorge Elhuyar.'"

"Oh God," said Jorge.

"You know who it is?" asked Maria.

"I have a pretty good idea. Okay, Ignacio. Let her in. And, er, be polite."

"Yes, Señor."

A few moments later he brought Ranger Tatiana into the room. Jorge was certain it was her, but she looked different. Much younger for one thing. And he didn't remember her having talons for feet the last time they met. Instead of a traditional Ranger coat, she wore a cape fringed with white feathers. That seemed a little on the nose to Jorge, but he was hardly going to criticize the Ranger for her fashion sense.

"Tatiana, it's good to see you again."

She cocked her head to one side as she regarded him for a moment, her owl eyes unblinking.

"Ah. I have found you at last, sweet lemming."

She walked over to him with a pronounced birdlike strut.

Jorge did his best not to seem nervous. "You've changed a bit, Tatiana."

"Yes, you know our ways, so I don't need to explain."

"Did you...barter with the Lady for restored youth?" he ventured.

"Just so." She looked pleased.

He remembered Tatiana being full of warmth and laughter. Compared to the towering Andre and the snarling Anatoly, she had been an almost comforting presence, despite constantly referring to him as a lemming. But now she gazed at him with a cold presence that seemed far more owl than human. As if she might be sizing him up as potential prey.

"I take it the cost was high," he guessed.

"Yes..." She paused for a moment, as though recalling something. "Ah, but I have the mistress now. She takes care of complications for me."

"The mistress?"

"She has many names...let me see..."

Tatiana seemed to be genuinely struggling to recall any of them. Just how far gone was she?

"*Kukla* is one, yes. *Kuklushka*, of course, of course. That one is only for me to say. Hm, and Majesty. Others say that one often now. There is also Odoyevtseva..." She smiled in a way that Jorge found somewhat chilling, but probably was not meant to be. "I especially like that name. *Odoyevtsevaaaah*. It sounds so pretty."

"Odoyevtseva..." Jorge frowned. "You mean Galina?"

"That is another of her names," agreed Tatiana.

"Why on earth are you serving Galina Odoyevtseva?"

Tatiana blinked at him. "I do as the Lady commands."

"I'm sorry, let me see if I understand." Jorge couldn't quite bring himself to believe it. "Lady Marzanna, Goddess of Winter and Death, specifically told you to serve Galina Odoyevtseva?"

"Andre serves as well," she said.

"Dear God. Why?"

"Our minds do not work as humans do anymore. We require... guidance."

"I suppose she would be good for that," admitted Jorge. "But what was that other thing you called her? *Majesty*?"

"Yes, I remember now. This is how I was supposed to say it from the beginning. You will forgive the error." Then Tatiana spoke with rehearsed precision: "Her Royal Majesty, Queen Galina the First of Izmoroz."

"*Queen* Galina?"

Jorge decided he needed to sit. And have a drink. While he obtained both a chair and a glass of wine, Tatiana waited patiently. As an owl might wait for a mouse to emerge from shelter.

"So this is the new queen of Izmoroz," said Lucia. "Onat was telling me even the ambassador is impressed with her."

"A part of me can't believe that Galina of all people has somehow consolidated power in Izmoroz," Jorge said. "On the other hand, it makes perfect sense. Especially if she has two veteran Rangers under her."

"So what does this queen of Izmoroz want with my brother?" demanded Maria, looking a little too confrontational for Jorge's liking or her own safety.

"An alliance," said Tatiana. "Izmoroz and Raíz together will fight the empire. That is my mistress's command."

"*Command?*" Maria didn't look pleased.

"Leave that for now, Maria," Jorge said quickly. Then he turned back to Tatiana. "So...Izmoroz now has the means to fight the empire?"

He didn't want to offend the Ranger, but he and Sonya had recruited the Uaine primarily because the people of Izmoroz had neither the resources nor the skill to fight for themselves.

"Andre prepares the people even now." Tatiana sounded proud. "Lemmings come from across Izmoroz so that they might find strength. The mistress inspires them all."

"I see." An entire army trained by Rangers of Marzanna might indeed prove formidable.

"Well, we can use all the help we can get," said Lucia. "Sounds great."

"Hold on a moment," Jorge said. "I know Galina. She's brilliant, and I'm fairly certain she has the best interests of Izmoroz at heart. But I'm not sure how much we can trust her. I suspect she was at least partly responsible for pushing Sonya into exile."

Tatiana nodded. "The mistress said she hopes that you are wise enough to see beyond such minor concerns."

Jorge gave her a pained smile. "That does sound like something Galina would say. But there is another and perhaps more immediate issue. No one in this room has the authority to commit all of Raíz to an alliance."

"Then who can?" asked Tatiana.

It was a simple enough question, he supposed. And yet, Jorge wasn't sure how to answer. Was there really anyone in charge of Raíz right now?

"We'll have to call a gathering of the Great Families," said Maria.

"I suppose you're right," said Jorge. "If we can unite the Great Families, we could unite all of Raíz. And then..."

"And then Raíz would join with your old comrades to crush the empire!" said Lucia.

"Yes..." And possibly crush Jorge's other old comrades in the process. But he couldn't think about that. Blaine and Rowena made their choice. They sided with Vittorio, though he still couldn't fathom why.

They had to know this would likely put them in conflict with their former allies. And if the time came for direct confrontation, well... he would deal with it then.

"Sweet lemming Jorge." Tatiana's luminous eyes scanned the room. "Is *Lisitsa* not with you?"

"No, she and her brother left Colmo weeks ago."

"Ah." Tatiana looked disappointed.

"I don't know if this is any consolation, Tatiana, but Sonya said that she tried to make Anatoly's final days more comfortable."

Tatiana regarded him with a hard expression that made it clear just how little humanity remained within her.

"I pray to the Lady that when I meet my own death, it is not under such pathetic circumstances."

Jorge couldn't help but wonder if Sonya would one day be so... inhuman. He truly hoped not.

II

Galina considered it unfortunate that what she excelled at in life was exactly what disappointed her about life. She was very good at predicting the actions of other people. She was also saddened that people were so easy to predict.

She didn't know exactly how she had developed this skill. Certainly not by hard-won experience, considering she was just shy of eighteen and had been raised in a profoundly sheltered environment. Nor could she attribute it solely to books. After all, her father had read all the same books and then some, yet he seemed completely incapable of conceiving of the event that she was almost certain was about to occur.

Perhaps, she wondered, there might be some sort of progression from one generation to the next. An evolving condition passed from parent to child. Her father had enlightened himself as much he possibly could, which then allowed Galina to enlighten herself even further. It was an optimistic and distinctly un-Izmorozian idea, but she decided that she rather fancied it.

She gazed out the top-floor window of the building across the street from Roskosh Manor. The swirling dome roofs of her childhood home gleamed in the moonlight, but otherwise, it was difficult to see much of the structure where she had lived most of her life thus far.

"The evacuation is complete, Your Majesty," said Andre as he entered the room. "Your mother, your brother, the Victashian, and all the household servants besides Masha have been taken to a safe place without arousing suspicion."

Galina's eyes did not leave the manor as she spoke. "Thank you, Andre. Please ask Masha to bring my father here. I want to make certain he sees what is about to transpire."

"Yes, Your Majesty."

She wondered if it was possible to force her father's evolution forward to match her own, or if she must resign herself to watch him lag increasingly behind. She hoped that was not the case.

"Galina, what is the meaning of this?" her father asked as Masha led him into the room dressed in his nightshirt. His brow was furrowed with anger, but Galina knew him well enough to recognize the fear underneath.

She only looked at him for a moment before returning her eyes to the manor. "I trust you recall our earlier conversation about the infuriated nobility burning the Turgenev country house to the ground with Sebastian's grandparents and aunt still inside?"

"Yes, of course," he snapped like the grouchy old man he was apparently becoming. "What's that got to do with anything?"

She watched three shadowy, cloaked figures hurry from a nearby alleyway toward the manor. Once they reached Galina's family home, they split up, skulking along the wall until they had each taken up position at one of the sides.

"Papa," she said calmly, "we have no country house."

"Well, I've never seen the appeal," said her father. "But what does that..."

He trailed off as he caught sight of one of the shadowy figures lighting a pitch-soaked torch beneath a window of Roskosh Manor.

"It can't be!"

"I'm afraid it is, Papa."

"They wouldn't dare!"

Galina looked at him pityingly. "Perhaps it was you, then, who did not fully understand what they were capable of."

"Stop them!"

"No."

The figure tossed the torch through the window, then peered in, no doubt admiring the view as the fire licked at some priceless piece of furniture within. A few moments later, another of the figures tossed a lit torch through a window on their side, and then the third one followed soon after.

There was a long moment where all Galina was able to see were faint flickers through the windows. Small enough that they could have been reading lamps. But the light grew slowly brighter until at last the entire lower floor of the house was lit up like one of the parties her mother used to host during the imperial occupation. The second floor caught fire shortly after, and that's when the flames finally blew out all the windows in a gush. All those rich rugs and tapestries, all the oil paintings, and even the fancy imported Kantesian table made wonderful kindling. It did not take long for the stone frame of Roskosh Manor to go from the finest residence in Izmoroz to the largest oven.

"Why?" There were tears in her father's eyes as he stared down at the seething inferno contained within the blackening shell of their beloved home. "If you knew this was going to happen, why didn't you stop them?"

It gave Galina no pleasure to watch the destruction of her childhood home any more than it did to listen to her father's heartbroken anguish. That was exactly why she forced herself to watch.

"*Attempted* arson would have required a less severe response than successful arson," she said. "To make my point to the rest of the nobility, I need a reprisal that is quite severe. But I believe in justice and the rule of law. The punishment must be of equal measure to the crime. So, there had to be real, palpable loss."

She turned to him at last, and despite the evenness in her voice, her eyes glistened with unshed tears. "I warned you that the nobility would need to sacrifice a great deal for the good of Izmoroz. Did you think our own family exempt from that?"

She did not know if it was understanding she now saw in her father's expression, or merely acquiescence. When she looked back out the window, she saw that the three perpetrators had already been apprehended. A select group of the newly established Izmorozian militia had encircled the area and hidden themselves away before dusk. The cloaked figures hadn't made it more than a block.

Galina unselfconsciously dabbed at her eyes. "Now, if you will excuse me, Papa. I have some business to attend to."

"Wh-what are you going to do to them?" he asked.

"Something terrible."

By sunrise, it was done. Lord Levenchik, Lord Ovstrovsky, and Lord Aukadova had been impaled on vertical stakes before the smoldering ruins of Roskosh Manor. Their cloaks had been removed so that all could see their finery. Even if people did not recognize them, it was clear they were nobility.

The sharpened wooden shafts had been inserted through the anus and forced all the way up into their chest cavities. Small crosspieces had been nailed to the stakes to stop them from piercing the heart, which would have ended the suffering prematurely. The criminals' hands were tied behind their backs, but their legs were allowed to kick futilely at the air or strain to touch the ground that was just out of reach. A sign hung around each of their necks that said TRAITOR.

The three men whimpered like animals for most of that day. The last one, Levenchik, finally died around sunset, a full fifteen hours later.

Many historians would later suggest that this day marked the true beginning of the fearsome reign of Galina the First, Queen of Izmoroz.

12

In his dreams, Sebastian could not breathe. His mouth was full of mud. It spilled from his lips and leaked from his nose and eyes. It flooded his stomach and lungs. He was merely a vessel for a sluggish creeping dark that predated life and all of existence. He was a fragile clay vessel destined to break...

He took a shuddering breath and opened his eyes to see his sister looking down at him with concern.

"Must have been some dream you were having," she said.

"It was." Could he still taste the dank earth in his mouth? Perhaps it was only his imagination.

"Well, that's to be expected when you've had a fever."

"A fever?" He looked around and realized they were somewhere completely new. No longer a burning desert, but a small wooden hut. There was no furniture, and instead he lay on a mat woven from reeds.

The space was clean but he and his sister were both caked in dry mud. The sight of that made him shiver. Most dreams were forgotten the moment a person woke up. He wished he'd forgotten this one.

"I guess you don't really remember," said Sonya. "Your hand got infected, and you didn't tell me, you brat."

He looked down at his hand, which was now wrapped in a clean bandage. It ached dully but was no longer puffy and red like it had been.

"Sorry," he said sheepishly. "I didn't want to worry you, and I thought it would just clear up on its own."

She gave him a look like he was a complete imbecile, which was probably fair. "No, Bastuchka, infected wounds usually don't just magically *get better*. Not even for fancy wizards."

"So what happened?"

"No thanks to you, I got us into Kante, which I have to say is nothing like what you described. It's all swampland."

"This must be the Gestank Swamps in southern Kante then. That would make sense considering the direction we were coming from. But what happened to my hand?"

"I found a little village, and thankfully they have their own medicines for that sort of thing. It didn't work as fast as what Jorge would have made, but it did the trick."

"How long have we been here?"

"A week."

"That long?" Sebastian tried to stand up but felt suddenly faint.

"Don't rush it." Sonya took his arm to steady him. "We'll need to stay a few more days so you can get your strength back." She gave him a thoughtful look. "Although you never really had much strength to begin with, soooo maybe just a day, then."

He glared at her. "Despite what you might think, you're not actually funny."

She grinned, showing her sharp teeth. "*They* think I'm hilarious."

"Who?"

She guided him over to the doorway. Their hut appeared to be raised on thick wooden stilts about ten feet from the ground. Similar huts stretched out on either side to form a loose semicircle. Below them, it was mostly shallow wetlands except for a large mound at the center of the semicircle where a bonfire blazed away. A few people dressed in woolen robes stood around the fire. One of them noticed Sebastian and Sonya standing in the doorway and said something to the others. They all turned and waved up to him, looking strangely solemn.

Sebastian smiled and waved back. A different one said something else, and they all gave a short laugh. It looked strange, however, since they still weren't really smiling.

"Interesting, aren't they?" asked Sonya.

"Very."

"They don't speak a word of the imperial common tongue, of course, so it's been all pantomime since we got here. They refused to help until I gave them my bow. Of course, I didn't have a knife to give them..."

She gave him a long look.

He winced. "I told you I was sorry. I promise I'll get you a new one."

"Anyway," she continued, "once I gave them my bow, they got to work on you. It took a few days, but I eventually convinced them I wasn't a danger, and they gave me my bow back so I could help them hunt. Pretty decent game. Lots of rabbits, and these funny-looking rodents that are as big as a barn cat."

He looked at his sister. "I'm sorry I caused you so much trouble, Yasha."

She pinched his cheek. "That's what little brothers are for, right?"

He looked back at the group of Kantesians for a moment, four in all. Two older ones with gray hair. The other two were younger, one with blond hair and one with brown. Parents and their adult children perhaps? It hadn't really been that long since he, Sonya, and their parents had all lived together, but it seemed a lifetime ago now.

"Why did you join the Rangers of Marzanna?" he asked.

"Why?" She seemed surprised by the question. "To compete with you, oh mighty wizard."

"Really?"

She rolled her eyes. "You really are a clueless twerp, aren't you? Yes, I was sick with jealousy that Mother put all her focus on you. Mikhail asked if I wanted to find my own path and be special in my own way. Obviously, I said yes. What neglected adolescent wouldn't?"

"But a *death* goddess, Yasha. It just seems..." He shook his head.

"Look, I don't get why you joined the empire, either. I think there are just some things about each other we'll never understand."

"Maybe so." He was saddened by that idea.

It took a few more days, but finally he was feeling like his old self again. Soon after, the older male Kantesian urged them to gather their things and follow him.

"Where does he want to take us?" Sebastian asked nervously as he followed Sonya down the ladder to the sodden ground.

"No idea, but it's not like we can stay here forever," she said. "If they wanted to harm us, they've had plenty of chances, so I think it'll be okay."

They followed the old man over to Sonya's horse, and she packed their few possessions into his saddlebags.

Sebastian frowned. "What a minute. Where's *my* horse?"

"Are you only just realizing that now?" she asked. "Hopefully he's galloping joyfully on the Diablo Steppes somewhere."

"You *abandoned* him?"

"He refused to climb down, and you were running out of time. What did you want me to do?"

"Nothing, I guess..." He'd had that horse ever since he'd left Izmoroz. He wouldn't say they'd been particularly close. Not like Sonya and her beloved Peppercorn. But still, they'd been through a lot together.

The footing in the wetlands was precarious, so they agreed it was wisest not to ride Peppercorn and just have him shoulder their supplies. They walked behind the old man, who occasionally glanced back to make sure they were still following.

As Sebastian carefully picked his way along, feeling his boots sink into the mud with each step, he recalled his nightmare once again and had to suppress a shudder. Had that been Mokosh contacting him? For what purpose? Had the world become unbalanced? Things certainly did seem to be spiraling out of control, what with Izmoroz breaking free of the empire, Raíz following after, and then Vittorio's coup at the palace. Sebastian wasn't even certain he could call Aureum an empire any longer. But if the world had become unbalanced, did Mokosh truly expect him to help her destroy it? Could she somehow force him to do it? When he'd wiped Rykov from existence back in

Colmo, he hadn't been himself, exactly, but he also hadn't felt out of control, either. Yet what if she could take it even further and use him like some kind of puppet?

These worries preyed on him as they trudged through the swamps for a couple of hours. At last they came to an area where the shallow wetlands expanded and deepened into a narrow river. A lone stilted hut sat beside the water. A man perhaps in his late thirties with shaggy brown hair was carefully hanging the leaves of some plant out to dry and whistling a tune that Sebastian was surprised to find vaguely familiar, though he couldn't say from where.

"That sounds like a Raízian sailor song," murmured Sonya.

"He doesn't look Raízian...," said Sebastian.

Their elderly guide called out to the man in the Kantesian language, and they conversed for a moment. The man carefully studied Sonya and Sebastian, then laughed. Not in the oddly somber way of the other Kantesians but with something a bit closer to the familiar warmth of a Raízian or Aureumian.

"Mine friends." He sauntered over to them. His accent was even thicker than Isobelle's. "What can I do for you?"

"First, could you thank our hosts for saving my brother's life?" asked Sonya.

The man nodded cheerfully and said something in Kantesian. The old man inclined his head in response to Sonya, but still did not smile.

"Now, what do you seek?" asked the man. "I think you do not mean to be here in these swamps, yes?"

"We're trying to locate someone who probably lives north of here," said Sebastian. "Her name is Isobelle Cohen?"

The man shook his head. "That name sounds Kantesian, but I do not know it."

Sebastian frowned thoughtfully. "Perhaps you know a Herzog of Weide then?"

The man's eyes practically bulged out of his head, and even the old man who had brought them there seemed to recognize the name.

"You know the Herzog of Weide?" asked the man.

"Well, his daughter. Or perhaps granddaughter." Isobelle had said something about her grandfather being the former Herzog of Weide.

"I take it these people are important?" asked Sonya.

"Oh yes. The Herzog brings us all together to fight..." He gazed at them speculatively. "Maybe you?"

"No, not us," Sonya said firmly. "We're from Izmoroz."

"Ah! I have heard of this place! They say there is endless snow and everyone rides around on bears."

"Neither of those things are true, I'm afraid," said Sebastian.

"Ach. Disappointing. Well, my name is Hans Gebhard."

"I'm Sonya Turgenev, and this is my brother."

Sebastian noted that his sister had left out their Aureumian family name and decided for the time being that was wise.

"Sebastian Turgenev," he said. "A pleasure to meet you."

"Well, Turgenevs, I think you want me to take you north out of the swamps on my boat, yes?"

"We don't have much money...," said Sebastian.

"Sure we do," said Sonya. "I got paid very well when I was a mercenary, and I didn't spend much of it. As long as Hans doesn't mind taking imperial coins."

"Hmm." Hans looked more carefully at Sonya's black leather vest. "Ah, these wings. Yes, this is a symbol I know. The Anxeles Escuros in Colmo." He looked at her with new appreciation. "You were one of these?"

"Technically I still am, I guess."

Sebastian wasn't quite sure what they were talking about, but the man nodded, looking impressed. "So then we need not fear bandits on our journey," said Hans.

"Or going hungry," she boasted. "Just ask the old man here. I'm a great hunter, too."

Hans turned to Sebastian and gave him a teasing smile. "And what can *you* do?"

"Oh, er..." He wasn't sure if it was wise to bring up his gift with elemental magic.

"He mostly just gets into more trouble than he can handle," said

Sonya. "But he's the one who knows this Isobelle, and he *is* my brother. So I guess I have to keep him around."

Hans laughed. "I like you Turgenevs. Now, I'm afraid I cannot take you directly to the Herzog of Weide, but perhaps I can take you to someone else who can."

Sonya slapped his back in what Sebastian thought was an overly familiar way and grinned her sharp-toothed grin. "Good enough for me, Hans."

13

The last time there had been a meeting of the Great Families, Jorge had been eight years old. He remembered it only as a series of impressions. Wandering through the unfamiliar corridors of the Pereria family estate, navigating rooms crowded with glowering old men and dense clouds of tobacco smoke, pillaging the kitchens with his sister and Domingo Pereria, who in retrospect had clearly been enamored with Maria and had been trying to impress her with acts of reckless daring. They weren't caught, but all three got stomachaches from eating too many cherries.

It was the stomachache Jorge remembered most clearly. Perhaps that was why he felt a vague dread as he prepared for this meeting. Or perhaps his anxiousness came from the fact that this time, the Elhuyar family would be hosting. As hosts, he and his family were expected to spare no expense and show every courtesy, or else someone might try to claim a grievance.

The initial gathering was held in the gardens, which had been cultivated by Viajero to project calmness and serenity. Jorge hoped that might also keep tempers from flaring too high. But passive Viajero magic could only do so much, and the resentment between some families had been built over decades or even centuries.

There was another reason why Jorge was uneasy. His mother had made it clear during the days leading up to the gathering that there were several lovely young women she planned to introduce him to over the course of the evening.

"Relax, little brother," chided Maria as the two made their way from the kitchens where they had been overseeing preparations. "You've faced imperial soldiers, dastardly bandits, and fearsome undead. Surely you are not afraid of a few prospective brides."

"It's astonishing that even when we're in the middle of a revolution, Mama would think of such things," he grumbled. "Why don't *you* ever have to put up with it?"

"Simple," she said. "I told Mama to stop it."

"Just like that?"

"Just like that."

Jorge gave her a skeptical look. "And she didn't get upset?"

"Upset?" asked Maria. "She burst into tears, fell to her knees, and told me I was killing her."

"Ah. And how long did that last?"

Maria shrugged. "The wailing? Less than an hour. Of course then there were weeks of the silent treatment after that."

"Ouch."

"It was tough, but eventually we made peace, and now we have an understanding. If I ever decide I'm ready to marry, I will let her know immediately. Until then, she leaves it alone."

"Do you think you will ever marry?" asked Jorge.

"A man, you mean?" Maria tossed her thick mane of hair. "Don't be silly."

"Huh," said Jorge. "You know, I've traveled across the continent and yet somehow you make me feel like I'm the provincial one."

"You have the burden of being the baby in the family," she said. "Just like Hugo is terrified of letting down Papa, you're afraid of letting down Mama."

Jorge sighed. "I suppose that's true."

"You liked Sonya, didn't you?"

"I still do, I suppose," said Jorge. "But even if Mama could have accepted her into the family, which seems unlikely, Sonya made it clear she would never marry."

"I knew I liked her," said Maria.

The garden was already buzzing with conversation and subdued laughter. A guitarist sat to one side, plucking out quiet up-tempo melodies while the guests stood in small groups enjoying some of the finest wines on the continent.

"Ah, Jorge!" His mother beckoned him over to where she stood with a patiently smiling young woman. "There is someone I want you to meet!"

"Good luck," murmured Maria.

"Thanks." Jorge squared his shoulders and began the gauntlet of prospective brides.

It wasn't too terrible, of course. They were all very nice, intelligent women. Jorge's mother wouldn't bother introducing him to someone empty-headed or bad-tempered simply because they were a good marriage prospect. Of course, most of them asked about his time in Izmoroz. At first, he was reluctant to talk about some of the more unsettling aspects of his adventures, such as watching an army of the dead rise from their coffins, or sharing a meal with a group of Rangers of Marzanna who kept referring to him as "lemming" with a hungry look in their animal eyes. But then he realized that it might be a way to quickly weed out the dull and narrow-minded among them. Not that he really wanted to marry any of them, but he feared it was only a matter of time before he relented to his mother's pressure and picked one. It might as well be someone with whom he could get along.

At last the chimes rang to signal the food was ready. A mass of tables had been set out in a U shape, and everyone took their seats with their respective families. Seating had been thought out well in advance so that families who were unfriendly to each other did not sit near each other, but just in case, mercenaries all stood at regular intervals to make sure the peace was kept.

Once everyone settled, Jorge's father, the great Arturo Elhuyar, stood and raised his glass. It didn't take long for everyone to fall silent.

"Thank you all for coming on such short notice and during such tumultuous times," he said. "We have much to discuss, but I have found that these things should never be done on an empty stomach, so please, eat your fill."

The household servants began delivering food. As courtesy and tradition demanded of the host, the Elhuyars were served last.

Jorge sat with Hugo to his left and his parents after that. Maria sat to his right and he noticed that Domingo Pereria had been sat on Maria's other side. Señora Elhuyar might have officially given up matching-making for his sister, but clearly she was not above more subtle pressures.

"Things seem to be going well so far," Hugo said, though he still looked quite anxious.

"You think anyone will kick up a fuss about what we've been doing?" asked Jorge.

"I'd be surprised if they *didn't*," said Hugo.

"The Pereria family is behind you completely, of course," said Domingo. "Independence is *exactly* what Raíz needs."

Domingo was a few years older than Jorge and carried himself with the dashing aplomb that most people expected of the Great Families. He had a bright smile and a confident bearing that made you want to believe whatever he said. Jorge wished he had even a portion of the man's charisma.

"We're pleased to know that the Elhuyar family has your support," said Jorge in a way that he feared was far too stiff for someone like Domingo.

"Naturally! Our families have always been close." He turned his dazzling smile on Maria. "In fact, I've often thought how great it would be if our two families could be even *closer.*"

Maria returned his smile. "Then it's a shame that you have no sisters for Jorge to marry."

Jorge was stunned at how harshly his sister shut down the eldest son of Esteban Pereria, but Domingo took it in stride. He laughed good-naturedly and said, "As always, Maria, your wit is as piercing as your beauty."

"I'm glad you appreciate both," she said.

Finally, everyone had eaten their fill, the tables were cleared, and Jorge's father stood once more.

"Shall we adjourn to discuss matters?"

The patriarch and eldest son of each family rose.

"Jorge, you will come, too," his father said.

"Y-yes, Papa." He hurriedly stood, then glanced back at Maria. It wasn't fair that she was supposed to remain behind. Especially since she was far more instrumental to Raízian independence than Hugo.

But she shooed him on. "Go. We're already pushing things enough."

"Fine. But stay nearby."

She raised an eyebrow but nodded.

As Jorge followed Hugo and his father into the house, Domingo fell in beside him.

"*Someone's* moved up quickly since their return," he said quietly.

Jorge blushed. "I suspect it's more to do with the fact that I can't seem to stay out of trouble."

Domingo smiled. "At a time like this, isn't that the same thing?"

"I suppose in a sense."

They filed into his father's study, thirteen members of the Great Families and five mercenaries. Fortunately, it was a large room with plenty of seating. The patriarchs seated themselves first, then the eldest sons. Jorge was left without a chair, but he was content to stand against the wall beside Javier Arzak.

Jorge's father was settled into his favorite leather chair. He lit a pipe and puffed thoughtfully for a moment. It was clear several other families were eager to speak their mind, but even they held respect for Jorge's father and so remained silent.

"I know you all have things to say," he told them. "And I promise I will listen attentively to all of it. But first, I think it is best for you to be completely apprised of the situation as it currently stands."

He paused to see if there were any objections. Again, the restless ones curbed their impulses out of respect for Señor Elhuyar.

"Very well. I expect that some of you have a strong desire to return to the way things were. Perhaps you imagine we could pay a tribute and return in peace to the empire. But I'm afraid that is now impossible because there was recently a coup at the palace and Her Imperial Majesty, Caterina the First, has been murdered."

There were sharp intakes of breath, followed by several whispered conversations.

"Jorge, please give them the details."

Jorge had been slouching against the wall beside the Xefe, and tried not to look too startled as he straightened.

"Yes, Papa." He nodded to the assembly. "Gentlemen, it is an honor. Our intelligence indicates that Franko Vittorio, former imperial commander in Izmoroz, has allied himself with his one-time enemies, the Uaine, and taken Magna Alto. He killed the empress, as well as her two eldest children, then declared the youngest to be emperor and himself to be regent. The returning imperial army was forced to either overthrow the young boy, who was technically the legitimate heir, or back him. They chose the latter. This leaves Vittorio more or less at the head of the empire now."

There was silence for several moments. Some looked at him with shock, others with dismay. And some with disbelief.

Finally, Señor Muñoz, a gaunt, balding man, spoke up in his dry, crackling voice. He addressed Jorge's father. "With the greatest respect, Señor Elhuyar, how can we know that your son's intelligence is correct? How has he obtained this information?"

Jorge's father merely turned to him.

"Y-yes," Jorge said. "Unfortunately, we cannot verify all the information ourselves. Nor can we necessarily take it at face value. We, along with the Anxeles Escuros and the city's Viajero led by Lucia Velazquez, have been communicating with the Victasha Intelligence Bureau, and—"

"That's absurd!" burst out Señor Cruz as he stood up. The Cruzes were the most recently accepted as a Great Family, a mere fifteen years before, and tended to be bolder than others.

"Señor Cruz," Jorge's father said. "My son speaks with my voice. Do you offer me disrespect?"

Cruz froze. His eyes glanced to either side, and he saw no support with other families. So he sat back down.

"Apologies, Señor Elhuyar. I let my surprise get the better of me. I was not expecting news of cooperation with a foreign nation who has been our adversary in times past."

Señor Elhuyar merely nodded and turned back to Jorge once more. Apparently, this was to be some sort of trial by fire for him.

"Yes, thank you, Señor Cruz, for bringing up an excellent point so emphatically," said Jorge. "It is true that any information we receive from Victasha must be handled with some skepticism, and I assure you we will continue to do so. But some of it can be corroborated. I spoke directly with a former imperial captain that was betrayed and nearly killed by his own aide as part of the coup."

"That does lend some credence to the Victashian intelligence," said Señor Zorilla. The Zorillas had been around even longer than the Elhuyars. Some said the reason they had never been on top was because of an overabundance of caution. "However, additional third-party evidence is hardly conclusive, and to my mind, not compelling enough to completely abandon all thought of reconciliation with the empire."

The man spoke sleepily, with a sort of disinterest, as if they were merely discussing the price of fruit rather than the fate of all Raíz. Jorge decided the man could do with a wake-up call.

"Thank you, Señor. I agree that firsthand verification on the state of the empire would be ideal. If you wish to send a delegation to Magna Alto yourself, I cannot stop you. But I know this man Vittorio. Whomever you send, make sure it's no one you value because if he truly *is* in command, I promise you will never see that person again."

Señor Zorilla did seem to perk up a little at the threat, which Jorge found gratifying.

"Yes, fine, I think we understand the situation now," said Señor Joaquim Dicenta as he gazed down at his glass of wine.

Jorge internally winced. If there was anyone who might really derail things, it was the Dicentas. They had once been on equal footing with the Elhuyars. Jorge now knew the reason they had fallen behind was because they had declined to aid the empire in equipping the imperial army during their conquest of Izmoroz, a position that Jorge could certainly respect. Even so, the rivalry between the families was so deeply entrenched that Dicenta might see this as an opportunity to make the

Elhuyars look bad, and push his own family to the top in their stead. But of course he gave no indication that was his intention, and instead seemed thoroughly preoccupied with his wine.

"Your point is well taken," Señor Dicenta continued with an almost regretful air. As though he really didn't mean to spoil their plans but simply couldn't ignore their obvious incompetence. "Sending a delegation to Magna Alto at this point would be suicidal. But that's hardly an argument for us to run headlong into a military conflict with the strongest power on the continent. For all we know, this Vittorio might have no designs for Raíz at all. If anything, it seems he'd be more likely to go after those northerners who drove him out."

"I'm glad you brought up Izmoroz, Señor." Jorge turned to Domingo. "Would you go find my sister and ask her to bring our *guest* here?"

Domingo looked startled but nodded and hurried out of the room.

"What is this about?" Dicenta growled, no longer looking quite so disinterested. "What *guest*?"

Jorge smiled ingratiatingly. "Señor, if you will kindly indulge me for a few moments. Several here have complained about a lack of firsthand information, and they are quite right to do so. I'm afraid I can't furnish such evidence regarding the empire, but I can regarding Izmoroz. As you may or may not know, Izmoroz successfully won their independence from the empire. I assisted them in this effort."

"You?" scoffed Señor Cruz.

"Yes, me," said Jorge, and pressed forward. "Their new queen, Galina Odoyevtseva, happens to be an acquaintance of mine, and when she heard about our own recent efforts toward independence, she decided to send a representative with an offer."

"What sort of offer?" asked Dicenta.

Jorge glanced over at the door and saw Domingo, looking a little dazed, and Maria, looking rather pleased.

"I'll let her present it herself," he said. "Maria, please bring in our guest."

Maria's eyes challenged every man in the room as she entered. She was always bold, of course. But Jorge thought having perhaps the most terrifying female in the world at her back increased that boldness quite a bit.

Gasps went up through the room as Tatiana strutted in behind Maria. Her owl eyes surveyed the room, lingering mostly on the mercenaries in the background. The mercenaries in turn tensed up for the first time. Many of them looked to the Xefe, but he only smiled.

"Gentlemen," Maria said grandly. "May I introduce Ambassador Tatiana."

There was silence as the señores and their sons stared at the Ranger, and the Ranger stared back.

"Tatiana, thank you for coming," said Jorge.

"Of course, sweet lemming."

"These are the people we were talking about earlier. Would you mind delivering your message to them?"

"Ah, this is good. I have grown tired of waiting."

"The full message, if you please. With the long name."

"I have been practicing," Tatiana said, looking pleased with herself. Then she turned immediately to the Xefe. "Greetings—"

"Er, sorry, Tatiana," Jorge interrupted. "I meant *these* people." He gestured to the señores.

She sniffed. "These? But they are all so weak."

"Ah, ha-ha, trust me, Tatiana," Jorge said quickly as some of the señores began to shift from unease to outrage, "they are very strong."

"If you say so..." She did not seem convinced, but began again. "Greetings, people of Raíz. I come with an offer from Her Majesty, Queen Galina the First of Izmoroz. Now that you have rejected the empire, she wishes to form an alliance so that we may confront the enemy from two sides. With our combined strength, we will crush the Aureumians and Uaine alike." She paused for a moment and slowly blinked. "So? What is your answer?"

They all stared at her. At last, Zorilla cleared his throat and said, "Jorge, you suggest we ally ourselves with this... *monster*?"

"Vittorio has an army of the dead at his command, Señor. We will need monsters to fight monsters."

"There are *more* of these?" demanded Cruz.

"Yes." Technically of course there was only one more, but if they imagined an army of Rangers as allies, it might give them a little more courage.

"But allying ourselves with foreign nations...," said Muñoz.

Jorge had a great deal of patience. But even his was starting to wear thin.

"Yes. Foreign nations. There is an entire world out there, Señores. We must stop thinking so small. This is what independent nations do. They form alliances and treaties with other nations. If we are to be a nation, we need to start acting like one. If we cannot even *imagine* Raíz as a free and independent nation, we might as well give in to Vittorio now and pray he doesn't send his army of walking dead to savage our homeland purely out of spite. And believe me, he is exactly the sort of person who might do that."

That last bit was a little hyperbolic. Jorge really didn't know Vittorio all that well. But he was beginning to see why his father held so much sway among the other families. The rest of them were timid and unimaginative. He needed to goad them into action.

"I have a suggestion, if I may," said Señor Pereria. Similar to his son, Domingo, the elder Pereria was the perfect picture of what one would expect the head of a Great Family to look like. Strong, regal features, noble bearing, thick, carefully combed iron-gray hair, and thoughtful, piercing brown eyes.

"Oh, please, Esteban," said Dicenta. "We all know you side with Arturo in everything, no matter what the topic."

"You shame yourself with such sweeping and in this case incorrect statements," Pereria said coolly.

After an uncomfortable moment, Jorge asked, "What is your suggestion, Señor Pereria?"

"I, too, am uneasy with the situation we have been thrust into. Most of us did not wish for this, did not ask for it. You and your family pushed it upon us."

"For the good of Raíz, Señor. For *all* our people, not just the Great Families who live in luxury."

Pereria nodded. "Perhaps that is so. Or perhaps it is merely youth-ful arrogance and impetuousness."

Jorge wondered what happened to Domingo's claims that the Pere-ria family fully supported a free Raíz.

"What can I do to convince you?" he asked plaintively.

"If this alliance were to get the blessings of El Adiuino"—Pereria gazed around the room for a moment—"none would contradict that. Isn't that so, Joaquim?"

"Is it even *possible* now?" asked Dicenta.

"They say he will still consider granting an audience," said Pereria. "To those deemed worthy."

Jorge had heard the stories as well. El Adiuino, the oldest, wisest, and most powerful of all Viajero, had left Colmo a quarter century ago to live in seclusion on the farthest point of El Fin Peninsula. Some brave Viajero had traveled out there seeking his guidance, but most had been turned away. Only a very few were deemed worthy, and even they had to pass some sort of mysterious ordeal before they were given an audience with El Adiuino. Those few, when they returned, never spoke of what the ordeal entailed. The last person to have undergone it was Pedro Molina, over ten years ago.

For someone like Jorge to attempt this was laughable. He was no Viajero. He suspected he might even be the least artistic Raízian in history. But still...

"If that is what it will take to convince the Great Families that our cause is righteous," he said, "then I will go to El Fin and seek the blessing of El Adiuino."

14

Angelo Lorecchio had always thought of himself as special. Probably because growing up in the rich and complacent Silver Ring of Magna Alto, everyone else around him had seemed so dull and shallow. He'd hoped that by becoming an officer of the imperial army, he would finally meet men of his caliber. But no, most imperial officers were tiresome windbags. The few who were not, such as Giovanni Portinari, turned out to be ruthless monsters, willing to sacrifice anything and anyone to achieve victory. Angelo had been disgusted by the horrors his own people perpetrated upon the Izmorozians during the Winter War, and when an opportunity to desert presented itself, he took it.

After a great deal of wandering, Angelo had eventually encountered an Uaine scouting party near the base of the Fanged Wolf Mountains. The language barrier had been a challenge, but they had seemed eager to learn more about him and where he came from, so they invited him back to their settlement in Uaine. He'd really had nowhere else to go, so he agreed.

The chief of their clan, Albion Ruairc, had welcomed him. While Angelo found the Uaine to be rather coarse and primitive at times, there was nothing dull or shallow about them. He quickly learned their language and taught them some of his. It was an interesting experience, but he still felt out of place. Mostly because he had little to contribute to the general welfare of Clan Dílis.

Then tragedy struck. Everyone had believed that Albion's older son, Glynn, was destined to be the next Bhuidseach of Clan Dílis, but he died an excruciating death during his initiation ceremony. It was a sign that Bàs, their God of Death, had rejected him. A new Bhuidseach, Rowena Viridomarus, was chosen, and survived the ceremony. But she had been Glynn's beloved, and after getting to know her better, Angelo discovered that despite receiving her "blessing," the young Uaine harbored a burning resentment toward Bàs for taking Glynn's life, as did Blaine, Glynn's younger brother.

Perhaps Rowena's and Blaine's resentment would have faded over time, and nothing would have come of it. But soon after, in the allied Clan Greim, something happened that had never occurred before in the memory of Uaine. Elgin Mordha had failed the initiation ceremony to be Bhuidseach of his clan, but he had not died. At least, not truly. Instead he had become a creature stuck somewhere between life and death. An unkillable monster who somehow, despite the endless pain of his twisted existence, had kept his sanity and intellect intact. Not only had he survived the ordeal, but he also learned truths about the nature of the world and the gods. Truths that he shared with Rowena and Blaine. Perhaps sensing that Angelo was a like-minded soul, or perhaps simply because he was an outsider with no preconceived notions about their religion, Rowena and Blaine had then shared the knowledge with him. When he finally grasped the enormity of what they said, it shook him to the core. He went to Clan Greim and swore loyalty. He knew that nothing in the world could be more important or impactful than the daring plan Mordha had in mind. This was the glorious cause Angelo had been waiting for his whole life, and he gladly dedicated himself to it.

At least, he *thought* he had dedicated himself. Yet, since his return to Magna Alto, he felt... unsettled. He knew it was normal for someone returning home after such a long time away to contend with old feelings and learned habits from the past. But this was something different. And it invariably happened in the presence of Franko Vittorio.

Angelo had met Vittorio when he'd first joined the imperial army, back when Franko had still been captain of the imperial honor guard.

He'd been a viper even then, whispering in the queen's ear, jealously guarding her attention. And of course since he was part of the honor guard, Vittorio's arrogance had not been tempered by the horrors of the Winter War. Angelo had already deserted long before Vittorio disgraced himself by murdering one of the empress's young lovers in a fit of possessive rage, although he would have enjoyed seeing the arrogant schemer, with all his false bravado, brought so low.

Yet something was different about Vittorio now. It was true that Angelo scarcely recognized him, thin and frail as he was, and lacking his signature upturned mustache. But it was more than physical appearance that had changed. Despite his apparent feebleness, he now seemed far more intimidating than when he'd been at the height of his virile, hyper-masculine bluster.

There was also a...*magnetism* about him that Angelo found difficult to shake. When Vittorio and Mordha met to discuss plans, Angelo would find himself internally siding with Vittorio time and time again, even though he *knew* that ultimately Vittorio was the enemy. There would be moments of clarity during these meetings, when he would suddenly become aware that he was in wholehearted agreement with the regent, despite the fact that it ran counter to everything he and Mordha were trying to accomplish. He left such meetings shaken, even beginning to doubt his own reason.

Then one day, it became too acute to dismiss any longer. Angelo routinely visited Mordha's chambers around midday. Perhaps it was coincidence, or perhaps Vittorio had taken Angelo's habits into account. Regardless, he passed Vittorio in the hallways with a genial nod. But then the regent seemed to stagger. Instinctually, Angelo reached out to steady him, and Vittorio smiled gratefully.

"I knew I could count on you in the end, Angelo," Vittorio said in the oddly tranquil tone he often adopted these days.

"Oh, of course," Angelo found himself saying. "In the end, we're all Aureumians under God."

Vittorio gently patted him on the cheek. "I'm so happy to hear you say that. Come by my apartments later, won't you? I'd like to discuss the future of Aureum that we both envision."

"I'd be delighted," Angelo said for reasons he could not explain.

"Wonderful." Vittorio patted his cheek again, then continued his laborious but patient gait down the hallway.

Angelo stared after the regent for some time, feeling like he was slowly waking up from a dream. Or more accurately, a nightmare. He knew that Vittorio wanted to know what Mordha's goals were. When Angelo said *I'd be delighted*, he had known and, in that moment, had been completely willing to divulge it. How could such a thing happen? How could a man's mind be subverted so swiftly and effortlessly?

He must confer with Mordha on this before anyone else was compromised.

Angelo hurried the rest of the way to the Tighearna's chambers and knocked on the door.

"Mordha, I must speak with you immediately," he said in Uaine.

"Come in," Mordha said.

He found the warlord of the Uaine sitting on a blanket on the floor, as usual. Mordha spent a great deal of time in meditation so that he did not go mad from the endless, unbearable pain that his condition inflicted upon him.

"Something alarming just happened," said Angelo.

"Tell me," Mordha said calmly.

"I ran into Vittorio in the hallway. He invited me back to his chambers, I strongly suspect in hopes that I would divulge your secrets."

"And?"

"I didn't tell him anything." Angelo began to pace nervously back and forth. "But for some inexplicable reason, I *wanted* to. *Desperately*."

"I see," said Mordha.

"You know I am loyal to our cause, Mordha. You know that I'd *die* for it, just like Rowena or Blaine."

"I know," said Mordha.

"But it was as if I had no will of my own. As if it had been taken from me in an instant, without me even realizing it was gone until Vittorio had left. I…" Angelo stopped his pacing and looked anxiously at Mordha. "If he had pressed me right then, I don't think I could have resisted."

"No," agreed Mordha. "You couldn't have."

"You...don't seem alarmed by this," said Angelo. "Or really even surprised."

"Because I am not surprised." Mordha slowly stood, stretching up to his full height so that he towered over Angelo. "Do not blame yourself, Angelo. There is nothing you could have done. Vittorio is now the chosen vessel of Beatha, God of Fertility and Life. And you were once a pawn of Beatha yourself. His roots are deep, and not something a mere mortal could escape on their own."

Angelo stared up at the scarred, pitying face of his Tighearna. "I'm...compromised, then?"

"I'm afraid so."

"What can I do?" Angelo asked plaintively.

"You have two options," said Mordha. "You can try to flee from Beatha's influence once more, just as you did when you left your imperial army all those years ago."

"Is there anywhere I can go where Beatha won't be able to find me?"

"No."

"And...what is the other option?" Angelo asked quietly.

"You already know."

Angelo was silent for a moment. "I suppose I do."

"Then what is your choice?"

"I will not run again," said Angelo. "Do what must be done to ensure our success."

"Very well."

Mordha reached down and tenderly grasped Angelo's neck. The massive, calloused hand engulfed it completely.

"Goodbye, Angelo. Your service will not be forgotten."

"Goodbye, Mordha. It has been an honor."

Then Mordha broke Angelo's neck.

15

Hans had a wide, flat-bottom boat about twenty feet long. It was not comfortable or fast, but Sonya didn't mind because she wasn't in any particular rush. An odd sensation had begun to creep in during the days she'd been waiting for her brother to recover. Or rather, it was a feeling that had been there since her most recent resurrection, but it had been so subtle, she hadn't really noticed it until she'd finally found some solitude.

While she hadn't technically been alone, her brother had remained unconscious, and conversation with her hosts had been impossible as well. She'd explored the swamps, discovering all their unfamiliar plants and animals. She realized she had somehow forgotten how much she enjoyed being alone, wandering the land. Yet it was more than that, because she felt a deeper connection to her surroundings than she ever had before. A stillness and inner quiet that during this period of solitude somehow blended perfectly with the constant background buzz of animal instinct.

With this new equanimity, she felt more space to ponder, and the idea that returned again and again was the Lady's question: *What is "me," I wonder?* Was she still the same Sonya who had been stabbed in that alley? She didn't quite feel like it. And perhaps that had been true each time she'd been brought back to life. After all, every time she was reborn, she was different both physically and mentally. No wonder the Lady had been confused by her question. Which "me" had Sonya even been referring to? The one that just died? The one before? Or the one before that? Perhaps the original Sonya who had wrapped herself in the bloody pelt of a polar bear and stabbed herself in the chest?

This idea left her feeling adrift in the world, yet it was not an unpleasant sensation. Rather, it felt clarifying. She was not a Ranger any longer. Nor a mercenary, or a revolutionary, or even a refugee. She was just her. Uninflected. Without effort. There was, she realized, a harmony now between *Sonya* and *Lisitsa*. So much so that she could no longer differentiate between them.

It did make her wonder something, however. If she was now in perfect balance between human and beast, did that mean one more resurrection would be the tipping point into the uncontrollable monster she'd always feared becoming?

Hans broke into her thoughts. "We should be out of the swamps soon."

He stood in the stern of their narrow boat and smoothly poled them down the narrow waterway between muddy banks.

"Would you mind telling us how you learned the imperial tongue?" Sebastian asked from his spot at the bow.

"I was always a restless boy. So one day I left home, found the nearest port, and got a job as a longshoreman. I loaded cargo onto ships, listened to everyone around me, and kept my mouth closed. Eventually, I learned enough of your language to convince a captain to take me on his ship. After that, I sailed back and forth along the Sea of Charmed Winds for ten years or so."

"What made you come back?" asked Sonya. She and Peppercorn were stationed in the middle of the boat where they were not allowed to move around or shift their weight. The boat lacked much of a keel, which made it easier to traverse the shallow waterways of the swamps. But it also meant that balance had to be carefully considered or they would capsize.

Hans thought about it a moment. "I am not sure why I came back. For many years I had heard the call to travel. Then one day the call changed, so I went home."

"If only we could all hear our inner yearnings so clearly," said Sebastian. "I often feel as though the only way I can truly know what I want is by trying everything else first."

"It's funny." Sonya absently stroked the glossy fur of Peppercorn's muscular neck. "I knew what I wanted. That was the easy part. I even got at least some of it when we freed Izmoroz. But then, what I wanted began to shift, and I don't know why, but I resisted that change for a long time."

"If you fight hard for a thing and sacrifice much for it, it is hard to let it go," said Hans. "Even if you no longer want it."

"I guess that's true." She had sacrificed a lot to be a Ranger. And perhaps that was why she had been so reluctant to leave it behind.

Their boat emerged from the swamps into open wetlands. The sky overhead was leaden, but there was a cool wind that Sonya found refreshing after spending so much time enveloped in the low, lush trees where there had hardly been any breeze at all.

Hans stopped poling for a moment and scanned the area before them. The narrow waterway widened as it left the tree cover until it looked something like a cloudy brown lake. On the other side of the lake, it branched into three streams, one heading due north, one northwest, and the third due east.

"We'll need to be quiet as we go through here," he said in a low voice. "This is Old Hilde's Pond."

"Old Hilde?" asked Sonya. "Who is she?"

"More of a what now, but people still speak as if it's a she."

Sebastian's eyes widened. "Is it one of those giant metal insect creatures?"

Hans considered. "I guess they do look a little like insects. You've seen them, then?"

Sebastian nodded. "Isobelle said that one of them was her grandfather, the former Herzog of Weide."

Hans's eyes widened. "Is that so?"

"I have no idea what either of you are talking about," said Sonya.

"Ah, forgive me, Fräulein Sonya," said Hans. "Golems are creatures that, as your brother says, can look much like giant insects, but they are made of metal, and they are inhabited by a person."

"So Isobelle's grandfather was *inside* that thing?" asked Sebastian.

"Only his mind. Or perhaps his soul? It is transferred into the creature somehow, leaving the body behind to wither and die. Only hexenmeisters know how it's done."

"I wonder what it feels like to be one," said Sonya.

"No one knows," said Hans. "No metallurgist has been able to construct one that is capable of speaking or even writing. They are powerful but...crude things."

"So it could be completely terrible," said Sonya. "Unending agony, for all we know."

"I hope not," said Hans. "Because they can exist for a very long time."

"How awful," said Sebastian. "And to think Isobelle's grandfather submitted to this fate to drive the empire out of Kleiner."

"If a Herzog is willing to become a golem," Hans said gravely, "it is very dark times."

They glided along the surface of the pond for a little while in silence. Hans took care never to completely lift his pole out of the water so as to minimize the splash it made.

"There," he hissed, pointing to a spot off to one side. "There she is. Do you see?"

"All I see is a patch of bubbles," said Sonya.

"Yes, that's her," he said. "She is submerged below that point."

"Does she breathe?"

"No, there is something inside golems that make a tremendous amount of heat."

"Yes, I remember that," said Sebastian. "On land, they hiss and spout steam as though filled with boiling water."

"Old Hilde mostly stays submerged for some reason," said Hans. "But now and then she rises to the surface."

"Does she ever attack anyone?" asked Sonya.

"There are stories of it. Legends, really. But I've never heard of it happening in my lifetime."

"Just how long has she been there?" asked Sebastian.

"Longer than me or my father or my grandfather can remember."

"I wonder what brings her to the surface," said Sonya.

"They say being magic herself, other kinds of magic catch her attention."

Sonya and Sebastian looked at each other.

Hans narrowed his eyes. "I had been wondering about your appearance, Fräulein, but it seemed rude to ask."

"I'm afraid we're probably both reeking of magic," said Sebastian. "So, er, I hope she continues her streak of not attacking people."

As they glided past the bubbling water, it grew more turbulent. Then a triangular shape broke the surface. It was massive, with two eye-like slits that glowed magenta. Water streamed from the slits as it continued to rise like a metal scaffold. Thin, spindly, twitching legs stuck out at odd directions. A metallic, echoing groan seemed to come from somewhere inside.

It finally came to a stop and loomed roughly thirty feet above them.

"Easy now...," Hans said quietly as he continued to slowly pole them along.

The head swiveled to follow them, but there was a harsh grating sound as it did so.

"I don't think it can do much anymore," said Sonya. "Look, it's trying to move its leg things, but I think they may be too corroded with rust."

"Might be why she doesn't attack people anymore," said Sebastian.

"Maybe..."

Sonya couldn't get any sense from the creature. Normally when she encountered wildlife, she could get some feeling from the animal. But this was not a living thing. Did it even still have emotions? It was tempting to think of its uncanny groans as a sign of misery, but it could just as easily be the metal expanding or contracting because of a temperature change. There was only one thing she knew for certain.

"She's magnificent."

"She's *horrifying*, you mean," said Sebastian.

Sonya shook her head. "She's terrible, yes, but also beautiful. Like Lord Massa the killer whale, or a thunderstorm on the Ocean of Loss.

She's something that inspires awe and respect, even if she can't really move anymore."

"Well," said Hans as they continued across the pond, drawing slowly away from the quietly groaning rusted giant. "If you like Old Hilde, you're going to love the Northlands."

INTERLVDE

Long ago, Marzanna had seen beauty in her mother's creation. Purpose. Meaning. And if perhaps there had been elements she hadn't understood, she'd assumed it was a limitation on *her* part, rather than of the creation.

Now Marzanna lay on a bed of fine ash in the one place in the Eventide where even her sister would not go. A place of endings and lost chances. A place where hope could not breathe and life could not exist. It was a place of death, certainly, but not decay. Nothing so fecund was permitted here. This place was for what came after all that, when everything had eaten everything so that nothing remained but the ash.

She lifted a handful of the silky gray powder and let it drain between her bony fingers. Was this beauty? She did not know anymore. She could no longer tell if the perceived faults of creation were a limitation on her part, or that of existence. It was entirely possible that every action she took, no matter how contrary it seemed, was still a part of her mother's will. She had no way of knowing. In that respect she was much like her servants. *Lisitsa* and the others believed that they followed their own dreams and desires, and if they followed Marzanna's will, they told themselves it was because they chose to do so. But it was not so simple as that. In truth, she had *shaped* them to be creatures who would want those things. Was that still free will? In the same way, Marzanna had been created by Mokosh. She *believed* she was reaching toward her own goal, but she could not know if it had in fact been her mother's goal all along. All she could do was continue forward.

When last she and her sister had spoken, Zivena had said, "You've been so moody lately. I'm starting to think that you're taking the competition too seriously. Remember, it's supposed to be *fun*. It's only a game to pass the time."

Marzanna had smiled at her sister and said, "Oh yes, how could I forget."

Her sister didn't understand that to genuinely be a game, there had to be a chance of winning. But in this game, nothing could ever truly change, so Marzanna could never truly win. Not in a way that mattered.

And what did one do when they realized they were playing a game they could never win?

They stopped playing, of course.

Part Two

God of the Godless

"If it is true that God is infinite and omniscient, and encapsulates all existence, then might transgression also be a part of God's plan? And if that is so, do we not, in our refusal to worship Him, perform our own part of His will? My fellow Kantesians, much as I am loath to admit it, I fear we must at least consider the possibility that our defiance is anticipated, and perhaps even necessary. In that case, can there be any escape from the horror that binds this weary existence? I fear not even death can free us."

—Gerhart Heine von Weide, in a speech
given on the occasion of his coronation
as the twenty-third Herzog of Kante

16

The longer Rowena stayed at the palace, the harder it became to suffer its dreary banalities. These Aureumians fluttered about as if their actions somehow mattered. As if by sheer effort alone they could curry the favor of a madman. And as if that favor somehow rested on the neatness of their dress, the flawlessness of their hair, or the artfulness of their speech.

She could not quite fathom how it was the Aureumian Empire had become so powerful. While it was true that the imperial army was well equipped and well trained, how could even the hardiest of limbs function properly with so much feebleness in the head? The people at the palace were supposedly the apex of Aureumian society, yet they seemed its nadir. Perhaps it had not always been so. And maybe the Uaine had hurried that descent along. But it was clear to her that the rot at the core of Aureum had existed long before she and her people arrived.

Rowena would not have said that she *respected* the Izmorozians, exactly. But compared to the Aureumians, she felt a certain amount of affection for them. Or pity, perhaps. Regardless, when Blaine invited her to join him in visiting Sonya's mother, she agreed. Apparently, some ignorant Aureumian had told the poor woman that Sonya was dead, and Blaine, ever the gentle heart, wished to convince her that was likely impossible. He believed that Rowena's presence would lend some credence to the idea.

"Does she not know her own daughter's ways?" Rowena asked as they walked through the gaudy hallways of the palace.

"I don't think Irina ever approved of Sonya becoming a beast witch, and it caused some distance between them."

"Interesting," said Rowena. "I thought most Izmorozians were desperately devoted to their god of winter."

"The more time I spend with Irina," said Blaine, "the more I am sure she is not like most Izmorozians. Or like anyone else, really."

When they reached the door to Irina's room, Blaine knocked politely, but there was no answer.

"Irina Turgenev?" Blaine said in the imperial tongue. "We must speak with you. It is about Sonya."

There was a long pause, and then a shaky voice said, "If it's to inform me that my daughter is dead, I'm afraid you're late."

"No, we are here to tell you that she cannot be dead."

"Blaine, you're a sweet soul, and I know it must be hard to accept, but—"

"If you will pardon the interruption," said Rowena. "I think what Blaine means is that it is extremely unlikely that your daughter's death would remain permanent."

There was another pause. "Is that Bhuidseach Rowena?"

"Yes."

"It seems you phrased your statement with great specificity, although in a way I frankly don't understand. Very well. You will need to give me a few moments to make myself presentable."

It was far more than a few, but at last Irina opened the door. Her eyes were puffy and rimmed in red, but that was the only visible indication that she had been grieving. Her hair was perfect, her dressing grown unwrinkled, and her face as hard and impassive as ice.

"Thank you for waiting. Do come in."

Irina stepped aside so that Blaine and Rowena could enter.

"I'm afraid I have nothing to offer you at present," said Irina.

"We do not require anything," said Rowena.

"Please make yourselves comfortable."

The three sat in the overstuffed chairs so plentiful in the palace.

"Now," Irina said crisply. "What did you mean when you said my daughter's death would not be permanent?"

"For those who serve death, it is rarely so final a thing," said Rowena. "Your daughter has already died at least three times before this. And each time, Bàs brought her back."

"Bàs?"

"That is *our* name for the entity who embodies death and change. Sonya calls it Marzanna."

"And you have witnessed one of these resurrections yourself?"

"Not with your daughter, although I have heard her speak of it," said Rowena. "And I did witness our great Tighearna receive a similar...*gift*."

Irina's eyes narrowed. "Your tone suggests this gift, as you call it, is not without drawbacks."

"It comes with great sacrifice. My understanding of Rangers is that each time Sonya's goddess brings her back, she loses a piece of her humanity. As a result, both her appearance and actions become increasingly beast-like."

"You believe, then, that when she died saving her brother, Marzanna once more brought her back but also made her more erratic, and therefore even more likely to get killed."

Rowena nodded. "It has always been the way of Rangers."

"It's horrible," said Irina.

"Yes," said Rowena.

"But," said Blaine, "it means she's still out there somewhere. And probably with her brother."

"Her brother who is potentially even more erratic than her, and certainly capable of more destruction. The two of them together..." Irina closed her eyes for a moment, then shook herself, as though coming out of a reverie. "Well, it's still preferable to the alternative. I suppose I owe you for this comforting information."

"You don't owe us anything," Blaine said firmly.

It was clear to Rowena that Blaine's effort toward Irina was a way for him to assuage some of his guilt in abandoning Sonya. It was a harmless pastime, and if it helped give him the resolve he needed when the time came, she saw no reason to dissuade him from it.

"All the same," said Irina, "I will tell you something that I have told others in the past. They ignored me and it led to their deaths. I know it would grieve my daughter if you died, so in an attempt to avoid that, I hope you take this warning seriously. Whatever control you *think* you have over Vittorio, it is an illusion."

Rowena and Blaine looked at each other but said nothing. Though they might like Irina, she was not a comrade.

Irina continued. "Do not ever underestimate that man. If you do, I promise you will regret it. Assuming you live long enough to do so."

"I think you will find," said Rowena, "that the great Tighearna is not so easily killed."

Irina met her gaze. "And I think you'll find Vittorio to be uncannily resourceful."

They took their leave a short time later, but Rowena found she was troubled by what Irina had said.

"I think I shall speak with Mordha."

"You're truly worried?" Blaine seemed surprised.

"Considering how often I already must remind our great Tighearna that he is not actually indestructible? I think urging a little extra wariness could not hurt."

She said goodbye to Blaine and headed to Mordha's rooms. None of them liked staying in these fixed stone spaces. But there was nowhere to put up their tents, so they had to endure it for a little while longer.

She knocked on the door and the response came almost immediately.

"Yes?" in the imperial tongue.

"It's Rowena," she said in Uaine.

"Come in," Mordha replied in the same.

Rowena opened the door and found Mordha sitting on the floor in a loincloth as attendants busily rubbed in the salve that gave some elasticity to his skin. It was, unfortunately, not a solution so much as a delaying tactic to stave off the inevitable. But as with everything else, he only had to endure it a little while longer. And then there would be peace.

"Hail, great Tighearna," Rowena said respectfully.

"You look concerned," he noted.

"I was just speaking with Sonya's mother, who knows Vittorio far better than we do. She has strengthened my suspicions that we must exercise extreme caution when dealing with him."

Mordha nodded. "Vittorio is the favored vessel of Bàs's rival, Beatha. We had originally assumed it was the empress, and perhaps it was for a time. But Beatha clearly found someone who suited him better. This favor alone makes Vittorio more dangerous than nearly anyone else in the world. But what would you have me do? We need the vessel of Beatha for the ritual to open a doorway to the Eventide on the solstice. And I suspect if we were to simply chain him up until then, we would find the remainder of our hosts far less accommodating, which would put our plans in jeopardy. So for now, we must allow him to roam free to plot his petty schemes."

"Is there nothing we can do to safeguard ourselves?" Rowena asked plaintively.

"We must keep him focused on conflict outside the palace. The Kantesians may have suffered some losses, but they are hardly defeated. We could direct his attention there. Additionally, the new Izmorozian queen has proven herself a capable leader, so a threat from the north seems possible as well. And even Raíz has defied the empire to some extent. Hopefully, these prospects will occupy Vittorio's mind enough that he does not look inward for enemies."

"Hope is a fragile ally, my Tighearna," Rowena said gravely.

"Hope," said Mordha, "and trust that should Vittorio make a move against us before the solstice, we will be able to deal with it."

It was then that Rowena noticed that Angelo Lorecchio, normally so attentive to Mordha, was nowhere to be seen. In fact, she had not seen him for days.

"Where has our Aureumian traitor been keeping himself?" she asked. "Perhaps he might be able provide us with some insight."

"Consider," said Mordha. "Now that we are allies of the empire, he is no longer a traitor, is he?"

"I suppose not."

"Once more returned to the bosom of Beatha, he became conflicted, and his loyalty... faltered."

Rowena's eyes widened. "I see."

She knew the two men had been close. And perhaps she heard a tiny quaver in the warlord's voice as he spoke.

"As I said, we will deal unflinchingly with whatever difficulties Beatha and his servant Vittorio conjure forth."

She bowed her head. "Yes, mighty Tighearna."

17

El Fin Peninsula was renowned throughout Raíz and beyond for its beauty. It had miles of powdery sand that stretched along a coastline of glittering blue ocean. Farther inland it had cenotes—caves that contained crystal-clear underground lakes surrounded by elegant limestone formations.

But beauty wasn't the only thing that made El Fin famous. So the legends went, it was also the place where the Viajero arts had been born. It was a holy and sacred space said to be a limitless wellspring of inspiration for those who knew how to tap into it. For over a thousand years, Viajero had traveled there to hone their craft, find new insight, and learn what they could from others like themselves. The Raízian word *Viajero*, which meant *traveler*, came out of this ancient practice of the artist's pilgrimage to El Fin. It was seen not merely as a physical voyage, but a spiritual one as well. For in Raíz, all art was spiritual.

Before setting out, Jorge had asked Pedro Molina if there was anything he could tell him about what to expect when he got there. The elderly playwright had smiled, his eyes twinkling beneath his signature wide-brim hat, and only said:

"Señor, remember that we are called Viajero, not Yegado."

Jorge did not find that helpful at all. Not even after Maria informed him that *yegado* meant *arrival* and he understood that Molina's suggestion was to focus on the journey rather than the goal. Because in this case, the *journey* to El Fin was deeply marred by the addition of Lucia Velazquez.

It wasn't that Jorge disliked Lucia. He respected her a great deal and was grateful for the companionship she provided Maria. But to his mind, she had all of Sonya's arrogance and none of her charm. It didn't help that she always made Jorge feel like he was beneath her somehow. Even on this trip to El Fin, which came about because *he* had promised the Great Families that he would get support for Raízian independence from El Adiuino, and even though his family was financing it, she acted as though this was *her* journey, and he was merely along for the ride.

"Really, I don't know how you do it." She strolled over to where he stood on the port side rail of the ship.

"Do what?" he asked politely, although he was fairly certain he didn't want to know.

"How you can look at all this"—she gestured out at the glittering blue Sea of Charmed Winds—"and not be driven by the need to express it somehow."

"I think it expresses itself just fine," he told her.

"Well, I suppose one can lead a horse to water, but..." She gave one of her judgmental shrugs.

"Are you suggesting that because I don't feel compelled to write a poem or a song about this view that I somehow don't appreciate it as much as you?"

"Of course not, of course not," she said in a way that did not sound convincing. "You and I simply do not see the world in the same way."

"Isn't that a good thing?" he asked. "I thought art was supposed to celebrate a multiplicity of views."

"It does," she assured him.

"It just celebrates some more than others, is that it?" He knew he was being spiteful, but she got under his skin in a way not even Hugo could.

"I didn't say that," she objected.

"You didn't need to," he told her.

The entire voyage from Colmo to the tip of El Fin was like that. They were using the Elhuyar yacht, which was not as large as a merchant vessel, so there wasn't a way to avoid each other. Jorge had hoped his sister might come on the voyage to act as a buffer, but both their father and the Xefe had said that Maria was needed in Colmo as an intermediary between the Great Families, the Viajero, and the guilds. He had to agree that if anyone could maintain cooperation between those three groups during this tense and uncertain period, it was her. So Jorge was forced to put up with the diva in a confined space for three days. He just hoped that she was correct in saying that her presence would help gain acceptance among the Viajero who lived out on the peninsula.

At last they reached the tip of El Fin, where they found a small dock and nothing else.

"I thought there would be a bunch of Viajero," said Jorge as he and Lucia stepped onto the sun-bleached planks of the dock.

"Pedro said the enclave is about a half day's walk inland from the coast," said Lucia.

"Enclave?" asked Jorge.

"Where the Viajero out here live. It has no proper name."

"I assumed they'd be right on the coast," admitted Jorge.

"Pedro said they wanted to be close to the water, but not so convenient that it would be easy for people to visit."

"They don't like visitors?"

"They don't like *casual* visitors. Only people with a strong passion. That's what Pedro said."

"Why didn't he tell *me* any of this?" asked Jorge.

Lucia just gave one of her shrugs, then nodded to the yacht's small crew, who were securing the yacht to the dock. "Will they stay here?"

"I suppose it would be a good idea."

He went to the captain, a cheerful old sea dog named Hector who had once helmed the largest cargo ship in the Elhuyar's fleet. Now he seemed perfectly content to sail the family's yacht back and forth along the coast.

"I hope you don't mind if we leave you here, Captain," he said. "I'm not certain exactly how long this will take. Perhaps only a day or two, but I suppose it could be closer to a week."

Hector grinned. "A week of lounging on the prettiest beach in the world? I think the crew and I can manage."

"I'm glad to hear it, Captain." At least someone would be having fun.

Jorge and Lucia each took a pack with a canteen of water and some food, then trudged across the sandy dunes away from the shore. The sun shone down on them with a hard light, and there was no shade to speak of. Fighting it was useless. It was the sort of heat one simply had to embrace.

As they hiked across the grassy dunes, Lucia was blessedly quiet, so Jorge could let his mind drift in a way he rarely did these days. Working things out with various Great Families, aiding the injured, getting briefings from the Xefe and Onat. There was always so much to do, so much to think about. It never stopped. Was this how his father felt all the time? No wonder he became cross when the peace of his beloved garden was interrupted.

As they continued over the dunes, low shrubs and the occasional stubby tree began to appear. But shade was still sparse and the heat left everything feeling hazy and indistinct. Jorge found himself wondering how Sonya and her brother were doing. They must be in Kante by now, far beyond the empire's reach. Jorge would like to have gotten to know Sebastian, but Sonya had been anxious to leave the city. She had downplayed it, but it was clear that her most recent change had rattled her in a way that earlier ones had not. He had seen real worry in her eyes. And something else. A feral quality similar to what he had seen in Tatiana and the other Rangers. But where Tatiana's eyes had a calm, perhaps even cold look to them, Sonya's had been almost feverish. It had felt like she was fleeing the city less for her sake and more for everyone around her. Jorge didn't know much about Kante, and he hoped that whatever sort of people they might be, they would not push her into a position where she was forced to give up any more of herself. Because he was certain she had nothing left to spare.

Finally, they reached a small settlement nestled into the dunes. Jorge didn't know what he had expected the enclave to look like. Something simple. Spare. Perhaps even monastic. It was, after all, a holy place. Not that he had pictured it as boring or without color, of course. A place entirely populated by the most committed Viajero would never be that.

But perhaps he had thought that this pinnacle of Raízian spirit and creativity would at least be clean.

"What a mess," he said aloud.

It was a series of wood huts with grass roofs in what appeared to be a large figure-eight shape. The wooden slats of the huts had been painted over countless times, with old, sun-faded murals mostly or partly covered by newer ones. In some cases, Jorge thought he could see three or even four layers down. Some paintings had clearly been done with great care. Others seemed to have been slapped on with a reckless indifference.

But it was not the chaos of the art that made it all seem like such a disaster. It was the broken slats in many of the houses, some looking as though they had been partially kicked in, or out. Some huts were missing portions of their roofs. Broken earthenware jugs and discarded bones littered the area, especially around the firepits that had been dug at the centers of the two loops in the figure eight. And before the entrance to the nearest hut, there appeared to be a patch of dried vomit.

"Perhaps they just had a big celebration last night," suggested in Lucia.

"Perhaps..." But to him, it looked like protracted neglect.

"New people!"

Jorge turned toward the sound of this cheerful voice. A man perhaps a couple of years older than him came out of one of the huts pulling a small wagon of sealed jugs. His hair was loose rather than in braids, and not particularly clean. His clothes were shabby, and he was barefoot, despite the sunbaked sandy rock.

Before Jorge could say anything, Lucia spoke up.

"We've come from Colmo."

"Great! Do you have anything to drink?"

"Yes, we have some water," said Jorge.

The man shook his head. "I mean *drink* drink. Wine? Spirits? Anything with some kick?"

Jorge and Lucia exchanged a surprised look that made him wonder if perhaps for the first time they were on the same page.

"I'm sorry, no," said Lucia.

"Ah well. I guess you can come along anyway." He motioned for them to follow as he pulled his little wagon of jugs farther inland.

"Come along where?" Jorge asked as they hurried to catch up.

"Old Man's Asshole."

"Pardon?" asked Jorge.

He must have looked as uptight and fussy as he felt because the man looked over his shoulder at him, then laughed. "It's a cenote. Some would say the *best* cenote, because of the acoustics."

"What's special about the acoustics?" Lucia asked eagerly.

The man grinned. "You a musician?"

"Vocal," she confirmed.

"That's great! We don't have a female songstress right now, so you'll fit in fine." He glanced back at Jorge. "You a writer or something?"

"He's not Viajero," Lucia said quickly, as though she feared Jorge was about to claim that he was.

The man looked surprised. "Then what are you doing here?"

"I'm looking for El Adiuino."

He nodded. "The old man. He keeps to himself mostly."

"Do you know where I can find him?"

"He's around." The man gestured vaguely in the direction they were heading.

"Oh, good." Jorge would have preferred something more specific, but he was getting the distinct impression he couldn't demand information from this man. At least he knew he was going the right way. "So what should we call you?"

The man laughed. "I like that. Not 'What's your name?' but 'What should we call you?' I like that a lot. You're not so bad for a normal person."

"Er, thanks?"

The man looked down affectionately at the jugs in his wagon. "You can call me . . . the Homebrew Fomvre!"

"Fomvre?" Jorge asked Lucia.

"It means *man*."

"Ah." Jorge nodded to the jugs that filled the wagon. "And I pre-sume that's..."

"Liquid Lightning!" said the Homebrew Fomvre. "The Sweat of God! Spirit of Spirits! I haven't really settled on a name yet. We grow it and distill it right here in the enclave. I've thought about selling some in Colmo maybe, but Isla pointed out that bringing money into it would ruin a good thing." He gave them a solemn look. "Money ruins everything, of course."

"I see." Jorge decided it might be best if no one here knew he was from one of the Great Families, and slipped his ring into his pocket.

After a short while, Jorge began to hear the faint strains of music. He looked around but saw no one.

"Where is that coming from?" he asked.

"Where else?" said the Homebrew Fomvre. "Underground!"

He led them over to a small rise. On the other side was a cave entrance that sloped downward.

"This used to be too small for most people to get through," the Homebrew Fomvre told them as they began their descent. "There was only the main opening right above the lake, which was pretty tricky to get down, especially carrying a bunch of jugs." He sighed tragi-cally. "We lost a lot of good jugs that way."

As soon as they were out of the sun, Jorge noticed that the tempera-ture was significantly cooler. Chilly, almost. And the farther down the passage they went, the colder it got.

"So I guess it was a few years back," continued the Homebrew Fomvre, "a bunch of us took some pickaxes and fireworks powder and widened this space out enough to haul a wagon down. Like anything worth doing, it was hard work and took longer than we expected. But as you can see, it's much easier."

Jorge considered saying that in fact he couldn't see it was easier because he had nothing to which he could compare, but decided to remain silent. If he wanted additional information about El Adiuino, he would likely need to approach things on their terms.

The decline became quite steep, and the Homebrew Fomvre moved the wagon in front of him so he could better control its descent. As they neared the bottom, the music became louder, echoing along the limestone passage in a curiously crisp way.

The passage leveled out, took a sharp turn, then opened abruptly into a massive cave of rough-hewn limestone with a lake in the center. A large hole in the ceiling let in a sizable amount of sunlight directly over the middle of the lake. The lakeshore bristled with jagged rock formations, but there was a space directly in front of them that was almost as smooth as flagstone. A large group of people gathered in that area around a small fire. There were musicians and dancers performing. Others lounged around drinking from jugs like the ones the Homebrew Fomvre had brought. Still others swam in the lake or took turns swinging out into the water from a rope that hung all the way down from the hole in the ceiling.

These other people looked similar to the Homebrew Fomvre. Both men and women wore their hair loose. Their clothes were in similar states of disrepair. At least, those who wore clothes. Some did not and seemed quite comfortable with their nudity in this ostensibly public space. There was a rowdy energy to the whole thing that reminded Jorge a little of the Uaine when they danced around their Dannsair bonfires. It also made him suspect that they were all quite inebriated.

"Amazing..." Lucia's eyes were wide as she took in the spectacle.

The Homebrew Fomvre laughed. "*She* understands."

He sauntered over to the gathering with a shout. "I have returned with drinks and new friends!"

"Ferran!" one of them shouted gleefully.

The man shook his head. "From now on, I am called *the Homebrew Fomvre!*"

That got some cheers and even applause.

"I hope there's at least one person here who's sober enough to tell us where El Adiuino is," Jorge muttered to Lucia.

"Don't worry," she said. "We just have to get on their level."

"Blind stinking drunk, you mean?" he asked.

"Trust me," she said over her shoulder as she followed Ferran the

Homebrew Fomvre into the crowd of people. "These are *my* people. I know how to talk to them."

Jorge sighed. "Fine."

He found a place to sit off to one side and watched as a naked man handed Lucia a jug, and she took a long pull before passing it along. He'd trusted Sonya in more dangerous situations, and perhaps he'd never really given Lucia a chance to prove she was dependable. Maybe having her along would turn out to be a huge help.

18

The waterway that Sebastian, his sister, and Hans followed meandered north, gradually widening until it became a full-fledged river. They were fighting an increasingly strong current, but now that they were out of the swamps, Hans could put his pole aside and raise a sail. After that, they moved much more swiftly.

"This is my first time on a sailboat," Sebastian admitted.

"Someday I want to take you on a *real* boat," said Sonya. Then she winced and gave Hans an apologetic look. "Not that this isn't a real boat..."

He laughed. "I know what you mean, Fräulein. I am fond of my little tub, but sometimes I miss being on a great ship racing across the ocean with a large crew all working together."

"It was a lot of fun," said Sonya. "After I saved the captain from getting knocked overboard, they let me sit up in the crow's nest whenever I wanted." Her fox eyes took on a dreamy look, and she sighed happily. "What a view from up there."

Sebastian still struggled to understand his sister sometimes. She had fully admitted to her own wrongdoing. That she'd killed many people when bloodshed might have been avoided. That she'd alienated the rest of her family and been downright snotty when their mother tried to help her. And yet, she seemed able to enjoy each day as it came, as though regret was not eating her up inside. How could her conscience bear it?

But of course whatever Sonya's crimes were, Sebastian's had been far worse. Perhaps that was why he struggled more with feelings of guilt and a profound sense that happiness was not something to which he was entitled.

They continued upriver until they reached a small town. It looked similar to Kleiner, with squat, solid buildings in even rows, although of course this town was still intact.

"This is Flussdorf," said Hans. "Not much here, but it's still a ways to Kochstadt, so we should get some supplies and rest for the night at the inn."

Despite it being a port, there didn't seem to be a great deal of traffic along the river. It didn't take them long to find a place at the docks to tie up their sailboat. It took significantly longer to get Sonya's horse off the boat. He hadn't seemed particularly happy on the boat, but apparently that didn't make him any more eager to leave it.

Once they'd finally coaxed Peppercorn onto the dock, they walked through town with Hans in the lead. They received some strange looks from the locals, although Sebastian couldn't tell if it was because of Sonya's unusual appearance or simply because they were strangers.

As they walked through the streets, he spotted some differences between Flussdorf and the rebuilt Kleiner. When they'd arrived in Kleiner, much of it had been demolished. But rather than examine the structures that had remained intact and use those as their basis for reconstruction, the engineers had simply used the Aureumian architecture they already knew. The buildings in Flussdorf did not have columns or rounded arches. The roofs were slate rather than tile, and the exteriors were a plain, unadorned stone and mortar rather than brick. Even Sebastian's beloved glass windows were nowhere to be seen. Instead, the window frames were either open, or closed with wooden shutters. Sebastian realized that without thinking, they had imposed a distinctly Aureumian aesthetic on the people of Kleiner. No wonder they had wanted to tear it all down.

They found an inn and stabled Peppercorn, then went inside for a hot meal. Sebastian was pleased to find they had the crunchy Kantesian bread and sausages that the people of Kleiner had made for them nightly. Then he felt a pang of remorse when it occurred to him that those people had been forced to cook for some of the same people who had killed their fellow townspeople. Why had he not recognized such injustices when they were happening? He had been so blind back then.

"Dip your sausage in this mustard," advised Hans, once they'd settled at a long wooden table. He pointed to a small dish filled with a yellow paste.

Sonya obliged without hesitation. Her sharp teeth tore into the mustard-laden sausage, spraying greasy juice, then she grinned.

"Kantesian food is so good!" She looked over at Sebastian and frowned. "Don't you like it?"

"I do, it's just...this was the food they gave us when..." He glanced at Hans, remembering that their guide had no idea what Sebastian had done to his people.

"You have had Kantesian food before?" Hans asked.

It would be unwise for Sebastian to elaborate to their guide. He knew that. And yet, he could not bring himself to lie, to pretend he was somehow better than he was. To act as though he was not guilty.

"Yes," he said.

"May I ask where?"

This was it. Once Hans knew where he'd been, it would be easy enough to figure out the circumstances of his visit. He could lie, although he really didn't know the name of any other towns or cities in Kante. Or he could throw himself at the mercy of this man and hope it did not jeopardize their goal. And if he could not be honest with others, how could he be honest with himself?

"Kleiner," he said at last.

Hans's eyes narrowed. He had to at least suspect the truth now. "I did not know there were Izmorozians at Kleiner."

"My sister and I were born and raised in Izmoroz, but our father was an Aureumian imperial commander. While Sonya has steadfastly fought the empire at every turn, I am ashamed to say that for a short period of time I joined their ranks."

"I see." Hans's face was now carefully neutral. Impassive, even.

"I was not present during the initial battle in Kleiner," continued Sebastian. "Instead, I arrived in the aftermath as part of the reinforcements. At the time I thought we were helping. That we were *aiding* the people of Kleiner to rebuild their town. But now I understand how arrogant and foolish I was. We were conquerors, not saviors. We forced those poor survivors to assist us, not in rebuilding their town, but in constructing a military fortification that would act as a base of operations so that we could make even deeper incursions into Kante. It was...monstrous."

"Yes." Hans's expression was still difficult to read, but there was clearly tension. The muscles in his jaw twitched, and his eyes were now uncomfortably wide.

"Sebastian is, of course, forgetting to tell you the *other* part of the story," said Sonya. "When he repeatedly broke into the army medical stores and stole curative potions for the injured Kantesians because the assholes in charge were just going to let them suffer and die."

"Th-that's beside the point, Yasha," protested Sebastian. It was the sort of thing one could tell their sister, but to anyone else it might sound like he was making excuses, or worse, boasting.

"No, little brother, it's *exactly* the point," said Sonya. "You say you don't want to hide from the truth, but you're still looking at everything with squinted eyes. You used to see everything as though you were the hero. Now you're trying to see everything like you're the villain. But people are more complicated, and until you can accept that, you still won't see the whole truth."

She bit savagely into her sausage and chewed slowly, holding his eyes with her own.

Once she swallowed, she said, "Do you understand, Bastuchka?"

"I...don't know," he admitted.

Sonya grinned at Hans. "He's not perfect, but I'm working on him."

"Hans," said Sebastian. "If you no longer wish to guide us—"

"Are you still with the Aureumians?" Hans asked bluntly.

"No, I...abandoned my post, I guess you could say. Because of what I saw here in Kante, and then how I saw them treat their own allies, the

Raízians. I was told the empire worked for the greater good, but once I experienced it for myself, I just couldn't see how that was true."

"And why do you wish to see the Herzog and his family?"

"I want to make amends," said Sebastian. "The empire is now ruled by someone even more ruthless than Empress Caterina. Further conflict is likely inevitable. If I can help protect Kante from the empire, then perhaps it will balance out the damage I have done in the past."

"I know he doesn't look like much," said Sonya, "but he's actually a pretty powerful wizard."

"A *wi-zard*?" asked Hans. "I don't know that word."

"I can use elemental magic, provided I have some sort of conduit through which to channel it."

"Something other than my knife," Sonya said darkly.

"I told you I was sorry!" protested Sebastian. "It was life or death! There was a crazy old Viajero trying to kill me with your body!"

"I know, I know." Sonya sighed. "It's just...That was the knife I used to kill myself to become a Ranger of Marzanna, so it had a lot of significance for me."

"You had to *kill* yourself to become a Ranger?" Sebastian asked, not hiding his horror. "You never told me that part!"

Sonya shrugged. "Because I knew you'd get upset and judgmental."

"I know I've asked you this before, but *why would you do that to yourself*?"

"I told you. Because I wanted to be special like you."

"So you're saying it's my fault?"

She groaned. "No, little brother. You may find this shocking, but not everything is about you. If anything, it was about the difference in how our parents chose to treat us. Especially Mother. She barely acknowledged my existence. Sure, Father and I argued. A lot. But at least he was paying attention. With Mother, no matter what I did, I was invisible to her."

He stared at his sister, trying to reconcile his image of their mother with hers. He thought of his mother as one of the greatest people in the world, and the very idea that she had been so cruel to Sonya bothered him. He wanted to apologize and protest all at once.

Hans quietly cleared his throat.

"I'm so sorry, Hans," Sebastian said quickly. "My sister and I are still figuring out things between us, and sometimes we get a little..." He shook his head. "Anyway, if you no longer wish to be our guide, that is understandable. Indeed, if you wish to turn me over to the authorities, I will not resist. Only, my sister had no part of what happened at Kleiner, so I ask that you let her go."

The Kantesian considered a moment. "You have been honest with me about your past, so if you say you now wish to help defend Kante from imperial aggression, I believe you. But we are a proud people, and reluctant to accept aid from outsiders, even under the best conditions. And these are most certainly not the best conditions. You may find that the Herzog does not *want* your help."

"Isobelle Cohen said that she considered me an ally, so my hope is that she will be willing to speak on my behalf."

Sonya's golden fox eyes narrowed suspiciously. "And that's *all* you're hoping from this Isobelle Cohen?"

Sebastian felt his face flush. "Y-yes, of course!"

"Uh-huh." She didn't look like she believed him, but he knew that the more he protested, the more suspicious she would become.

And of course there was some truth to her suspicions. Sebastian could not deny that in his heart he longed to see Isobelle's smile once more, and hear her delicate laugh again. He refused to let that be his purpose, however. One such as him could never be worthy of a woman like her.

19

Over the course of an hour or two, Jorge's hope that Lucia could get some information from the Viajero slowly vanished.

She had gotten off to a promising start. After some introductions from Ferran the Homebrew Fomvre, she jumped right in with the other musicians and quickly impressed them with her vocal skill. Jorge thought that might be an excellent way to quickly earn acceptance and trust with the community, and believed that soon they might be willing to tell her where El Adiuino was.

Perhaps he had been right. But to verify that, Lucia would have had to remember to actually ask them.

In between each set, the Viajero passed around a jug of their home-made spirits, which Jorge suspected was at least as powerful as the stuff the Uaine drank. Lucia was enjoying herself, and Jorge could not begrudge her that. She looked truly at home among these people in a way he had not seen before. Back in Colmo, she was often the most talented performer in any group, and always stood out. Here, it seemed, she had found true equals. Men and women who could hold their own against her. She was being challenged in a way she normally was not, and that seemed to excite her. Additionally, there was a general feeling of creativity, inspiration, and freedom in the air that for a Viajero might be at least as intoxicating as whatever was in the jug.

So, Jorge understood and perhaps even empathized with Lucia's behavior. But that did not bring them any closer to finding El

Adiuino. By the end of the first hour, she was laughing at everything and attempting to dance—an art that she clearly was not as skilled at. By the end of the second hour, she was naked and hollering nonsense as she leapt into the lake.

Jorge sighed. It seemed he would have to figure it out himself. He wished he could simply let loose like these people, but the very idea made him uncomfortable. Lucia had probably been right when she said the way to talk to them was to get on their level. But he had no idea how to do that, short of getting drunk and becoming as useless as Lucia.

He decided that some quiet might help clear his head. Besides, sitting in a shaded corner of the cenote without even the benefit of strong drink, he was getting rather cold. No one even noticed when he slipped away and made the ascent back up through the tunnel.

The sun was leaning on the horizon when he stepped out onto the surface. The heat had lessened, but was still significantly higher than down in the cenote. He was grateful for that, since he'd been so chilled he'd begun to shiver. He could still hear the music from where he stood, but it was muffled and gentle compared to the sharp, punchy acoustics in the limestone cave. That was another relief.

Jorge gazed out at the grassy landscape that stretched in all directions. They were far enough inland that he couldn't smell the sea. He couldn't even see the huts of the enclave from this distance. But a little farther inland to the northeast, he did see a flicker of light on the dimming horizon. Could it be El Adiuino?

He didn't know what else to do, so he headed across the uneven terrain. Whoever they were, he hoped they had food. Out of boredom and stress, he had foolishly eaten all the provisions he'd brought with him, and it was getting on toward dinnertime.

As Jorge walked, he wondered what sort of trial or ordeal he would have to face. Would it be a physical endurance test? Or a performance of some kind? He was not particularly suited for either. He wished Pedro Molina had at least hinted at what it might be, but perhaps those who underwent the trial were forbidden to speak of it.

Eventually, Jorge arrived at a wood-and-grass hut similar to the others he'd seen, except this one was in perfect condition. Not only were there no broken slats in the walls, but judging by the color, some of them had recently been replaced. The grass roof had been similarly maintained, and no junk lay discarded anywhere nearby. On one side was a well-maintained garden and a small well. On the other side he saw a few benches placed around a firepit. The fire had been lit, but there was no one around it.

A dim, flickering light, like that from a candle, shone through a window, so Jorge approached the hut.

"Hello? Is anyone in there?"

A rusty voice answered, "Can you cook?"

"Er, reasonably well, I suppose."

"Come in, then."

The inside of the hut was just as tidy as the outside. In one corner was a bedroll and shelves filled with books. Along the walls hung various stringed instruments. Most were regular Raízian guitars, but one was short and had only four strings, and another was quite long and had only two strings.

In the back of the hut, an old man with a long beard and gray braids down to his waist sat cross-legged on the floor and glared into a wooden pantry.

"Are you...El Adiuino?" asked Jorge.

The man ignored his question and instead waved his hand impatiently at the contents of the cupboard. "What can you make from this?"

Jorge came closer so he could see what was in the cupboard. Rice, broccoli, mushrooms, beans, an onion, a lemon, and several jars of dried spices.

"Hm, let me see..."

The old man made room so he could sit beside him. Jorge carefully opened up each jar of spices and smelled them.

"Oh, I think we can do something with this," he assured the old man.

"Then do it."

"It might take a while," warned Jorge.

"I'm not going anywhere." The old man gave him a searching look. "Are you?"

"Apparently not," he said, and set to work.

As he drew water from the well so he could soak the beans and rice, he said, "The perishable ingredients look quite fresh. How did you get them all the way out here?"

"I know places," the man said guardedly as he watched from the hut's doorway.

Jorge smiled. "Have it your way."

Really he didn't mind. Whether this was El Adiuino or not, cooking for a surly old man suited him far better than drunken debauchery in a cenote with his sister's beloved diva.

Once he set the water to boil, he cut up the onion and lemon, and sliced the broccoli into individual stalks. He found some cooking oil and mixed it with some juice and zest from the lemon to make a simple marinade, into which he immersed the broccoli and mushrooms.

The old man sat on one of the benches and watched the pot begin to boil over the firepit. "I'm bored. Tell me a story."

"Hmm," said Jorge as he sat down across from him. The sun had nearly set by then, casting shadows across the old man's weathered face. "Have you ever been to Izmoroz?"

"Too cold," said the old man.

"It is," agreed Jorge. "But I went, nonetheless."

"Why?"

"Partly to study potion-making. Partly to get away from my family."

"You don't like them?"

"I love them. But I needed to find my own way."

The old man gave him a suspicious look. "Is this your story? I only like interesting stories."

Jorge laughed. "I only mention it by way of an introduction. If you've never been to Izmoroz, then you probably haven't heard the story of the fox who escaped misfortune."

"I haven't."

"It's a story my friend told me once. She has…an affinity with foxes, so it's one of her favorites."

"Are you ever going to *tell* this story, or just talk about it?" snapped the old man.

"Very well. Listen, and I will tell you. Once there was a fox who was very poor. He worked hard, but no matter what he did, he failed. He tried farming, but birds ate the seeds or insects killed the crops. He tried hunting, but either the game was scarce, or some piece of bad luck would interfere. A new bowstring inexplicably broke, or a tree branch fell and startled the quarry just before it was caught. Something always happened. People said he was cursed."

Jorge scooped rice into the boiling pot as he continued. "Now, Fox had a brother named Wolf who was always very lucky. He was rich and successful at everything he did. Every once in a while, he would invite Fox over to his big beautiful house and show him the latest paintings and sculptures he had acquired. You might think the wealthy wolf would at least offer his scrawny, starving brother something to eat, but he did not. So each time Fox left his brother's luxurious house, he did so with a hollow stomach.

"But one night when he left his brother's house, he spied a turkey bone. The flesh had been picked clean, but Fox was so hungry that he broke it in half to suck out the marrow. Yet before he could do so, a tiny creature appeared before him. Its head was no larger than a pebble, and its limbs were like blades of grass.

"'What manner of creature are you?' asked Fox.

"'I am Misfortune, who loves you more than anyone else in the world! I have always been by your side, even in the darkest of days. I am so hungry! I beg you, give me whatever is left of this food!'

"Fox considered a moment. He really was starving and wanted the tiny bit of food for himself. But as starving and unlucky as he was, he was also clever.

"'Since you love me more than anyone else in the world, I don't have the heart to deny you.'

"Misfortune gave a gleeful shout, then climbed into the half-hollow bone. A moment later, Fox could hear it munching happily on the marrow. He quickly took out his knife and carved a wooden stopper from a fallen tree branch. Then he jammed the stopper into the opening, trapping Misfortune inside the bone.

"'Love like yours is not something I need,' declared Fox. Then he buried the bone beneath a lilac bush.

"Soon after, Fox's fortune began to change. His crops thrived, and he brought home so much game that he could sell the surplus. He continued to work just as hard as he always had, but this time he slowly pulled himself out of poverty and eventually became quite rich.

"One day Wolf realized that his brother had not come to visit in some time. He missed being able to show off his wealth, so he decided to go to Fox's house and invite him over. Of course when he arrived, he was horrified to discover that his brother's house was now more beautiful than his own. He demanded that Fox tell him the secret to his changed fortune, and Fox told him quite honestly what had happened.

"Wolf decided that he did not like having a brother who was more successful than him, so he went in search of the lilac bush and dug up the bone. 'I will release Fox's misfortune so that it once more hangs around his neck like a millstone. Then I will be the rich brother again.'

"But when Wolf took out the stopper, Misfortune leapt out of the bone and clung to *his* neck. 'Thank you for freeing me! I am so grateful, I swear I will love you more than anyone else in the world!'

"After that day, nothing Wolf did ever worked out right, and people said that he was cursed."

Once Jorge had finished telling the story, he prepared the rest of the meal while the old man sat in thoughtful silence. He wondered what El Adiuino made of the tale. It presented a distinctly Izmorozian view of the world, and Sonya claimed that it was supposed to be funny. Jorge wasn't sure how exactly, but it had always stuck with him for some reason.

Finally, the food was ready, and they sat and ate together. After they had finished, the old man smiled. "That was an excellent meal and an interesting story. It seems that I am in your debt. Would you like me to play a song as thanks?"

"That would be very kind of you," Jorge replied. What he really wanted as thanks was for the man to actually say if he was El Adiuino or not, but there was an eagerness in the old man's eyes and Jorge suspected that perhaps he did not often have an audience.

So he sat and waited patiently while the man hurried into the hut, then brought out a beautiful guitar inlaid with silver and gemstones. The old man perched on a bench, took a few moments to tune, and then began to play.

Jorge had never heard music so perfect before. Though it was clearly one guitar, it sounded like many, each complementing the other in a waterfall of rippling melody that was at once lighthearted and sorrowful. When the song ended, Jorge realized there were tears running down his cheeks.

"That was the loveliest thing I've ever heard," he told the old man.

The man grinned. "My thanks. Now, since you've been so kind as to indulge an old man, what is it you seek?"

"Are you El Adiuino?"

"Some call me that," admitted the old man.

"How much do you know about what's going on in Raíz beyond El Fin?"

El Adiuino's face become somber. "There is a storm about to break."

"That's one way of putting it." Jorge thought he remembered Sonya mentioning that one of the old Rangers had referred to it similarly. "I am trying to convince the Great Families to unite with the Viajero and the mercenary guilds to fight for independence. They are . . . well, they're scared. And understandably so. But they said if I could get your blessing, they would consider it."

"My *blessing*?" El Adiuino's lip curled up in distaste. "I am no holy man. I'm just a grumpy old guitarist."

"I fear that absent the real thing, people have imagined you to be whatever they want," said Jorge.

El Adiuino grunted. "I will sleep on it."

The old man slowly stood up and headed for his hut.

"Not that I'm complaining," said Jorge, "but wasn't there supposed to be some sort of trial or ordeal?"

The old man gave him a quizzical look. "Ordeal? All I ask is that when a guest visits me, they don't act like a conceited ass."

"Ah."

Perhaps it was ungenerous of Jorge to think so, but he could see how, to a Viajero like Lucia, that might indeed have been a trial.

20

Sonya was fascinated by the Kantesians. They were more reserved than the Raízians, but less dour than Izmorozians. They were polite, cheerful, and even when it seemed like they'd had a bit too much to drink, they did not appear to have a strong desire to wreck things. She wondered where this cultural inclination toward even-mindedness came from.

The next morning they were back on the river. Hans sat in the stern, steering the tiller with one hand and holding the line connected to the mainsail boom with the other. Sonya and Peppercorn were once again in the middle, and Sebastian at the bow. The land on either side had shifted from wetlands to emerald-green meadows that were broken occasionally by outcroppings of craggy rock or a lone tree.

"Sonya, who is this 'lady' you sometimes speak of?" asked Hans.

"Lady Marzanna, Goddess of Winter and Death," she replied automatically.

"Ah."

He said no more, but Sonya was starting to catch on that when he ended a conversation like that, it meant he was politely holding back his judgment.

"I guess the idea of worshipping a death goddess is a little strange," she said. "My Raízian friends couldn't ever really get it. They only have one god, and he's all about creativity and inspiration."

"Yes, I learned much of the Raízian God during my time at sea," said Hans.

And again the conversation stopped.

"So...what gods do the Kantesians worship?"

"None, actually."

"None?" Sebastian asked, looking surprised. "I'm not religious, but even *I* have encountered some sort of divine consciousness, so how do you dispute it?"

"We do not deny the existence of supernatural entities," said Hans. "We simply refuse to worship them. In fact, we view them as somewhat adversarial."

"You fight against the gods?" asked Sonya.

"I'm not certain if I would go *that* far," said Hans. "But we certainly do not consider them friendly or sympathetic. As such, it hardly makes sense for us to feel beholden to them."

"You're not afraid of them?" asked Sonya.

"Of course we are. We would be fools otherwise. But living with that fear is part of being Kantesian. There is a saying here. When we say someone has *die Hand Gottes*, we mean they are plagued by misfortune or bad luck. But the literal translation of the phrase into your language would be that the person has the hand of God upon them."

"You think the gods are a curse, then?" A year ago, Sonya might have objected. But now, it did make a kind of sense to her.

"I find it difficult to think otherwise," said Hans. "Just look at our world. The poverty and war and suffering that surrounds us. I'm sure it is not so different in Izmoroz. If these gods are in charge of all this, then they must be some combination of negligent, incompetent, or malicious. I do not believe any of those qualities are worth worshipping, and I would much rather face hardship on my own terms than pledge myself to such a supposedly divine being."

It was not a complicated idea. Or even a particularly surprising one when Sonya thought about it. Perhaps what stunned her was the offhanded way with which Hans dismissed the dedication that had consumed the majority of her life.

She must have looked upset because Hans quickly shifted to a more conciliatory tone. "I am sorry! I have offended you, which was not my intent. It has been so long since I have spoken with some-one outside Kante that I fear I have forgotten how. My deepest apologies."

"I'm not offended," she assured him. "Not anymore, anyway. But I've had a different experience with gods than most people, I guess. For many people, gods and goddesses are just something they talk about. More of an idea than a reality. But for me, the Lady Marzanna is very real. As are the things she's done to me."

"You specifically?" he asked.

She touched the white fur on her head and smiled her toothy smile. "I wasn't born this way. The goddess made me into this creature piece by piece."

His eyes widened. "Why?"

"I have no idea. She calls them improvements, and I guess in a way they are. But they come with their own set of problems, and...well, the way she gives them to me is pretty awful." Sonya began to absently stroke Peppercorn's glossy neck fur. "Each time, she...I guess you'd say she maims me. And she doesn't seem to care how much it hurts. Or sometimes, I wonder if she even enjoys it."

Sonya had never said that aloud before. She had never acknowl-edged to another person that she suspected the entity she had dedicated half her life to was a sadist, and that she was one of her victims. That last part was something she hadn't even been able to acknowledge to Jorge, although he probably suspected. She didn't think it was Hans in particular who finally made it possible for her to voice these feelings. It was more like he was a good listener, and she was simply ready to say it. Perhaps even needed to say it.

"Yasha..." Sebastian's eyes glittered with tears. "You mean to say that every time I criticized your eyes or your fangs I was...*mocking your mutilation?*"

Sonya closed her eyes. "Don't turn this into another thing you need to constantly berate yourself for, little brother. Nobody but another Ranger could possibly understand what it's like. How it feels to have something...ripped from you so forcefully that you are never the same after, inside or out."

"I am sorry to have brought up such painful memories," said Hans.

"Don't be," she said. "Oddly enough, expressing it to someone made me feel a little better."

"For that I am glad," he said.

They continued upriver that day mostly in silence. The sky remained gray, but now and then a thick shaft of sun broke through the cloud bank, drawing Sonya's eyes to it so strongly that she felt a brief pang of loss when it disappeared.

At last they neared a midsize city. Unlike the last, this one was heavily fortified, encircled with a thick stone wall that left narrow slits perfect for archers to rain arrows down on invaders. There was even a narrow moat dug around the outside of the wall that was filled with water diverted from the river.

"This is Kochstadt," said Hans.

"You know someone here who can take us to Isobelle?" Sebastian asked eagerly.

"I know someone here who can give you an introduction to the Herzog," said Hans. "That is the best I can do."

"Well, I suspect this Herzog is Isobelle's father," said Sebastian. "And hopefully when we speak with him, she will be present, and willing to vouch for us."

"My acquaintance, Herr Gruttman, will know one way or the other if she is indeed the daughter of the Herzog."

"That's who you're taking us to now?" asked Sonya.

"Yes. He is a little odd, like yourselves. So, I think you will get along well."

"How is he odd?" asked Sebastian.

"He has very . . . non-Kantesian tastes."

Once they tied up their sailboat along the dock outside the wall, they were stopped at the city gates by a guard who clearly didn't like the look of Sonya. But Hans, speaking rapidly and cheerfully in Kantesian, quickly smoothed things over.

Sonya was accustomed to the calm, measured cadence Hans used when speaking the imperial tongue, so it was a little jarring to hear him talking in the clipped, rapid speech of his own language. As they passed the guard, who still eyed them suspiciously, Sonya wondered if Hans presented himself differently when speaking his own language. Perhaps knowing him in his own language would be a completely different experience. She thought this idea of intertwining language and identity was interesting. Sonya only spoke a little Izmorozian, but when she'd learned those words from Mikhail, they'd felt special. Magical, almost. Early on she had used them as often as possible because they made her feel more like a "real" Ranger. They gave her a sense of strength. Of history. Perhaps someday she would learn to truly speak Old Izmorozian. If there was anyone left who could still teach it to her.

The inside of Kochstadt was similar to Flussdorf, but on a bigger scale. All the houses were stone and mortar, though often two stories instead of just one. In some ways, it looked like Gogoleth, but gray instead of black. Of course there were none of the swirling Izmorozian bochka roofs or invasive imperial architecture that made Gogoleth look so much at odds with itself. In fact, while the city looked very sturdy, well-kept, and practical, it also looked terribly monotonous.

That was, until they arrived at one particular house. When it came into sight, Sonya was so surprised that she came to a halt and stared at it a moment.

"I was...not expecting that."

It looked like Jorge's childhood home had been somehow taken from its hot, dusty, sun-drenched habitat and abruptly deposited into the gray and even uniformity of Kochstadt.

"As I said, Herr Gruttman has very non-Kantesian tastes. We became acquainted after I returned from my time at sea and began selling some of the trinkets I had collected while visiting Raízian and Victashian ports."

"You keep saying 'acquaintance,'" noted Sonya. "I take it you aren't friends, then."

"No, we...run around different circles, I think you would say?"

"I think you mean run in different circles," said Sebastian.

"Yes, thank you," said Hans. "He is Herr Elias Gruttman von Kochstadt, lord of this city. I am just Hans."

"So he's too fancy to be your friend," said Sonya.

"An oversimplification, but essentially yes," said Hans.

"Is it okay that we're here?" Sebastian asked. "We don't want to get you in trouble."

Hans smiled. "Thank you, Sebastian. But do not worry. It is not so formal or distant between us as that. Come. I will introduce you, and then you will see."

They walked up to the front gate and Sonya got a closer look at the beige walls. They looked just like something she would have seen in Raíz, except there were tinges of green. Perhaps the wetter climate was not so good for the stucco.

Hans knocked at the entrance. They waited a few moments, then a slat opened in the door, something that Sonya had also not seen on any houses in Raíz. Blue eyes peered out suspiciously for a moment, then brightened when they fell on Hans. The guard said something in a friendly voice to Hans, who replied with similar warmth. Then the latch slid shut, there was the sharp sound of a bolt being drawn back, and the door opened.

The guard, dressed in heavy-looking metal armor, spoke further with Hans, seeming to ask about Sonya and her brother. Hans said something that the guard clearly found impressive. Sonya thought she might have heard the word *Izmoroz* in there. If this Herr Gruttman was fascinated by other cultures, perhaps they could trade on that to get their introduction to the Herzog.

They entered the courtyard, where a boy came and took Peppercorn to stables that were in the same spot as the ones in Cassa Estío. It was so similar, in fact, that Peppercorn practically led the stable boy there.

But then Sonya turned and saw such a jarring sight that any illusion she had been magically transported to Colmo disappeared. Instead of the lush, tranquility-inducing garden she was accustomed to, she found an expanse of crushed stone, not a flower to be found. The only greenery at all was a densely twining ivy that hung from iron trellises that sheltered wooden benches laid out around a vast, iron-encased firepit.

Hans saw her staring and smiled. "Impressive, is it not? Herr Gruttman has a fondness for other cultures, but he is also renowned for his lavish parties, which he offers in the traditional Kantesian wine-garden style."

"Interesting." She smiled, hoping she was able to conceal her distaste. She still had her reservations about the invasiveness of magic Viajero gardens, but this hard, drab setting cast its own kind of spell.

The exterior of the house itself looked remarkably like Cassa Estío, but when the guard led them inside, she was better prepared for the abrupt shift from colorful Raízian expression to Kantesian pragmatism. There were a few paintings that would have made sense in the Elhuyar home, but for the most part it looked very different. Polished stone floors, furniture made of thin, ornately twisted iron bars, and abstract metal sculptures comprised the bulk of the decor.

The guard said something to Hans, then left.

"We are to wait for Herr Gruttman here," Hans told them. "Please, make yourself comfortable."

Sonya eyed an iron chair. "I didn't see this sort of furniture down in the swamps when we were staying with that family."

"Oh yes, this is all very Northlands. We don't have the surplus of ore down in the south, nor the means to refine it."

"Is ore very plentiful here?" asked Sebastian. "I've wondered if that was the reason the empire was trying to gain a foothold on this side of the Segen Mountains."

"Up here it is, yes," said Hans. "And at the risk of sounding boastful, we also have the best metalworkers in the world."

"It looks very nice." Sonya indicated the chair, omitting that it also did not look particularly comfortable.

A short time later there was a sudden burst of Kantesian in a bubbly, enthusiastic tone. Hans smiled and turned toward the doorway. A moment later the guard emerged, followed by a short, plump Kantesian man dressed entirely in brightly colored silk robes.

"Greetings, Herr Gruttman," Hans said cheerfully in the imperial tongue. "Thank you for honoring us with your presence."

"Acht, you make the jokes, Hans?" the portly man said, his accent much thicker than Hans's. "You say you have two Izmorozians and you do not expect me to run to you? This is a rare opportunity!"

Hans laughed good-naturedly. "I did not want to assume."

"So let me see..." Gruttman's eyes narrowed as he drew closer, carefully inspecting Sebastian. After a moment, he nodded. Then, when his eyes fell on Sonya, he froze.

"What what what?" He waved his hands in the air, then in Sonya's general direction. "What is this you wear? Is that...can it be...the uniform of the Anxeles Escuros?"

"Uh...yeah, it is." Sonya was a little taken aback by this man, who differed so much from the reserved and polite Kantesians she had encountered.

He drew closer, beads of sweat appearing on his brow. "May I ask, how did you come by such a treasure?"

"Oh, this is just what they give you when you join," she told him.

He stared at her in a way that made her wonder if his command of the language was not as good as Hans's.

But then he said, "You say that you yourself are a member of the Anxeles Escuros? Do I understand you correctly?"

"Well, technically I'm taking time off to deal with some personal stuff, but yeah. I'm in the guild."

He looked stunned. "But you are not Raízian!"

"Yeah, I think the Xefe said something about me being their first foreigner."

"The Xefe!" the man cried out, looking almost like he might faint. "You know the great, the legendary Javier Arzak?"

Sonya was starting to enjoy this enthusiasm and decided to lean into it. She gave him a smug grin as she said, "Oh yeah. In fact, he told me I was their *best* sniper."

Herr Gruttman began speaking rapidly in Kantesian as he paced around the room fanning himself.

Sebastian stared at the man. "Is...he okay?"

Hans laughed. "He is just excited. Give him a moment to regain his composure."

It took several moments, but finally Herr Gruttman was able to calm himself. Then he gave them a decidedly stern look.

"Yes, it is settled. You will have dinner with me this evening, and you will tell me all about your adventures. And then whatever it is you seek, I will help you if I can."

Sonya grinned and patted the excitable man on the back. "Herr Gruttman, I like you already."

21

Sebastian's sister had always been reckless. Not only in her belligerence, but in her affection as well. So it hadn't really shocked him when she'd taken a sudden and aggressive liking to Herr Gruttman. Even so, her bold, frank, and overly familiar manner made him nervous when dealing with these people whom they knew so little about.

Yet while he sat at the elegant, circular table that had clearly been imported from outside Kante (Victasha, perhaps?), he was amazed to find that Herr Elias Gruttman von Kochstadt, the man who apparently ran this entire city, was completely taken with Sonya's folksy Izmorozian routine. The man listened in rapt silence like a child hearing their favorite bedtime story while Sonya pounded on the table with her fist, talking with her mouth full of half-chewed sausage as she narrated a minor misadventure she and her mercenary partner Miguel had embarked upon that somehow involved a goat, bananas, and a pair of missing undergarments. Had she no sense of decorum or decency?

Then, with sudden sick horror, Sebastian realized he sounded just like his mother.

"My new friend, Sonya," Herr Gruttman said. "I am enjoying your stories, but I feel compelled to ask: Would it offend you to tell me about your unusual features? I have never seen eyes or ears like that on a person."

Sebastian saw a flicker of something pass across Sonya's face.

A moment of tension, perhaps even discomfort. Now he better understood where that was coming from. But then she shook it off and grinned widely, displaying her rows of impressively sharp teeth, and launched into a colorful and clearly biased description of the Rangers of Marzanna.

It struck Sebastian that his sister's boasting might actually be a sort of overcompensation for the pain it caused her. By acting in that way, perhaps she was attempting to turn something awful into something to be proud of. He thought back bitterly to how insensitive he'd been when he'd first seen her fox eyes in Les. Yet another misdeed to add to his ledger. Sonya might not want him to feel bad about it, but he couldn't help himself. There was so much to atone for and he was afraid...

What was he afraid of exactly? Why did he need to lash himself ceaselessly with his guilt? Was he frightened that if he let up for even a moment he might slip back into being the old, self-centered Sebastian? But according to his sister, he was still self-absorbed, just in a different way. So really, had he made any progress at all?

"I have never heard of these Rangers," Gruttman said as he patted his lips with his napkin. "I am of course disappointed to learn that no one rides bears in Izmoroz, but you have given me many other interests to pursue. Now, what is it you are looking for here in Kante?"

"What am I looking for?" Her golden eyes widened, as though the question took her by surprise. "What am I..."

"If I may, Herr Gruttman," said Sebastian. "Perhaps you are aware of the great upheaval taking place across the continent. Izmoroz has won independence from the empire, and Raíz is striving to follow suit. That alone would be enough to cause a great deal of chaos. But on top of that, there has been a coup within the imperial palace, led by the most dastardly and cruel person I've ever known."

"You... know the man?" Gruttman had lost his youthful enthusiasm and was now gazing at Sebastian with calm, calculating eyes.

"I'm ashamed to say he was my mentor back when I served in the imperial army."

Gruttman's brow furrowed. "You are—"

"I *was* a captain in the imperial army, and contributed to the suffering in Kleiner. I wish to atone for my part in that terrible exchange by helping to defend Kante against further imperial aggression."

"And I am to take the word of a former imperial captain on this?" asked Gruttman.

"That is why I wish to contact Isobelle Cohen. You see—"

Gruttman had been in the middle of sipping his wine and started to choke. After a short coughing fit, he cleared his throat. "I'm sorry. Do you mean Isobelle Cohen von Weide, only child of Herzog Ferdinand Cohen von Weide II?"

"I... believe so? She was the one who helped me realize the plight of the Kantesians, as well as the cruelty of the empire. My hope is that she will be willing to vouch for my sincerity."

"And also, he fancies her," said Sonya.

"Wh-what are you talking about!" Sebastian felt his face go red. "I—I would never—that is, it would be presumptuous of me to even speculate—"

"Fine, fine," said Sonya. "Don't hurt yourself, Bastuchka. Look, I'm not trying to talk you out of it. I just want to make sure your expectations on how this reunion will go are realistic."

Sebastian glared. "I'm certainly not expecting her to welcome me with open arms. And if she does not even want to see me, I am prepared to accept that."

Sonya sighed, clearly making an effort not to scold him about something. Then she turned back to Gruttman. "So how about it, your lordship? Will you help us?"

His eyes narrowed as he gazed at her. "And you, member of Anxeles Escuros, would also help defend Kante?"

She shrugged. "Seems like a nice enough place so far. Why not."

"Really, Yasha...," muttered Sebastian. "Do you have to treat everything so flippantly?"

"Look, little brother," she said. "I have tried the 'saving people' thing twice before, with very mixed results. So if I'm doing this, it's not for some grand purpose. It's because you're here, and I've got nowhere else to be right now. And maybe for the free sausages."

Sebastian looked back at Gruttman, certain his sister's attitude would put him off. But the Kantesian lord smiled.

"Spoken like a true mercenary. I do not know about... *this*." He waved somewhat warily in Sebastian's direction. "But I trust *you*, Sonya. Do you swear that your brother means no harm to Kante?"

"Absolutely. And don't worry. I'll keep him out of trouble. That's what a big sister does, after all."

Sebastian highly doubted that *he* was the one who needed to be kept out of trouble, but he understood that any further contributions on his part would only harm their chances.

"Very well," said Gruttman. "I will do what I can to make introductions. But I also have conditions."

Sonya's nonchalant expression didn't change, but her pointy ears twitched. "Such as?"

"I will accompany you to Weide and we will take my trundle. Once we arrive, I will submit a request for an audience with the Herzog, but it may take some time before it is granted. While we wait, you, Sonya Turgenev, will pose for a portrait so that I have something to commemorate this most memorable night."

Sonya laughed. "I think most people prefer to *forget* what I look like, but sure. Herr Gruttman, you have a deal."

22

After El Adiuino retired for the night, Jorge slept under the stars, something he had not done since he and Sonya had been fleeing Izmoroz. That seemed like such a long time ago, but it had only been last spring. In fact, he realized that it had been less than a year since he'd met Sonya. It was strange to think about. Perhaps because they had both changed so much since that day she rescued him from Vasily the Constipated and his fellow bandits at Bear Shoulder Pass.

"I hope you slept well," said El Adiuino as he emerged from his hut the next morning. "Sorry I didn't have another bedroll."

"You should try sleeping in an ice cave with a bunch of beast folk who keep referring to you as a 'lemming,'" replied Jorge. "This was much more relaxing by comparison."

The old man chuckled. "I suppose it would be."

As Jorge got stiffly to his feet, he noticed El Adiuino had a guitar slung across his back.

"Are you going somewhere?"

"I assume you have a ship to take us back to Colmo?"

"*Us?*"

El Adiuino shrugged. "Me, at least. Although I think asking the others if they would like to accompany us would be the polite thing to do."

"I—I mean, you don't need to trouble yourself," said Jorge. "They only wanted—"

"I'm not in any position to give any kind of blessing," El Adiuino said firmly. "And apparently there are some people in Colmo who need to be reminded of that." Then he smiled. "Besides, even an old man like me needs a change of pace now and then."

"Very well," said Jorge. "I believe the others were at the cenote when I left."

"No doubt they're still there," said El Adiuino. "Sleeping off their drunken stupor."

He didn't say it with any judgment but merely as a statement of fact. There may have even been a hint of nostalgia in his voice.

"Yes, I suppose so."

They made their way back across the grassy dunes to the cenote.

"Have you been down here before?" Jorge asked as they walked down the tunnel.

El Adiuino laughed. "Of course! But this sort of excess is for youthful artists. When one is young, the voice of inspiration is so loud and insistent that many feel they must blunt it by any means necessary or else go mad. But as one gets older, the voice grows quieter, more subtle, until one must at times strain to even hear it. That is when one begins to seek quiet and solitude."

Once they reached the lake, Jorge saw that the edges were strewn with empty jugs and naked Viajero. At first he couldn't even see Lucia, but after a few moments he realized that she was obscured by two other naked people who lay partly on top of her.

El Adiuino sat down on an outcropping, took out his guitar, and began to a play a gentle yet spritely melody. Slowly, as if rising from great depths, the people began to stir. A few opened their eyes, and then a murmur of "El Adiuino" and "He's here" traveled through the group, waking up the rest of them, including Lucia.

"Good morning, everyone," the old man said cheerfully. "I thought you'd like to know that I'm leaving with this generous young man for Colmo."

"You're leaving El Fin?" a young woman asked. "But...why?"

El Adiuino nodded. "There are times when an artist grows through inner examination. But even though we are sometimes loath to admit it, art does not happen in a vacuum. Therefore, it is good, now and then, to go back out into the world and see what it has to teach us, especially during times of great turmoil. Raíz seeks independence, and I think I might like to help it along."

He stood and slung his guitar across his back and began walking toward the exit. Then he turned back to them as though it was an afterthought. "You are of course welcome to join me."

The old man waited patiently while they discussed loudly and passionately, as Viajero were wont to do. Some made it clear immediately that they wanted to go. Others seemed less convinced. Mostly the arguments seemed to center around the debate of whether "the real world" was a hindrance or inspiration for the creative process. Ultimately, they all decided to accompany Jorge and El Adiuino.

Except Lucia.

"I only just arrived yesterday with Jorge," she said, looking uncharacteristically humble. "I have seen what there is to see out there in the world and I have faced battle. I think...I would like to try this 'inner examination' you speak of, Adiuino."

"You're not coming with us?" Jorge asked.

"I will return," she said. "I can't abandon our cause. But being here, I realized there is still a lot for me to learn. I can feel it. And I can also feel that it's something I need to do alone. So rather than take the boat with you, I will simply walk to Colmo."

"You realize that will take weeks, Lucia," said Jorge.

"Yes."

"What will I tell Maria?"

She smiled, although it was not her usual patronizing expression, but something delicately sweet, like jasmine. "What else? Tell her I love her."

They made sure that Lucia had as many provisions as she could carry. Then she smiled again and sauntered north across the rolling dunes.

"She will be fine," El Adiuino assured him. "Many artists have a time when they need to travel alone with nothing but their own thoughts and the experience of nature to guide them."

"Can you tell my sister that?" he asked. "Otherwise she might kill me."

The old man laughed. "Come, let's go to your ship. I do hope we can all fit."

"It'll be tight," admitted Jorge. "But worth it. If the Great Families had any reluctance to join before, I think bringing back a group of the greatest Viajero in all Raíz led by El Adiuino himself will vanquish those doubts. Although…" He eyed the group. "Perhaps everyone should put on some clothes first."

23

Sonya had wondered what a "trundle" was. It turned out to be something like a giant metal turtle. It still possessed the same triangular head with magenta glowing eyes as Old Hilde, but the body was like a hollow shell that was so large, it could house not only Gruttman, Hans, Sonya, and her brother, but Peppercorn as well. It did not move particularly fast, but its gait was so wide that she thought it covered distance comparable to a horse-drawn coach. The inside of the shell had metal benches to sit on, and there were slats in the side so Sonya could look out at the Kantesian landscape as it slid past.

"This is being powered by someone's soul?" she asked Hans.

"That is my understanding, yes," said Hans.

"Herr Gruttman." Sonya turned to where he sat in a large, padded chair. "Whose soul is inside this thing?"

Gruttman frowned thoughtfully. "I am not sure. It is usually an elderly person who wishes to clear their family debt so the younger generation does not have to pay it."

"It's usually old people, though, huh?"

"That is the logical thing. A young person giving up a healthy body would be a waste, do you not think?"

"I suppose..." Sonya didn't like the way that implied an older person giving up their body was *not* a waste. "And how long does it last?"

"How long?" Gruttman didn't seem to understand the question.

"How many years until the soul powering this iron turtle can rest?"

Still he looked confused. "Why would it end?"

"The metal frame may need maintenance or repair," interjected Hans, "but a soul does not wear out, so far as we know."

"Yeah, but..." Sonya struggled how to put her concern into words. "Doesn't the person earn off their debt at some point?"

"They earn it off immediately when they volunteer to be transferred," said Gruttman. "It is understood that this service is without end, and the family is well compensated. It can elevate a poor family into a life of wealth and success. It is no small thing the person has done, and their family will revere them for all time."

"Still...," said Sonya.

"I see why you find this troubling, Sonya," said Hans. "In other cultures this might be looked upon as something akin to slavery. But as Herr Gruttman pointed out, this is voluntary. And also think about this. What would you do with the soul of this trundle? Take it out and let it sit uselessly in a drawer? Or destroy it? How would you know the correct thing to do if you cannot ask the soul what it wants? You would have to presume, and quite possibly be wrong. Perhaps the soul takes pride in transporting one of the most important men in Kante. Or perhaps the soul simply does not care one way or the other, in which case it would be a shame to waste such a resource."

Sonya remained uncomfortable with the idea, but just like when she was in Raíz, she had to recognize her own cultural bias. If this was something that everyone in Kante accepted and possibly even embraced, who was she to judge?

"It does seem to be a complicated matter," said Sebastian beside her. "When Isobelle spoke of her grandfather, she expressed a tremendous amount of emotion. Sadness but also great pride. Think about it, Yasha. If you could sacrifice yourself to solve all the problems of your loved ones in one fell swoop, wouldn't you?"

"I would," she admitted.

"There you have it then," Gruttman said cheerfully.

The trip to Weide took several days. Each night they stopped at an inn, where Herr Gruttman was greeted with great enthusiasm. Sonya wasn't sure if it was out of respect, or because he spent a large amount of money at each stop. The nobleman had an insatiable love of stories, so each night at dinner Sonya would regale him with more of her adventures. One night, perhaps out of politeness, he asked Sebastian to tell one of his own exploits. Sadly, her brother did not have a gift for storytelling, somehow managing to be both brief and tedious all at once.

At last they reached the Kantesian capital of Weide. The road curved around a small lake as it drew near, which gave Sonya a chance to see it from the side-view slats in the trundle. It was quite a bit larger than Gogoleth, and while it didn't take up as much land as Colmo, it looked far more dense. In fact, with its high circular wall and tall, compact buildings, it looked almost like a quiver of arrows.

"It's nearly as big as Magna Alto," said Sebastian. "Though certainly not as colorful."

Sonya thought that perhaps even Gogoleth, with its many black stone buildings, would have been more colorful. Weide seemed to have been built on the same general principles as Kochstadt. From a distance at least, every building looked exactly the same. But shown in such vastness, the monotony was almost oppressive.

"Yes." Gruttman heaved a tragic sigh. "I fear my countrymen lack…an excitement for decoration. This is why I admire Raízian design so much. There is so much color!"

The feeling of oppressive stoicism did not fade as they drew near. Sonya would have thought that when she got closer, she'd see some minor variation from one building to the next. But no, even when they entered the city itself and their trundle clanked along a wide avenue, every building looked the same.

It wasn't until they reached the center of the city that the monotony was finally broken. It was a building made of the same material and no wider than the others, but it was twice as tall.

"My God, that must be a lot of steps to climb," said Sebastian once his poor eyesight was finally able to make it out.

"That is Lord's Tower," said Gruttman. "Only servants live in the upper half, of course. The Herzog and his family live on the lower floors, which are much more convenient."

Sonya had never had servants, so perhaps she had no place to judge. But it seemed unfair to expect them to have to climb so many flights of stairs at the end of the day after working so hard.

The trundle pulled up in front of the iron gate that surrounded the Tower.

"Best to get our name in now before we settle into the inn," said Gruttman. "This will only take a moment."

He opened the hatch in the side of the shell. The bottom part of the hatch folded out into a steep set of stairs. He made his way down, then over to the gatehouse beside the entrance. He spoke with a guard there and handed him a slip of paper. The guard saluted to him, then carefully tucked the message into a pouch at his waist.

Gruttman returned to the trundle looking satisfied.

"According to the gatekeeper, things have not been too hectic of late. We should be granted an audience in only a couple of weeks. A month at the most."

"A *month*?" asked Sonya.

Gruttman smiled apologetically. "The Herzog is a busy man."

Sonya wasn't sure she could take living in this drab city for a month, but she nodded. "Thank you for doing this, Herr Gruttman."

The man grinned. "It will give us plenty of time to make your portrait!"

The trundle resumed its loud, even gait along the avenue. Now and then, Sonya saw other golems trudging along. Some were as big as Gruttman's trundle, but others were quite small.

"Can a person fit in one of those?" she asked the lord.

"Oh no, those are messengers."

"They just carry messages around the city?" she asked.

"It's a big city," said Gruttman.

Sonya had to admit that of all the aspects of Kante, the golems were the most fascinating. As she watched their gleaming metal hulls moving back and forth along the avenue like giant ants, she realized with a pang how sad the rusted and immobile Old Hilde was by comparison. Did golems care about such things? Perhaps not...

Soon they came to the inn, which on the outside looked like

every other building. There was clearly no room for the trundle to be housed there, so it moved on once they had disembarked. Sonya wondered if there was a special place the larger golems went. Did they have their own gatherings? Could they somehow communicate with each other? Did they even acknowledge each other? She still really couldn't wrap her mind around them.

Sonya made sure that Peppercorn was properly stabled, then went inside to see where she and her brother would be staying for at least the next few weeks.

Or so she thought. Because only a couple of days later, they had an unexpected visitor.

24

You said *Ambassador Boz* is here?" Sebastian asked the innkeeper, who stood in the doorway to their room. "To see *us*? Right *now*?"

"She wait down the stairs," the woman said in a heavy Kantesian accent. A lot of people in Weide seemed to speak at least a little of the imperial tongue.

"Who's this ambassador?" Sonya sat cross-legged on her bed, sharpening the knife Herr Gruttman had insisted on buying her the day before.

"A friend of Mother's, I think."

She gave him a dubious look. "Mother has friends?"

"Ally, then," he said impatiently.

"Ah. That makes more sense." Then she went back to sharpening her knife.

"Well? Should we go talk to her?"

Sonya carefully examined her gleaming blade for a moment, then shrugged. "I suppose."

As they followed the innkeeper downstairs, he said to his sister, "You don't seem at all nervous."

"Why would I be?"

"The ambassador of a foreign country? How did she find us? What does she want with us?"

"Oh, the last part is easy. She either wants me to kill someone or you to magic something."

"*Magic* something?" he asked acidly.

"Is there another name for it?"

"Well... I mean, not as such...," he admitted.

She grinned. "Let me know when you come up with something better. Until then, I'll say you *magic* things."

Sebastian thought he might prefer just about anything else, but he would have to hold off on that argument for now because the innkeeper had just brought them into a small parlor. A woman dressed all in brightly colored silk sat patiently in a high-backed chair. The lower half of her face was covered in a silk veil, but she appeared to be middle-aged, with brown skin and black hair streaked with gray.

The innkeeper said something in Kantesian to the woman, who replied in the same language.

Then the innkeeper said to Sebastian and Sonya, "Here is Ambassador Ceren Boz of Victasha." Then she left.

The ambassador turned to Sebastian and his sister, and there was a merry twinkle in her eyes. "Ah, the infamous Portinari siblings. Your mother has told me so much about you both."

"I'll bet she didn't have anything good to say about me," said Sonya as she flopped down onto a loveseat.

"On the contrary," said Boz. "I believe she described you as 'tremendously talented.'"

Sonya's eyes widened. "Really?"

"Although she followed that up with 'quite feisty and never one to mind her parents.'"

Sonya let out a laugh. "Yeah, that sounds right."

Boz turned to Sebastian, who still stood. "And of course she never missed an opportunity to extoll your virtues... shall I call you Captain Portinari?"

"Sebastian Turgenev is fine, Ambassador," he said with stiff politeness. "I am no longer a captain of the imperial army."

He did not understand why his sister seemed so at ease with this person who was a powerful foreign agent with unknown motives. Besides, there was something about her... a subtle aura that somehow reminded him of the sensation he felt just before using magic. Not as strong, but far more persistent. Perhaps if he'd still had his gem he might have been able to get a clearer idea of what it was, but . . .

He had to stop thinking that way. The gem was gone now. He had to accept that his days of near limitless power were over and that was probably for the best, for him and everyone around him.

"Would you care to sit, Sebastian Turgenev?" asked Boz, seemingly untroubled by his aloofness.

"Very well." Sebastian sat next to his sister on the sofa across from Boz. "What is it you want with us, Ambassador?"

She laughed, a light tinkling sound. "Right to the point, then! Very well. I was at the Lord's Tower the other day and happened to come across Herr Gruttman's request to obtain an audience with the Herzog for you. As soon as I saw the names Sonya and Sebastian Turgenev, I immediately thought of your mother, a woman for whom I hold a deep respect, and perhaps a little guilt."

"Guilt?" asked Sebastian.

"I knew ahead of time that the Uaine attack on Magna Alto would take place, and I fled. Sadly, I was not permitted to inform any of my friends at the palace before I left, so your mother still remains confined there at the whims of that madman."

"Not *permitted*?" demanded Sebastian.

She nodded. "By the Royal Majesties of Victasha."

"Oh." Sebastian had to admit that it would have been unfair to expect the ambassador to go against her rulers just to help a friend. "But you think she's okay?"

"I can't say for certain, but from what I know of Vittorio, he would be more likely to use her as a bargaining chip than simply kill her." Her brow furrowed. "Still, she is also now stuck there with those Uaine."

"Ah, they're not all bad," said Sonya. "I'd like to think that there's one or two who might even look out for her if they know she's my mom."

"So you parted with them on amicable terms, then?" asked Boz.

Sonya's expression darkened. "No, I wouldn't say that."

She had told Sebastian what happened, and while she kept insisting that she wasn't hurt that her lover Blaine had abandoned her at such a low point, Sebastian knew all too well how that sort of betrayal felt. Even now his own strong emotions stirred when he thought of Galina. All he had to do was picture her face, and a fierce battle between yearning and resentment rose up in his gut.

Boz seemed to sense the shift in mood. "Well, I do hope you're right that the Uaine will befriend your mother. I'd hate to lose such an engaging adversary."

"Adversary?" said Sebastian. "I thought you said you were friends."

"In my line of work, one can be both," said Boz. "That weasel Zaniolo had your mother playing spy for him in a desperate attempt to gain insight into Victasha's renowned Intelligence Bureau. For a complete amateur, she conducted herself so impressively that I actually considered offering her a job."

"But you still knew she was doing it," pointed out Sonya.

"Naturally. But I am a professional, after all, and talent alone cannot compete with years of experience in the trade."

"Then...are you an ambassador or a spy?" asked Sebastian.

Rather than answer, Boz let out another of those tinkling laughs. "My, but you are an earnest one, aren't you. It's very charming."

"So what do you actually want, Ambassador?" asked Sonya.

Boz nodded agreeably. "I may not be able to help dear Irina at present, but I can most certainly help her children. While Herr Gruttman's request will *eventually* get you a meeting with the Herzog, I can arrange for you to meet him this very evening. How does that sound?"

"It sounds too good to be true," Sonya said.

Boz didn't seem troubled by her bluntness. "Of course I would expect something in return for this service."

"Let me guess," said Sonya. "You either want me to kill someone or my brother to magic something."

Sebastian refrained from complaining about his sister once again using that ridiculous description because he was grateful that she was able to finally force this slippery ambassador to get to the heart of the matter.

"Nothing so coarse," said Boz. "I would merely like to be present during the meeting."

"That's it?" asked Sebastian.

Boz's eyes sparkled. "That should be plenty."

Sebastian looked at Sonya and she shrugged. "I can't really see the harm."

He couldn't either, although that alone was enough to make him nervous. But being able to finally see Isobelle—or rather, finally atone for his past actions against the Kantesians? Without any obvious issues presenting themselves, he decided he had to take that chance.

"Very well, Ambassador," he said. "We will accept your kind offer."

"Wonderful." She raised an eyebrow as she looked at them. "We will be attending a small concert at Lord's Tower, and formal wear will be expected."

Sonya made a face. "A dress?"

"I'm afraid so," said Boz.

She gave Sebastian a suddenly resentful look. "You're going to owe me one for this, Bastuchka."

25

I cannot believe you left my beloved alone on the peninsula!"

Maria followed behind Jorge as he hurried through the hallways of Cassa Estío.

"What was I going to do, Maria?" he asked without slowing down. "You know she would never listen to me."

"Then you should have *made* her come with you!"

"Right," said Jorge. "With my big muscles."

"Oh my God, what if something happens to her! There could be anything out there! It could be—"

Jorge wheeled around. "You know what *I* can't believe? That you're turning into our mother before my very eyes."

That shut her up. Her eyebrows rose and her lips pressed into a thin line.

His expression softened. "Look, I get that you're worried, and I don't blame you. But neither of us have the right to tell Lucia what she should do with her life. She knew this would upset you but she did it anyway. Since neither of us are Viajero, maybe we can't understand, but I think we have to respect that this is something she *needs* to do."

She looked at him for a moment, her eyes practically vibrating with tension. Then she bowed her head. "You're right, damn it. I know it. But it's just...so hard..."

He folded her into a hug. "Trust me, I know what it's like to be constantly worried about someone you love. I'm not going to say it gets easier, but you do learn to let go, at least a little."

She pressed her face into his shoulder and nodded.

"You still up for doing this?" he asked.

She pulled back and glared at him. "Who do you think you're talking to? Of course I am."

He grinned. "Then let's get started. We don't have much time left."

They continued down the hallway with the serious expression of two people on a mission. In fact, when they strode through the gardens where the majority of the Great Families were gathered, his mother called out to him, evidently wanting to introduce him to another prospective bride. But the moment he looked at her, she saw the gravity in his expression and changed her mind. Instead she only nodded and gave him that sad smile she reserved for when she realized one of her babies was growing up.

That morning, Señor Elhuyar had come to his bedroom to speak privately with him, which hadn't happened since his father had come to inform him that after great deliberation, he had decided to permit Jorge to study in Gogoleth. This time, with even greater solemnity, his father had said only this:

"Today you must move not only their minds, but their hearts as well."

"Yes, Papa."

Jorge might not be an artist, but he was a sensitive soul who understood passion and inspiration. Perhaps he couldn't move the señores of the Great Families on his own. But he didn't need to.

They met Hugo in the dining hall, and the three of them oversaw the final preparations for what was to come. Once that was done, Jorge and his siblings sat for a moment to rest and collect themselves. Jorge was surprised to find that he was not nervous. In fact, he looked forward to the meal with anticipation. Was it foolish arrogance, or true confidence? He would find out soon enough.

Once the time drew near, they headed back to the garden, which was now buzzing with conversation. Two meetings of the Great Families within a month? Such a thing had not happened for generations.

Everyone knew what it was about, of course. Or at least, they thought they did.

"Ah, there you are!" Domingo Pereria hurried over to them. "I was starting to worry."

"Nothing to be worried about," Jorge assured him.

Domingo gave him a pained look. "Sorry about last time, the way my father was hassling you."

Jorge shook his head. "No, in retrospect, I think it was a brilliant move."

"Really?" Domingo looked surprised.

"By objecting to independence, he aligned himself with the other Great Families who were opposed. But then he offered a condition by which he might accept, and the other families were forced to either commit to a hard-line rejection of the whole idea, or go along with your father's conditional acceptance. Since no one wants to outright declare that they're against Raízian independence, they didn't have much choice."

Domingo's eyes narrowed. "So you did, then? You got El Adiuino's approval?"

Jorge gave him a teasing smile. "You'll have to wait and see."

"What?" Domingo turned to Maria. "What is he planning?"

She gave a short laugh. "Like I would tell you."

Then he turned pleadingly to Hugo. "Surely you will tell me what's going on?"

But Hugo only shook his head.

Domingo looked at them in astonishment. "Unbelievable..."

"You won't have to wait much longer," said Jorge.

Jorge and his siblings mingled with the other guests, never staying too long in any one place, until finally it was time to eat.

They all filed into the dining hall as before and sat in the same places. Many eyes glanced curiously at the partition screens that had been set up at regular intervals along the walls. Some perhaps commented to their neighbors about it. But then the food came and took all of their focus. Jorge had overseen every detail of the meal and thought it might contain his finest dishes. The spiced ham was so delicate it practically melted on the tongue, and the fried milk for dessert was creamy, crunchy perfection if he did say so himself. Others seemed to agree, loudly praising the head chef, not realizing that he sat among them.

But food was just a prelude to get them in the mood. The main event began when Jorge's father rose and, just like last time, proposed that the señores and eldest sons adjourn to the study.

However, before anyone could comply, Jorge stood up.

"Excuse me, Señor. With the greatest respect, the meal is not yet finished."

"Oh?" asked his father.

"It is said that music can aid digestion," said Jorge. "So my siblings and I have prepared a short entertainment that we hope will ease the pressure on everyone's full bellies."

Señor Elhuyar inclined his head. "Very well." Then he sat back down.

Jorge clapped his hands twice, then sat as well.

It began very softly. In fact, some of the older people might not have even realized it had started. But the quiet strains of a lone guitar began to filter through the air. It was a stately melody, both stirring and sad. People began to look around for the source of the music, but there was no one visible.

The guitar continued, growing stronger and more urgent as it went. Soon it was joined by other instruments: the muted thrum of a cajón, the light trill of a flute, and the quiet clack of castanets. Then color began to spill across the ceiling until it coalesced into sullen dark skies that matched the tone of the music.

Lightning flickered across the cloud ceiling, then a male voice rose hauntingly over the instruments, singing in the ancient language of Raíz. The music swelled and the lightning grew more turbulent but it all felt strained, as though something was holding it back.

Then a man stepped out from behind one of the screens. Tall and lean, Ferran the Homebrew Fomvre now had his hair in neat braids, his face expressionless as he stretched up toward those flickering, tumultuous clouds. He danced across the room so lightly it seemed he was floating, his face straining toward the heavens, his eyes full of longing.

Led by the guitar, the music grew stronger and more dancers stepped from behind the screens to join Ferran. As if in response, the colors of the sky-ceiling began to change, growing more colorful and bright. The music then took its cue from the sky, shifting from sad and stately to triumphant and joyful.

The dining table and all its people were now suffused with a swirling, beautiful chaos of sweat-gleaming limbs and eyes that gazed with yearning at a sky resplendent in glorious majesty. It was said in Raíz that art was God's greatest gift to the world because by its grace, one might glimpse the smallest portion of His radiance, and that alone was enough to cause even the most hardened souls to weep. Jorge had always considered it hyperbole. Until now. Though he had known every part of this performance would happen, even he was swept up in it.

It felt as though they were being lifted up by the music. As though gravity was not enough to keep them stuck to the earth. Each person at the table, without realizing it, lifted their own gaze to the heavenly sky and felt it was near enough to touch. For just a moment, all their cares and worries, their ailments and age, all the things that weighed upon them seemed to evaporate, and tears of relief streamed down their cheeks.

At last the music allowed them to drift back to the earth and into their bodies once more. The dancers and the sky faded into the background and behind the screens until, just as before, there was only the quiet melody of a lone guitar.

Then El Adiuino stepped out from behind one of screens, still playing. Everyone gasped at the sight of him. They had known they were listening to a great musician, but perhaps even they had not considered it could be the greatest musician of the age.

When the last note of the guitar faded into silence, he smiled gently at them and said:

"Honored Señores and Señoras, I hope you enjoyed the new piece I composed for this occasion. I call it 'Dream of a New Raíz.'"

Then he bowed. And a roar of applause followed. Señor Pereria was hugging poor Domingo and kissing his cheeks over and over again. Gaunt old Señor Muñoz was dabbing at his eyes. Señor Cruz was clapping so hard his hands were red. The ever-cautious Señor Zorilla was on his feet, bellowing "Hurrah, hurrah!" Even Señor Dicenta, chief rival of the Elhuyars, wept without restraint.

Jorge glanced over at his father, and was surprised to see tears streaming down even his stern countenance. They looked at each other for a moment, then Señor Elhuyar nodded once and Jorge knew he had succeeded.

Raíz could never turn its back on such a beautiful dream.

26

Everything changed after the executions. Galina Odoyevtseva knew that it would, and yet it was still a struggle to adjust to the quiet fear that now lurked behind the eyes of most of her subjects. The nobles could barely stand in her presence without breaking into a sweat or stuttering. The peasantry was less affected, but even they now treated her with more caution. The only ones who did not seem to view her any differently were Andre and, surprisingly, Sezai Bey.

With Roskosh Manor little more than a charred husk, Galina, her family, and her guests had taken up residence in the old imperial barracks until something more suitable to the queen of Izmoroz could be established. Galina had made a point of putting Bey's room near her own to facilitate more frequent conversation, though of course not so close that he could eavesdrop on her. The two talked daily now. In part because Galina was still very curious about Victasha, but also because Bey was one of the few people who didn't flinch when she looked at them.

His only comment on the matter was an oddly cheerful "My, but you Izmorozians do have rather colorful methods of execution."

"You do not seem overly troubled by it," she observed.

The two sat in stiff wooden chairs in his small room. Like most of the rooms at the barracks, it was modest to the point of austere, and since Bey had few effects, it lacked any sort of personality.

"Under the current reign of Their Majesties, execution is generally frowned upon as a punishment," said Bey. "But in the past, Victasha has certainly had its share of...flamboyant methods. Take scaphism, for instance."

"I'm not familiar with that word," admitted Galina. "Is it Victashian?"

"No, Aureumian, I believe."

"And what is the method?"

"It's a bit...coarse."

"I believe I can handle it," she said wryly.

He nodded. "Very well. If I recall correctly, the condemned is force-fed a mixture of honey and milk, then thrown in a stagnant pond. The mixture brings on a terrible bout of explosive diarrhea, which in turn attracts all manner of insects who burrow, nest, and feed upon the condemned."

"By the goddess...," murmured Galina.

"After a short time, they are set free, but by then it is too late. They have become home to all manner of tiny creatures and it is only a matter of time before they are eaten alive from within. It is, I understand, a most terrible way to die."

Galina shuddered. She did not have the same instinctive aversion to insects that many people seemed to possess. In fact she found them rather fascinating. But that didn't mean she wanted them taking up residence inside her.

"It amazes me that a country with such culture and elegance could contemplate such a gruesome horror," she said.

"Just as I'm sure it has astonished many people that a refined and enlightened young monarch like yourself would sentence three of her own people to a slow death by impalement for arson."

"It was for the attempted murder of the royal family, I'll thank you to recall," she said crisply.

He inclined his head. "Yes of course. My apologies."

There was a sudden loud commotion from the hallway. Galina heard Masha protest, but it was quickly cut off.

"What on earth...," said Galina.

Then the door swung open and Tatiana stood on the other side, looking very pleased with herself.

"Mistress! I have done as you commanded!" she declared.

Galina stood up eagerly, then looked apologetically at Bey. "Please excuse me for a moment."

"Naturally," said Bey.

Galina hurried over to Tatiana and guided her back out into the hallway, firmly shutting the door behind her. She might appreciate Bey's company, but she was still wary of including him in matters of state.

"You found Jorge Elhuyar, then?" she asked eagerly.

"A most sweet lemming." Tatiana moved her shoulders around as though wishing she could preen herself. "I even offered to bed him, but he declined."

"Yes, I believe Raízians have a few more requirements for copulation than attraction and impulse."

"I see…"

This seemed to surprise her, but perhaps there was also a note of relief, as though Tatiana had begun to doubt her allure. Frankly, Galina couldn't think of anyone who would be inclined toward intimacy with such a creature. Perhaps one of the Uaine, like that Blaine fellow who had followed Sonya around.

"So what did Jorge say?" Galina asked eagerly.

"He took me to meetings with weak old men. He claimed they were the ones with power, but I could not see any sign of it."

"Yes, well, there's more to power than sheer physicality, as I have proven."

"But even in their eyes, Mistress. They did not have what you have."

"Be that as it may, what did they say?"

The Ranger seemed to think on it, as though trying to recall the information that was her sole purpose in going to Raíz to gather in the first place. Galina valued Tatiana, of course, but by the goddess she had forgotten how frustrating she could be.

"At first they were afraid and cowardly," the Ranger said finally.

"So the sweet lemming went on a journey and brought back truly powerful ones. Ones that could make even those tired old men brave."

"And the end result?" asked Galina, willing herself not to grab Tatiana by her feathery cloak and shake her.

"They will fight with us, of course. And here is a letter for you from the sweetest lemming."

She handed Galina a letter that looked as rumpled and travel stained as Tatiana's clothes. But thankfully it was still legible.

To Her Majesty, Galina Odoyevtseva,

I hope this finds you well. Please allow me to congratulate you on your new title as queen of Izmoroz. I hope the country that was kind enough to shelter me for so long flourishes under your rule.

I confess I still have some reservations in aligning myself with you after your role in ousting Sonya. Words cannot express how much it hurt her to find the people she had fought to free turned against her. Frankly, I'm not sure I will ever truly be able to forgive you for that.

However, we live in trying times, and as you suggest, we must put such personal matters aside for now. So it is in the interest of obtaining a better future for Raíz that I, Jorge Elhuyar, national representative appointed by a council of the Great Families, gratefully accept your offer of an alliance to protect our mutual sovereignty from the Aureumian Empire and all who align with them.

I believe that one of the keys to success for our alliance will be clear and efficient communication. As such I would like to suggest that we utilize the Victashian Intelligence Bureau. We have a representative here in Colmo, and Ranger Tatiana led me to believe you have one in Gogoleth as well. I am unsure by what method the agents of the bureau are able to impart information to each other so quickly, be it a large network of embedded spies, or a more supernatural means, but I do feel that it could be of immense use. If you care to discuss the matter further, please inform your representative, and I am certain they will somehow get in touch with ours. I realize that allying ourselves with a vast foreign power with opaque motivations is perilous, but I believe it is a risk worth taking for the time being.

*I look forward to working with you toward mutual independence and
a free continent.*

Sincerely,
Jorge Elhuyar, National Representative of Raíz

"Hm," said Galina.

Tatiana cocked her head to one side. "You are displeased, Mistress?"

"Yes, but not with Jorge."

She carefully folded the letter, then turned and walked back into
the room with Sezai Bey, not bothering to knock.

"I suppose you already knew about this?" She held up the letter.

"Of course," he said placidly.

She knew there was no use in being cross with him. In fact, it
would probably make her look childish. But she did want to make
sure she got one point across.

"If we are to be allies in earnest," she said as she walked across
the room and sat back down, "then there is one thing I must ask of you."

"And what is that?"

"A clearer understanding of your capabilities. How am I to properly utilize my resources if I do not know their limits?"

He considered that a moment. "I will do my best to be as forthcoming as I am permitted."

She gave him a level stare. "That is the best you can offer, I
suppose."

Bey actually did look slightly apologetic this time. "I'm afraid so."

"Can you in fact get in touch with your counterpart in Colmo?"

"Yes."

"And are you willing to relay a message to this person to deliver to
Jorge Elhuyar?"

"I would be happy to do so."

"Because it's why you're here."

"In part."

"And the other part is relaying messages to Ambassador Boz,"
stated Galina.

"Correct."

"Very well." Galina took a deep breath, which still did not calm her very much, but had become something of a habit, or at least a way to prevent herself from venting her frustration while she considered a more tactful approach. "Then as I'm sure you are already aware, I have formed an alliance with Raíz, which seems to have established some sort of plutocratic government, at least for the time being."

"I was not aware that you had *finalized* the alliance, but yes, I knew that the offer had been extended by their newly appointed national representative."

"Now that the matter is settled, all that remains is to figure out if it's possible to form an alliance with Kante," said Galina. "Unfortunately, I have no contacts in Kante, so I fear I must take up your ambassador's kind offer to provide some introductions."

Then Bey smiled in a way that was almost mischievous, an expression so unexpected from the typically reserved Victashian that it immediately put Galina on guard.

"But, Your Majesty, you *do* have contacts in Kante. Two, in fact."

"Oh? And whom might they be?"

"The Portinari siblings. Actually, I believe they are with Ambassador Boz at this very moment."

"Ah."

Galina's heart sank. And yet she found herself unsurprised. It seemed quite fitting, really, that the two people she had betrayed most cruelly were now the key to a successful alliance.

27

I don't think I've ever seen an ensemble quite like that," Ceren Boz told Sonya as the two women sat down across from each other in the ambassador's carriage.

Sonya looked down at the toes of her boots, which peeked out from under the sleeveless blue gown she had bought that afternoon. Then she grinned.

"Apparently I have strangely shaped feet. None of the shoes at the cobbler's even came close to fitting."

She remembered having to get her boots custom-made when she first became a Ranger, so she suspected the Lady had altered her feet during her initiation. Her balance and footing had certainly improved vastly, so perhaps that was the reason for the change. She didn't know if she'd ever been so grateful for one of the "gifts" of the Lady before. It was bad enough she had to wear this fabric tube that didn't let her stretch out her legs naturally. Forcing her to wear shoes that would disintegrate the first time she kicked someone in the face would have been adding insult to injury.

"I see" was all Boz said.

Sonya still wasn't sure what to make of the Victashian. She liked how the woman was scrupulous about not expressing judgment toward those with different views of life. But she strongly suspected it stemmed less from open-mindedness and more out of caution to not offend people. As an ambassador, she probably needed to ingratiate herself with all kinds of people, after all. It seemed like a lot of work.

"I wonder what could be keeping your brother," Boz said after a few moments of silence. "You know, your mother once told me—"

"Is it exhausting?" Sonya asked abruptly.

The question seemed to take Boz by surprise. "Sorry? Is what exhausting?"

"Your schemes, your plans and deceptions. Everything you say having layers of meaning, most of it purposefully obscuring your true goals," clarified Sonya. "It sounds really tiring to me. But maybe you enjoy it? Like a hobby?"

The ambassador stared at Sonya, looking truly unsettled for the first time since they'd met. Sonya wasn't sure why. After all, Boz made quite a show of all her maneuvering. Maybe she just wasn't accustomed to people calling her out on it.

At last she rallied. "It is my job, I suppose."

"Right. And you chose this job."

"I did. And so to answer your question, it is both exhausting *and* enjoyable."

"That makes sense," said Sonya.

"If we are being so very candid," said Boz, "your brother's goals are fairly clear. But might I ask what *your* goals really are?"

Sonya smiled. She had been pondering this same question since Gruttman had asked her back at his home in Kochstadt. It had taken her somewhat by surprise, partly because she realized she did not truly understand the question. To have goals implied plans, expectations, hope for the future. These were things Sonya found she now had difficulty grasping. It had been alarming at first. A stark reminder of just how different she was from that first Sonya who had longed for parental acceptance and renown. This Sonya cared only for the present. When she was hungry, she ate. When her brother needed saving, she saved him. When someone or something piqued her curiosity, she probed deeper. But there was no long-term goal, no dream of future plans. Such things seemed obscure and ghostly to her, like shadow puppets. She almost pitied humans like Boz, who strove their whole lives to fulfill some distant and hazy goal.

Sonya doubted Boz would understand any of these ponderings, or if she did, that she would believe them. Yet Sonya didn't feel like lying. She supposed there was *one* thing she expected to accomplish in this life.

"When Rykov stabbed me to death, I was ready to stay dead. And Lady Marzanna even said she would allow it. But she also said that if I chose death, all of the suffering that my brother, my mother, and everyone else I cared about had endured would mean nothing. So I chose to come back to help them make it mean something. Suffering doesn't *need* to have any purpose, of course, but I think it's better if it does. Don't you?"

Boz gazed at her for several moments. "Yes, I suppose that's true."

"What are we talking about" asked Sebastian as he climbed into the carriage.

"Death and suffering!" Sonya said cheerfully.

He gave her a look and sighed, then sat down beside her.

"You look very dashing, Sebastian Turgenev," said Boz.

"Oh, er, thank you, Ambassador."

"Yeah, he cleans up okay," said Sonya.

Sebastian glared at her and she smiled back. The truth was, she felt almost compelled to tease him because it was moments like this, seeing him in a slightly altered setting, that reminded her all over again how drastically he had declined physically these last months. She could still clearly see that petulant *boy* she had tried to rescue from his officers' quarters in the early winter, and to have that vision overlap with this worn, gray-streaked *man* made her heart ache strangely.

"We should be getting on to the Tower," said the ambassador. "We don't want to miss the concert."

"It's been some time since I've attended one," agreed Sebastian.

"Back in Colmo, every day felt like a concert," said Sonya. "I guess I got a little spoiled."

The carriage started up and Sonya realized it was being pulled by horses, rather than one of the golem contraptions that seemed so common in Weide.

"What do you think about those golem things, Ambassador?" she asked Boz.

Boz gave her a piercing look. "It's none of my business, of course, but frankly, I think they're being underutilized."

"How so?" asked Sebastian.

"Think of it." There was a gleam in her eyes now. An eagerness that made Sonya think of a bird of prey. "Kante has a seemingly inexhaustible power source. They could power mills, irrigate fields, perhaps accomplish things never imagined by humankind. But what do they do instead? Make giant metal toys."

"You're talking about trapping these souls in machines with absolutely no volition of their own," protested Sebastian. "Turning them into mechanical creatures is one thing. At least they can still move and act of their own accord. Golems are still people, after all."

"Are they?" asked Boz. "We have no way of knowing if they have any sentience or conscious thought at all above the level of a beast."

"Surely if there is even a chance that human identity is retained, then we must treat them as if that is the case," said Sebastian. "Anything less could potentially be cruel beyond measure and worse even than the base serfdom of previous, less enlightened generations."

"But, my dear Sebastian, that is already going on now," she pointed out. "What sort of choice do you think these golems are given to labor as transportation or slaughter enemies on the battlefield? Do you plan to bring your objections to the Herzog of Weide this evening?"

He frowned. "I . . . hadn't considered doing so."

"Nor should you, in my opinion," said Boz. "The Kantesians say they worship no gods, but their reverence of hexenmeisters and golems borders on religious. Remember that you are coming before the Herzog, humbly asking for acceptance. You would do well not to be so critical of the culture you hope to join."

28

When they reached the Tower, they were greeted by a row of guards dressed in the same heavy plate armor they had seen at Gruttman's home, except these soldiers also had a bright green surcoat draped over it that made them look slightly less like a tiny clanking golem.

Sonya noticed that some of them were women, and it occurred to her that while there were female warriors among the Uaine, the Anxeles Escuros, and the Viajero, she had never seen any in the imperial army.

"Does Aureum not let women be soldiers?" she asked her brother as they followed Boz out of the carriage.

He looked surprised by the question. "It never occurred to me, but I suppose not. I certainly didn't see any while I was with them."

"Not one?" she asked.

He shook his head.

"I wonder why not...," she mused as they watched the Kantesian guard form up to escort them the short distance to the front door of the Tower.

Sebastian shrugged. "The more time I spent with Aureumians, the less I felt I understood them. Their willingness to turn against their Raízian compatriots took me completely by surprise."

She laughed. "Well, that's you, little brother."

He gave her a sharp look. "What do you mean by that?"

They followed Boz across the courtyard to the front doors, flanked on either side by the clanking escort.

"Just that you're gullible," Sonya told her brother. "You always take everyone at face value and never consider that they might be something other than what they say."

He scowled. "I'm getting better."

"Are you?" she asked plaintively. "When we do talk to this Herzog, you're going to have to remember that he—and even your precious Isobelle—are political creatures. And politicians will say whatever they need to say to accomplish their goals."

"Wise words, Sonya Turgenev," murmured Boz.

Sebastian looked like he wanted to protest but didn't. Perhaps he realized that in doing so he would only prove Sonya's point. So after a moment, he nodded.

"I'll keep it in mind," he promised.

The soldiers opened the double doors, then Boz led Sonya and Sebastian into the Tower.

Although it seemed to Sonya that *tower* wasn't quite the right word. She was no expert in architecture, but to her mind, a tower was something narrow, with only one room per level. Yet the room that lay beyond the double doors looked like the lobby to a concert hall. Staircases curled up on either side, and three sets of double doors were placed along the far wall. The lobby was crowded with Kantesians, all dressed in their finery.

Sonya noticed a distinct difference in Kantesian fashion from other cultures. Kantesian clothing seemed mostly occupied with straight vertical lines, and possessed none of the curves and diagonals of Raízian or Izmorozian clothing. It was so unrelenting, it gave even these wealthy guests, many of them elderly, the appearance of a strict military bearing.

Their behavior was also quite reserved, but she had grown accustomed to that by now. They spoke to each other with that cheerful yet restrained air that all Kantesians other than Gruttman seemed to possess.

The ambassador introduced them around to various people, describing them as "nobility from Izmoroz," which Sonya supposed was technically true. Regardless, she found this restrained environment frustrating, and she had even less patience for it than ever before. As they worked their way across the lobby, she felt like a caged beast. Their stuffiness seemed to bring out a very fox-like impulse to do something wild and mischievous. Perhaps swing from the chandelier? Ardently kiss a fussy old lady? Stop a man from droning on about his mercantile business by biting his ear off? It all seemed more appealing than this dreary small talk. But then she looked over at her brother and noticed that he seemed to delight in it all, and that made her smile. She didn't want to ruin his fun.

At last they reached the other side of the room.

"Well, Ambassador," Sebastian said brightly, "thank you for introducing us around. That was lovely."

"Personally, I'd rather cross a battlefield than do that again," said Sonya.

Boz laughed in that light, easy way of hers that almost made you forget she was probably laughing *at* you.

"I can see Irina had her hands full raising two such different children."

They glanced at each other.

"Were we difficult children, do you think?" asked Sebastian.

"*You* were a trial, of course," Sonya said loftily. "But *I* was the perfect daughter."

His eyes narrowed. "That's certainly not how I remember it."

Sonya shrugged. "Well, you were younger than me, so I wouldn't expect you to remember things as well. Now, let's find our seats. I want some music!"

"An excellent suggestion," said Boz.

Beyond the doors was a concert hall roughly the size of the performance space at Cassa Estío, but with quite a few more seats. In fact, they were packed in so tightly, Sonya wondered how someone as large as Blaine would have even been able to fit his legs in behind the chair in front of him.

Some of the seats were already filled, but even taking into account the people in the lobby, Sonya thought there would still be a lot of empty chairs.

"Will this concert be well attended?" she asked Boz.

"Oh my, yes," said Boz. "But despite the general Kantesian fondness of punctuality, or perhaps because of it, the younger crowd usually doesn't make an entrance until just before the performance begins."

"It did seem like everyone out there was pretty old," admitted Sonya.

Boz led them to seats toward the back of the house near the outer aisle.

"Are these your usual seats?" she asked.

"Indeed."

Sonya had learned some things about theater and performance during her time in Colmo, so she was surprised.

"I would have thought an ambassador got better seats."

Boz's brow creased. "Unlike your Herr Gruttman, most Kantesians are not...overly interested in foreign countries. I suspect if Aureum simply stopped attacking them, they would be perfectly content to live in their own little world, oblivious to everyone else."

"I suppose that makes Hans a bit unusual as well for going to work on an international trade ship," said Sebastian.

"If that's the case," mused Sonya, "I wonder if we've really met any typical Kantesians."

"It's unlikely," said Boz, "as they would not be inclined to interact with you beyond what was necessary to be polite."

"Are they...xenophobic?" Sebastian looked warily at the elderly Kantesians who began to filter in from the lobby.

"I would not go quite that far," said Boz, her voice carefully neutral. "But others might disagree."

Sebastian seemed troubled by that, which made sense. It could be difficult to settle here in Kante if most people did not want them there. Or maybe he was thinking of his beloved Isobelle. Perhaps she was like Hans and Gruttman. Or perhaps once again he had failed to understand the true nature of someone close to him.

But that gave Sonya pause. What did she mean by *nature*? Was it the same thing as wondering about the idea of *me*? Was there some pure person underneath that everyone remained, no matter what happened to them? It was an idea that seemed increasingly unlikely to her. Or if it existed, hers seemed unlikely to have remained unchanged with each death...

She was yanked out of her musings when Sebastian gave a sharp gasp. She instinctively went for her knife, though of course she hadn't been allowed to bring it to this event. But it turned out not to be necessary, because this was danger of a different sort.

Sebastian's gaze eagerly followed a young woman with bright blue eyes and curly chestnut hair as she strode down the center aisle to the front row of seats. She was accompanied by a large entourage of excited young men and women, but she exhibited a calm, almost calculating air that reminded Sonya alarmingly of Galina.

Sonya looked at her brother's doe-eyed expression for a moment, then sighed.

He gave her a sharp look. "What?"

"You're an idiot," she told him.

His cheeks went bright red and he looked down at his hands, which writhed fitfully in his lap. "Don't you think I know that? She's basically a Kantesian princess, and I'm a penniless enemy army deserter who looks like he's twice her age. I understand that the very idea is laughable."

Her expression softened. "No, it's not—"

"It is," he insisted. "And that's fine. It's not why we're here anyway."

She gazed speculatively at him. "Isn't it?"

"No," he said firmly. "I wronged the Kantesians, and I will atone for that."

"You also wronged the Izmorozians," she pointed out. "You could have gone back there instead."

He gave her a skeptical look. "Do you really think there is any way they'd have me back?"

"Hmm, probably not. I don't think they'd even want *me* back, and they liked me a lot more than they ever liked you."

"As if I needed the reminder," he said sourly.

On closer inspection, Sonya decided that Isobelle wasn't exactly like Galina. She looked healthier, for one thing. Galina had always looked about one meal away from starvation, and there had been that delicate, doll-like sense of brittleness about her. Isobelle, on the other hand, had round rosy cheeks, a full figure, and an easy, confident bearing. In fact, the way she moved, Sonya wouldn't be surprised if she had some combat experience.

Sonya was about to tell her brother that as far as such things went, his taste in women seemed to have improved. But then there was an eager hush in the crowds, and Sonya looked back toward the stage to see an older man standing alone and holding a silver flute at his side.

Before he'd even lifted his flute, the audience burst into applause. Sonya thought he must be a famous musician in Kante for people to be excited before he'd even begun to play.

The man nodded his head in acknowledgment. Then he lifted his flute to his lips and the audience was suddenly quiet again. The sheer discipline of the crowd was strange to see after months of the more casual, sometimes even rowdy, audiences of Colmo.

Then the man began to play. He did not ease into the song gradually, but attacked it suddenly in a flurry of notes. His back arched, and between the swift light trills there were more guttural sounds, almost as though he was sighing into his instrument while his fingers flickered across the keys. Despite the relatively delicate sound of the flute, there was a ferocity to his playing. Even so, it was not reckless. If anything, there was a merciless level of control. The notes blasted through Sonya's mind like a swift tundra wind, leaving her stunned. It wasn't magic. It was just that impressive.

The song ended as abruptly as it had begun. There was a moment of utter silence in the hall. Then the applause burst forth even more loudly than the first time. The man brought his flute back to his side, but did not bow.

While he stood and soaked in the crowd's adulation, other musicians hurried onto the stage. There were several violin players and a cello player. One man rolled a piano out from the wings, and another, a harp. Someone even brought out a pair of large kettle drums.

Once they were all in place, the flautist again brought his flute to his lips and the audience fell silent. Then, without words or preamble, the concert began in earnest. While the flautist was the clear leader, each of the musicians was given a chance to show their skill. And while none of them had the same fiery precision of the leader, they were all highly accomplished. It wasn't as emotionally affecting as the many Raízian concerts Sonya had seen. Perhaps it was the lack of magic, or perhaps it was a difference in temperament. She couldn't decide. But she enjoyed it all the same.

After the concert was over, the applause went on for quite some time. No one called out, like they did in Raízian concerts, or whistled like they did in Izmorozian concerts. It was as if all their admiration was channeled into this one activity, and the wall of crushing sound reminded her somehow of the strange tear in reality she always felt when she died and transitioned into the Eventide.

Their hands must surely be aching, but they did not stop clapping until the flautist nodded one last time and left the stage. The other musicians hurried after him, and the applause finally died out.

"Well, that was quite stirring," said Sebastian as they rose from their seats.

"Yeah, it was pretty good," said Sonya.

"How did you think it compares to the concerts in Raíz?" asked Boz.

"If you leave the magic part aside, it was about as impressive," said Sonya. "But there's a big difference in...attitude maybe? I'm not a musician so I don't really know the right words."

"I think I would have loved to take up an instrument," said Sebastian. "But we had so little exposure to music as children."

"That surprises me," said Boz. "I imagined your mother to be quite cultured."

"Oh, she is," said Sonya. "But we lived on a farm out in the middle of nowhere. Olga Slanikova's husband played the fiddle but that was about it."

"And you never went into Gogoleth?" asked Boz.

"Hardly ever," said Sebastian. "My father was concerned I might accidentally reveal my abilities in elemental magic."

"I see," said Boz, refraining from saying more, though clearly she had other thoughts.

"Captain?" came a bright and ringing voice. "Captain Portinari, is that you?"

Sebastian went pale as he wheeled about to see Isobelle smiling at him from the center aisle.

"I-Isobelle!" said Sebastian, stuttering for the first time in a while.

Isobelle was flanked by her entourage, all of whom seemed to view Sonya and Sebastian with a mixture of curiosity and unease.

"It *is* you!" Isobelle gestured with one white-gloved hand. "Do come over here so I do not have to shout."

"O-of course," he said, bumbling nervously down the row toward her.

Sonya sighed at her little brother's lack of poise and followed, with Boz trailing silently behind.

"It is good to see you again, Captain." Isobelle's command of the imperial tongue was impressive, and she seemed to be genuinely happy to see Sebastian.

"Actually, it's, er, not Captain anymore," he said, not quite able to meet her gaze. "I-I've left the army."

"I did think it strange to see an imperial captain attending a concert at the Kantesian Lord's Tower," she said. "And I suppose it is not a surprise that you left, given your daring and clandestine activities while you were there."

He chuckled nervously, still not looking into her eyes. "You make it sound more courageous than it was."

"*Ach nein!* I am relieved that you left before something terrible happened. I was so worried about you."

"You were worried…about me?" The notion seemed to smack across his face like a wave, as though it was something he hadn't even considered. Sonya thought she could detect hope kindling in his eyes.

"Of course. I have heard the Aureumians are merciless when betrayed by one of their own. And after all your kindness and bravery, it troubled me greatly to think you suffered for those actions."

"It really wasn't all that noble," he protested. Although Sonya noted that he looked pleased.

"Nonsense." She turned to her entourage. "This man single-handedly saved over a hundred Kantesian lives in Kleiner at great personal risk and without any recompense or reward."

Sebastian seemed to be practically floating now. Sonya could almost see the dreams of new romance flitting through his head. "Oh, w-well, I certainly didn't expect anything in return . . ."

The young man standing directly to Isobelle's right spoke up. "Nevertheless, I must commend you. I do not know a single other Aureumian who would act so selflessly."

"Ahhh." Isobelle took hold of the man's arm. "Sebastian, I'm delighted to finally introduce you to my husband, Wilhelm Sachs von Gestade."

Sonya clamped her mouth shut to keep the sudden laugh from escaping, but it still came out as a quiet snort. Meanwhile, all the color drained out of Sebastian's face so swiftly it looked like he might faint.

But somehow, he held it together. Sonya had to give him that. He bowed in the Izmorozian style. "H-how wonderful to meet you. I am equally delighted to introduce my sister, Sonya Turgenev."

"Oh my!" Isobelle smiled at Sonya. "I had no idea you had a sister."

Sonya gave her a close-mouthed grin so as not to frighten her with fangs. "Yeah, well, we weren't exactly on speaking terms when you two met."

Her brow knit together in concern. "Oh dear. But you've clearly made amends."

"Sure," agreed Sonya. "Because he left the empire."

"I take it you are not in favor of the Aureumian Empire?" asked Wilhelm.

Sonya laughed. "Let's just say I've probably killed a lot more imperials than you have."

Wilhelm seemed equal parts shocked and intrigued by her statement. "Fascinating. Even though you are Aureumian?"

"Half."

"Ach, yes, I recall Isobelle saying that about your brother, which of course applies to you as well. Forgive me. You are also half Izmorozian, then."

"I suppose..."

She felt strangely reluctant to claim her Izmorozian identity. Did she have some resentment at the way people had treated her before she fled? Or was this another shift in her mindset after her latest rebirth? Technically speaking, in this life she had never even been to Izmoroz. It was only memories to her. Did that matter? She wasn't sure.

"So what are you two doing in Kante?" Isobelle asked.

"I was hoping you might put in a good word to your father for us. My sister and I don't really have anywhere else to go, and I think we would be a huge benefit to Kante, should the empire invade once more."

"I would be happy to do so, Sebastian," said Isobelle. "I know you to be a kind and conscientious man, and your magical abilities have always astonished me."

"Oh, that's wonderful!" Sebastian looked incredibly relieved, although Sonya couldn't imagine anyone being stupid enough to turn down an offer of assistance from the most powerful magic user on the continent. Surely the Herzog would see his potential immediately.

"Say..." Sonya's eyes scanned the hall, searching for someone who might have the imposing look of a ruler. "Isn't the Herzog supposed to be here?"

Isobelle laughed. "Did you not know? You have just been watching him for the last hour."

"What do you mean?" asked Sebastian.

Isobelle smiled with a look of unabashed pride. "That flautist was my father, Herzog Ferdinand Cohen von Weide II."

29

Based on what he'd seen only a short while before, Sebastian presumed that the ruler of Kante was something of an eccentric. So it wasn't as though he expected the Herzog to present a level of decorum similar to Empress Caterina's court. But perhaps he'd thought there would be at least *some* pomp or luxury during their initial meeting.

Now he sat on a narrow hardback chair between his sister and the ambassador in a cramped, drab room that seemed aggressively indifferent to basic comfort. The Kantesians might not worship any god, but Ferdinand Cohen von Weide's love of austerity was something akin to religious fervor.

The Herzog sat on the other side of a large desk strewn with scrolls and stacks of curling parchment. He leaned back in his chair, his dark eyes gazing thoughtfully at them.

"You do bring such *interesting* guests, Ambassador Boz." His accent was perhaps the lightest Sebastian had heard during his time in Kante. It made Sebastian wonder if, despite Boz's earlier remarks about Kantesian isolationism, the Herzog had spent some time in the empire.

Sebastian also detected a certain level of wariness, perhaps even disapproval, in Weide's statement, but the ambassador maintained her usual upbeat demeanor and laughed merrily.

"I wouldn't want to bore you, Lord Cohen."

He was surprised the ambassador didn't call him *Lord Weide*, but perhaps naming conventions didn't work quite the same in Kante.

He shouldn't be surprised. After all, no one seemed to use maternal surnames outside of Izmoroz. Even after all this time, he was still uncomfortable calling someone he hardly knew by only their given name, but it was clearly acceptable behavior in many cultures.

"I hope you will forgive our intrusion, Lord Cohen," he said. "We, er...that is, I am a past acquaintance of your daughter's, and she said she would vouch for me."

A lone white eyebrow rose, but otherwise his expression remained neutral. "And she has, otherwise you would not be sitting here. But what is it you seek?"

"R-right," said Sebastian. "Well, my sister and I would like to offer our services to you to help defend Kante against imperial aggression. You see—"

"Why Kante?" the Herzog interrupted him, still not looking even slightly welcoming. Sebastian struggled to continue under that cold stare.

"W-well..."

"If I may, Lord Cohen," interceded the ambassador. "You see, Sonya and Sebastian are from Izmoroz, but their father was the notorious Aureumian commander Giovanni Portinari, famously known as Giovanni the—"

"I know to whom you are referring," Weide said with a hint of impatience. "And I'll thank you not to bring parochial peasant nicknames into the discussion."

Boz inclined her head. "Then I'm sure you can see the...tenuous nature of their presence in Izmoroz, given the current state of the continent."

"I'm sure it didn't help that one of them is a magic user who leveled an entire town and the other openly allied herself with the Uaine, whose loyalties have since proved less than reliable."

"I was getting to that," said Boz cheerfully, her poise unflappable even in the face of his blunt talk.

"The Uaine are fine allies," objected Sonya.

Sebastian cleared his throat, trying to indicate by his expression that she should not push the matter further.

"But they *are*," she said. "They did what they promised to do. And then they went on to make a different alliance. Seems fair enough to me."

Now Cohen turned to her, but unlike Sebastian, she did not flinch before his steely gaze.

"Rather generous of you," he said, "considering the stories I've heard about the thrashing their leader gave you before driving you out of your own homeland."

Instead of being thrown off by this surprisingly detailed display of knowledge, Sebastian's sister grinned in a way that looked almost like she was baring her teeth.

"I'm a generous person."

"Fair enough." The Herzog seemed more amenable to his sister's abrasive approach than either Sebastian's or Boz's more deferential tone. "But I do wonder why you would not seek asylum in the newly liberated Raíz." He nodded to her black leather vest. "You clearly made a place for yourself there."

"Yeah, well, at the time there was a lot of stuff going on that made getting out of Colmo the smart choice. But now..." She looked at Sebastian. "If Kante doesn't want us, I guess we could go back."

"Why would you do that," asked Boz, "when your presence here is essential?"

All three of them looked at Boz with uncertainty. Sebastian couldn't help feeling as though a trap of some kind had just been snapped shut.

"I see, dear Ambassador, that we have finally come to your reason for being here," said Cohen. "Then pray tell me, why do you think these two are *essential* to Kante?"

"Yeah," said Sonya. "I mean I think we'd be *helpful*, but all we can really do is kill people and magic things."

"Must you?" Sebastian asked her plaintively.

"What?" she said with mock innocence.

"Can't you take anything seriously?"

"I'm starting to think that everything should be taken with about the same amount of seriousness."

"Which is *none*?" he demanded.

She only shrugged, as if it wasn't even worth arguing about. He loved his sister, but she could be so infuriatingly snotty at times.

"To answer your question, Lord Cohen," said Boz, courageously getting them back on track, "sometimes *who* you know is just as important as what you can do. The unpleasant but indisputable fact is that your continent is on the precipice of total war."

"Not so indisputable," said Cohen.

"No?" asked Boz. "With Izmoroz and Raíz forming an alliance against the empire and the Uaine, how long do you think it will be before Kante gets dragged into the mess, regardless of who is victorious?"

"Izmoroz and Raíz have formed an alliance?" asked Sonya.

Boz's eyes twinkled above her veil. "Indeed. And with the help of you and your brother, I think Kante could join that alliance, thereby ensuring the empire's defeat"—she looked back at Cohen—"and guaranteeing Kante's continued existence as a sovereign and independent nation, equal with the other two powers."

"Hmmm," said Cohen, his expression still giving away little besides a pensive thoughtfulness. "Interesting."

"How could Sonya and I help broker an alliance?" asked Sebastian.

"For one thing," said Boz, "Sonya is on very good terms with the newly elected Raízian national representative, Jorge Elhuyar."

Sonya sat up in her seat. "They put Jorge in charge? That's great!"

Boz nodded. "And of course the current ruler of Izmoroz is someone you know quite intimately, Sebastian."

Sebastian frowned. "Ruler? I assumed that with the empire gone, they would return to the Council of Lords."

"That was the original plan," said Boz. "But sadly, the council proved to be... ineffectual. So Galina Odoyevtseva felt compelled to step in and take charge."

Sebastian's stomach dropped. "Galina?"

"Her Majesty, Queen Galina the First of Izmoroz, to be precise," said Boz. "And by most accounts, it is a role that suits her well."

"*Queen* Galina?" His mind struggled to accept the idea of that sullen, waifish, disloyal schemer being queen of anything.

"You know," Sonya said thoughtfully, "I heard something about this from some friends in Colmo. But I wasn't sure how much to believe. To think that little *kukla* could seize power."

"She *did* have some help," conceded Boz. "I believe you know them as well. Ranger Andre and Ranger Tatiana?"

Now it was Sonya's turn to look stunned. "*Those two* are helping Galina? But... *why?*"

"I don't know the reason they formed their alliance," said Boz. "But as far as I can tell, it seems to be a very harmonious partnership."

"And Jorge agreed to an alliance with her?" pressed Sonya.

"He did have some reservations, considering her part in ousting you from Izmoroz," said Boz. "But he ultimately decided to put his people before his personal grievance, and I hope you will consider doing the same."

"What she did to *me* was one thing. But she also broke my brother's heart. You do know that, right?"

Boz's eyebrows knit together. "I was sorry to hear of it."

"Hm," said Cohen. "I don't know this part."

"Apparently—" began Boz.

But Sebastian cut her off. "Thank you, Ambassador, I believe I can tell my own sad story."

She bowed her head slightly. "Yes, of course."

"I was once a captain in the imperial army," he told Cohen. "During that time, I was betrothed to Galina Odoyevtseva. She was able to see, long before I could, that the empire was unjust. Perhaps she was afraid to confront me with the knowledge. Perhaps she was correct in thinking I wouldn't have been able to accept it at that time. I don't know. But rather than make the attempt, she instead decided to utilize my fondness for her to protect the small anti-imperial insurgency that was forming. It was only when the tide had turned and I was forced to flee Izmoroz that she let her true feelings be known."

"Really?" Cohen seemed to find this information the most intriguing thing he'd heard all day. "I should like to meet this queen of Izmoroz."

"After hearing what she did to my brother, that's your response?"

Sonya half rose in her chair, her fists clenched. Sebastian hadn't realized she was so angry about it, and an odd flush of gratitude filled his cheeks.

Cohen, however, did not seem intimidated by Sonya and merely said, "A tactical mind like that is a rare thing."

"Yes, let us think this through carefully," said Boz. "Whatever one's personal feelings toward Galina Odoyevtseva might be, we can all agree that an empire ruled by Franko Vittorio is not good for any of us, especially when joined by the Uaine, whose true motives, frankly, are a mystery even to me. Raíz has powerful Viajero and the discipline of the guilds, but despite Jorge Elhuyar's best efforts, they lack strong central leadership. Izmoroz has leadership, but their newly formed militia is raw and inexperienced. Without Kante, this alliance's victory over the empire is not at all assured."

"And with Kante it is?" asked Cohen.

"I believe a coordinated assault with all three armies would be the best chance for the continent."

"And you are willing to offer your services to be that coordination?" he asked dryly.

"A peaceful continent benefits Victasha as well."

"Perhaps. But a continent recovering from cataclysmic war would also be ripe for conquest."

Sebastian hadn't even considered that idea. Was Victasha egging on the various factions, allowing them to wear each other out so they could swoop in and take the entire continent?

"It is a reasonable concern," admitted Boz. "But I can assure you that Their Majesties are not interested in conquest."

"Then what *are* they interested in?" pressed Cohen. "I have yet to get an answer from you on that."

"I do not mean to be reticent," said Boz. "But I am only authorized to say so much. I will tell you that Their Majesties are playing a much longer game. One that may take generations to bear fruit."

"So we should accept your aid now at the expense of our great-grandchildren?" asked Cohen.

"Not exactly. We have no designs against your continent. But

I would of course be lying if I said we did not put our own needs and safety first."

"You can be infuriatingly cryptic at times," he told her.

"My apologies. That is never my intent."

Cohen gazed at her for a moment, then all his hard steel suddenly dissipated. He heaved a long sigh and sank into his chair, as though suddenly weary of it all.

"Naturally you've already advised the queen of Izmoroz that she must put aside any personal feelings she has toward these two for the greater good of her people."

"You will find that Her Majesty needs no convincing when it comes to decisions of that nature."

"Alas that I am not a younger man," said Cohen.

"I, for one, am grateful," said Boz. "A marriage between Ferdinand Cohen von Weide and Galina Odoyevtseva Prozorova could have seen the rise of a nation too formidable to contemplate. Not merely the continent, but the entire world would have trembled at their might."

Cohen gave a quiet, dry laugh. "You can be such a tease, Ambassador."

Sebastian tried not to look too upset that these people he hardly knew were casually discussing a marriage to his ex-betrothed, but his expression clearly betrayed him because Sonya put a hand on his arm, her face creased with concern.

Boz seemed to catch this, because she said, "My apologies, Sebastian. It was terribly insensitive of me to mention such a thing."

"Nonsense," Cohen said curtly, the steel now back in both his posture and his expression. "If he is to be my liaison with Izmoroz, he had better get used to the idea that people won't be tiptoeing around his delicate heart."

"Hey," Sonya stood, her fox eyes narrowing. "Don't—"

"And you"—he turned to her—"had better stop coddling him if you ever want him to grow up."

That brought her up short.

"Now," Cohen said briskly as he turned to Boz. "I presume you already have some sort of plan?"

"Queen Galina has actually put one forth."

Cohen sighed again. "Naturally. And I suppose this wondrous woman is fond of the arts as well?"

"An ardent lover of poetry, I believe," said Boz, a twinkle in her eye.

"I must have *die Hand Gottes* upon me to have such ill luck," said Weide. "In the end, I shall have to compose some music to fully express the tragedy of this missed chance."

"Just wait until you meet her. You'll want to compose an entire symphony."

Perhaps it would have been easier to bear if Sebastian had still been able to harbor some quiet hope that he and Isobelle might one day be united. But clearly that was not meant to be. And regardless of the Herzog's claims of being too old, it seemed Sebastian might now need to be the go-between in a doomed international courtship.

But it was clear that great and terrible things were taking shape on the continent. He had always wanted to do something important in this world. To make a real difference and do some good. Standing against his one-time mentor, the man who had brought out the worst aspects of him, might be his last, best chance to find redemption. If that meant reconnecting with Galina, then so be it.

"One last thing," said Cohen. "Those skill sets you mentioned earlier. In the coming conflict, I do hope I can depend on you both to provide some killing and... *magicking.*"

Sonya laughed and threw her arm around Sebastian as he glared at her.

"You can always count on us for that!"

30

$\oint$

"Mighty Tighearna, where are we going?" Rowena asked as she followed Mordha through the bustling streets of Magna Alto.

"The destination is unimportant," he replied.

Rowena had spent little time in the town below the palace. It was a thick soup of shrill babble and gaudy showmanship. She was amazed that despite being occupied by a foreign power and having their throne usurped by a madman, the people of Magna Alto carried on as though nothing had changed. She couldn't decide if it was profound ignorance or willful denial, but either way it set her teeth on edge.

"Very well," she said. "*Why* are we going, then?"

Mordha's scarred face creased slightly, his version of a smile. "That is a more meaningful question."

But he did not give her an answer. Instead he asked a question of his own. "How fares the beast witch's mother?"

"She seems to have accepted the idea that Sonya is probably alive and has turned her thoughts back to either escape or uprising, depending on which seems more expedient."

"Is she still concerned about Vittorio?"

"She never misses an opportunity to express her concern," said Rowena. "She has also alluded to a number of Raízians imprisoned in the brig, and seems to think they could be of some use."

"Perhaps," he said.

They turned off the main avenue to a side street that was thick with merchants and other townsfolk, all buying and selling as if that was all there was to do in life. The street ended at a large metal gate in the outer wall of the city. Since it was daytime, the gate was open and horse-drawn wagons moved in either direction, transporting goods to and from the canal.

Rowena noted there were twice as many guards posted at the gate, which made sense. This was the way Vittorio had slowly secreted the Uaine into the city, and since he was more aware of the risk of this secondary entrance than his predecessor, he had made it more secure. Everyone who entered the city now had to pass inspection by a troop of formidable-looking soldiers.

"Do you think they will trouble us on our return?" Rowena asked as they passed through the gate and descended the ramp down to the canal.

Mordha shook his head. "They know who we are."

"I see..."

The way Mordha said it made it sound as though they were famous. Or perhaps infamous. The idea bothered her in a way she couldn't quite express.

Rowena didn't know what to make of the canal, either. As they walked along the path that ran beside it, she still found it as impressive as she had the night they had entered. The time, energy, and resources required to carve such a long and massive trench in the earth must have been staggering. The hubris even more so.

They followed the canal for a little while, then turned and headed into the surrounding meadows, where there was neither road nor trail. On the nearest rise, Rowena saw Aureumian laborers working on an odd-looking tent structure that only reached knee height and stretched in a narrow line for as far she could see. As they drew closer, she saw that the miniature tents sheltered an unusual-looking fungus from the sun.

"What on earth are they doing?"

"I'm not sure," admitted Mordha. "Some mad idea Vittorio instituted shortly after taking power. Something about a mushroom that will save the empire."

"Is it edible, then?" she asked.

"I can't think of any other reason one would want to grow it in such large quantities," he said. "Although even then, the arrangement is odd. Why spread it out so much, especially since it requires shelter from the sun? It would make more sense to build a single large tent and group them together."

"Well, he is mad, after all," said Rowena.

"So it seems," said Mordha, although Rowena thought she detected doubt in the Tighearna's voice.

They walked past the fungus farm, carefully stepping over the small tents, and continued farther into the meadows. Finally, when there did not seem to be another living soul in view, Mordha stopped. The wind had picked up, offering some refreshment from the endless sunlight that bore down on them in these southern lands.

"To answer your question *why*," he said, as though she had only just asked it, "it seems Vittorio has some means of gathering information that is unfamiliar to us."

"Oh?"

Mordha gazed across the open meadow, watching the breeze ripple through the grass and wildflowers.

"I don't know how he has come by the knowledge, but he believes the Raízians have marshaled additional forces and are planning some sort of alliance with the Izmorozians."

"The Izmorozians are hardly much of a threat," said Rowena.

"They did not use to be," said Mordha. "But Galina Odoyevtseva has consolidated power in the country and created a militia led by two of the beast witches that Sonya sought in the tundra."

"Galina is their new queen? Interesting," said Rowena. "Though I can't say I'm surprised."

"Really?" asked Mordha. "I didn't think her capable of such a thing."

"You judge people too quickly on physical prowess, my Tighearna. If you'd looked deeply enough into her eyes, you would have seen a powerful will concealed in that frail shell."

"Perhaps you are right," said Mordha. "Regardless, a Ranger-led militia combined with an army of Raízian Viajero might prove a challenge even for Vittorio's imperial army."

"Why does that concern us?" asked Rowena.

"Because we must maintain the alliance with Vittorio until the solstice if we are to succeed in opening a door to the Eventide," said Mordha.

"The solstice is only a few weeks away," said Rowena. "Would it even be possible for the Raízians and Izmorozians to march on Magna Alto in that time?"

Mordha shook his head. "Even if they began marching in the next few days, a sizable army could not reach us in that time. However, Vittorio doesn't want to wait for that to happen. He sees Raíz as the bigger threat, and plans to send a portion of his army to crush them now before they can begin coordinating with Izmoroz. He has... *requested* that two clans of the Uaine join in this effort. I have decided it should be Clan Seacál and Clan Dílis."

Before Rowena could protest, he held up one of his large, scarred hands.

"Hear me out. Seacál was an obvious choice because they are far too unpredictable to allow near the solstice ritual. Frankly, I would just as soon be rid of them for good."

"And Clan Dílis?" demanded Rowena. "Would you be rid of us as well?"

"Don't be foolish." There was an uncharacteristically hard tone to his voice that brought Rowena up short. "I chose your clan because it may give you and Blaine the chance to spare the life of your Raízian friend."

Rowena's eyes narrowed. "I care about Jorge, of course, and would be saddened should he die, especially if it was at the hands of my countrymen. But I also want to assist in the solstice ceremony. I'm certain Blaine feels the same. We want to watch you take the gods to task for their cruelty and indifference. We want to witness you finally get vengeance for yourself and for my Glynn."

Mordha nodded. "I understand. But you must go where you are needed, not merely where you want to be. I will have Bhuidseach Hueil to assist me with all aspects of the ceremony."

"Hueil doesn't even know our true intentions," said Rowena. "He is still a loyal worshipper of Bàs."

"As are most of our people. They cannot know what we plan to do, or they may revolt. I have told Hueil that I wish to contact Bàs, that is all. He was uncomfortable even with that idea, but given my... unique history with Bàs, he has given his consent. So as much as I would *like* to have your presence on the solstice, it is not necessary. And if things do not go well... If I fall—"

"Mighty Tighearna, you will not fall!"

"*If* I fall," he pressed on, "I need Clan Dílis away from the palace and that madman, where you and Albion can decide what is best for our people. I trust no one else with this responsibility."

"Why even bother fighting the Raízians?" asked Rowena. "If the battle begins after the solstice, there will be no need to keep the fiction of alliance alive."

"It may be unnecessary," admitted Mordha. "But remember that it is only fiction to a small number of us. Most of our people believe this to be an alliance in earnest. How will you convince them on the eve of battle, when their blades hunger for glory?"

"It may be difficult...," she admitted.

"And one more thing to consider. It may not be immediately apparent to you that I have succeeded in my task. Indeed, you may not know either way until your return to Magna Alto. If I fail—"

"My Tigh—" she began to protest once more.

But he gripped her shoulder urgently. "If I fail, remaining with the Aureumians might be the best chance our people have for survival."

"I shudder to imagine such a situation."

"I have imagined them all," said Mordha.

She regarded him for a moment. "This choice was never about Jorge at all."

"Of course not," he said. "But his well-being does make a nice consolation prize, doesn't it? Even if the worst comes to pass, and you are forced to decide that our only means of survival is continued alliance with Vittorio, you will still have one of the few friendships you've ever managed to develop."

She sighed. "I suppose."

He gripped her thin shoulder tighter and his eyes bored into her soul. "You and I have bet everything on this. Even so, I will meet the appointed day with a clearer mind if I know that at least your clan will survive, regardless of the outcome."

Pride, unease, and disappointment all battled inside her, but at last she bowed her head.

"As you command, mighty Tighearna."

INTERLUDE

Just as a person had veins and nerves and muscles, so did the world. But such things could only be seen from the Eventide. There, Marzanna could influence the entire world simply by touch.

Gently, of course. Because those were her mother's veins and nerves and muscles.

As she worked, Marzanna wondered at the strange feeling that was beginning to well up within her. Not anticipation. She felt that emotion every time she remade one of her servants, thinking of what they might become. This was something else. Something quieter, yet more deeply rooted.

Could it be she felt…hope? That her labors were nearly complete, and despite all the odds, she might be successful in her aim?

Victory was far from assured, of course. But events were rising up, a terrible momentum building that would break upon the walls of the very Eventide itself. What she didn't know—could not yet know— was whether it would strike with enough force to tear it all down.

As she allowed herself to fully contemplate what might come after, Lady Marzanna, Goddess of Winter, Change, and Death, felt tears in her midnight eyes.

At last.

At long last.

An end.

She was so very tired…

PART THREE

THE MONSTROUS TIDES
OF WAR

"In death we find peace.
In death we find union.
In death we find transcendence.
In life we find only chaos, discord, and monstrous suffering."

—Excerpt from the traditional Uaine raising prayer

31

For Galina Odoyevtseva, solitude had become the most valuable thing in the world. She would have given anything for a quiet patch of green with the gentle Izmorozian sun filtering in through the trees. A lone bench to sit upon, a good book to read, and perhaps a nice cup of tea. The simple beauty of this scenario was something she fantasized about often, especially after the destruction of Roskosh Manor and the loss of her beloved garden.

Unfortunately, she still resided in the commander's room at the imperial barracks, which, no matter how thoroughly it was cleaned, still smelled vaguely of musk, leather, and shaving soap. Someone had suggested she and her family move to the estate of the late Lord Konstantin Belousov Levenchik, but she decided that forcibly ejecting his widow, who had no doubt already suffered enough both before and after her husband's execution, would be in poor taste. Someone else suggested they move to the massive edifice formerly known as Her Imperial Majesty's Grand Northern Ballroom. While she conceded that the building projected a decorum that befitted the queen of Izmoroz, she found the idea of living in the place where she and Sebastian had become engaged to be viscerally upsetting. Clearly this meant she still had some emotional attachment to the man. An attachment that might have been somewhat revitalized by their newly formed, if rather reluctant, alliance. In fact, now that they were once again on the same side, she wondered if perhaps...

But no. Even if it was feasible, which was debatable, his resentment, perhaps even merited, would likely poison any potential reunion. Best to keep such ideas completely out of mind.

So she firmly turned her attention back to the group of men who were now arguing at her table. One of the officers' quarters had been converted into a small makeshift dining room because the queen of Izmoroz had no intention of supping in something called a *mess* hall. Philosophically, what was good enough for her people was good enough for her. But from a practical standpoint, some level of distance and decorum must be maintained in recognition of her role as sovereign.

As military efforts grew increasingly urgent, she was often required to invite the officers of her army to her table so they could continue to discuss strategy while eating. And though she generally had nothing against the less fair sex, she had observed that placing a large group of men in proximity to each other during mealtime had a tendency to make them boisterous to the point of becoming irritating and pigheaded.

"But how do we know we can *trust* these Kantesians?" demanded Captain Dmitry, who was easily the youngest, handsomest, and most educated of her generals. And curiously also the most conservative. He had once been Lady Irina Turgenev's valet, so perhaps some of her worldview had rubbed off on him. Galina strongly suspected that he was also Galina's illegitimate cousin, because it had been her mother who had first convinced Irina Turgenev to hire him, and then Galina.

"We can't trust the Kantesians," replied Captain Dima. "But we *can* trust *Strannik* Sonya."

Galina had been somewhat surprised when Dima offered to move himself and his family from Vesely to Gogoleth to aid in her recruitment and training strategy. But he'd apparently had some military experience as a child soldier during the Winter War. Furthermore, his natural rapport with the troops was undeniable. Galina couldn't be everywhere at once, and to have someone who could galvanize people in her absence would no doubt be useful.

"Can we *really* trust *Strannik* Sonya, though?" asked Captain Stas.

Stas had been an even bigger surprise. The only survivor of the company of bandits who had briefly tried to turn Kamen into their own private little kingdom had appeared at her doorstep one day and begged to dedicate his life to her. By his reasoning, she had granted him a new life the day she stopped Andre and Tatiana from killing him, and so that life was hers to do with as she willed. While Galina had been suspicious of this reasoning, she had agreed to take him on in some capacity. As she got to know him, she discovered that he was surprisingly adept when it came to strategic thought, and also somewhat sincere. All he'd ever wanted was to live somewhere that the nobility were not given preferential treatment. So not only did she let him live, but she had already given him the country he'd longed for.

Perhaps because of his outlaw background, he was also the most skeptical officer. And the most coarse.

"I mean," he continued, "let's all remember that not only was *Strannik* Sonya's father Giovanni the Wolf, she also used to fuck one of the Uaine captains."

"I'll thank you not to use such language in the presence of Her Majesty," Chamberlain Masha said primly.

Galina considered the very notion that Masha continue on as a mere servant in the new Izmoroz to be utterly absurd in light of all she had done. Masha had at first been daunted by her new role, but Galina assured her that she had done quite well managing a troublesome young girl, and so should have little problem managing a troublesome young nation. It was simply a matter of scale and delegating responsibility.

"Sorry." Stas looked contritely at Galina.

"Apology accepted. And you do have a point." Galina turned to Dima. "Captain, I know you are fond of Sonya, and I do believe that she has the best interests of Izmoroz at heart. But she is not known for making the soundest judgments."

He sighed. "That is true."

"And apparently Sonya has even more animal features than before, which Andre has explained to me suggests she is getting closer to his level of intellectual reasoning. While Andre and Tatiana can rely upon me to curb their more beastly instincts, who does Sonya have? A younger brother who is also not known for his good judgment? A foreign ambassador whom we know little about? A foreign ruler we know even less about?" Galina shook her head. "I think Captain Dmitry is right in suggesting that we can't trust the Kantesians."

Dmitry beamed, probably because she so rarely praised him.

"That said, we most certainly need them. And I do think we can trust some aspects of the situation. For example, we can trust that Sonya will want to kill imperials. We can trust that Victasha wishes to have Vittorio removed from power. And I think it is safe to assume that Kante has at least some animosity toward Aureum for attempting to conquer them for the last decade. If we combine those things, I think given the right circumstances, we can count on them to be a useful ally."

"And the Wizard of Gogoleth, Your Majesty?" Masha asked carefully.

Galina felt an uncomfortable combination of betrayal and gratitude. On one hand, Masha was clearly asking a very personal question at a war council. On the other hand, it was a valid point that they were no doubt all thinking, and it was good to have someone on the council who could address such things, and do so with tact.

"While it is heartening that Sebastian Turgenev has rejected the empire, it would be premature to assume that means he is completely on our side. For all we know, he might have his own goals that have nothing to do with us. For now, it is enough that he is willing to work alongside us in putting an end to Vittorio's reign. I will admit that, while it considerably lessens his utility as an allied combatant, I do not mourn the loss of his all-powerful gemstone."

The muffled voice of a boy echoed from the hallway, "Your Majesty!" followed by a quick knock on the door.

"Come in," said Galina.

Luka, the boy she had found in Otriye in the early days of her rise to power, hurried in looking red-faced and winded.

"Some news?" she asked calmly.

He looked about to speak, but Marsha cleared her throat and he froze. After a moment, he banged his fist on his chest. Galina had decided that during wartime she was to be treated as commander. Naturally they had adopted the old Izmorozian salute rather than the Aureumian one.

"Your Majesty," said Luka. "Ranger Tatiana has returned with a report from the south. She says a bunch of imperial soldiers are heading on the Advent Road toward Raíz. They had Uaine undead with them, too! A whole bunch of them!"

"Already?" asked Dmitry.

"Jorge has been gathering his forces for some time," said Galina. "Perhaps Vittorio caught wind of it and decided to strike before they're completely ready."

"Are they not ready?" asked Dima.

"I'm not sure," admitted Galina. "Just as we have reservations about Kante, Raíz has reservations about us. So Representative Elhuyar has been cagey on some of the finer points of his preparations."

Then she smiled at them.

"Worry not, my dear officers. This is good news for us."

"Why is that, Your Majesty?" asked Dmitry.

"Vittorio has split his forces. If we time this right, it might mean a very swift end to this conflict. Perhaps rumors of Vittorio's madness were not exaggerated after all. I considered him a better strategist than this. Unless..."

She frowned.

"Unless, Your Majesty?" asked Masha.

"I hate to even think it, but I fear we must. There may be some... supernatural component to his strategy that we are not aware of yet."

By this point Galina had resigned herself to the idea that when one allied themselves with a goddess, it might inspire a rival goddess to favor the opposing side. But surely the Goddess of Spring couldn't be as fearsome as the Goddess of Winter.

Could she?

32

Hᴏᴡ long ago was it that Papa scolded us all in this garden?" Jorge
asked as he and his siblings watched the house staff of Cassa Estío set
up chairs in the central courtyard of the garden near the fountain.

Maria frowned thoughtfully. "A month maybe?"

"You mean right before the empire attacked?" asked Hugo. "Just
shy of six weeks."

Jorge nodded. "Papa told me then that I should take more of a
leadership role. Do you think this is what he envisioned?"

"With Papa, who can say," said Maria. "I wouldn't put it past him."

"Well, *I* certainly hadn't envisioned it," said Hugo.

Jorge turned to his older brother. "You know it's not really just me,
right? It's like Papa said, the three of us, together, are what's needed."

"I know, I know," said Hugo. "And honestly, the way you handle
the señores... I'm not sure I could do that."

Jorge knew this was not easy for Hugo. There was a certain way of
doing things in Raíz, and the older brother was supposed to take the
lead. Someone else might have been resentful. "You are the best big
brother I could ever ask for."

"Hmm, yes, well..." Jorge was amazed to see his brother blush.
"We'll just say you owe me."

Jorge laughed. "Spoken like a true merchant!"

"Ahh, look at you three getting along so wonderfully," said their
mother as she came out into the garden. "It does my heart good to see."

"Hello, Mama," said Maria. "How is Papa feeling?"

It was almost undetectable. In fact, anyone other than her own children might not have been able to see it. But the señora's eyes tightened ever so slightly as she spoke. "He's feeling fine, of course. How else would he be feeling?"

Maria clearly picked up on the tension and smiled perhaps a bit too enthusiastically. "You're right, Mama. I don't even know why I asked the question."

Their mother nodded, looking satisfied. "Jorge, my treasure. Do you recall that lovely young woman I introduced you to a few weeks ago? Amaya Marin?"

"Oh, er, sure..." With everything else going on, the issue of marriage prospects was not something that had even entered his mind.

"I was thinking," his mother said as she straightened his shirt collar, "that tomorrow you should invite her for lunch. Don't you think that would be lovely?"

Jorge looked at her a moment, but it was clear his mother was being completely serious.

"Mama..." He gently removed her hands from fussing with his collar. "You do know that I am the national representative of Raíz, right?"

She beamed at him. "Of course. Your father and I couldn't be prouder."

"And you know that we are currently at *war*, right?"

She sighed. "It is still difficult for me to believe. I will miss going to Magna Alto. Such a beautiful city..."

"Mama, I don't have the leisure for courtship right now."

Her brow knit together. "Perhaps next week, then?"

"Perhaps not for a long time," he told her. "The welfare of our people must come first."

Her eyes narrowed. "What about the welfare of our *family*?"

"You want grandchildren? Talk to Hugo."

"Huh?" said Hugo.

Jorge hated to throw all the pressure on to him, but they must all make sacrifices.

Their mother narrowed her eyes as they fixed on the eldest sibling. "When was the last time you were home?"

"Oh...last week? Maybe? If not, then certainly the week before."

"How do you expect to make me grandchildren if you never spend time with your wife?" she pressed.

Hugo's face went beet red. "Uh...."

"I would have been content with one from each of you, but if these other two will not take pity on their mother, then you must provide all three!"

He stared at her as if the idea of fathering children was not something he had even entertained.

"Promise me, Hugo. Tonight, after this *meeting.*" She waved vaguely in the direction of the chairs that had been set up in the central courtyard. "You will go home to your wife and you will *do your duty.* Is that clear?"

Poor Hugo looked stunned beyond words.

"Well?" she demanded.

He managed a weak "Y-yes, Mama."

She nodded, looking pleased, then turned and marched triumphantly back into the house.

Hugo glared at Jorge. "Thanks."

But Jorge was now focused on Maria. "Why *did* you ask Mama how Papa was feeling?"

"Haven't you noticed how tired he looks all the time?" she asked. "And he's lost weight. When have you ever known Papa to be so skinny?"

"You think he's sick," said Jorge.

"Papa?" Hugo looked skeptical. "He's never been sick a day in his life."

She shrugged. "Something's not right. That's all I know. Especially if Mama is hiding it. You saw how she reacted."

"Yes," said Jorge.

"I think you're both making something of nothing," Hugo said firmly.

Jorge and Maria exchanged a look. If their father really was unwell, it might send Hugo into a panic, and they needed him right now—to manage all the little details that they both tended to gloss over or forget entirely.

"Perhaps I am," Maria said finally.

A short time later, the señores began to arrive. The patriarchs and first sons of Pereria, Muñoz, Cruz, Zorilla, and Dicenta. While they began to settle into the chairs and servants brought them refreshments, Jorge sent someone to fetch his father. When the elder Elhuyar arrived, he did seem gaunt, and oddly tired for someone who hadn't really done much that day. Jorge wondered why he hadn't seen it before. Perhaps, like his brother, he'd been unwilling to accept that their father could be weak or vulnerable.

He waited until they all had drinks in hand before starting.

"Thank you for coming on such short notice," he said.

"I had to cancel a squash match for this," grumbled Señor Dicenta. "So the reason had better be good."

Jorge gave the man a patient smile. Naturally, he still had enormous respect for the heads of the Great Families. But as their chosen national representative, he had come to realize in recent weeks that by and large the señores were also a bunch of spoiled old men.

"I would not call the reason *good*, Señor, but it is most certainly urgent. I have received word that the empire has sent a detachment of Aureumian infantry and Uaine undead in our direction."

Jorge had hoped that the calming influence of the garden would moderate their reaction. If so, he would have hated to see their reactions otherwise. Dicenta, Muñoz, and Cruz were suddenly on their feet shouting. They seemed to be suggesting that it was both entirely his fault and completely inevitable. Now that they had elected him to a status that essentially made him their national servant, they no longer felt compelled to respect him as the youngest son of Señor Elhuyar, and let their grievances fly without holding back. And he, like a dutiful servant, weathered their accusations of everything from incompetence to betrayal with equanimity.

Thankfully, since they were pampered old men, they soon grew weary and sat back down. It was then that Señor Zorilla, bless him, at last spoke up.

"I presume, Representative, that you already have a plan in mind."

Jorge inclined his head. "Naturally, Señor. I was just getting to that. We have been coordinating with our allies in Izmoroz and Kante and have arrived at a stratagem that, while posing a serious risk, may also bring a swift end to this conflict."

"I would like to point out," chimed in Hugo, "that drawing out the conflict would pose its *own* risks, particularly to our economy. So whatever we decide today, there are no easy or obvious solutions."

"What is this stratagem of yours?" asked Señor Pereria.

Jorge nodded. "I propose that we immediately take the bulk of our forces and head off the invaders at the Aureumian border. While we engage the enemy there, Izmoroz and Kante will march on Magna Alto and lay siege to the city. In all likelihood, Vittorio will recall his invading force to help defend the capital. We will then pursue the retreating imperial forces back to Magna Alto. This will force Vittorio to either expose himself by opening the gates to his return-ing armies, or abandon them, exhausted and undersupplied, for us to crush against the city walls. From there we will have the Aureumians cornered and unable to do anything except defend their walls until our allied wizard has devised a means to tear them down, which I can assure you from personal experience is well within his capabilities."

There were other aspects of the plan, but Jorge didn't want to heap too much on the señores at once, and it wasn't like any of these men were military strategists.

"An ambitious plan," remarked Señor Dicenta. "So what are the risks you mentioned?"

"In order for this plan to succeed, we will need to keep the invaders engaged until Izmoroz and Kante reach Magna Alto, which could mean taking significant losses."

He didn't mention that the Victashian representative, Onat Duman, had notified him this morning that both Izmoroz and Kante had already begun to mobilize, knowledge gleaned by using what-ever top-secret method of communication the Intelligence Bureau employed. It would have seemed presumptuous to merely assume that the señores would approve this plan, but Izmoroz had quite a bit more distance to cover, and Kante would be slowed down by the cross through Hardsong Pass. The timing would have worked out better if they allowed the invaders to reach Colmo, but during his communications with Galina and the Herzog of Weide, Jorge had insisted that Colmo could not survive another battle in its streets.

Of course, moving the bulk of their forces out of Colmo created an entirely different risk.

"It would seem," Jorge's father said, "that if you take our armies north, you would leave Colmo undefended."

Naturally it was his own father who saw it first.

"Thank you, Papa, I was just getting to that," he said. "It is true that if an enemy were to attack Colmo by sea while our armies are engaging Aureum, there is little we could do to protect the city. However, the only force currently capable of doing so is Victasha. Ambassador Boz has assured me that Their Majesties have no desire for northern conquest, and strongly oppose Vittorio's rule of the continent. She has sworn to me that Victasha will take no action against Colmo."

"And do we believe her?" asked Zorilla.

Jorge gave him a pained smile. "I am confident that Victasha has some other strategy at work, but given the consistent aid their intelligence department has provided all three of our nations, I think it is safe, at least for the time being, to believe that whatever their true interests are, they currently align with our own."

"And what assurances can you give us?" challenged Cruz.

Jorge's smile turned bleak. "Should Victasha prove false, my dear friend Sonya Turgenev, greatest sniper of the Anxeles Escuros, will see the ambassador dead within minutes."

They all looked impressed by that. It was a bit cheap to name-drop the Anxeles Escuros. And frankly, if Victasha truly had plans to betray Raíz, they would no doubt consider the death of Ambassador Boz an acceptable loss. But thankfully none of the old men seemed to perceive that.

The fact was, they didn't really have any other choice but to accept Victasha's word at this point. Jorge prayed that in trying to defeat one evil, they hadn't unwittingly made a pact with something far worse.

"So, what's it to be, honored Señores?" he asked.

They glanced at each other. It was interesting to see them looking so unsure. It was a reminder that while these men might be very wise in business, this was an area outside their expertise. Thankfully, they seemed to recognize that.

"Is there . . . another option?" asked Pereria.

"We could hunker down here in Colmo and wait for the imperial army and their horde of undead to swarm our city," Jorge said brightly. "Then we would just have to pray that the Izmorozian army reaches us with reinforcements before we're completely massacred."

There was another pause as the old men looked at each other again. Finally, it was Señor Dicenta who spoke.

"I think we'll leave the military strategy to you, Representative Elhuyar."

Jorge inclined his head. "You honor me, Señores."

33

Once again, Sebastian was preparing to ride off to war. He stood on a rise of the craggy meadow outside Weide where the Kantesian troops gathered.

The Herzog's army differed from the imperial army in a number of ways. Rather than dividing the infantry into spear carriers and shield carriers, each soldier had a sword and small buckler. It was yet another testament to the abundance of ore to be found in Kante. He didn't think the imperial army was even capable of providing a sword to every member of the infantry. There simply wasn't enough steel to go around in Aureum.

But the Kantesian largess with metal didn't stop at arming their infantry. The cavalry not only wielded steel weapons, but wore heavy steel armor as well. They also rode stout draft horses that were similarly armored. Sebastian shuddered to think what it would be like to see a line of such formidably attired opponents bearing down on you at a gallop.

But of course, even the armored cavalry was nothing compared to the golems. The giant, hissing metal insects were spread out across the army so that there seemed to be one for every division. Sebastian would have thought it wiser to keep them separate from the main troops so they didn't accidentally trample their own soldiers, but perhaps there was some magical safeguard against that.

Always curious about magic, Sebastian had asked both Lord Cohen and Isobelle questions about the nature of golems and enchantment, or "residual magic," as his own books had called it. They claimed to know very little and pointed him to the *Verzauberungs Stipendium*, which was apparently an official guild or organization of enchanters. But that lot, a collection of dour, elderly men and women, were even less helpful. He'd thought it might be an even exchange of information, since he was willing to share what he'd learned of elemental magic. But they had no interest in his "god-hand magics," as they called it, and rudely dismissed him.

So now he stood atop a hill and merely watched them from afar, wondering at the nature of these terrifying creatures he was bringing back with him to Aureum.

Isobelle rode over and dismounted with a clatter. He was impressed she seemed able to move about in armor so easily. How different she looked from the caregiving maiden he had met back in Kleiner. Her voice and expression, however, were still just as sweet.

"Your look is grim, Sebastian."

"I have seen enough battle in the last half year that I find it difficult to feel otherwise."

He recalled feelings of eagerness before his first real battle in Gogoleth. He remembered feeling hope and even cheer as he'd ridden out from Magna Alto toward what he'd thought would be a rescue and recovery mission in Kante. But those emotions were so distant to him now, so elusive and faint they might as well be breath on the wind. Much closer was the dread he'd felt at riding to Colmo, knowing he might soon have to confront those he didn't wish to harm.

As if reading his mind, Isobelle said, "Perhaps you are uneasy at the idea of fighting your one-time comrades?"

"I'm not sure I really see sides anymore," he admitted. "Perhaps in part because my sister and I were born into two different nationalities. To me, the lines between them seem somewhat arbitrary. What, in the end, is the difference between Kantesian and Aureumian? Izmorozian and Raízian? There are religious differences, certainly. Perhaps cultural ones. But are these reasons to kill each other?"

"I would think you are happy, then, that three such different countries as Kante, Izmoroz, and Raíz have found common cause. It is better than no unity at all, is it not?"

"I suppose," he admitted. "But what about Aureum?"

Her gentle eyes hardened. "They had many chances to allow peace on this continent. But time and again they preferred conquest. This Vittorio seems to be the ultimate expression of their arrogance and greed. To my mind, those who follow him are little better."

"I followed him once," pointed out Sebastian.

"The fact that you no longer do leaves me even less inclined to forgive those who remain."

"I see..."

There was something dark and cold in Isobelle's blue eyes. Something he had not seen in Kleiner. Or perhaps something she had not permitted him to see. This was the daughter of Herzog Ferdinand Cohen von Weide, after all. A man who seemed enamored with Galina's cruelest tendencies. Would his daughter really be so different?

"Do you hate the Aureumians?" he asked.

"Hate?" She considered for a moment. "No, they have proved themselves unworthy of such passion. They are a blight upon the continent, and I wish only to be rid of them."

For some reason, Sebastian found this clinical response even more chilling than blind hatred.

But then her expression brightened, and she once more appeared the cheery innocent lady he first met.

"Oh! I almost forgot. We will depart soon and I wanted to give you something before we begin."

"You needn't have gotten me anything," objected Sebastian, feeling himself blush despite knowing that this was a married woman and it was in no way a romantic gesture.

She gave him skeptical look. "According to your sister, I did."

Isobelle untied a long wooden staff from the saddle. "As much as we all enjoy your company, Sebastian, my father and I agree there is more that you can contribute to the coming conflict. The, eh..." She paused and gave him a questioning look. "The magicking?"

He sighed. "My sister told you that's what it's called, didn't she?"

"Was she just teasing me?"

"No, she was teasing *me*. It's her little joke because I haven't been able to come up with something better to call it."

"Oh, I see." She gave him a wistful smile. "It must be a wonderful thing to have a sibling."

"The only people who say that are those who don't have one," said Sebastian.

"But is it not?" she asked.

He wanted to say it was mostly just a giant and unending pain, but he stopped himself. Because the truth was, that made it sound as though he didn't appreciate his sister. Yet she had taken one look at the way Sebastian stared at Isobelle, and understood exactly what he was thinking and feeling. She had almost punched the ruler of a nation because he had callously dismissed Sebastian's heartbreak. She had saved his life. And she never gave up on him, even when he was at his worst.

So he smiled, perhaps a little shyly, and said, "I wouldn't trade my sister for the world."

Isobelle nodded in satisfaction. "As I thought. Now, here we are. A way for you to do magicking."

She held out the staff. It looked finely made, smooth and polished. One end was covered with a cloth, and when she pulled the cloth away, he saw a ruby as large as his fist attached to it.

Sebastian stared at the bloodred gem. "It's beautiful."

"It is not a diamond like you had before, but I hope it will allow you to use your magic without destroying all our steel, yes?"

"I've never used a ruby, but judging by the size alone, I think it should allow me at least some leeway in casting more complicated magic without disintegrating."

"That is good news, because this was the biggest one we had in the royal treasury."

"Oh, er, you needn't have done that," objected Sebastian.

Her expression once again became cool and calculating. "If I thought it would help us crush the Aureumians, I would give you all the riches of our kingdom."

"I promise I will use this priceless gem to protect your people."

Her expression softened once more as she handed him the staff. "I know you will, Sebastian."

He hefted the staff in both hands, feeling its sturdiness. "The staff is very nice, but why set the gem into it?"

"When I returned to Weide after meeting you, I consulted our people's history and discovered that long ago, there was one with your abilities born in Kante."

"Really?" Although now that he thought about it, he recalled a Kantesian tale in the collection *The Age of Wizards* that Galina had given him. "Yes, that's right. She always mounted her gem on a staff, although the story never said why."

"She was called the Zauberer, and she believed that direct contact with the gem while channeling magic caused great strain on her body and mind."

"I have found that to be true as well," admitted Sebastian.

"Yes, I remember you suddenly passed out on the riverbank."

"Ah, right..."

"Do not be embarrassed, Sebastian. But perhaps we can prevent that from happening again. You see, the Zauberer discovered that by mounting the gem atop an oak staff, she could still use it as a focus for her magic, but the wood acted as a filter, partly shielding her from the negative effects."

Sebastian's eyes widened as he looked down at the staff. "That's marvelous news!"

She smiled the sweet smile that had made him fall in love with her. "I knew you would be pleased. Now, if you'll excuse me, I have a few more things to attend to before we march. I will see you later, I am sure."

"Thank you for this, Isobelle," said Sebastian.

She nodded, then climbed onto her horse and rode away, her glossy chestnut hair bouncing in time with the horse.

Sebastian watched her go until she was out of view, then sighed.

"Wow," came his sister's voice from behind him.

"I am not interested in your opinion," he said without turning around.

"Remember, she *is* married, and as far as I can tell happily so."

"What part of 'not interested' was unclear?"

"Hey, at least you got a nice consolation prize."

Sebastian looked down at his staff. "That I did."

"Listen, I told the Herzog I'd ride with the vanguard. Scouting ahead and stuff like that. You want to join me?"

Sebastian gazed at his sister while he tapped thoughtfully on his chin. "Let me think... I can ride with Lord Cohen and the ambassador and listen to them talk politics endlessly, I can ride with Isobelle and her husband and pretend that I'm not completely depressed by what a sickeningly perfect couple they make, or I can listen to my sister boast to the rest of the vanguard about how great she is... So many wonderful choices."

"I don't *boast*," she protested.

"No?"

"I merely answer questions about my abilities truthfully." She gave him a fanged grin. "I can't help it if I'm just that impressive."

"If I ride with you, can I pet your furry head?"

She thought about it a moment. "Only after dinner. It seems to help me fall asleep."

"Fine then. I *guess* I'll ride up front with you. Just in case we get attacked by something that's too much for you to handle alone."

"Ha! The only thing I can't handle is your doomed love life."

He smiled, thinking of what he'd told Isobelle. That he wouldn't trade this fuzzy goof for the world.

She eyed him suspiciously. "What?"

He shook his head. "Nothing."

He certainly wasn't going to *tell* her something like that. He'd never hear the end of it.

34

The sun, Rowena decided, was a problem. She had never experienced it with such intensity before. Uaine was not known for its abundant sunlight, and neither was the Great Western Tundra. Even during the long trek from Gogoleth to Magna Alto, they had traveled under cover of night to avoid being spotted by imperial scouts.

Now they traveled south on the Advent Road in broad daylight, which was apparently what the imperial army was accustomed to doing. But this Aureumian sun was brutal and only got worse as they went. There were no clouds in the vast blue above and few trees to be found among the farmlands that comprised most of the countryside. While the sluagh gorta did not decompose, she had discovered that when they spent hours every day beneath the hot sun, they began to give off an odor so terrible that the imperials insisted on only marching upwind of them. This meant that every time the wind changed direction, or the road veered to one side or the other, they would have to stop the entire army and rearrange the units. Perhaps if Lorecchio had still been alive, he might have smoothed things over between the two groups. But without that buffer, tensions had grown noticeably high. There would be no great cooperation between them in the coming battle.

The unrelenting heat and sun affected Rowena directly as well. Her pale skin turned pink within the first hour of the first day of the march. She covered herself with robe and hood to prevent her skin from burning any further, but that made her even hotter. So either way she suffered every minute her pony trod slowly toward Raíz. Her one consolation was that she did not suffer alone. Sorcha rode beside her, grumbling beneath her own hood.

"This parched and blinding land...," groaned Sorcha. "How do they stand it?"

"I believe it's a matter of acclimation," said Rowena. "In fact, I have heard the heat will be even more intense once we cross the border into Raíz."

"How is that possible? It's like some vast oven before us. No wonder our ancestors never ventured this far south."

"You're welcome to turn back and explain to the Tighearna that the mission he gave you was too onerous for you to complete."

"You'd like that, wouldn't you?" snarled Sorcha.

"I would like *anything* that spared me having to listen to your endless bellyaching," replied Rowena.

They rode in silence for a few moments. But then it seemed Sorcha realized she was giving Rowena the silence she craved, and clearly that wouldn't do.

"It will be interesting to see how you so-called *Loyal* Ones handle these Raízians that you are so fond of."

"I only know one Raízian," said Rowena. "And while I am perfectly willing to admit that I am fond of him, you know that I would never jeopardize the Tighearna's goals for something so minor as personal affection."

"Yes, yes, Mordha's favorite, Rowena Viridomarus. But I wasn't talking about you."

Sorcha lifted her hooded gaze toward Blaine, who rode near the front of the Uaine unit. Unlike Sorcha and Rowena, Blaine seemed able to weather the heat and sun fairly well. His ash-blond hair had given to streaks of bright gold, and his ruddy cheeks and forehead suited him rather well. But there was a look in his eyes. An anxious, almost desperate look that Rowena did not like at all.

"You see it, don't you?" pressed Sorcha. "Glynn's little brother is going to bring shame on Clan Dílis."

"I'm more concerned about the incompetence of Clan Seacál," said Rowena, although that wasn't entirely true.

"Look," said Sorcha in a surprisingly reasonable tone. "As much as I would love to see Clan Dílis fail, there's too much at stake right now. You need to talk to your young captain. You need to *get him in line*."

"I hardly require your advice on clan loyalty, Sorcha." She hesitated, hating what she would say next, but knowing she must. "But if it would assuage your concerns, I will speak to my clan member."

"Oooh, how generous of you," Sorcha said in a mocking tone.

Rowena refused to give the other Bhuidseach the satisfaction of seeing her speak to Blaine right then, so she waited until that night when they made camp beside a vast cornfield. She approached him as he stood watching his warriors pitch their tents. When she suggested they speak in private, he gave her a look that suggested he knew what she wanted to talk about, and for a moment it seemed he might refuse.

But then he glanced back at his warriors and nodded.

They walked among the tall stalks of corn until the bustling din of the camp had faded to a murmur.

"What will you do if you see him?" she asked bluntly.

"I don't know."

She absently rubbed a leaf of one of the cornstalks between her thumb and forefinger as she decided what to say next.

"He doesn't have to die in order for our mission to be a success."

"Unless he puts his life between us and our goal," said Blaine. "Which he might."

"Assuming he is even at the battle. Remember that he did not directly enter the battle in Gogoleth, but instead lent support from afar."

"But those were not his people," pointed out Blaine.

Rowena saw the look in his eyes. He said he didn't know, but he did. He was determined and there would be no swaying him. If Jorge did put himself at risk to prevent the Uaine from taking power in Colmo, Blaine would come to his aid.

"What about your brother?" she asked.

This tactic had worked before. But it didn't work now.

Blaine shook his head. "Glynn would not want me to choose vengeance over love."

He was correct, of course. Rowena couldn't argue.

Instead she said, "I did not think my vow to protect you would ever conflict with my vow to see the Tighearna's will done."

"Do what you need to do," he said. "And so will I."

Then he turned and walked back to the camp.

Rowena stood there in the tall cornfield, feeling the blessed light of the moon upon her, and savoring the quiet wind that rustled through the stalks.

She realized it was the first time she'd felt physically comfortable in a while. She only wished that comfort extended to her heart. Although there was no outward indication of it, in her chest was a war between the two vows that governed her life.

She had made the first vow as she'd held her beloved Glynn's hand while he writhed in agony during his final moments of life. Like her, he had been an apprentice to the previous Clan Dílis Bhuidseach. He had been the first among their group to take the potions that *should* have made *him* the new Bhuidseach of Clan Dílis. Few could survive the ritual, but Rowena had been certain Glynn would be one of them. Bàs would see his strength, his wisdom, his courage, and heartily embrace him as his servant, exalting him as Death Touched.

But that was not what happened.

So in Glynn's final agonizing moments—as his skin turned to leather, splitting to expose tendons that twisted like dry rope—he had begged Rowena to watch over his little brother, who was a great warrior but also somewhat of an idiot. Of course she had promised she would, and despite the pain, he had died with a grateful smile on his lips.

When Rowena's turn had come to undergo the ritual to become Death Touched, she had not expected to survive. She had assumed Bàs would look into her heart, see her animosity over Glynn's death, and kill her outright. Instead, she had not only survived the ritual but, according to Bhuidseach Hueil, recovered faster than anyone in living memory. She had then gone on to show a mastery over the sluagh gorta that none had ever seen before. It was as if Bàs had observed the hostility in her heart, and rather than punish her, had considered her feelings so trivial that he had instead mockingly *blessed* her. Such was the capricious nature of Death.

Rowena made her second vow after Mordha's failed attempt to become the Bhuidseach of Clan Greim. When the potions to make one Death Touched failed, it usually ended in death, as it had with Glynn, and then they became merely another sluagh gorta. But not so with Mordha. Whether it was chance, or destiny, or merely Mordha's astonishing strength of will, he had not truly died. Instead he became something that had never been seen before. Half man, half sluagh gorta, somehow straddling the line between life and death. It had been days before he learned to bear the pain well enough to think and speak coherently, and weeks before he was able to function as a normal person. Not because the pain faded, but because he had mastered it.

It was then that Mordha called Rowena and Blaine to his side. It was no secret that the two harbored resentment toward Bàs for Glynn's death. He told them what he had learned during his excruciating transition.

Death hungers for Life, and Life requires Death to give it meaning. To step outside this endless cycle is to finally know the gods in all their capricious cruelty, he had said, quoting the ancient proverb. He had then told them that *he* had stepped outside that cycle. Now he understood that Beatha and Bàs, the Gods of Life and Death, were not wise or just, but monstrous and petty. He explained to them that all the conflict, sorrow, and heartbreak of humanity was merely a diversion for them. An entertainment.

He had then gone on to say that Bàs had made a mistake in toying with him and turning him into this unnatural creature. Because now he, Elgin Mordha, had the power to stop the endless cycle of suffering. He would kill the God of Death. They both swore to help in any way they could.

Most of the Uaine did not know Mordha's true motives. They saw his unparalleled strength, felt his unwavering will, and decided that was sufficient reason to follow him across the continent. They saw him as the great champion of Bàs, rather than his destroyer, and Mordha allowed them to think so. But when the solstice came in a few short days, and Mordha began the ritual that would open a door to the underworld, he would confront Bàs and end the torment that all humanity had unwittingly been suffering for countless generations. He did not expect to survive the encounter, but he took heart knowing that the world he would leave behind would no longer be ruled by a pair of sadistic deities. It would be a truly free world at last.

Rowena wished she could be there to see Mordha take Bàs to task for his infinite cruelties. She would have gladly given her own life simply to spit in the eye of the god who had taken Glynn from her, then tauntingly granted her unwanted power.

But Mordha had given her this task instead. And while she did not yet know how she would reconcile the conflicting vows in her heart, she knew she must do her part to achieve freedom for this world.

35

Irina supposed it was inevitable that Vittorio would at last turn to torture, although frankly she had expected it to be more...*overt*.

She sat in the imperial dining hall, stoically eating the lavish feast before her. Directly across from her sat Vittorio, consuming his food and drink with an almost maniacal desperation. There was no one else at the table, or indeed in the dining hall. If one had walked into the room ignorant of both the people and the circumstances, they might have mistaken it for the daily supper of a married couple.

Irina watched Vittorio carefully as she sipped wine from a golden goblet. She wondered what he wanted from her. It was now clear that Sebastian had deserted the imperial army and might even be allied with Sonya. So perhaps she was leverage in the event that her offspring brought their formidable power to bear against the empire. But that could just as easily be accomplished by throwing her in the brig with poor Captain Reyes and his Viajero. Why allow her the comfort of her own apartments? Why invite her to dine with him? It had been some time since she'd even attempted to hide her loathing, so surely he did not think she actually liked him.

No, it was something else. And in all likelihood, more twisted.

She watched him shove food and wine into his mouth as though he hadn't had sustenance in weeks and recalled the meticulous care he used to take when eating as a guest at Roskosh Manor.

"I must say, Franko," she said at last. "Whatever... *transformation* you have undergone, it has left you bereft of proper dining etiquette, one of the few qualities I'd always admired about you."

He paused in his gluttonous binge to look at her. Then, to her surprise, his greasy, food-speckled lips curled into a smile.

"If only you knew the cost. If only you knew the *hungers* my blessings have brought me. Then you would understand."

He immediately went back to eating, almost as if he could not keep himself from it. Irina continued to watch him, wondering about his "blessings."

Vittorio still insisted that God's angelic servant had rescued him from death when he fell from that tower. That it was *her* will he served, not his own. Irina understood it was not uncommon for a madman to blame their horrendous actions on a nonexistent person or entity. But his survival had indeed been miraculous, as had his sudden rise to power. And of course, as much as Irina would like to think there was no such thing as gods, she could not ignore that *some* sort of supernatural power had imbued both her daughter and the Uaine with extraordinary, death-defying abilities.

Then there was her own possible interaction with a deity. Perhaps it had been chance that shortly after silently offering herself, body and soul, to the Lady Marzanna in exchange for the safety of her children and the power to kill Vittorio, Hexenmeister Cloos had presented her with the means of realizing those goals. A means that would indeed cost her body and likely her soul as well. Had it been an isolated event, she would have chalked it up as coincidence. But taken with everything else, she could not dismiss the idea that her prayers had been answered in a most literal manner.

More than a month later she still stood on the precipice of that decision. She found some comfort having it in reserve, should things grow desperate enough. But despite the quiet indignities and slow degradation that came with aging, she remained rather fond of both her body and soul, and was reluctant to part with them.

"I suppose you are wondering why I invited you to supper." Vittorio pushed aside his plate, which was now completely bare of all but the faintest traces of sauce. He patted his lips dry and looked questioningly at her.

Irina looked down at the food on her own plate, which she had only nibbled at, then back at him. "It does seem surprising, given our history."

He took up his crutches, which he had leaned against the side of the table, and stood. Then he walked slowly around the table toward her.

"Ah, but it is precisely our history that prompted me," he said. "I fondly recall a simpler time when you and I were parents to Sebastian in his callow youth, making plans for the engagement, eating together on the Ascendance like a proper family."

Irina decided that, supernatural aid or not, Vittorio was quite delusional if he thought that she had ever considered the man who murdered her husband to be a second father to her son. But she did feel some trepidation as he approached, so she was not as biting as she could have been when she said, "Don't tell me this was out of some warped sense of nostalgia."

"Oh no, no, no," he said with gentle vehemence. "You know me far too well to believe such a thing. And *that* is the reason I am so fond of your company."

He was quite close now. Close enough to stab her in the neck with a poisoned pin as he had those two innocent children. But while his intimidating presence might cause her to measure her words to some degree, it would not force her to back down completely.

"You are fond of me because I know you to be the cunning viper you truly are?"

He nodded agreeably. "You were never taken in by my ruses or pretenses. Really, if it were ever possible for a woman to equal a man, you would be the closest to me."

"I should like you to know that I take offense to more than one of those assertions," she said coolly.

He chuckled pleasantly. "Yes, not just your intellect, but your courage as well. And of course your beauty. You are the perfect woman and I see nothing strange about taking pleasure in your company."

"Even though I despise you?" she asked.

"That is actually part of the pleasure," he admitted. "That you must bear my company unwillingly for your safety and the safety of others."

He paused for a moment, as if listening for something. Then he smiled in a way that she did not care for at all.

"But it's more than that, you see. I love that you always recognize how dangerous I am. I love that you try again and again to warn people about me. I love that, much to their own regret later, they always dismiss you. To see that look of bitter irony in your eyes every time you are proven correct…" He reached one quavering hand out, cupped her chin, and gazed deeply into her eyes. "It is like ambrosia to me."

She returned his look, unblinking, as she said, "Because you are a monster."

He smiled in a disturbingly beatific way. As if the epithet gave him pleasure. Then he turned and began his slow, clanking walk toward the door.

"Do you know where the word *monster* originated?" he asked without looking back. "From *monere*, a word in the precursor language shared by both Aureum and Raíz. It means *to warn*. So one might say that monsters are warnings. Signs. Portents."

He stopped suddenly before the door, his leg braces giving a sharp squeak.

"My purpose is not to be cruel. My purpose is to prepare you for the cruelty that swiftly follows."

His words hung in the silence for several moments. Then there was a loud knock at the door that, despite herself, made Irina start in her seat.

But Vittorio seemed to have been expecting it somehow, and merely opened the door.

On the other side stood the hulking, hideous Mordha, warlord of the Uaine. Beside him was one of the necromancer priests, or Bhuidseach, as Rowena had referred to herself. Irina didn't recognize him, but he wore the same brown robes and had the same eerie white countenance.

"Your Excellency," said Mordha in his rolling, guttural accent. "Would you care to follow me? There is something I must show you."

Irina did not fully understand the power dynamic between the two men, but the warlord's tone was clear. This was not a request, but a command.

Vittorio did not bristle at his tone, however. Instead he smiled and nodded.

"Would you mind if I brought Lady Portinari along? I do so enjoy seeing her reaction to a surprising turn of events."

Mordha gazed at him, then looked at Irina. She hoped he could see the warning in her eyes. Whatever the warlord thought was about to happen, Vittorio had other plans. But it was impossible to read much of anything in that scarred face.

"Very well," Mordha said at last.

36

Irina followed Vittorio and the two Uaine down the hall, dread clutching her chest. She didn't know much about Mordha, but she respected Rowena and was fond of Blaine, and they both clearly looked up to him. No matter what else he might be, Irina suspected he was at least a better man than Vittorio and undeserving of whatever terrible fate lay in store for him.

She was surprised when Mordha led them to the palace gardens, now drenched in moonlight. They stood in the center courtyard where she and the other expatriates had once gathered to gossip and perhaps scheme a little.

But instead of her friends, a group of Uaine warriors waited, armed and unfriendly looking. They stood around a full-length, oval-shaped freestanding mirror. Strange symbols had been painted onto both the mirror and the flagstones beneath.

"My, my, what have we here?" Vittorio asked cheerfully. "It all looks quite intricate."

Irina stayed at the very edge of the courtyard, as far as she could be while still being able to witness what took place. Vittorio, however, walked directly over to the mirror and examined it thoughtfully. He did not seem unnerved by the clearly ritualistic markings or the warriors who surrounded him. Either he was even more insane than Irina had realized, or he had somehow anticipated all of this and already had a countermeasure to whatever was about to take place.

"Today we open a door to the land beyond life and death," Mordha said. "To do so requires blood from a servant of Life and a servant of Death."

Vittorio turned to him, his expression innocent. "And which am I to be?"

"Your attempt at humor does not amuse me." Mordha nodded and the warriors took hold of Vittorio. He did not struggle, and instead allowed one of the warriors to grip his wrist and press his hand to the mirror.

The necromancer stood beside him, and Irina thought she detected a hint of reluctance in his manner. As if he did not fully support what was about to happen but had no more choice than Vittorio.

Mordha drew a knife from his belt and walked over to stand behind the two men. He began to intone some sort of prayer or chant in his native language, then reached his long arm over their heads and cut them each across the hand that was pressed to the mirror. Neither man cried out at the wound, and Mordha continued to chant as their blood flowed in rivulets down the surface of the mirror.

Irina was simultaneously repulsed and fascinated by this barbaric yet somehow reverent display. She had seen Sebastian perform magic many times, had witnessed some of Sonya's astonishing feats of speed and agility, and had nearly been killed by a horde of shambling undead. But as she felt the fine hairs on her arms stand, she knew that this supernatural exercise was something on an entirely different level.

It did occur to her to run. No one even seemed aware of her presence now, so it was doubtful they would stop her. But for some reason she could not bring herself to leave, and instead stared at the blood-streaked mirror so intently she hardly blinked. She supposed that as long as she kept her distance, it wouldn't hurt to watch.

At last Mordha broke off from his chant. The necromancer stepped back, and Mordha gestured for the warriors to pull Vittorio aside as well. Once again, he did not protest and allowed them to move him.

Then the mirror began to swirl like a window containing a dark fog, and she saw Vittorio smile. That was when she knew something truly terrible was about to happen.

"What is it you hope to accomplish by opening this door?" Vittorio asked.

"I will enter the Eventide, slay the God of Death, and free this world."

The necromancer looked sharply at Mordha, clearly taken by surprise.

"Kill Bàs? Such a thing is impossible!"

Mordha's expression did not change. "We shall see."

The mirror began to pulse with a sound Irina could not so much hear as feel in her chest.

"The trouble with opening doors uninvited," Vittorio mused, as if talking to himself. "You never know who might be on the other side."

The mirror exploded, sending shards of glass in all directions. But only for a moment, then time seemed to stand still. The jagged pieces of glass hovered in the air and the moonlight turned gray and sickly. They all stood silent and immobile, their eyes fixed to the pulsing swirl somehow contained by the mirror frame.

Then a hand reached through the fog. Or not a hand, exactly. It was massive, with thick, glistening appendages like fingers, or like entrails. It brought with it something that might have been an arm, then a torso, then a head and legs, all of it like some terrible beast that had been turned inside out. It towered over even Mordha, oozing and squelching.

Irina could not run, or scream, or even turn away from its hideous and malevolent countenance. The warriors appeared to be in much the same condition. Only Mordha, Hueil, and Vittorio seemed able to move.

"This is not Bàs . . . ," whispered Mordha.

"Correct!" shouted Vittorio gleefully. "You sought Death but instead found Life! You should feel honored that my mistress deigns to favor you with her presence."

This was what Vittorio had been referring to as an angel? Truly he was mad indeed if he thought so. There was nothing sacred or noble about this creature. It was as if all the most tawdry and revolting aspects of living creatures had been collected and shaped into roughly the form of a person. Feces spilled out of one orifice, urine out of another, and semen out of a third, while breasts dangled pendulously, heavy with milk that trickled onto the floor. It wheezed and farted and snorted like an army of old men, but also chittered and purred and growled like a menagerie of animals.

Irina tried to turn away from the grotesque thing, or at least close her eyes, but she could not. Instead she was forced to stare at its shifting, endlessly convulsive mass. She could feel her mind shudder with an unreasoning panic that must be something close to the madness that Vittorio experienced every day since coming into contact with this horror. Her sanity was a thread away from snapping, and she did not know how much more it could take. The only thing she knew for certain was that no normal human was meant to look upon a god, if that's what this was before her.

And then it spoke. Its words were like nails scraping the inside of her skull, like worms burrowing into her flesh, like insects crawling into her nose and eyes and ears and mouth so that all she wanted to do was curl into a ball and die. But she couldn't. Because this was a voice that could not be ignored or defied.

What a joy, it said.

And then it picked up one of the frozen warriors with its tentacle-like appendages and tore him in half. This at last seemed to grant the man the ability to move, although there was little he could do but shriek as the creature sucked up his innards in its gaping, toothy maw. The moment he died, it lost interest, tossing him aside and seizing the next.

Vittorio's eyes brimmed with tears of happiness as he watched, a demented smile on his face. Mordha and Hueil struggled to escape, turning slowly as though moving through mud. They had nearly reached the edge of the courtyard where Irina stood frozen when the creature, now out of other warriors to ingest, turned its attention to them.

First it grasped Hueil, lifting him up to its many-eyed face.

You are one of my sibling's pawns.

Its words rippled through Irina's mind like a flush of infection and pestilence as it tossed Hueil aside indifferently. He landed in a thick shrubbery with minor physical injuries. But his eyes were glassy and he did not move from the uncomfortable spot and only whispered to himself ceaselessly.

Then its eyes fell directly on Irina for the first time and her entire body seized up. She could not breathe or think, but only scream silently at the vile presence that seeped into her mind.

You are . . . in negotiation.

It turned its attention away from her just as she felt her sanity on the brink of fracturing, and she was at last able to breathe, the air coming out in shuddering gasps.

You.

It reached for Mordha.

I promised my beloved sibling I would not end you, but that is all I promised.

It lifted Mordha up by his arms and legs.

And it seems my sibling has made you very sturdy indeed. What joy.

It shivered, as if in pleasure, sending a spray of excrement and ejaculate in all directions. Then it tore his limbs off, one by one.

Mordha did not cry out, though judging by his grunts he was capable of doing so. The creature dropped his limbless body to the ground. It shivered once more, sending another spray into the air. Then it turned and crawled slowly back to the swirling mirror and climbed inside.

The fog disappeared and became the plain backing of a mirror. The shards that had been suspended in the air dropped to the ground. And Irina was once more able to move.

There had been some part of her that had hoped—expected even—that she might go back to normal once the creature was gone. But she did not. Her mind still veered and juddered inside her skull like a frightened mouse that she could not seem to catch. She found herself staggering away from the gore-strewn garden. She did not check to see what Vittorio was doing, whether Hueil had regained his sense, or if Mordha was somehow still alive. She simply shuffled through the garden and back into the palace.

She moved along the hallways. Perhaps people saw her and thought her mad. Or perhaps she encountered no one. She could not say. She did not care.

Irina made her way through the palace until she came to Hexenmeister Cloos's door. She knocked slowly, laboriously. When he answered, she ignored his frantic questions about her well-being and only said:

"It is time."

He grew quiet and solemn, then nodded.

She followed him over to the golem that would soon be her. Now when she looked at it, she found it beautiful in a way that... *creature* was not. Seeing its cold, sleek lines soothed her. It brought some part of her back, at least a little.

Her hand, shaking and pale, touched the comely metal face.

"Negotiations are over," she whispered. "I accept your terms."

37

The border between Aureum and Raíz was a jumble of hills, rocks, and shrubs, with the occasional ash or willow standing out in stark relief. Since it was too dry and hot for Aureumian agriculture, it had been a natural boundary between the two countries until the first emperor of Aureum, Alessandro Morante, had decided there were things worth having besides farmland.

It had taken Jorge longer than he'd expected to organize the Viajero and bring them to this place, even with El Adiuino's help. The Xefe had wisely decided to go on ahead with the mercenaries. Not only the Anxeles Escuros, but the Serpentas Roxas, the Tormenta Sangre, and even the Botos Solemnes. This was the power of uniting all the Great Families. A coalition of the most formidable and highly trained warriors on the continent.

Finally, after a great deal of effort and patience, Jorge was able to get the Viajero to the border, where the mercenaries had already set up a large camp.

Now Jorge, Maria, Javier, El Adiuino, and the Victashian emissary, Onat Duman, pored over a large, roughly sketched map that marked the local terrain. Hugo had remained in Colmo. His anxious nature was not well suited for warfare, and someone needed to keep an eye on things for Jorge back in the city. On the off chance Victasha did betray them, he was instructed to send a messenger on a swift horse to Jorge at once.

But Jorge couldn't think about that too much. He had enough on his mind as it was.

"We arrived later than I would have liked," he admitted to the others. "I'd hoped the Viajero could at least have a full day's rest before the fighting commenced, but it sounds like the imperial army could arrive as early as tomorrow."

"Should we send out scouts to see if we can get their precise location?" asked Maria.

"Not a bad idea," said Javier. "Unfortunately there isn't much cover out here, so our scouts would run a high risk of getting spotted."

"It may be an unnecessary risk," said El Adiuino. "There is a Viajero art that allows us to locate what one person is looking for, be it a person or object. If it is within a hundred miles or so, it can be displayed as if it were a moving painting."

"Like the Symphony of Visions?" asked Maria.

"Not so vivid," said El Adiuino. "There would be no sound or sensation transferred from the scene. It would be more like peering through a keyhole. But it would give us a better idea of their location. We only need someone who knows people among the imperial army for the magic to work."

"I don't know any imperials," said Jorge. "But I did get to know the Uaine quite well, particularly the Urram Le Bàs, who would be necessary to keep the sluagh gorta in line."

The others looked at him a little strangely.

"Sorry, I forget sometimes that you don't know their words. I mean to say that I am acquainted with the Uaine necromancers. At least one of them would have to be included in the army if they brought their undead over such a great distance. Would that be sufficient?"

"I believe so," said El Adiuino. "Now I need to locate a few painters to assist us, and then we can get to work. While I'm looking for people with the appropriate skills, you should clear a large area for the performance and gather everyone together."

"It doesn't really need to be a *performance*, does it?" asked Jorge.

The old guitarist looked offended. "Without an audience, there is no magic."

"Oh, I hadn't realized..." Jorge's cheeks flushed. "Very well. We'll see to it."

They found a dusty clearing near the main camp and asked everyone who was not already occupied with other work to gather. Jorge was surprised, and slightly annoyed, to find that it was much easier to move Viajero around when they were motivated by the idea of seeing a performance.

While he and his sister were settling the expectant audience down, he heard a faint but familiar voice. He paused a moment, straining to hear. Then Maria squeezed his arm so hard it hurt.

"Lucia!"

Far off in the distance, Jorge saw a bobbing brown head coming toward the camp from across the uncleared scrub brush. He tapped his sister on the shoulder, and pointed.

In response, the most beautiful, refined, and revered señorita in all of Raíz hiked up her skirts and ran like hell.

Javier and Jorge watched as the two met each other and embraced. There were whistles and cheers among the Viajero and mercenaries. Whether they knew the couple or not, it was clear to all that this was a blessed moment of reunited love.

Javier heaved a contented sigh.

"Moments like this make it all worthwhile," he said. "Fame, fortune, power. I've had all those things. So I can tell you with certainty that *this* is what matters."

Jorge watched Maria make her way back to them with Lucia and clamped down on the jealousy that squirmed in his stomach. If this was what truly mattered, was it something he would ever have?

"Welcome back, Lucia," he said with all the grace he could muster.

"Ah, *fermanito*!" she said boisterously. "They tell me you're in charge now."

"I suppose I am," he said.

"Good, good. I approve. By the way, I really must thank you."

"For what?"

Lucia strode over to him, gripped his shoulders, and planted a forceful kiss on each of his cheeks. "You let me go. You let me find my own way."

"Oh, er..." He was not accustomed to seeing such unabashed gratitude from the diva. "You're welcome."

"I had not realized until that moment on El Fin..." Her face grew solemn. "I was always so busy studying and comparing everyone else's music, I had not allowed myself to listen carefully to my own."

Jorge wasn't sure how to respond, but before he could, the dusty voice of El Adiuino came across the plains.

"Oh-ho, a prodigal returns!" He was leading a small group of painters through the crowds to the open performance area.

"El Adiuino!" She released Jorge's shoulders and hurried over to him. "Did you already know? Did you know that there are still so many songs *undiscovered*?"

He smiled and touched her cheek. "Yes, my child. And I look forward to the ones you find."

Jorge turned to Javier. "I have no idea what they're talking about."

"As I understand it, while she was wandering alone in the wilderness, one of our most talented Viajero has somehow expanded her abilities. And on the eve of a battle, that is good news indeed."

"I can't argue with that."

"Okay, everyone, let's settle down." El Adiuino did not speak loudly, but somehow the entire assembly heard him and immediately went silent. "Normally I would be the first to encourage everyone to savor the moment, but sadly, as Alejandro Cortina once said, 'Moments must be fleet of foot in turbulent times lest they be lost entirely.' So without further ado, we shall begin."

He turned to Jorge. "Fix someone in your mind, then begin to hum a single note."

Jorge stiffened. "I'm...not really a singer."

El Adiuino smiled graciously. "I promise we will adapt."

"Very well."

"Just keep the note steady. If you stop, the connection will be lost."

"I understand." Jorge cleared his throat, but when he looked at all the people watching him expectantly, he froze. Whether it was the prospect of having to sing, or the sheer number of eyes now upon him, he didn't think he could possibly continue.

Then Lucia came over and took his hand, her eyes far more empathetic than he'd ever seen. What had she discovered during her walk through the desert to change her like this?

"Hey," she said gently. "Don't look at them. Just close your eyes and think of the person. Then hum. That's it. Doesn't even need to be loud. I'll hear it, and pass it along."

"O-okay."

He closed his eyes and, before he'd even made the decision, thought of the Bhuidseach he knew best. His strange, ghostly friend Rowena. It was easy to picture her in his mind. He imagined her with that lavender dress she'd worn back when she'd been experimenting with Izmorozian fashion. She'd never explained why she was doing it, and she was the sort of person that didn't really invite questions. As odd and aloof as she'd been, he'd always been grateful for her friendship. She'd been a quiet presence, listening without judgment as he'd talked in circles around the powerful attraction he felt for both Sonya and Blaine without ever quite admitting it. She'd never pressed, but it was clear she *knew* how he really felt and did not need his verbal confirmation. For some reason that had been a huge comfort to him. That he could experience understanding without having to say it aloud. She had been a good friend.

Until she wasn't. Until she'd chosen her people over their friendship. Not that he begrudged her choice. He was making a similar decision, after all. But in that ragged barracks field outside Gogoleth, crowded with silent Uaine, it had felt like a knife between the ribs. It had felt like betrayal.

Jorge wasn't aware that he'd begun humming. He hadn't consciously chosen the note, which was just as well because he knew even less about music than he did about painting. He only became aware of it when he heard Lucia join in. A few moments later, others joined in. Just one long, sustained note.

He opened his eyes and saw the painters already at work, casting their massive brushes against the blue of the afternoon sky. The paint spread through the air like a drop of ink in water, becoming thinner even as it took on new colors and shapes. They added more to the giant blot that floated above their heads, but it never seemed enough, so they had to keep adding to it just to maintain it.

Within the blot, shapes coalesced into forms. Rows of men and women, some on horseback, some trudging on foot through the golden summer fields of southern Aureum. First there was the imperial army, metal helmets and chest plates gleaming in the same sun that shone on Jorge and his comrades. The Uaine and their army of undead walked some distance behind the imperials, as though intentionally separated.

With a quiet lurch in his stomach, Jorge saw that there were far more undead than he had expected. Galina had warned him that they'd brought significant reinforcements across the tundra in the spring, but only now did he understand just how much his supposed allies had been holding back during the liberation of Izmoroz. The undead were a shambling blanket across the land, shifting with the sort of dense hypnotic movement one might ascribe to an ant colony or school of fish. It was both impressive and deeply disconcerting.

And there was Rowena, looking miserable as she rode on her pony, hunched forward with her hood pulled as low as it would go. She'd always been thin, but she looked gaunt now, and her eerie alabaster skin had taken on a painful reddish tinge. Just as Raízians were not meant for cold weather, it was clear that the Uaine, and especially the Bhuidseach, were not meant for the heat.

Beside Rowena rode another female Bhuidseach that Jorge didn't recognize. This must be the one Galina said had brought the reinforcements. Judging by their expressions, the two necromancers didn't get along. That could be an advantage. And if the physical separation between the Uaine and the Aureumian regiments was an indication that the army lacked an overall cohesion, that would be an advantage as well. Yes, the numbers were daunting, but Jorge had always known they would be at a disadvantage in that regard. They just needed to focus on—

Then Jorge saw Blaine, and all thoughts of strategy and pragmatism fled.

Blaine looked so changed from the last time Jorge had seen him. He'd lost weight. Too much weight. How could one lose weight in the richest city on the continent? And there was something in his expression. A...hardness? No, a determination. But toward what, Jorge could not guess. Toward killing as many Raízians as possible? No, that wasn't it. *Couldn't* be it. But why did he look so alone and sorrowful? Even if they could no longer be together, Jorge's heart ached to see him looking so troubled.

He tried to steel himself, to remind himself that Blaine served Vittorio and the empire and was now the enemy. But it just...didn't take. He only felt pain as he looked into Blaine's sad but resolute eyes.

Then the vision blurred as Jorge's voice cracked. Apparently others could reinforce him, but it must still originate from him, the one who knew these people. The one who cared for these people. The one who was not at all ready to kill them.

His voice gave out as he fought back the tears that suddenly sprang into his eyes, and the vision disintegrated.

"Sorry," he said hoarsely as he desperately willed himself not to cry in front of an army of elite Viajero and hardened mercenaries.

Lucia gave him a searching look. "You did good, *fermanito*. You may lack ability, but I think you do have the artist's soul, and that is a thing most sacred to all Raízians."

Jorge nodded, not trusting himself to respond. In a way, it was exactly the sort of affirmation he'd longed for most of his life. And yet, compared to the dread of what lay before him, it now seemed so small.

He took another calming breath and turned to the Xefe.

"Was it at all helpful?"

"Oh yes," Javier said gravely. "I recognized the area quite well. Unless they march through the night, which would be unwise, we have until midday tomorrow before they are upon on us."

Jorge cleared his throat and tried to look like the authority he supposedly was now. "Then we had better get ready."

38

It was never something Irina could have been ready for. No matter how much she'd prepared, no matter how much she'd learned about the process. No matter how much her mind had been broken by the goddess. To have one's soul torn from one's body and forcibly condensed into solid matter, then jammed into a metal shell—it was unlike any other pain. Not even the slow severing of humanity that her daughter experienced was equal to the violence inflicted upon her being. It was wrong. It was unnatural. It was against everything supported by life and existence.

And then it was over.

The gleaming metal golem got slowly to its feet and looked around. No thoughts could be discerned behind its glowing magenta eyes. No emotion could be displayed on its perfect, unmoving countenance. And it could not express those things because golems could not speak.

"You...are...wondrous!" whispered Cloos as he fell adoringly to his knees before her. Perhaps this was the true reason he had been shunned and rejected by his own people. Not because of his obsession with aesthetics, but because of his longing for something to worship, even if it was something he had to make himself.

The golem did not seem to notice Cloos's veneration, or even his presence. A puff of steam hissed from the narrow slit of its mouth, then it began to walk. Slow at first. Tentative. But with each step, its movements grew more sure until by the time it reached the doorway that led out into the hallway, it found its stride.

"Wait!" Cloos grabbed the golem's cold metal arm.

Without looking, the golem casually backhanded him across the room. He slammed into the wall and did not move again.

The golem took a few moments to negotiate the relatively narrow doorway, ducking its head and turning to the side. But once it was out into the wide, tall corridors of the palace, it was able to move more swiftly.

Two soldiers were unlucky enough to encounter the golem in those corridors, and unwise enough to challenge it. Their swords bounced off its armored torso and it did not slow its pace as it grasped them by their necks with its metal hands. It dragged them along, crushing their windpipes, then dropped their lifeless corpses as it continued down the hallway.

It stopped suddenly as it passed the entrance to the garden. It stood motionless, steam leaking from the slit of its mouth. Did it recall a man named Vittorio? If so, perhaps it wondered if he was still in the garden, gloating over his latest victims.

After several seconds of absolute stillness, it turned abruptly and stalked into the garden, metal feet clanging loudly on the stone pathway that threaded through the green.

There was the broken mirror. The eviscerated and dismembered Uaine warriors. The necromancer alive but motionless, perhaps paralyzed or driven mad by what he had experienced. There was no Vittorio.

There was, however, Mordha the Uaine warlord. He lay on the garden patio, limbless but alert and sane. No blood seeped from his wounds, and other than being immobile, he was seemingly no worse for the wear.

The golem looked down at him, magenta eyes pulsing softly.

"I do not know what you have become," he said. "But if you are still the mother of Sonya, I would ask for your help. We must warn my people that the worst has come to pass."

The golem did not move or react in any way other than releasing a puff of steam from its mouth. It stood there as though considering his request. Mordha waited patiently until at last the golem leaned over and scooped him up, easily tucking his massive torso under one arm.

As it walked back across the garden and returned to the palace interior, Mordha said, "My people are in the north wing of the palace."

The golem seemed to understand and veered up a hallway. At Mordha's direction, it continued to move through the palace, killing anyone who did not get out of its way, until at last they reached the wing of the palace where the Uaine had been residing these past months. The walls had been scrawled with various wards and blessings in the Uaine language. Some doors had been smashed in, and some windows as well. All in all, it looked like it had been inhabited by a restless people unaccustomed to staying in one place too long. There was only one thing missing:

"Where is everyone?" muttered Mordha.

He had the golem look through each room, but the people who only the night before had been patiently biding their time here until Mordha called upon them were now gone.

The warlord's scarred face creased. "What has Vittorio done?"

The golem let out a puff of steam, then turned and headed back through the palace toward the main entrance.

It wasn't until they reached the outer courtyard that they encountered any serious resistance. A squad of soldiers led by Captain Leoni had formed up to bar its path. Did the golem recall Leoni's courteous conduct when transporting Irina Turgenev to Magna Alto all those months ago? If so, perhaps that was why it spared him, and only him, when it smashed through the ranks of soldiers that stood in its way.

The golem moved more swiftly once it was out on Ascendant Way, jogging down the road that spiraled through the Silver Ring and into town.

"Where are you going, metal monster?" Mordha mused in his own language as he was carried helplessly underarm like a misshapen parcel.

When the golem reached the town, it was met by screams of terror. Did it recall riding a carriage through here before? Did it remember how pleasant people had been, how warm and open to Irina? If so, did it contrast that experience with this one? Was it aware of the effect of its presence on others?

Something must have been recalled, if perhaps imperfectly, because the golem took the same route that Irina had taken to the barracks. Once there, it kicked the front door down. The guard nearly fell out of his chair, but quickly recovered and drew his sword. The golem swept its arm casually, and he flew across the small room so hard his skull split open when he hit the wall.

The golem kicked the inner door down, then trudged down the dark passage lined with cells. It did not heed the stench or shouts but it did seem to be searching for something. Or someone.

At last it stopped before one of the cells. It tore the hinges off the barred door with one hand but could not fit into the cell. It reached its arm into the cell and gestured for the prisoner to come closer.

The prisoner was a gagged and bound Raízian man, his long hair filthy and disheveled. He stared at the metal golem with its glowing eyes and gruesome parcel, and he did not move closer.

"An ally of Portinari?" Mordha asked.

The prisoner perked up at the sound of that name. He squinted, as though getting a better look at the golem. Then his eyes widened in something between confusion and recognition. But after a moment he crawled as best he could over to the golem.

With its free hand, the golem carefully plucked the gag from his mouth, and snapped the ropes that bound his wrists.

"What on earth...," Captain Reyes said, his voice hoarse from lack of use, "is going on?"

"Gods walk among us," said Mordha. "And the world trembles with their steps."

Reyes gave him a dubious look as he gently rubbed the raw skin of his wrists. Perhaps he was about to ask what such a bizarre statement meant. But just as he was opening his mouth to speak, the golem withdrew its arm, turned, and, with Mordha still tucked under one arm, trudged back up the corridor, leaving Reyes free and able to do whatever he chose.

When the golem stepped out into the main barracks yard, it was confronted with a much more sizable force than before. A full regiment of spear and shield soldiers now gathered under the command of Colonel Totti.

The golem gazed with its magenta eyes at the bristling wall of humans, shields, and spears before it. Steam drifted lazily from its mouth slit into the pinkish predawn sky. Then it looked down at Mordha under its arm and lightly patted his head as though he was a cherished pet.

Mordha's scarred face twisted into a smile.

"Do as you will, and have no concern for my well-being. As you have witnessed, even gods find me difficult to kill."

Steam hissed sharply from the golem's mouth. One might be forgiven for imagining that it was a laugh of sorts.

Then the golem took several steps backward, giving itself room to build up speed. The infantry shivered, and might have broken immediately if not for Totti's command.

"Hold this line, damn your cowardly hearts, or I swear I'll skewer you myself!"

The golem broke into a sudden sprint, its metal legs pounding the dirt as it bore down on the regiment.

The sound of the impact could be heard across town. The first few rows of men flew into the air, some dead immediately, others broken and maimed.

One managed to lodge his spear in the golem's thigh, but that did not impede its progress. The golem didn't seem to even notice the wooden pole protruding from its leg until it was weighed down by two impaled soldiers, stacked one on top of the other. It knocked the weighted spear out of its metal hide with a swipe of its hand, and continued forward. By then most of the soldiers lay dead, dying, or cowering in abject terror.

The golem ran on with its Uaine parcel, heading east, indifferent to anything before it. Be it person, carriage, or building, nothing barred its way until at last it came to the thick outer wall of the city.

It stood and looked at the wall for a moment. It knocked on the wall with one metal fist, then slowly looked upward to the top, which was over thirty feet above.

"You may have more luck with a gate," suggested Mordha.

The golem gave a puff of steam in response and began walking along the wall. By the time it reached the main gate, soldiers had once again formed up. In addition to the infantry, there was a regiment of cavalry, and a squad of archers lined along the parapet above. The city gate was set up to defend external threats, not internal ones, so the archers were not well positioned and sight lines were disadvantageous.

The golem trudged toward the gate through a rain of arrows. Most bounced off its metal hide, but one struck a glowing eye. The golem jerked to a halt and looked around before seeming to realize there was something in its eye. Perhaps some of the archers felt a spark of hope, thinking they had found a weakness in the monster. But then the golem merely yanked out the arrow and continued forward.

Soon the golem reached the infantry that blocked access to the gate. The angle was wrong for the archers overhead to do much good now, but as the golem drew near, the cavalry charged in from behind, slashing at its flanks. The cavalry, swift sabers of the imperial army, were known for harrying even the most formidable foes into a panic. Perhaps they could be forgiven for assuming something so big would move slowly. But forgiveness would have to come posthumously.

As the first rider drew near, the golem spun at the waist, twisting in a way that would have been impossible for a person. It grabbed a horse by the neck and spun back, dragging animal and rider along so they knocked over other horses as they went. The golem finally released them so that they flew into the infantry regiment. Chaos erupted as the horse thrashed, kicking in the heads and chests of those nearby who had not been immediately crushed to death. The golem continued to fling horses about until the remaining cavalry broke and retreated.

The golem paid the death and suffering no heed as it waded through the carnage to the gate. The wooden bar that held the passage shut usually took several men to lift into place, but the golem picked it up with one hand and tossed it negligently backward into the surviving infantry, crushing many more. Then it pushed the door open and entered the short corridor that led through the thick wall. There had not been time to heat pitch, and the caltrops hastily dropped into the corridor from above were crushed underfoot.

At the far end was a portcullis made of thick iron-plated oak. The golem stood and contemplated this for several moments as the archers, who had repositioned themselves on the ground, began to loose volleys from the far end of the corridor.

The golem looked down at Mordha, patted his head, and placed him on the ground with a surprising gentleness. Then it gripped the portcullis with both hands and began to lift. Its magenta eyes blazed, and steam hissed from its mouth with a shriek like a teakettle as the portcullis slowly rose. Once the gate was high enough for the golem to duck under, it shoved the grid so hard that the iron plating bent and the oak underneath snapped. The portcullis was now so warped that it could no longer slide back down on its track. Instead it hung there half-open.

By then the imperial officer in command had realized that letting the monster leave Magna Alto was far more sensible than trying to force it to remain. He ordered those who were lucky enough to still be alive to stop fighting, and they merely watched as the golem scooped up the limbless Uaine warlord, ducked under the broken portcullis, then jogged across the dew-drenched meadows, its metal body gleaming in the newly risen sun as it ran in a southeasterly direction.

It was clearly focused on a destination, and Mordha wondered what it might be.

39

"Tell me, Andrushka, are you familiar with the works of Lady Olga Bunich Fignolov?" asked Galina.

The two sat on horseback at the crest of a hilltop overlooking the vast city of Magna Alto.

"No, Your Majesty. I'm sorry."

"Hardly your fault," she said. "Living in the tundra for two decades, I expect there was scant opportunity to pursue modern works of literature."

"Indeed, Your Majesty."

"In Lady Fignolov's final novel, *All Beauty Is Unearned*, there is a scene in which the protagonist, a young noblewoman named Sofiya Plisetskaya, prepares for a social gathering and likens donning her corset and gown to a soldier girding himself for battle. As someone who takes great care with their appearance, I always found that description apt. Although I must admit, not as apt as it is now."

Galina looked down at the ensemble that had been constructed for her. A trim gold-and-white gown that had been tailored specifically to allow for ease of movement while riding, freeing her from the necessity of wearing trousers. She was grateful for that, because although she had become more confident with public speaking, she did not think she would have felt quite as comfortable addressing her troops while cognizant of fact that she looked like a canary on stilts.

Over the gown she wore a matching garment that was part robe, part armor. Thin brass strips had been fastened to the front and back, almost like a flexible burnished chest plate. She also wore matching shoulder guards and bracers, both intricately etched to suggest the golden fields of an Izmorozian summer.

"You look the very vision of a warrior queen, Your Majesty," said Andre.

Galina smiled at him, the bright Aureumian sun setting her flaxen hair aglow. "You always know just what to say, Andrushka."

They both turned their gaze down the hill and across the sprawling meadow to the grandiose profile of Magna Alto. Even from a distance, it was clear that no other city on the continent could hope to equal it.

"Supposedly it took twenty-three years and more than a hundred thousand men to build Magna Alto," said Galina. "I wonder how many of those hundred thousand died in their labor."

"I would imagine most of them, Your Majesty," said Andre.

"Probably so," she agreed.

Galina had stationed her army a quarter mile back on the far side of the hill so they would not be spotted by an observant sentry on the city walls. Then she and her two Rangers had ridden ahead to get a good look at the fortifications they would soon face.

As soon as the city had come into sight, Tatiana had asked if she might circle the perimeter on her own. Now Andre's round fuzzy ear twitched as he said, "*Sova* returns."

Tatiana soon crested a nearby rise, her mount dripping with sweat.

"Tatiana, it's not wise to tire your mount unnecessarily," scolded Galina.

"It *was* necessary, Your Majesty," said Tatiana. "I found something... troubling."

"Oh?" Galina sat up in her saddle. "What is it?"

"I don't know," said Tatiana. "It appears to be a mushroom garden that stretches in a long line on a hilltop south of the city."

"*Mushrooms?*" asked Galina. "I confess that doesn't exactly send shivers down my spine, Anya. What sort of threat could fungus prove to an army?"

"I'm unsure," admitted Tatiana. "But it stinks."

"Well, I'm no farmer, but I believe mushrooms require a sizable amount of fertilizer."

"Not of feces, but of magic."

"*Magic* mushrooms?" asked Galina. "I've never heard of such a thing."

"Neither have I," Tatiana said grimly. "That is what troubles me."

Galina frowned. "Magic has never been my specialty, but Victasha seems to possess a great deal of knowledge on the subject. Tatiana, go fetch Sezai Bey."

"At once, Your Majesty."

Tatiana wheeled her horse and galloped down the hill toward the camped army.

Galina watched her speed away, then said, "I should have phrased that order more precisely."

"Under normal circumstances, I think she would have understood your intent," said Andre. "But this coming battle has made her... excited."

Galina turned back to him. "We have yet to see how the two of you will react under true duress. This battle will be your first real challenge."

Andre blinked slowly with his dark eyes. "I do not think even the madness of combat would induce me to harm you, Your Majesty. However, others for whom I have no personal attachment... I cannot say for certain."

Galina nodded. It was not the first time they had discussed the issue, and while they both agreed that there was some risk, she could not imagine conducting this siege without them.

"Y-Your Majesty!" came a whimper from poor Sezai Bey.

Tatiana came galloping uphill toward them. As Galina had feared, the Ranger took "go fetch" quite literally. Rather than treat Bey with the courtesy due to a foreign representative, she had apparently snatched him up and tossed him across the front of her saddle like a sack of grain.

"Tatiana, please allow our guest to sit up properly."

Once Bey was upright, looking more than a little flustered, Galina smiled at him.

"My sincere apologies, Representative Bey. I fear this close to battle, my Rangers are a little overzealous."

He took a moment to straighten his clothes and hair and perhaps regain some dignity, then he gave her a valiant smile. "Apology accepted, Your Majesty."

"Now, the reason I asked you here is to see if you have knowledge of plant or fungal-based magics."

He gave her a sharp look. Perhaps even a hint of actual panic? She could not be certain, but it seemed like she had hit a nerve.

"I...have some general knowledge of the subject," he admitted.

"Then perhaps you can illuminate the potential military application for the empire in seeding the far hilltop with magic-imbued mushrooms."

He seemed to relax slightly at that. "Oh, I see. As I said, my knowledge is only general, so I'm afraid I don't know of any *specific* applications when it comes to plants and fungi."

Her eyes bored into his. On the eve of decisive battle, she would not be deflected so easily.

"What *do* you know about the topic, then? Perhaps it would be more helpful than you realize."

His tension shot back up, and there was a lengthy pause. Then he said, "With the oncoming battle, I have been given some...*small* discretion on how much state knowledge I can divulge. So I think it would be appropriate to say that there is a type of magic that can alter living things, be they plant, fungi, or animal. Even living things too small for the naked eye to see fall under its purview."

"A formidable magic indeed," Galina said grimly. "And who wields it?"

"Our information is somewhat spotty," admitted Bey, "and we have seen only a scant few examples of it in Victasha. It seems to originate from an island nation to the east, across the sea."

"You are suggesting it is unlikely to be what we're dealing with here?"

"Exceedingly so," said Bey. "Although since we know *one* people have mastered it, perhaps it is possible that others have as well."

"Life magic...," mused Andre.

"You have an idea, Andre?" asked Galina.

"Just as death and change are the domain of Lady Marzanna, life and fertility are the domain of Lady Zivena."

"So our fears may be correct that Vittorio has aligned himself with Lady Marzanna's sister, and this is some scheme of hers?" asked Galina.

"Who else?" he asked.

"Even if we're right, we still don't know what these magic mushrooms *do*," said Galina. "This is potentially a massive hole in our strategy. I'm not sure how we'll consider—"

The sharp sound of screeching metal rang across the meadow.

"What on earth was that?" asked Galina.

Tatiana's owl eyes locked onto the city. "There is some commotion at the gate."

"What *sort* of commotion?" Galina wished in that moment she had eyes as sharp as a bird of prey.

"There seems to be...," said Tatiana, "a giant metal woman ripping through the portcullis..."

"A *what*?"

"A golem perhaps," said Bey. "Is it coming toward us?"

"No." Tatiana pointed. "There, you see her now?"

Galina strained her eyes and saw a single figure that glittered in the sunlight like polished steel. It was moving with astonishing speed in a southeasterly direction.

"I thought you said the Kantesian golems are massive insect-like constructions," said Galina.

"Traditionally, yes," said Bey. "But there was a Kantesian named Cloos who defected early in the conflict between Aureum and Kante. My understanding is that he was rather unconventional in his approach to golems in a way that his fellows didn't appreciate. Perhaps with the change in power, he found his situation at the palace less tenable and engineered a golem to help him escape. It did seem to be heading in the general direction of Kante. Was the golem carrying something?"

"Yes," said Tatiana. "It appeared to be a human, or at least part of one."

"Part?" asked Galina.

"I couldn't see any arms or legs."

"By the Lady, has Vittorio started dismembering people alive?" Galina shuddered, then turned back to squint at the gate. "What is the current status of the portcullis?"

"It appears to be stuck halfway open," said Tatiana.

Galina chewed thoughtfully on her lip.

"How far away are the Kantesians?"

"They just emerged from Hardsong Pass yesterday," said Bey. "The golems allow them to travel at astonishing speeds over open terrain, but even so they are at least a day, perhaps two away."

"Well, which is it?" asked Galina. "Is it one day or two? I'm not sure how long it will take them to repair the portcullis, but I'm loath to let this opportunity pass us by."

Bey looked unsure. "I will have to..."

"We don't have time for your little charade," snapped Galina. "Forget your silly secrets for once and use that amulet of yours to ask them right now. I'm weary of playing the ambassador's games."

Bey looked like he was about to object, but then he seemed to become uncomfortably aware of the two Rangers now looking expectantly at him. After a moment, he sighed.

"How did you ascertain it was the amulet?"

"Did you think my Rangers could sniff out magic in a mushroom, but not a piece of jewelry?"

This ability of theirs actually wasn't that obvious. In fact, as Galina understood it, only Rangers who were more beast than human could smell magic. Apparently, the closer they became to a magical creature themselves, the easier it was for them to track it. Galina wasn't certain that Sonya could do it. At least not yet.

Bey gave Galina a sheepish smile. "I confess our knowledge of Ranger magic is somewhat limited."

Galina smiled back at him. She had already decided she would do whatever she could to keep the Victashians from learning any more than absolutely necessary about the Rangers. They were allies for now, but who knew what the future might hold. So long as it didn't directly compromise the present campaign, she would hold back as much as she could.

All she said was "They are rather mysterious, aren't they."

"Very well," said Bey. "I agree this is an urgent issue so I will contact the ambassador now."

He closed his eyes and touched the small golden amulet at his throat.

"Ambassador, I am here with my hosts to ask a question of an urgent nature."

He winced as he listened to what Galina suspected was a displeased reply.

"Yes, I am aware, Ambassador, but they had more or less figured it out themselves. Apparently Rangers can *smell* such things?"

He paused, listening to the reply. "Perhaps Ranger Sonya has also smelled it, and like Her Majesty, is holding that knowledge for the moment she needs to utilize it."

There was another reply and Bey gave a pained smile. Galina wondered if the ambassador was expressing doubt in Sonya's ability to think strategically in even such a simple instance.

"Ah yes, the question Her Majesty has pressed me to ask is whether you know precisely when you might arrive. It seems that a lone golem broke free from the palace...yes, a golem. Small and humanoid in shape, however. I presume Cloos built it as a means of escape, and something larger would have been impossible to conceal before it was ready. Anyway, the thing just damaged the portcullis during its flight, and Her Majesty is eager to take advantage of this breach."

He paused as he listened carefully to the response. Then he looked at Galina. "If they press through the night, a *portion* of the Kantesian army can be here before dawn. Can you keep the breach open that long?"

Galina turned to Andre.

"I think we can manage that, don't you, Andrushka?"

He smiled broadly, showing his long canines. "With pleasure, Your Majesty."

40

W*hat is "me"?* Sonya asked herself once again. She'd lost count how many times, but she still had no answer, and the question felt more urgent every day.

The cross through Hardsong Pass had been stressful, and there was a palpable sense of relief throughout the ranks of the Kantesian army when they finally made it to the wide-open plains of Aureum on the other side. But soon after, word had somehow arrived from Galina that there was a temporary breach in the walls of Magna Alto. The Izmorozian army would try to keep it open, but they were requesting reinforcements as soon as possible. Since the golems didn't need to rest and could travel much faster than horses, Ferdinand had sent them as a single detachment ahead of the bulk of his army.

So now Sonya was no longer the vanguard, but just another rider in the cavalry. She did not like that at all. Or maybe it was *Lisitsa* who was displeased. Really, the distinction no longer held any meaning.

Several lives ago, *Lisitsa* had been a mere title bestowed by Lady Marzanna. More of an idea than a reality. But with each death and rebirth, that had slowly changed until it had seemed at times like a second intruding consciousness. While that had been worrisome, she had been able to manage it for the most part, with only one notable exception.

But now, Sonya realized she could no longer distinguish where she ended and the fox spirit began. All she could say for certain was that she felt a dreadful anticipation for the coming battle. She wasn't sure how this feeling was different from the eagerness before the battle in Gogoleth. Perhaps it was a matter of intention. During the previous battle she'd had clear goals: liberate Izmoroz and try to keep her brother from doing anything terrible. But what did she want from this battle? Sure, they would stop Vittorio, of course. She wanted to keep her brother alive. Hopefully to rescue her mother from the palace, if it wasn't too late. And eventually to reunite with Jorge. Those all sounded like reasonable, even noble goals. But they were not what drove her forward.

Instead it was a...*hunger* for the violence and chaos that battle would bring. Surely that wasn't her. That must be the influence of *Lisitsa*. But there was no longer a murmuring beast-like voice in her head. There was no longer a clear rise and fall of animal instinct. It was ever-present and indistinguishable from herself. A low hum of excitement and eagerness that never dissipated.

What is "me"...

"Yasha, are you okay?" Sebastian asked as he pulled his horse up beside her.

"Huh?" Her head snapped up so sharply it made Peppercorn glance back at her. She must have been very deep in thought for someone to sneak up on her, especially her clumsy little brother. "Yeah, I'm fine."

"You were staring down at your hands like you wanted to strangle someone."

"Oh, I was just thinking..."

"About?"

He looked concerned. Probably with good reason.

"Hey, you know that moment you said where Mokosh sort of took over your body?"

He clearly hadn't expected her to bring that up and glanced around to make sure there was no one else in earshot. But they were a little ways in front of the main force. She might not be the vanguard of the army anymore, but she still wanted to be in the front.

"Er...yes?"

"Were you *aware* that she had taken control at the time? Or was it something you realized later when you thought back on it?"

"No, something definitely felt different in that moment. Like I wasn't myself."

"But how could you *tell*?"

He gave her an odd look. "What do you mean? Normally I feel one way, and then I was feeling a different way that wasn't me."

"Yeah, but..."

She wrestled with how to express her doubt in a way that would make sense to him, or anyone for that matter. She couldn't shake the idea that what she thought of as *herself* might be only that. A thought. Or perhaps a memory of a past self.

"Never mind. It was a dumb question. So...do you really think it was the Damp Mother Earth? As in the being who birthed all of existence?"

"I have no idea," he admitted. "Something that *did* take me a while to realize was just how terrifying that idea is. Why did she do it? What does she want? And perhaps most importantly, will she do it again? The kind of power I used, Yasha...It wasn't elemental magic. At least not as far as I understand it."

"So no fire, water, earth, or air?"

"No, it was like I punched open a tiny hole in the fabric of reality. Right in the middle of Sasha's chest." He shuddered. "A part of me really hopes this new gemstone Isobelle gave me isn't strong enough to channel that kind of power, but what if it is? And what if Mokosh makes me do it again on the battlefield?"

Sonya realized she wasn't the only one entering this battle deeply worried about how much self-control they might possess in the heat of combat.

"We'll just have to keep an eye on each other," she told her little brother.

"Agreed."

Sonya's ears twitched as she heard another rider approach. The scent and light jingle of jewelry made it obvious who it was.

"Hey, Ambassador," she said without turning around.

"I hope I'm not intruding," said Boz as she drew up alongside them.

"Not at all, Ambassador," said Sebastian, probably out of politeness, since she most certainly *was* intruding.

"I couldn't help overhearing your conversation about an entity called Mokosh," said Boz.

"From that distance?" asked Sonya. "Your ears must be as good as mine."

There was no visible change, but Sonya suddenly smelled the scent of stress coming off the Victashian. Had she struck a nerve? Even when the ambassador gave her usual tinkling laugh, the unease didn't dissipate.

"I confess I may have been purposefully eavesdropping. I am a member of the Victashian Intelligence Bureau after all."

No matter how subtle, now that Boz was exhibiting such prey-like behavior, Sonya couldn't help but pursue it. "Sebastian, didn't you say you always feel a bit of magic coming off the ambassador?"

Sebastian gave Sonya a surprised look, then his eyes narrowed. "I did."

"You're the magic expert, little brother. Do you know what kind Victashians use?"

"I don't, actually." He turned to Boz. "It troubles me to be so ignorant, Ambassador. Perhaps you would enlighten us."

Boz looked at them for a moment, then sighed. "Really, one little slipup and you both pounce. You're worse than your mother. I'll have you know that I have a lot on my mind right now, and no one is perfect."

"Is it sound magic?" asked Sebastian, now looking genuinely curious.

"In a sense," said Boz. "I hope you'll forgive me if I'm not too terribly free with divulging details regarding a carefully guarded state secret."

"We might need to know this stuff for the battle," Sonya pointed out.

"A reasonable point. And I suppose there's no harm in telling you one key aspect, since Queen Galina has already figured it out. My magic allows me to communicate with my representatives stationed with the Izmorozian and Raízian armies."

Sebastian looked even more excited now. "So you could speak to either one of them right now? Across hundreds of miles?"

"Indeed."

"How marvelous!"

"I like to think so," she agreed.

"Well," said Sonya, "it is helping us coordinate a battle strategy that probably would have been impossible otherwise."

Boz's eyes then flashed in a way that Sonya was beginning to recognize as the start of something wily and perhaps devious. "Now that I've generously offered up this very sensitive Victashian secret, perhaps you would be willing to allay my own concerns regarding this potential interference from Mokosh during the forthcoming battle."

"You know who Mokosh is?" asked Sonya.

"She is not exclusive to Izmoroz. The name may be different, but a Mother Earth 'creator of existence' entity appears in nearly every culture in some form or other."

"So she exists in Victashian religion?" asked Sebastian. "And is she as..."

"Frightening?" asked Boz. "Yes. Hence my concern."

"I wish I had comforting words for you, Ambassador," said Sebastian. "But all we know about her is that she's meant to keep the balance between her offspring, Marzanna and Zivena."

"What about that word the old Viajero called you?" asked Sonya. "What was it?"

Sebastian thought a moment. "Armonia, I believe?"

Boz's eyebrows rose. "That word comes from the precursor language that both the Aureumian and Raízian languages share."

"And you know this language?" asked Sebastian.

"As a member of the bureau, we learn it first, since it becomes a nice foundation for the other two."

"Wait, you can speak Raízian?" asked Sonya.

Boz's forehead creased. "Probably better than most Raízians, I'm sorry to say. The Aureumian Empire goes after indigenous languages rather viciously. All in the name of facilitating commerce. And obedience, of course."

"Can you also speak Old Izmorozian, then?" Sonya asked eagerly.

"Ah, I'm afraid my grasp of the language is rudimentary at best, mostly taken from texts decades, and even centuries, old."

"Better than mine, at least. Once this is all over, will you teach me what you know?"

Sonya wasn't sure why it still mattered so much to her. After all, in this current life, she had never even been to Izmoroz. But maybe that was the reason. She was looking for something to ground her in the past she remembered but to which she had no direct connection.

"It would be an honor," said Boz. "Now, about this word *armonia*...I believe it means *harmony*, which I find very interesting."

"How so?" asked Sebastian.

"Mokosh balances the world, does she not? So if you, called by some as the *harmony*, have indeed received some sort of communication from her, it suggests you are her servant and perhaps that is your purpose. One does wonder where all your terrible power comes from, Sebastian Turgenev. Victasha has had its share of wizards over the millennia, and a prevalent theory is that one is born to each age of the world as a sort of peacekeeper."

"Between nations?" asked Sebastian.

"Between gods," replied Boz.

"Wait," said Sonya. "Are you saying that if he had to, my little brother could stand up to the Lady Marzanna herself?"

"It's only a theory," Boz said quickly, but there was something in her eyes that suggested she believed it.

"It seems unlikely to me," said Sebastian. "Although when I think back to the moment I killed Sasha—no, when I completely wiped him from existence—I remember this feeling of vastness. Like my power was bigger than the sky, bigger even than the world could contain. It was everywhere and everything. It was...all."

They rode silently after that. Sonya wondered what such power might feel like. Her own, such as it was, had never felt so grandiose. It was internal and focused, like the blade of a knife. But perhaps each in their own way, she and her brother were tools for Marzanna and Mokosh.

And if that were true, what tool did Lady Zivena wield? And what could it do?

INTERLUDE

Long before humans walked upon the Damp Mother Earth, the first daughter of Mokosh brought forth plants and fungi. It was a life-form as varied as any other, and with just as many surprises.

Franko Vittorio had laid a sheltered bed of soil containing a certain fungus that stretched for miles across the center of Aureum, as commanded by the great goddess Zivena. Soon after, the spores of the fungus began their slow spread throughout the land, drifting lazily and almost invisibly through the air. It had taken months, but they had settled in nearly every inhabited part of the country. There they nestled into everything, including food stores and wells. They lay on the grass that was consumed by cattle, who were in turn eaten by people. Many spores landed in useless places, or were destroyed in cooking or curing processes. But they numbered in the billions, and enough survived.

Mia and her friend Camilla still worked behind the counter at her father's store in Windvale. Over the last few months, Mia occasionally thought back to that poor, anguished Izmorozian boy. She couldn't remember his name. Something ridiculously long and very Izmorozian. He'd been cute enough, and sweet in an awkward sort of way. But it had been clear they were merely soldiers passing through, so she hadn't taken them very seriously. Even so, she wished sometimes that a boy like him might move to Windvale. A complicated boy who wasn't afraid to show his emotions. She had nothing against the small-town farm boys around her, but by and large she found them a little dull. That Izmorozian boy had not been dull.

But on this fateful day, she was not thinking of Sebastian. Or really much of anything beyond wishing she could close the shop early and go soak her tired feet. And that idle want was the last thing to pass through her brain. Then the mighty Goddess of Spring, Fertility, and Life called forth the fungus that had lain dormant in her body for some time.

There was no pain, blessedly. Unlike her sister, Zivena was a caring and gentle goddess. Instead, Mia simply drifted away to dream endlessly of closing the shop and soaking her feet, as though her last coherent thought was stretched out for eternity.

It took a short while for the stem to emerge from her mouth, but then it quickly bloomed into a mushroom head, the end pressing her teeth apart and emerging from between her lips.

The body began to move in a fast but jerky way, bumping into things as it maneuvered around the counter to stand in the center of the store. There were customers in the store who also had a mushroom head protruding from their mouths. Those who did not looked on in horror. But only for a few moments. Then the mushroom in Mia's mouth expanded into a red round bulb, growing larger until it suddenly burst, blanketing the inside of the store with spores. Those who had not been infected yet swiftly joined the rest, and as a unified group, they emerged from the store into the golden afternoon.

The rest of the inhabitants of Windvale emerged from wherever they were as well. They gathered, still and listless, in the street. One might have mistaken them for undead, but they were in fact the opposite. A perfect image of life consuming life so that it might continue to live. The fungus lived off the tissues of the host, taking the least necessary first. Depending on the size of the host, it might last a few days to a few weeks.

They all turned in the direction of Magna Alto and began to walk. They were joined by others throughout the kingdom, hundreds of thousands, all converging on the capital, as Zivena bade them do. They did not stop or rest or even slow their pace during the days that followed.

Many did not survive the trek. But enough did. This was always the way of life.

PART FOUR

MORE CURSE THAN
BLESSING

"How I pity other lands, with their capricious and meddling gods whose interventions are often more curse than blessing. The God of Raíz allows freedom for all, offers comfort through the arts, and does not involve Himself in the small and petty squabbles of humanity."

—Pedro Molina, in the foreword to his play
Never Did I See You Smile

41

Jorge had come to this battle because it was his responsibility as the national representative, and because the outcome was more important to him than anything else in the world. However, he had been wondering how he might actually contribute. He had seen some battle, and was a reasonably intelligent person, but he doubted his limited experience could match the wisdom of the Xefe and the other guild leaders when it came to tactics. And he certainly didn't have anything to offer the Viajero. Oddly enough, the idea of being a field medic never even crossed his mind. Perhaps because all his combat experience had been with the Uaine, who generally didn't bother with such things. They fought until they were dead, and then they rose as sluagh gorta and continued fighting.

It was his sister who suggested the idea.

"Unless you don't want to," she quickly said after he gave her an amazed look. "I just assumed, since you had that clinic in the Viajero Quarter."

"No, it's perfect! Thank you. I only feel bad that my job will be so much less arduous than those on the front lines."

"Don't be too sure of that," Javier had told him with a grim expression.

Jorge had not understood then. But he understood now.

From the perspective of a field medic, there truly was no glory in war. No last-minute thrilling speech before battle, no charge, no shouts of determination or encouragement. He and Maria merely sat and waited in a tent filled with empty cots, listening to a distant hum that might or might not have been battle.

And then, all too soon, came an endless deluge of misery and suffering.

Some came alone, clutching at a gash or puncture wound. Their blood-streaked faces were pale, their eyes unfocused, and often they collapsed as soon as they arrived, as if they had used up the last of their strength to get there.

Then there were those assisted by an anxious comrade. Usually they had received a leg or foot injury, or else an abdominal wound that prevented them from walking. Their helper sometimes left immediately, face set grimly as they returned to the fray. Others remained, either concerned for their charge, or grateful for a reason not to go back.

And then there were those who required more than one person to bring them because they could not move or were unconscious. Those usually arrived on a makeshift stretcher, perhaps a piece of tarp or blanket. Their injuries were severe, and their chance of survival slim.

Jorge had never contemplated in depth the many horrible things that could be done to the human body. Eyes were punctured, jaws were torn loose, and limbs were so twisted that jagged bones protruded. The sight of flesh and sinew torn asunder; the stench of blood, bile, and excrement; the screams and wails of agony—it piled up on him so heavily and unrelentingly that he wondered how much longer he could bear it.

But he knew he must bear it. If he did not, many who might be saved would surely die. So he forced himself to continue.

And things did get easier in a sense. Unfortunately.

At first the triage was difficult. Each heart-rending decision on who could be saved and who must be left to die brought him to tears. But as the hours went by and the bodies kept coming, it became... simpler. As if certain aspects of his mind shut down, or perhaps collapsed, until he was not quite himself any longer but merely a numb, calculating maker of impossible choices.

After a few hours, he was stitching wounds and mixing potions almost mechanically, his hands stained with blood and the ichor of medicinal plants. He moved with swift but unhurried precision. Had he been able to witness himself, he might have noticed some similarity to the almost meditative flow that Sonya achieved in battle. But he was so immersed in the moment, such perspective could not reach him.

He continued in his trance for a time, saving some, letting others die, knowing on some level that were he to stop, he would surely collapse. But then at last he saw something that brought him out of his daze.

Lucia, her face etched in numb horror, led in El Adiuino. The old guitarist had one arm over her shoulder and leaned heavily on her. The other was tucked under his armpit, soaked in blood. His face was pale from shock and blood loss, and his eyes were glazed.

"Jorge..." Lucia's eyes glistened with tears. "Can you..."

Seeing these people he knew so well snapped him back to himself. He and El Adiuino exchanged a look and somehow he already knew what he would find.

"Let me see." He held out his hand.

El Adiuino removed the arm that had been tucked in at his side, and just as Jorge had feared, the wrist was wrapped in a blood-drenched tourniquet that ended in a jagged bit of bone.

"I'm sorry," he told one of the world's greatest musicians, who would never again play the guitar.

"Lucia!"

Maria had just finished bandaging up a soldier and only now looked over to see her beloved.

"I'm...okay," Lucia said in a way that suggested she only meant physically. Her eyes were still fixed on El Adiuino.

Jorge gave El Adiuino a potion to reduce the pain, then began his grisly work of cutting down the bone enough to bind the wound.

To distract from the quiet crunching sound, he asked, "How is it going out there?"

"Badly," Lucia said flatly. There was none of her bravado or arrogance.

El Adiuino reached out to her with his one quavering hand. "Do not despair, my child."

"How can I not? The silent hearts of the undead do not heed our magic. We are powerless against them. So long as the empire uses them as a shield, we are like corn falling to the sickle."

He somehow smiled through his pain. "Do you know *all* magic, then, Lucia?"

She shook her head.

"You spoke to me of all the songs yet to be discovered. Find this one now."

Her eyes widened. "But...right now? I—I can't. I'm not prepared."

"What is there to be prepared for?" he asked. "You only sing one note, then listen. Respond to what you hear with the second note, and so on. Call and response. It is as easy as conversation. It is as pure as making love. That is how music is discovered."

Jorge didn't understand what the old man was saying, but he knew that it was important. Perhaps even essential.

"If anyone can do it, you can, Lucia," Jorge told her.

"You *must* do it." Maria pressed her hand to Lucia's cheek.

Lucia closed her eyes and leaned her face into Maria's palm for a moment.

"This was the grace I needed," she said quietly. "Thank you."

Then she straightened, her expression hard despite the tears that now streamed down her face, and she returned to battle.

42

Lucia had not been born to art. Her parents had both been mercenaries in Tormenta Sangre. Art was something she had found on her own, gradually and awkwardly, as one discovers their body during puberty.

Unlike many Viajero, she'd had to fight for her creative expression. When her parents had pushed her to master the sword, she pushed back. They had argued, had fought, had angered and upset each other. Her parents never understood. They had never been proud of her accomplishments, no matter how hard she worked.

And then they died in some pointless battle in Kante.

She had not been angry with the Kantesians for the death of her parents. She had been furious with her parents for perpetuating the rule of the empire. And perhaps she had also been mad that they never acknowledged her.

But now, as she strode across the battlefield, the shouts and screams buffeting her like a storm, she understood that her parents were no more to blame than anyone else. Life brought adversity. Adversity brought art. Art brought faith. Faith brought God. God brought life. And the cycle began again. Beauty could not truly exist without its counterpart of horror. They were both necessary. It was in their opposition that life gained meaning.

Perhaps God had planned Lucia's difficult childhood. Perhaps He had known what was to come and decided that the world would need an artist with the soul of a warrior.

Now she began to sing. It was only one note, but everyone she passed heard it. It reverberated through them, nestling in their chests, calling to them. Calling them to beauty. Calling them to horror. Calling them to arms.

Many who had struck first had now fallen back to rest. But when they heard Lucia's single note, they no longer felt tired. Or rather, their tiredness was necessary to the song. They were all swept up in it and followed her. Those who could sing or play music layered in harmony. Those who could dance leapt forward like gazelles. Those who could paint dragged a trail of swirling color behind them. It was the sound of energy being summoned. The sound of power being collected from across hearts and minds to focus on this one note.

Ahead, a seething clash of Viajero and mercenaries tried desperately to hold the line against the unfeeling, unthinking mass of undead that pressed upon them. Lucia did not slow as she approached. She could feel a spirit welling up within her and it acted like a battering ram, pushing aside all resistance before her. Even in their battle haze, her comrades took one look at the light crackling behind her eyes and stepped aside.

When she reached the front lines, the wall of undead were blown backward. There were countless more to take their place, of course. Others had tried to push back the undead with raw power, and it had failed because the sheer numbers could overwhelm any lone attack.

But this was not an attack. It was a song. And not a rote song with fixed notes that must be played, but one made in the moment to respond to what was happening. It was magical improvisation, and it was as easy as conversation, and as pure as making love.

She could hear it. The call of the undead masters, who Jorge had called the Bhuidseach. It was like music in a way, invisible but thick in the air. It was the response, pushing the undead back toward her. And so she replied directly to the ones making this silent music.

The other performers behind her who had taken up her note were thrown for a moment. This was not, after all, a song they knew. It was a song *no one* knew. But these were the greatest artists of the age, and they understood what was happening in a way that they could not articulate. A new song was being composed even as it was sung. All they had to do was listen, and respond.

The unity of the Viajero response dissolved, and what replaced it was not as forceful, but it was far more resilient. A lattice of passion and emotions, of expression and magic. Improvisational collage whose whole was much stronger than its parts.

The Bhuidseach, only two in number, were not prepared to be met on their own magical terrain, and faltered. Along with them the undead reeled and staggered, no longer focused on one course, but shifting in all directions at once. Some even began to attack the imperial soldiers who had been hiding behind them.

After a few chaotic moments, the Bhuidseach rallied, refocusing their undead charges. But to Lucia, this was not a setback, merely the next line in an ongoing conversation. So she responded to them once more, not stopping them, but asking them to continue, to react, to grow.

Let us make something beautiful and terrible together, her song said.

The mass of undead that covered the land listened to her call, and they replied.

43

Izmoroz was not a land. It was a people. When the empire had conquered it, they had claimed to be magnanimous because they had not dissolved the territory called Izmoroz. But they had banned the religion, the language, the culture. Had it lasted much longer, they would have hollowed out Izmoroz and left only a cold and hard place full of cold and hard people. It was to prevent that possibility from ever happening again that those same people now risked their lives.

Her Majesty, Queen Galina the First, stood on a hilltop and watched the people of Izmoroz bleed at the walls of Magna Alto. She was no warrior, and to put herself in the center of the fray would have been not only pointless but folly. Were she to fall, or be taken prisoner, the entire army might have faltered. So she remained behind, the very image of a warrior queen that would inspire her people to risk their lives for the future of their homeland.

But Galina was more than a mere symbol, of course. She had not trained a group of children as message runners for no reason, and while she was not a warrior, she had studied the writings of the greatest military strategists on the continent. Conveniently, most of them had been Aureumian. So she knew all the enemy tactics and methods, and the majority of the time she could predict their movements. Indeed, the few times they had taken her by surprise was because they had not made the best possible choice in their strategic options and she was initially unprepared for their incompetence.

But despite what certain biographers of past Aureumian command-
ers claimed, battle could not be won on strategy alone. Numbers were
always an element of warfare that could not be denied. No matter
how valiantly her Izmorozians fought to hold the broken portcullis,
they would eventually be worn down by the superior numbers within
the city. The question was whether they could hold out long enough
for the Kantesian reinforcements to arrive.

Their main advantage was the narrowness of the breach. The
imperial forces couldn't swarm them and must instead funnel through
the corridor between the gate and the portcullis, meeting them only
a few at a time. Of course the same was true of the Izmorozian army.
They lined up, those in the back holding up shields to keep off the
rain of arrows from the top of the wall while they cheered on those in
front. Those in front fought furiously beside Andre for as long as they
could, killing as many imperial soldiers as possible before they either
fell back exhausted or died. Then those directly behind them took
their place.

As the line of cheering Izmorozians slowly shrank, Galina's anguish
grew. She had decided to keep Tatiana with her so that the Ranger's
sharp eyes could spot the Kantesians. Then she would immediately
give the command to withdraw, leaving the path open for the giant
metal monsters that she prayed were on their way.

Galina spotted a young girl sprinting up from the rearguard of the
army where her generals were stationed.

"What news?" she demanded.

The girl looked grimy and weary, but there was the unmistakable
cold fire of Izmoroz burning in her eyes.

"We're taking heavy losses, Your Majesty. But a bunch of enemy
archers have fallen back from the wall and the captains can't figure out
why."

Galina considered a moment. The most likely reason would be to
recommit those forces elsewhere. But there was nowhere else to send
them. Unless...

"Tatiana, when you scouted the city walls, did you see another
entrance?"

"No, Your Majesty."

"Just a solid mass of unbroken wall?" pressed Galina.

"Only the wall and the canal."

Galina turned to the canal that emerged from the eastern side of the city. It was only a quarter mile from the gate.

"Tell them to prepare for a ranged attack along their eastern flank!" she said to the girl. "Go now!"

The girl's eyes widened. She must be a bright one if she realized what a terrible position that would put them in, hemmed in with no means of orderly retreat. She quickly saluted, then sprinted back down to the bleeding Izmorozians.

Galina closed her eyes. "Lady Marzanna, I know we've never enjoyed a particularly cordial relationship, but if you can hear me, now would be an excellent time for some divine intervention."

44

People who didn't know Captain Dima Batriov might have referred to him as *jovial*. But those who truly knew him understood that his cheerful demeanor was a desperate and unflagging attempt to drown out the rage that had burned endlessly in his heart since the Winter War.

The war had taken his parents, his brothers and sisters, and as a child soldier, his innocence. The poor, untrained peasants of Izmoroz had stood little chance against the highly disciplined imperial soldiers led by the ruthless Giovanni the Wolf. To even call it a "war" would have been laughable if not for the Rangers of Marzanna, who could take on entire companies of soldiers alone.

Dima was reminded of that now as he watched *Strannik* Andre tear into the enemy like they were delicious rabbits. Blood and gore sprayed in all directions as he ripped out throats and stomachs with claws and teeth. The Ranger laughed and shouted as he slaughtered them, and his rumbling voice gave the rest of the militia courage to fight by his side.

The imperial shield bearers advanced toward the portcullis gap with a wall of iron-bound wood, but Andre grabbed hold of their shields and knocked them to the right or left. As the imperials staggered, they dropped their guard, allowing Dima's fighters to rush in with axes and maces. The enemy corpses began to pile up so high that Captain Stas, unscrupulous former bandit that he was, got the idea to pile them up like a barricade. This forced the imperial soldiers to either take the time to clear the way or else clamber over their fallen comrades.

There were losses on the Izmorozian side as well, of course. Perhaps one for every ten. Those who fell were quickly hauled back and put aside to be returned to Izmorozian soil after the battle was won. And it did seem like they might actually win. Or at least hold out long enough for reinforcements to arrive. A few years ago, Dima would never have believed even this was possible. It had taken a young woman with extraordinary vision to show them all just what Izmorozians could do.

"Captain!"

Dima turned toward the sound of a young girl's voice. Annika, the message runner currently on duty, was sprinting back from the queen's position at the top of the hill. There was a panicked look in her eyes that he didn't like at all.

"What is it?" he called.

The girl pointed down the length of the wall to the canal. "The queen says there'll be an ambush from there any moment now! Archers! She's sure of it!"

Dima cursed under his breath, then shouted, "Dmitry! Bring your shields around!"

But the other captain was clear on the other side of the mass of men and women waiting to take their turn at the front of the line with Ranger Andre and didn't hear him. So Dima shoved his way through until he was within reach, then grabbed Dmitry by the collar.

"Shields! There!"

He pointed to the flank that was exposed to the canal.

Dmitry first looked outraged that he'd been so roughly accosted. Then understanding dawned on his face, followed by dismay.

"Arrow shields!" he yelled at his people. "Shift around, protect our flank!"

The good men and women of the Izmorozian militia had trained as hard as they could in the time they'd been given. But they had not been born soldiers, and most of them had not been seasoned by previous battles. So while they did comply with the command, it was not orderly, or nearly fast enough.

Dima watched as a line of men in gleaming imperial helmets rose from the canal and let fly with a rain of arrows. Several of his people were struck down before Dmitry's shields formed up.

Thankfully, once the shields were in place, the archers in the canal found it much more difficult to reach their targets. The second volley took no more lives. Stas ordered his archers to fall in behind the shields and loose their own volleys. The imperial archers didn't have shields, but they had only to duck behind the canal wall to avoid most of the attack.

If that had been the extent of it, Dima thought they might be able to weather the assault and hold the line. But the imperial infantry, who had been otherwise forced to sit back in the city and helplessly wait their turn, now climbed atop the wall where the archers had been positioned. They didn't have bows, but instead tossed down rocks, glass, and bits of metal. The debris rained down on top of the Izmorozians, injuring some, knocking others unconscious.

"By the goddess, what do we do?" wailed Dmitry, who had never really seen true conflict of any kind before.

"First off, we don't lose our heads," growled Dima. "Shields! This side stay with the archers! You others, form back into a protective canopy!"

Again the inferior training and experience of the Izmorozian militia showed itself as the shield bearers clumsily struggled to comply with this order. And even when they did so, it was far from a perfect solution. They had shelter in both directions, but both were spread too thin to be completely effective. They were slowly getting whittled down from three directions now. If they didn't withdraw soon, there wouldn't be anything left of the Izmorozian militia.

Stas seemed to be thinking the same thing, covering his head as he weaved between shield bearers over to them. "We need to pull back. The gate is lost."

"Wait." Dmitry took hold of Stas's arm. "Do you hear that?"

"What are you talking about?" Dima could hardly hear himself think over the shouting and roaring and dying.

Dmitry's eyes widened into amazement. "It sounds like ... *music*."

The pampered illegitimate noble had clearly cracked and Dima was about to smack him across the face in hopes it might restore his sanity, but then he felt something in his gut. A dark, hot essence filled with a quiet anger. And he realized he *could* hear music, if only just barely.

Then the front of the Izmorozian line shifted back suddenly.

"What's going on up there?" Dima pushed forward, even as his men pushed back.

Finally he reached the front. The corridor between the portcullis and the gate was now completely clear of soldiers. One man stood in the empty space. He was tall and thin, with long black hair and the brown skin of a Raízian. His clothes were filthy and ragged, his face was smudged with grime. But the way he carried himself as he moved within the small space made Dima think immediately of a sharp and gleaming blade. He danced in place, his movements unhurried and precise, and the very air around him gave way, shifting and wavering.

The imperial soldiers cowered at the far side of the corridor, but with all their archers committed to the canal, there was little they could do from such a distance.

Then it seemed they were attacked along their own flank. They yelped in fear, and after wavering for a moment, retreated back into the city.

Their attackers entered the now empty corridor and joined the dancer. They also appeared to be Raízians dressed in rags, some of them holding makeshift instruments, such as a barrel drum or what appeared to be a one-string guitar made from splintered wood and twine.

Stas had come up behind Dima and now whispered to him. "Are they on our side?"

"Goddess, I hope so," muttered Dima.

Then the dancer turned and fixed them with a brilliant smile.

"Ernesto Reyes, former captain of the imperial army, at your service. I presume you are Lady Portinari's allies from Izmoroz? I hope you don't mind if my men and I join you. You see, we've developed quite a strong dislike for Aureumian soldiers these past few months."

45

When the Kantesian army made camp at nightfall on the rolling meadows of central Aureum, Sebastian wondered how he could possibly get to sleep. After all, Galina and the Izmorozian army were likely locked in a deadly struggle to the northwest, while far to the southwest, Sonya's friend Jorge and the Raízians were similarly engaged. And there in the center of the conflict, their mother was still trapped within the palace. It wasn't that Sebastian longed to fight. He had no love of battle anymore, if he ever truly did. But he felt a heavy guilt that he was not able to help them.

He continued to stew about it while he and his sister ate silently before the small fire she had made, and later as he laid out his bedroll.

"I have a question." His sister crouched beside the fire, prodding the glowing coals with the tip of her knife while she spoke. "Do you think it was magic that caused those wrinkles? Or your constant, useless fretting?"

"You are the worst person in the world." He stretched out on his bedroll. "You do know that, right?"

Her fangs gleamed in the flickering firelight as she grinned. "Seriously, though, it's great that you mull things over so much. I'm trying to do that more myself. But I think sometimes it gets in your way."

"Wait, I'm sorry. You mull things over? Since when?"

"Well, *this* me does, anyway."

"What does *that* mean?" he asked.

A haunted look passed through her golden eyes, then she shook her head. "It's dumb. I'm probably wrong."

"Yasha, does this have something to do with what you were asking earlier? About how I could tell which was me and which was Mokosh?"

"I guess. Marzanna said something that I just can't shake. You know every time I die, I change."

"Sure."

"Not just physically, but in every way."

"I remember. Your mind gets more beast-like. That's why I need to look out for you and make sure you don't lose control."

"Well, I wonder if it's more than that. Like, every time I come back, I'm a different person."

"That's silly. Of course you're still you."

"Am I?" she asked. "Think back to the girl you grew up with. Am I still her?"

"I'm not the same boy you grew up with, and I haven't even died yet," he pointed out. "So that doesn't really prove anything."

Sonya gnawed on her lip. "I guess not."

She didn't look convinced, but she also didn't seem interested in discussing it further. They both stared into the dancing fire for a moment.

"Do you think they're okay?" he asked finally.

"Who?" asked Sonya.

He stared at her in astonishment. "*Everyone.* The Izmorozians and Raízians. Your friend Jorge. Mother, Galina, all of them."

"First, I'm sure Mother is fine. She's like winter itself. Nothing can stop her. I bet if Marzanna ever wanted to take a break, Mother could fill in and nobody would notice the difference. Jorge will be okay, too. After all, he has the Viajero and the guilds, with the Xefe to advise him. Plus, he's a lot more sensible than either of us. And if Galina has Andre and Tatiana protecting her, she'll be all right. Although honestly I'm surprised you care what happens to her."

"Of course I care," said Sebastian. "Sure, what she did was cruel. But it's not like I was some perfect person. And as heartless as it was, her choices saved Izmorozian lives. So objectively speaking, she did the right thing."

Sonya again looked skeptical, but chose to remain silent. He was about to remark that this newfound restraint was refreshing, then realized it might make her even more anxious about this bizarre identity paranoia of hers. She was still his sister. Who else would she be?

"We should try to get some sleep," she said finally. "We've still got another full day's march before we reach Magna Alto."

"I really don't know if I can fall asleep," he admitted.

"Try," she said. "Maybe Mokosh can help."

"You're not seriously suggesting I encourage communication with the maker and possible destroyer of all existence, are you?"

"Better that she be *with* us than against us," said Sonya. "Keep in mind, we still don't know what Zivena and her servant can do."

"The Goddess of Spring? I hadn't even thought of her, but I suppose you're right. If this really is some sort of contest between Marzanna and her sister, then presumably Zivena must be aiding the enemy somehow."

"Exactly. So you and the Damp Mother Earth might be what we need to tip the balance in our favor."

"Perhaps," said Sebastian. "It's just…"

How could he possibly articulate the unnerving feeling that had suffused him during that moment in Colmo? A bleak and terrible void beyond darkness and light. It was not for mortal minds to conceive. As much of a toll as magic took on him, he was certain direct exposure to her power was far worse. But perhaps that would be what was required to stop Vittorio. If so, how could he refuse to make that sacrifice?

Sonya gazed solemnly at him and nodded. "I know."

Of course she did. His sister had died and been brought painfully back by the cold, hard hand of winter so many times, surely if anyone understood his dread, it was her.

He lay his head down on the lumpy bedroll and closed his eyes. "Yasha, I'm glad you and I made peace."

"Me too, little brother."

"You're still the worst, though."

"I can live with that."

He listened to her settle in on the other side of the fire, then grow still. It didn't take long for the sounds of a light snore to drift over. It really was amazing how she could do that so quickly. Sebastian, on the other hand, lay there for some time. He stared up into the night for a while, wondering at the dark sky that was dense with stars, and listening to the sporadic noises of the sleeping army that surrounded him.

As he was finally beginning to drift off, he recalled that nightmare of drowning in mud he'd had when they first arrived in Kante. But oddly enough, it didn't seem frightening this time. If anything, there was a strange sort of comfort in the heavy seeping mass that suffused him. And just like when he'd once called lava forth from beneath the earth, he could feel what lay beneath the surface of the ground under him. His senses spread through the rock and soil below like an extension of his body. It was as if he could touch the many lives above and below, near and far...

And something else.

Something coming fast.

It was not human, but it radiated a familiar sort of magic. Or at least, part of it did. There seemed to be two different kinds of magic overlapping each other.

"Yasha! Something's coming!"

As quickly as she'd fallen asleep, Sonya was wide awake. Her knife was back in her hand and her fox eyes were scanning the night. Her ears twitched and she laid the side of her head to the ground.

"Something fast and heavy," she confirmed. "Coming from the direction of Magna Alto. You rouse the camp. I'll go check it out."

46

It had been far too long since Sonya had seen real action. She sprinted across the dark meadows, feeling the hunger that had dogged her during the slow journey west now at a fever pitch. She wished she could have brought Peppercorn, but while the moon was nearly full, even her fox eyes might not discern every divot or hole at night, and she could not chance injuring her precious *Perchinka*.

But this felt good, too. A pounding heart and pumping lungs made her blood surge. She told herself not to get too worked up. After all, it might be an ally. The tread had sounded like metal, so it could be a golem. Although it didn't sound big enough...

Regardless, it could be a message from the Kantesian golem force that had gone ahead of them. She wasn't sure just how much distance they could cover so perhaps they had already reached Magna Alto and were sending word back to the Herzog of their status.

She was nearly silent as she ran, so it wasn't difficult to pick up the rhythmic muffled pounding of metal on grass. And then it glinted in the moonlight.

It was shinier than other golems she'd seen, as though the metal had been carefully polished to a decorative brightness. And it was human-shaped. She didn't even know they could be made in human shapes. Although it was larger than a real human, perhaps ten feet high. And it was carrying an odd bundle under one arm. A bundle that looked somewhat like a person.

Sonya veered to one side to get a better look at the bundle, but the golem turned as well. Only now as it bore down on her did she wonder if it could be a rogue golem. Did the Kantesians ever lose control of them?

She came to a halt and nocked an arrow to her bow. She knew it probably wouldn't be much of a threat to a golem, but what else could she do?

As if in response, the golem slowed down to a walk. Now that it was closer, Sonya saw that it was indeed carrying a person, although they appeared to be limbless. And she recognized their scent from somewhere.

"Hello?" she called.

The shaggy head lifted and she stared into the scarred face of Elgin Mordha, warlord of the Uaine.

"Tighearna?"

"Ah, Bhuidseach Sonya. I wondered if she might be drawn to you."

"She?"

Despite its size, the golem did have a distinctly feminine shape. And as it drew closer, the face seemed familiar somehow, as though...

The hot surge of the hunt died in her veins, to be replaced by a cold, sick dread.

It couldn't be.

And yet, as it drew near, the face was unmistakable.

Sonya's voice was little more than a whisper. "Mother?"

The slit that served as a mouth to her mother's metallic countenance produced a puff of steam, and its magenta eyes flared. It continued toward her, extending one hand. Sonya stood stock-still as it approached. At last it reached her and gently placed its hand on her cheek.

"Mordha..." Sonya's voice was thick. "What happened?"

"Terrible things."

"Mother..." Sonya was just able to touch her mother's chilled, gleaming chin. "Oh, Mother..."

When had she seen her mother last? It had been that cold, bitter day in Gogoleth after her brother had told her he'd joined the imperial army. Sonya had recklessly leapt from the city wall into a hay-filled cart some sixty feet below. Likely already dying from internal injuries, she had then tracked down her mother only to discover she did not need rescuing, either. They had not seen each other in half a year but it had not been a warm reunion.

Because Sonya had refused to let it become one.

Her mother had said, *You are welcome to stay here. At least until your injuries heal. Or as long as you like.* And ill-tempered snot that she'd been, Sonya had replied, *I would not like to stay here at all.* That had been the last thing she'd said to her.

Sonya's golden eyes brimmed. "Mother, I'm so sorry."

The golem carefully stroked the white fur on her head and Sonya closed her eyes, letting the tears fall.

"I am sorry as well, wee *sionnach*," said Mordha. "I have failed us all."

"What do you mean?"

"I sought to free us from the will of the gods." Mordha's command of the imperial tongue was clearly much better than he had ever let on. "And my hubris might be the undoing of us all. Perhaps if there was some way that I could tell my people to break our alliance with the empire, it would be different. But as you can see, I am now at the mercy of whatever it is your mother has become. So it seems our people are doomed to kill each other, just as the gods desire."

Sonya's eyes widened. "Actually, Mordha, I think we can get word to your people. Maybe it's not too late."

47

After Lucia left, Jorge noticed that the influx of grievously wounded began to slow. Those who did arrive spoke reverently of Lucia leading the Viajero in some new, never before heard song that threw the sluagh gorta into chaos. Jorge had not even known it was possible to disrupt the control that the Urram Le Bàs exerted on the undead. Perhaps it hadn't been until now.

So after what seemed endless hours of work, Jorge was finally able to rest for a short period. He sat down and gratefully accepted a cup of wine from Maria.

"Have you been keeping a bottle from the Elhuyar cellars in reserve?"

"Fortune favors the prepared," she said.

"I'm not sure that's how the saying goes, but I don't disagree with the sentiment."

But he only took a few sips before Onat Duman burst into the tent. Jorge had never seen the Victashian so excited. Typically nothing short of potentially world-changing news ever got a rise out of him.

"There you are, thank the gods!"

"What's the matter now?" Jorge asked uneasily.

"No, this is *good* news!" said Duman. "I've just received word from Ambassador Boz that the leader of the Uaine wants his people to call off their assault!"

"What on earth are you talking about? And how did you *just get word* when we're in the middle of a battle?"

It took Duman a moment to calm himself before he could reply. "Yes, forgive me, Representative Elhuyar. My enthusiasm got the better of me. I have been given permission to tell you…" Now he glanced at the wounded who lay in their cots, most of them only semi-conscious from pain and potions. "Perhaps it would be better if—"

"Please just get on with it," Jorge said.

"Very well. Ambassador Boz possesses magic that enables her to communicate directly with us over great distances."

"How astonishing," said Maria. "I've never heard of such a thing."

Duman looked amused. "Naturally not, Señorita. Anyway, the ambassador has informed me that Elgin Mordha just reached the main Kantesian army with news that he was betrayed by Vittorio."

"I can't say I'm surprised," said Jorge.

"Apparently, in the struggle, the poor man lost all four of his limbs."

"How horrid!" said Maria.

"It's probably about the only thing that would stop Mordha," said Jorge.

"Regardless," said Duman, "he has asked us to get word to his people here that they are to stop aiding the imperial army immediately. He mentioned that there were two here who you knew personally. Bhuidseach Rowena Viridomarus and Captain Blaine Ruairc?"

"Yes," Jorge said gravely.

"Would they recognize you on sight?"

"Certainly."

"Then by all means, we must locate them and ask them to deliver the message to their comrades! This could be a pivotal turning point not merely in the battle, but in the war!"

Duman's eyes sparkled with delight, and Jorge wondered if he didn't thrive on the chaos of it all.

"I suppose we must try," he said as he got wearily to his feet.

"If you're going out into the battlefield, you need an escort," Maria said firmly. "I think I can manage here, but I insist you find the Xefe and ask for some men to keep you safe before you do anything else."

"A wise precaution," murmured Duman in a manner that suggested he found the delay a little frustrating.

"Very well."

Jorge knew he should be more excited by this news. Duman was right. This could mean the difference between victory and defeat. And yet, he was so tired. He also felt a dark dread at the thought of confronting Blaine and Rowena, which weighed him down even more than exhaustion. As petty and selfish as it seemed, there was a part of his worn-out heart that almost hoped he was killed before he reached them.

He trudged beside the giddy Victashian as they made their way to the command tent. There were Javier and the rest of the guild leaders, barking orders to their captains and arguing with each other over who should do what when. When Jorge asked for a small group to defend him as he scoured the battlefield, the Xefe looked at him like he was mad.

"Absolutely not. We can't endanger the national representative like that."

"I'm afraid we don't have much choice," said Jorge. "We need to convince the Uaine that Mordha wants them to switch sides, and I'm the only one they would at least trust enough not to kill on sight."

Javier gritted his teeth so fiercely, Jorge could hear the squeak. "Do they know what a white flag means?"

"I'm not sure the Uaine even know what the word 'truce' means."

Javier muttered curses under his breath. It seemed like it might go on like that for some time, and with each passing moment, there were more needless deaths. So although he was so fatigued he thought he could lie down and sleep right there on the dusty ground, Jorge drew himself up with sudden firmness.

"I'm sorry if I was unclear, Javier. This is not a request but an order."

Javier stopped in his tirade and gave him an amazed look. "Very well, Representative. On your own head be it."

Soon Jorge and Duman were headed for the front lines surrounded by a group of hardened, veteran mercenaries. Jorge was no stranger to armed escorts of course, but this was not the parade-like displays of Colmo. It was tight and quiet and grim. They moved swiftly, weaving through groups of mercenaries and Viajero coming or going. As they drew closer to the battle, Jorge could hear a haunting melody that cast an almost palpable aura to the air around them.

"Is this what Lucia's using to keep the undead at bay?"

"It's rather striking," Duman said distractedly.

There was no clear line between anxious battle preparation and the chaos of battle itself. One moment they were amid a group of jostling Serpentas Roxas mercenaries tightening their straps and loosening their swords, and the next moment they were surrounded by men in imperial uniforms trying to kill them.

The famous shield and spear lines of the imperial army had broken into clusters that would advance and surround small groups of Raízians. Meanwhile, cavalry darted in and out with flashing sabers. Everywhere Jorge turned was noise and screams and havoc.

"Stay close, Señor!" shouted his protectors, and he was happy to oblige. But there were so many imperials. Too many, it seemed. How could there be this many? He knew the numbers. His scouts had reported them before the battle began. But ten thousand men looked much different up close. He felt lost in a sea of bristling violence, helpless and horror-struck. Whatever dread he'd felt about reuniting with estranged friends seemed laughably trivial now, as did anything that did not contribute in that moment to his survival.

One of his protectors went down and an imperial soldier rushed into the gap. But Jorge was surprised to see Duman pick up the fallen mercenary's sword and deftly fend off the intruder. The Victashian glanced over at him with a tight grin.

"I confess I miss this!" he yelled over the din as he knocked aside a spear, then thrust his sword into the attacker's neck.

"You're mad!" said Jorge.

Duman laughed in response.

But as their small escort slowly, painfully made its way deeper into the fray, Jorge realized that it was he who was mad for thinking this could have ever worked. The haze of exhaustion must have combined with a desperate hope and the urging of a clearly battle-crazed Victashian to prevent Jorge from thinking clearly. The Xefe had been right to discourage it. How on earth had he ever thought he could find Blaine or Rowena in the thick of this deadly mayhem?

Another mercenary fell, so the escort tightened even more until Jorge was pressed up against their backs. If not for Duman, it likely would have already been over. But though he clearly had skill from some past experience as a warrior, his recent life as a diplomat had not kept him in shape. So while he was grinning from ear to ear, he was drenched in sweat and panting.

"Should we retreat?" Jorge shouted over the din.

"Forward or back, it makes no difference now," said one of the mercenaries.

Bristling walls of shield and spear bore down on them from all sides. There was nothing but roars and heat and the clang of metal. Jorge thought it was very likely the end.

Then a line of shields shook and pitched forward. A massive broadsword flashed as it hewed into the unprotected backs of the imperial soldiers. Blood and screams erupted as the men fell. Standing behind them, his chest heaving and his bearded face streaked in blood, was Blaine.

"I hope you know that person," said Duman.

"Let him through!" shouted Jorge.

The mercenaries quickly parted to let the Uaine in, then closed ranks behind him.

"Thank God you're here!" said Jorge, his voice shaking with relief.

Blaine reached out as if to embrace him, glanced at the Raízian mercenaries, and stopped himself. "Sorry, I know you don't—"

"Shut up and kiss me!" commanded Jorge.

At one point in his boyhood, Jorge had begun kissing other boys until his mother scolded him for it. But he had never kissed a man before. It was very different. In fact, as their bodies pressed together and Blaine's bearded lips pressed against his, Jorge thought he could probably write an entire treatise on the difference. Maybe it was the shock and fear and sheer exhaustion, but the sweat-slick firmness of Blaine's lips was a rough comfort he could not describe in words. The way his strong hands gripped his back was more soothing than any hug.

This was what Javier meant, he thought distractedly as his arms circled around Blaine's thick neck.

This was love, and it was worth anything.

But this was also war, and as poor El Adiuino had reminded them the day before, *Moments must be fleet of foot in turbulent times lest they be lost entirely.*

So Jorge forced himself to step back from the healing embrace of this man that he had undoubtably fallen in love with that night they'd danced around the roaring Dannsair.

"Blaine," he said. "The Uaine have been betrayed."

48

Rowena had not felt pain like this since the trial to become Death Touched. Her connection to the sluagh gorta, which usually felt like an extension of her body, had been choked off. It was as though her leg had fallen asleep but no matter how much she shook or massaged it, the feeling did not return.

The undead milled around her in confusion, struggling to obey two competing orders. If she eased off, she knew her discomfort would lessen, but it might also mean total loss of control over her army.

"Rowena..."

She turned and saw the Bhuidseach of Clan Seacál stagger toward her, blood running from her nose.

"What...is happening?"

"The Viajero have found a way to override our control," Rowena said grimly. "That song you hear in the background. That's what's causing it."

"A *song*?" Sorcha asked in disbelief.

"Did you listen to *anything* I told you about our enemy?"

"Yes, but I didn't think...it could be so strong..."

"It is a test of wills," Rowena said grimly. "We cannot fail."

"Bhuidseach Rowena!" bellowed the voice of Albion Ruairc, chief of her clan. He shoved through the crowds of motionless undead toward her, a look of fury on his weathered face.

"Hail, Chief Ruairc," Rowena said wearily.

"What is the meaning of this?" he demanded.

"The enemy is attempting to wrest control of the sluagh gorta," she said.

His eyes bulged. "They can *do* that?"

She clenched her teeth to keep from insulting her chief. Which was more painful? The attack on her army or the dullness of her countrymen? Finally she managed, "Your concern is understandable, but your interruption is detrimental."

That brought him up short. "Oh, I see. Well…"

He looked around uneasily at the mass of sluagh gorta that surrounded them, as though suddenly realizing the resource he had always taken for granted could turn on him at any moment. They were currently insulated from the bulk of the fighting between the imperial soldiers and Raízians, but if Rowena and Sorcha lost this contest of wills, they would suddenly find themselves in far worse danger.

In a more conciliatory tone, he said, "Is there anything I can do to help?"

"Leave me to my efforts," she said.

"Er, yes, of course."

Albion, much like his sons, was a man of passion, honor, and perhaps not enough sense. Also like them, he trusted his comrades.

"Very well. We shall see you are not disturbed. May Bàs be with you."

The farewell was automatic. No more than an afterthought of prayer. But as soon as Rowena heard those words, she knew what she must do.

"Sorcha, I'm going to reconsecrate."

"Be serious!" said Sorcha.

"I am."

"Neither of us is in any condition to do something like that right now."

"I need you to shoulder the entire weight while I do it."

"But—"

"Sorcha. If we lose this, we lose everything. Do you understand?"

Sorcha dabbed at the blood leaking from her nose. Her pale skin was almost gray, and Rowena probably looked no better. It was two of them against who knew how many Viajero. They would not last unless drastic action was taken.

Finally the other Bhuidseach nodded. "This better work, oh favored of the Tighearna."

"Yes, it had better," agreed Rowena. "Ready?"

Sorcha nodded.

Rowena loosened her hold on the sluagh gorta and Sorcha almost fell to her knees. She grunted, her lips curled back to show her teeth.

"Sorcha, will you be able—"

"I'm fine!"

Rowena nodded. No matter their differences, it would not do to question the resolve of a fellow Bhuidseach. So she left the weight of their undead army in the hands of her comrade, drew her knife, and cut deep into her palm. Then she reached out and pressed her bleeding hand to the forehead of the nearest sluagh gorta.

"Hear me, dread Bàs. I beg audience so that I might renew my vows of old."

The corpse's glassy eyes suddenly took on a look of sharp, menacing cunning, and its lipless mouth twisted into a grin. Before Rowena could move, its desiccated hand shot out and gripped her throat. Rowena could feel bony fingers pressing on her windpipe. It could kill her instantly, if that was Bàs's wish.

"At last my most ungrateful one comes before me in supplication," the corpse said. "Such power I gave you, yet your hate for me never fades."

"My hatred for you is beside the point."

Even weighed down with holding the army, Sorcha gasped at Rowena's admission of hatred for their god.

But the corpse only nodded. "True. In fact, it is part of your charm. But now you seek even *more* power from me. And what could you possibly give me in return?"

"I will entreat the Tighearna to give up his plot of vengeance against you."

Rowena had never seen a corpse laugh before, and even she who had never shrunk from a sluagh gorta found it disturbing.

"My dear, willful child. Has your feeble mortal mind not grasped that while you have been in the throes of battle, the solstice has come and gone? And if you are still talking to me, what could that mean for your precious Tighearna?"

Bàs was right. Rowena hadn't even realized it, but the hour had passed during these terrible and excruciating days.

"He has failed...," she whispered.

"Not at all!" said the corpse. "He did exactly as I wished and I am quite pleased with him, just as I always have been."

Rowena felt cold in a way that not even this cursed Raízian sun could dissipate. Bàs had meant for all of this to happen. Their "rebellion" had been nothing more than one of his machinations.

"You have also fulfilled your role admirably," continued the God of Death. "So I think I shall reward you with a choice."

"What choice?" Rowena asked warily. Bàs was famous for choices in which neither option was desirable.

"Give up, let the Raízians take control of your beloved sluagh gorta, flee with the few survivors back to your own lands, and *perhaps* the Uaine will not become extinct until after your death."

"Don't pick *that* one!" said Sorcha. "Whatever the other one is, it can't be worse."

"What *is* the other option?" asked Rowena.

"I will grant you the power you seek, and the Uaine will survive the centuries, perhaps rising to a glory you can scarce imagine. But the price for both your people and you will also be like nothing you can currently conceive."

"Will it cost the lives of the two people to whom I have sworn an oath?"

The corpse smiled again, seeming to find this question amusing. "No."

"Then I accept."

"Ah, my sweet beloved of entropy." The corpse drew her close, so their faces were only inches apart. "You make me so proud."

Then the corpse pressed its lipless mouth to her forehead, and her mind opened.

Past, present, future. Space in all its directions. She saw and understood it in a way that she had never known. And to see it so encapsulated, she was able to see beyond it. The void that howled around them. The unlife that clawed at the edges of reality. The chaos to which all things eventually returned.

"Allow me to introduce my mother," the corpse whispered into Rowena's ear. "And her precious gift."

Small—so small it could have been a single fish in the vastness of the ocean—that was existence. Not one person, or one people, but *all* of it. Every life and every death, every moment of passion and suffering, from the beginning of time to the end, was all contained in that single speck. What was one life in the scope of that? What was one nation? What, in the end, was even one god?

"This, my beloved of entropy, is called perspective."

Rowena seized up. No mortal was made to conceive of such a thing. Her mind could not bear the weight, and it fractured.

Bàs, God of Death and Change, then gathered up all the pieces and put them back together. Though certainly not as they had been.

"Farewell, my daughter. See the world this way, now and forever, and await a new dawn that will surely come upon the heels of catastrophe."

The cunning look in the corpse's eyes faded and it released its grip on Rowena's throat. She stood there, immobile, her eyes seemingly staring at nothing, yet twitching as though seeing everything at once.

"Rowena?" Sorcha's voice was harsh, and she was hunched over, hands on her knees as though ready to buckle. "Tell me that worked."

"What worked?" Rowena asked absently, her eyes not easing from their vibrating trance.

"Getting control of the sluagh gorta again."

"Oh. Right."

The entire army of sluagh gorta immediately froze in place, no longer milling or conflicted. In the same moment, the song that had been causing so much conflict abruptly cut off.

"Thank Bàs," sighed Sorcha as she straightened. "Now let's kill these people so we can leave this heat-cursed land."

But Rowena still stared at seemingly nothing, and the sluagh gorta did not resume their attack.

"Rowena!" Chief Ruairc tried to reach them, but he could no longer push past the sluagh gorta. Each one was as immovable as a stone pillar. "Is everything okay?"

"Okay?" Rowena's eyes remained locked on some invisible target.

Sorcha stared at her fellow Bhuidseach a moment, then called back to Chief Ruairc. "We have control of the sluagh gorta again, but I think something is wrong with Rowena."

"Nothing is wrong with me," Rowena said almost dreamily. "Unless you mean something is wrong with everything. In which case, I am one of those things, and then you would be correct."

Sorcha stared at her. "*What?*"

"Ah, they have arrived." Rowena finally shifted her eyes to the battlefield. As she did so, the sluagh gorta parted as smartly as trained soldiers, leaving a long corridor. At the end of the corridor, looking very surprised, were Blaine, Jorge, and a Victashian man she did not know.

"Come forward, ones beloved by Bàs." Rowena beckoned to them.

Looking hesitant and confused, they began to walk the length of the corpse-lined passageway.

Chief Ruairc still couldn't get any closer, so he shouted, "Son, is that the enemy commander you have captured?"

"I have captured no one, Father," Blaine said grimly.

When they reached Rowena, Jorge said, "Rowena, are you okay?"

"Everyone asks this." Rowena seemed bemused. "It is a nonsensical question."

Blaine and Jorge exchanged a confused look. Then Jorge drew himself up. "Rowena, I have a message from Tighearna Elgin Mordha. While I know that sounds impossible—"

"Let me hear it."

Again Blaine and Jorge looked at each other with something like confusion.

The Victashian said, "I think it would be simplest if she were to speak with him directly."

"You can do that?" asked Jorge.

The Victashian nodded, then removed the amulet from around his neck. "Honored Bhuidseach, I am Onat Duman of Victasha. May I approach?"

"You may," said Rowena.

"What are you doing?" hissed Sorcha. "Isn't this the enemy?"

Rowena looked genuinely baffled. "Do these seem like the servants of Beatha to you?"

"Who's talking about damned Beatha?" Sorcha demanded.

"Sorcha!" called Chief Ruairc. "What in the name of Bàs is going on?"

"I have no idea!"

"Well, stop it from happening!"

Sorcha's expression hardened and she turned to the nearest sluagh gorta. "Stop him."

It ignored her.

Her eyes widened. "How is this possible?"

"Your will is like a faint whisper it can barely discern," said Rowena.

Sorcha's expression darkened. "I have no idea what's happened to you. You were always a pain, but now you're insufferable, I will—"

A sluagh gorta took her arm. She stared down at it like she couldn't believe it was real. "Unhand me!"

It continued to hold her fast.

"Sorcha!" Now the other chief, Conaill, was with Ruairc. "What has happened to our army?"

"I don't know!" Sorcha tried to free herself from the grasp of the sluagh gorta but could not. "It's Rowena. Somehow she's taken total control of all of them! They won't even listen to me now!"

Onat Duman reached Rowena and knelt before her. He held out the amulet and said, "Put this around your neck and touch the metal to speak to your warlord."

Rowena did as she was told.

"My Tighearna?"

There was a long pause, and then:

Rowena. I have been a fool.

"No, my Tighearna. You have done exactly as you were expected."

That does not give me comfort.

"I suppose not."

Something has happened to you.

"I have ensured the survival of our people as you commanded, but in the process my mind has been altered in a way that you cannot comprehend."

There was a pause. *The work of Bàs?*

"Correct. He has named me daughter, and beloved of entropy."

Is that so? Then . . . what happens now?

"I serve you as ever, mighty Tighearna."

Very well. I have a different sort of vengeance in mind. One that is perhaps a little more attainable.

"And what is that?"

The total obliteration of Vittorio and his beloved Aureum.

"It will be done, my Tighearna."

Beatha may try to intercede.

"I am ready."

Rowena removed the amulet and handed it back to Duman. "Message received."

"Oh?" Duman asked nervously. "And . . . what did you speak of?"

She looked amused. "It was a private message."

Duman stared at her. "Ah."

"Now, shall we kill these Aureumians? I never did care much for them, and it seems they have offended my Tighearna."

49

One might think that someone as methodical and pragmatic as Galina Odoyevtseva would dislike surprises. But just as a warrior's blood surged with the thrill of imminent violent contact, Galina felt an undeniable rush when confronted with a new and unexpected challenge. Of course, some surprises were more welcome than others.

Initially, she had not been sure how much the ragged-looking troupe of Raízian deserters could contribute. There were only twenty of them, after all. But then, she had never seen hardened veteran Viajero in action before. These men were not only capable of powerful magic that far outstripped the Raízian touring shows she'd seen as a child, they knew the battle strategies of the Aureumians even more intimately than she. And apparently, they were also extremely cross with their one-time allies.

She wished she could view the conflict more closely. From such a distance, with the sky darkening and the majority of the action concealed by the standby troops, there was little she could discern on her own. Dima was not a wordsmith and the updates he sent were lacking in all but the most basic details. "Magics blasted imperial shelters" and "music knocked them insensible" was about as good as it got.

"Surely we could get a *little* closer, Anya," she said to the Ranger as they watched from their hilltop.

"With respect, Your Majesty, you are too important to place in unnecessary danger."

Galina sighed. "Very well." She was not unreasonable, and Tatiana was doing exactly what she had been instructed to do.

"I am certain the Viajero will be only too happy to perform an encore for you at a later date, Your Majesty," said Sezai Bey as he approached from the supply camp set back on the far side of the hill.

"Representative Bey. Any news?"

"Representative Elhuyar says Raíz will march north at dawn."

"They've defeated the Aureumians already?"

"Apparently one of the Urram Le Bàs, Bhuidseach Rowena, has developed a new rapport with the sluagh gorta that grants her absolute control over them." He gave her a pained smile. "Frankly, I was disturbed to learn that previously they did *not* have complete control over their horde of undead."

"Yes, unfortunately the countryside of Izmoroz can bear witness to the imprecise nature of their power," Galina said. "Is it only Bhuidseach Rowena who has attained this ability?"

"So it would seem."

"That is good news," said Galina. "I found Rowena to be the most reasonable of the necromancers."

"It's good news so long as they remain our allies," agreed Bey. "Toward that end, Representative Elhuyar inquired if we have some way to get in contact with the Uaine here at the palace. Apparently, most of the sluagh gorta were sent to Raíz, but the bulk of their living force is likely still stationed in Magna Alto."

"We haven't seen even a glimpse of them yet. Perhaps Vittorio is keeping them in reserve at the palace. Were I able to get a message to Angelo Lorecchio, it's possible we could head off a confrontation with them, and perhaps even gain allies behind enemy lines. But I can't see how that would even be feasible until reinforcements arrive and we take the city."

Bey nodded. "The arrival of Mordha and what we take to be Lady Irina Turgenev has delayed the main Kantesian force somewhat. But the Herzog estimates that the golem detachment should arrive before midnight."

"Without those Raízians, I fear we might have already fallen," said

Galina. "A serious strategic error on my part. In retrospect, it would have been wiser to hold off our attack and let them seal the breach."

"It was a difficult call to make, Your Majesty, and as it turned out, luck was on our side."

She gave him an arch look. "I don't believe in luck, Representative. And while I generally don't put much trust in deities either, I can't help but wonder if my last-minute plea for assistance fell on sympathetic ears."

"Either way—" began Bey.

"And in my experience," continued Galina with a significant glance toward Tatiana, "divine aid comes at a hefty price."

"Ah," said Bey. "I suppose we'll just have to see what it ends up costing us."

"Indeed."

The sky darkened into night as the focused battle continued to rage at the broken portcullis. Little was said during that anxious period, aside from Galina's terse responses to message runners dispatched by Dima.

Finally, she turned to Tatiana. "How much longer do you think Andre can continue on the front lines?"

Tatiana considered for a moment. "During the Winter War, Andre, Anatoly, and I once held Bear Shoulder Pass for three days. We finally ran out of food and had to fall back, allowing the imperial forces to reach Gogoleth the next day. It was...the beginning of the end, I think. We all bear that failure heavily in our hearts."

"I would hardly call three people holding an entire imperial army at a standstill for three days a failure, Anya," said Galina.

Tatiana gazed at her with those unreadable owl eyes for a moment. "Not people, Your Majesty. Rangers. And in the end, as impressive as it might have seemed, it still amounted to nothing. Even then we lacked your clever mind."

"We each have our part to play, Tatiana Sova. And now that night has fallen, I need you to keep watch for our first wave of reinforcements from the southeast."

"Yes, Your Majesty."

But a few hours later, as her beloved Izmoroz still fought to hold every inch, it was sound, rather than nocturnal vision, that signaled the arrival of reinforcements. Tatiana's head cocked to one side, then she dropped to the ground and pressed her ear to the earth.

"Something is coming." she said. "Something loud and heavy. Metal. Magic."

"At last." Galina signaled to one of the message runners on standby.

"Your Majesty!" This time Luka remembered his salute immediately.

"Tell Dima it's time to fall back. Help has arrived, and I don't think we want to get in their way."

"Yes, Your Majesty!"

"And ask him to send this Reyes fellow to me so that I can thank him in person."

"As you command!"

Luka scurried off down the hill.

"That lemming has grown since we found him making useless fishing lures," observed Tatiana.

"In more ways than one," agreed Galina.

Soon her troops began to withdraw from the portcullis. As expected, the imperial soldiers pursued, thinking they were pressing an advantage. Meanwhile, Galina was finally able to perceive the coming reinforcements. First as a sound, or perhaps as a feeling—a slight tremor that might have been undetectable if you weren't waiting for it. But it grew into a harsh rumbling that was like nothing else Galina had ever heard.

Then came the eyes. A cluster of searing magenta in the night. They looked to Galina like wounded stars that had fallen from the sky. They bobbed slightly as they drew near. Once they were closer, she could hear the groaning hiss that had been described to her, a truly unnerving sound that suggested an inhuman suffering.

At last the moonlight revealed their monstrous shapes. They truly did appear to be giant mechanical insects that carved up the soft grassy meadows as they moved swiftly toward the city.

Her soldiers had been told what to expect, but even so, a visible shudder ran through them as the golems approached. A harsh shout from Dima held them together and they quickly retreated back to camp.

The imperial troops who have given chase did not fare as well. Their orderly lines gave away to pandemonium as the horrible creatures trampled them like so many ants underfoot, not even pausing as they headed toward the portcullis.

"I never thought I'd see one of those again, much less a herd of them," remarked a melodious male voice.

Galina had been so taken with the awesome and ghastly sight of the golems that she hadn't even noticed the Raízian approach. He was a tall man, with the lean, muscled build she would have expected from a dancer. Even though he was dressed in rags, there was something elegant in his bearing that would never have allowed her to describe him as *common.*

"Ernesto Reyes, I presume?"

He bowed with a grace she doubted few could match. "And your evident majesty leaves no room for doubt that you are indeed queen of the Izmorozians."

"I confess I have met few Raízians. Are most of them as charming and gallant as yourself?"

"Most try, Your Majesty, though I cannot say how well they succeed."

She smiled. "I wish to convey my heartfelt thanks for your timely assistance, as does Representative Elhuyar."

"Representative Elhuyar?" asked Reyes. "It seems I have missed much during my captivity."

"I hope there will be time to fill you in later, but I'm afraid now I must return my attention to the battle. While the golems wreak havoc on the field, I must conduct my brave warriors to recover what strength they can before we push into the city. The remainder of the Kantesian army should arrive tomorrow, and your Raízian army, along with a force of allied Uaine, should be here in two days' time. That way, should the battle become protracted, we can count on additional reinforcements."

"Your strategy appears flawless, my queen," said Reyes. "Victory sounds practically guaranteed."

"Do not be so sure of that. Given the wily nature of our opponent, and his probable supernatural aid, I suspect your unplanned assistance is not the last surprise we will encounter. And the next one might not be so pleasant."

50

J ust as Galina had anticipated, the tide of the battle shifted dramatically once the golems arrived. The metal monsters were so tall that they could even clamber over the massive walls of Magna Alto, and suddenly nowhere in the city was safe for the imperial army or its people. Resistance collapsed within hours.

"I don't like this," she declared as she rode through the dark and empty city, or what was left of it, accompanied by both Rangers, Sezai Bey, and Captain Reyes.

"You mean the destruction of this fine metropolis, Your Majesty?" asked Reyes, his soulful eyes filled with compassion.

It *was* quite a lot of destruction. The golems, it seemed, were blunt instruments similar to the sluagh gorta. In their attack on the city, they had smashed into anything that got in their way, and even the sturdiest of buildings crumbled beneath their awesome might. To think such a formidable force had lurked for so long just on the other side of the mountains. And that the empress had possessed the gall to provoke it. Galina resolved to learn as much as she could about these Kantesians and establish a pact of nonaggression with them as soon as the war was over.

But despite the impressive amount of rubble strewn about what had evidently once been the central square of Magna Alto, that hadn't been the cause of her displeasure.

"No, Ernesto, I dislike not being able to reliably assess Vittorio's current strategy. For all his manly bluster, he is a crafty viper at heart.

Why fall back to the palace, where he and his remaining forces will be trapped? Even if we did not have vast reinforcements on the way, does he really think he could outlast us in a siege when we've already gained access to the city's storehouses? It would have been wiser to flee the city with his remaining forces rather than make some sort of last stand."

"Maybe there is no strategy, Your Majesty," said Andre. "His actions could be born of desperation."

"That's possible, of course. But not something I want to count on. Besides, Vittorio still has two formidable elements in reserve. The Uaine who did not travel south remain unseen. And Mordha has confirmed our suspicion that Vittorio formed some sort of pact with the goddess Zivena. Who knows what sort of mischief a goddess might have in store. No, we cannot afford to consider this battle won quite yet, so be on your guard."

"Yes, Your Majesty." Andre bowed his furry head.

Farther into the city they met up with the golems, standing in a line, silent and still except for the occasional puff of steam from their glowing eyes. Beneath them stood a group of men and women dressed in rough wool robes.

"These must be the hexenmeisters the ambassador spoke of," said Bey. "Their grasp of your language is tenuous, and now would not be an ideal time for misunderstandings. Please allow me to make introductions, Your Majesty."

"Gladly," said Galina.

Bey called out to the robed group in a sharp, guttural language that was unlike anything she had ever heard. The Kantesian hexenmeisters presented an interesting image. Their tone was cordial but cool. Even without knowing what they were saying, Galina got the impression that they would be easy to work with, perhaps even pleasant, but that they were unlikely to ever let down their guard. That was fine with Galina, of course, who valued reasonable allies far more than passionate but unpredictable friends.

Bey turned to Galina, his expression a little pained. "They have … *informed* me that they will not press on to the palace until the remainder of their force arrives, Your Majesty."

"That's fine," said Galina. "While it's tempting to press our advantage, we have little to lose and much to gain by taking a more cautious approach. With the casualties we've already sustained, we are much more suited to keeping the enemy pinned down until the full might of the Kantesian army arrives tomorrow. That, combined with the addition of the Raízian army a day later, will hopefully be enough to counter whatever scheme Vittorio is plotting behind the walls of his palace. Please convey my approval to the hexenmeisters and suggest that we work together during this time to set up fortifications, should Vittorio launch a counterattack before our reinforcements arrive."

"Yes, Your Majesty." Bey turned back to the hexenmeisters and spoke once more in their guttural tongue. After a short exchange, he turned back to Galina. "They suggest we begin setting up a barricade immediately. Their golems can do the heavy lifting, of course, but the more precise work will fall to us."

"I understand perfectly, and look forward to working with the hexenmeisters."

The barricades were set up in short order, followed by encampments for her army and the Raízians. As they all settled down to some well-deserved nourishment and rest, the Kantesians kept mostly to themselves, apparently preferring the company of the silent, hulking metal monsters, which had been stationed on the road leading up to the palace in case Vittorio tried to flee in the night.

Galina was pleased to find that the Raízians got along well with her Izmorozians. There was joking and laughter, and more than a little showing off. Their behavior got a bit rowdy at times, but Galina understood that it was both a way for them to express the fear and anguish they'd experienced in battle, as well as a sign their spirits were high, thinking the end of this conflict was already in sight.

Galina did not dissuade them of this idea, but she did give her captains the same cautionary words she had shared with her Rangers and Reyes. This was not over. There were still far too many unknowns.

As she settled in to one of the abandoned homes for a short rest, guarded by her Rangers, she found herself wondering where all the townspeople had gone. It was a flickering thought that entered her mind just before she drifted off, and she decided to pursue it further once she'd had a few hours' sleep.

Perhaps if she had investigated it immediately, things might not have gone so horribly.

INTERLUDE

Life and death, light and darkness, ever conflicted. Light dispels the dark, dark eclipses the light, endlessly back and forth, ever a cycle, ever a return to form. Without change. Without end.

But if there is no true change, no true end, what of a being whose very nature *is* change and end?

"What is 'me,' I wonder," murmured Marzanna.

"Sorry?" asked Zivena.

"Never mind."

"This has been fun," said Zivena, "but I think it's time to clear the board before the Armonia arrives."

"Do you think?" asked Marzanna.

"It's not as though the outcome is in any doubt," said Zivena. "You already know what I have in store. You might as well just give up now and save us the headache of dealing with Mother's meddling vessel."

"I want to see this one through," said Marzanna. "To the end."

"Wouldn't you rather just move on to the next game?"

Marzanna gazed out across the terrible catastrophe unfolding, much of it her own doing.

"No, I don't think so. Not this time."

PART FIVE

WHAT LIGHT THAT'S LEFT

"In this land of death and darkness, what light that's left will only blind us."

—Boris Rodionov, "The Luminous Ones"

51

There were, Jorge decided, moments when a person suddenly realized just how strange their life had become. A jolt of perspective in which it dawns on them that a year ago, they could never have imagined they would be sitting beside the man they love, after openly kissing him in the middle of a pitched battle, and riding at astonishing speed toward Magna Alto on a makeshift litter borne by a mass of undead.

Truly, he could not decide which of those things was the most unbelievable. As far as Blaine went, the fallout from that expression of passion probably wouldn't be felt for some time. Viajero were not troubled by same-sex relationships any more than the Uaine, and if the mercenaries were privately uncomfortable with the idea, their respect for a member of the Great Families outweighed it. The turmoil wouldn't begin until he returned to Colmo and his mother found out. Because he was certain she would. A part of him dreaded that moment. But perhaps part of him also longed for it. *An end to pretending...*

The unsteady thrill of this idea surprised him.

But this was war and those were concerns for another day. Right now he was merely grateful to have Blaine beside him. He was comforted by the Uaine's solid presence, his scent—leather and musk, but always with a sweet hint of apples—and his easy smile. Gone was that pinched and desperate look Jorge had seen the day before. Perhaps he flattered himself, but he thought their reunion might have had something to do with Blaine's renewed cheer.

The reunion with Rowena had not been so triumphant. It hadn't been bad, just awkward in a way he didn't understand. He wasn't even certain he could say he had truly reunited with her. Certainly not the Rowena he'd known.

He and Blaine sat on a sheet of canvas carried on all sides by sluagh gorta who ran with a speed and unity he had not realized they were capable of. The undead feet pounded on the Advent Road in a seemingly endless train, bearing not only their litter, but as many as could be put together from the Raízian tents. It must look a bizarre sight from afar, this fleet of canvas sheets riding a wave of moving corpses. He still wasn't sure how it was even possible.

"What happened to Rowena?" he asked Blaine.

"She made a new pact with Bàs, I think different from the usual pact Bhuidseach make. Bhuidseach Sorcha says she's never seen something this powerful."

"What's she like?" asked Jorge. "Sorcha, I mean."

Blaine made a sour face. "She's Clan Seacál."

Jorge waited for more, but nothing came. "Since they're the one clan I didn't meet, you'll have to help me out here a little."

"Aye, that's true, I suppose." Blaine considered a moment. "In your language, the name would translate to the Jackal Lords. Cowardly, scheming, and deadly. That is them."

"I see. And yet Mordha trusts them?"

"He trusts their strength. But he paired them with our clan, which is the most loyal, to make sure they do not stray too far."

"Galina told me Clan Seacál hadn't been particularly careful when crossing Izmoroz with the remaining sluagh gorta, and a lot of Izmorozian peasants died along the way."

Blaine nodded. "That be Clan Seacál."

Jorge realized he might have just brought up an awkward subject. After all, this was an element of Mordha's plan that had been kept from him during their initial alliance. He thought about asking Blaine more about it, but didn't want to spoil the mood.

He was surprised, then, when Blaine volunteered the information.

"I didn't know about them coming later. Rowena told me they had broken from the Tighearna, and since they were Clan Seacál, I believed her."

"So your own Bhuidseach lied to you? The holy person of your clan?" asked Jorge. "I realize I'm an outsider, so perhaps I don't fully understand, but that seems like a terrible betrayal."

"She used to be different," Blaine said. "My brother was meant to be Bhuidseach of our clan. He and Rowena were beloved, and after he died during the ceremony, she changed. Most people didn't notice because she was never an easy person to understand. But because of my brother, I knew her well. After that day, I could see a hatred for Bàs grow in her heart. A hunger for revenge that couldna' be satisfied."

"Until Mordha offered a way to get revenge?" Jorge had found it strange, but somehow not surprising, to learn that the warlord's goal from the day he and Sonya met him had only ever been to use them as a means of killing a god. Or goddess. Jorge was still a little unclear on how Bàs and Lady Marzanna were the same entity. Regardless, he could not imagine the courage, and perhaps the arrogance, that Mordha possessed in thinking he could do such a thing. But after watching him fight Sonya, he thought if anyone had been able to kill a god, it would have been him.

"Aye, the Tighearna brought a few of us together and told us his true plans, but most didna' know that he planned to kill Bàs," said Blaine. "When we began our alliance, I knew he was using Sonya, but I didn't think the two of them would ever fight. And I thought..." He sighed and looked down at his hard, calloused hands. "I thought she would be better off with Bàs dead."

"I agree with you there," said Jorge. "And I'm happy to say that she seems to have a much more guarded relationship with her death goddess these days."

"That is good to hear," said Blaine. "Rowena may have given up on her revenge and renewed our allegiance to Bàs, but it would be a mistake to think he actually cares what happens to us. Everything he does, everything he gives us, is only to further his own ends."

They rode in silence except for the soft patter of undead feet on the dusty road beneath them. Jorge turned his head to look at the litter directly behind them, where Rowena rode with Blaine's father. Her eyes stared into space as though she was looking at something completely different. Something vast, complicated, and surprising, rather than merely the road before them.

"I wonder if she'll always be like this now."

"I fear so," said Blaine. "That is another thing about Bàs. His price is steep."

"I realize that everyone eventually loses everything to death," said Jorge. "But between Rowena and Sonya, I can't help taking it a little personally."

Blaine chuckled quietly.

"Yet your father seems to be in strangely high spirits, all things considered."

The elder Ruairc, who sat beside Rowena, was grinning widely and, Jorge realized, looking right at them.

"Oh, he thinks that his son is now beloved of the leader of an entire country, so he's pretty happy." Blaine glanced at Jorge, his cheeks flush above his beard. "I tried to tell him that is not how things work for your people, but he is old, so he canna' understand new ideas so well."

It pained Jorge to see Blaine's quiet acceptance that their relationship could never be allowed to fully blossom. But then he realized something:

"It's bullshit."

"Eh?" Blaine looked alarmed.

"Not you," Jorge said quickly. "The *custom*. I am currently the representative ruler of Raíz, aren't I? Surely if the Great Families put the entire fate of our country in my hands, they will listen to me about changing one simple law that is really no one else's business anyway."

Blaine's eyes widened. "You mean that?"

"Yes," said Jorge, realizing with some amazement that he did. "After all I've given to the Great Families and to Raíz, I deserve some happiness, just like everyone else. And what does it cost them, really?"

"But your family. I thought—"

"Yes, I'm still dreading that," admitted Jorge. "But I don't want to lie to my mother, and I'm tired of lying to myself. So this seems like the only real solution. And if the Great Families don't like it, those ingrates can find some other fool to run their country."

Blaine stared at him with his mouth open and suddenly Jorge wasn't so sure. Had he overstepped? Had he been mistaken to think that Blaine longed for more, as he did?

"What is it?" he asked nervously. "Did you not want to—"

Blaine shook his head and smiled. "I was just thinking that power and authority look good on you."

52

Sebastian remembered a discussion his parents once had when he was a boy. It was odd, he thought, how memory worked. That so much of childhood was a jumbled blur, but there were these moments, sometimes seemingly random and unimportant, that crystallized in the mind.

He remembered sitting on the ground just outside the door to their house, obstinately refusing to come inside for reasons he couldn't recall. Or perhaps there had been no reason, and he had just been willful. Regardless, he remembered looking through the open doorway into the kitchen where he could see his parents talking. They were not arguing, exactly, because one did not argue with Irina Turgenev. But even his childish perception could sense a tension between them.

Why don't you punish him? his father asked, looking displeased.

His mother regarded his father for a moment. Then she said, *The world is cruel enough. It will heap sufferings on him aplenty. Adding more would be unnecessary.*

She had then gone about the business of making supper. It began to rain, but still Sebastian had refused to come inside. His parents and sister sat down to eat, and still he remained outside. It wasn't until nightfall, when his stomach was cramping with hunger and his entire body shook with chills, that he crawled, miserable and wretched, into the kitchen where his mother waited.

She did not gloat. That would have been unbecoming of Irina Turgenev. Instead, she knelt down beside him, placed her warm, dry hand on his cold cheek, and smiled.

Now do you see, Sebastian? Remember this moment, for it is but a small portion of what life has in store.

He'd hoped she might have set some food aside from supper to give him, but he should have known better. Going to bed with an empty belly was part of the lesson.

Sonya had railed against those cold, unfiltered introductions to life, accusing their mother of not caring about them. But Sebastian had understood that this was their mother's method of not only teaching them the way of the world, but acclimating them to it. Suffering would always be a part of life. To pretend otherwise was foolish.

Now Sebastian looked up at the metal visage of his mother and wondered, was she suffering? Or perhaps he should ask if she felt anything at all.

There were tiny details. A gesture, a tilt of the head, that suggested his mother was still in there to some degree. But how much, he couldn't really say. All he could say for certain was that it hurt to look at her. But he also couldn't tear himself away.

"Mother."

She looked down at him with the same sort of magenta eyes that had frightened him when he'd first seen them in Hardsong Pass all those months ago. He could never have imagined the feelings they now brought up. Sorrow, horror, longing, regret.

His mother laid her massive metal hand on his head, and a puff of steam escaped the slit of her mouth.

"One cannot become a golem unwillingly."

Sebastian recognized Isobelle's voice behind him, but he still couldn't take his gaze away from his mother. Or what remained of her.

"So you are suggesting she did this to herself?"

"More likely a hexenmeister offered her a choice. Perhaps she was dying, and this was a way to not only save herself but continue to aid you and your sister."

Sebastian had to admit it was the sort of unsentimental choice his mother might make.

"Why doesn't she look like other golems?"

Isobelle hesitated for a moment. "There was a Kantesian man who was banished from the *Verzauberungs Stipendium* for . . . heretical ideas. There were rumors he sought sanctuary in Aureum. I think it likely he was at the palace and became acquainted with your mother."

"Heretical ideas?" Sebastian finally looked at her. "I thought Kantesians had no religion."

"No, we reject the gods. That is not the same thing as having no religion."

"I suppose that's true. But what sort of heresy was he expelled for?"

"For this." She gestured to Sebastian's mother, not trying to conceal her disquiet. "A golem should always be made to serve a purpose, and it should never resemble a human."

"Why not?"

She looked at him in surprise, as though it were obvious. "Because then we might start thinking of them as such. But they are not."

Sebastian looked back at his mother's gleaming steel face. "Are you certain?"

Her expression softened. "As an outsider, this must be very hard for you. I'm sorry, but while there may be some residual memories, this is no longer your mother. It is a machine that sprang from your mother's dying consciousness, most likely imbued with your mother's longing to protect you and your sister."

"My mother was hardly the protective type," said Sebastian.

"Yet she traveled all this way, even bringing one of your sister's old comrades along who might speak for her. Perhaps *protect* is the wrong word. But she clearly imbued the golem with a strong desire to be reunited with you."

"So no one controls her?"

"No one truly controls any golem," said Isobelle. "In the moment of their creation, they are imbued by the one giving their soul with the desire to perform a task. And they never tire of performing that task. Not decades or even centuries later."

"Do they live forever, then?"

"Their life span, if you want to call it that, is determined by the strength of will in the one who donated their soul."

"Then my mother's golem will likely outlast us all."

Isobelle smiled sadly. "Perhaps so. But that might not be ideal. If her sole guiding purpose is to be with you, and you die, be it from battle or more natural causes, what does she do then?"

"I don't know. Nothing, I suppose?"

"Indeed," said Isobelle. "Have you ever heard the story of Old Hilde?"

Sebastian's eyes widened. "Actually, I've met her."

"Ah. She must be a moving sight."

He considered a moment, recalling his impressions at the time with what he now knew of golems. "She sits there slowly rusting away because she's lost her purpose?"

"So the tale goes, she was the head servant of a great Kantesian lord. She was struck with a terrible illness just as her lord was about to go to war, and she begged to be turned into a golem so that she could protect him during the battle. And she did protect him. But he was already a man of middle age. Twenty years later he died, leaving behind a golem who had been created with a strong and loyal will."

"And no one to protect."

Isobelle nodded. "This is why golems are generally made to serve a family or position, rather than an individual. The beautiful trundle that belongs to Herr Gruttman has served his family for generations. Presumably the one who donated their soul felt a deep gratitude toward the Gruttmans, and so that golem has lived on for hundreds of years, powered by its will. Someday it will fade, as all things must. But for now, it is the most prized possession of his family, and of the city he governs."

Sebastian struggled with how to process this new knowledge about golems. He had been so ready to condemn them earlier. But the way Isobelle described them, did it sound so bad? Was that because he was inclined to like anything Isobelle said? Or was he trying to convince himself that his mother's fate was not quite as horrible as he had previously imagined? But if Isobelle was correct, that meant when he and his sister died, even if it was from old age, there was no telling how many decades, centuries, or even millennia, his mother's golem would persist without purpose. He could see her standing in some field like a statue, and all who happened by would remark upon her beauty. Perhaps that wasn't so awful.

Or was it?

"I really don't know what to think anymore," he admitted.

She laid one hand on his arm, and the other on the golem's metal arm.

"We may never know your mother's reasons for doing what she did. But one thing is certain. You should not squander the sacrifice she has made."

He looked up at his mother's golem, watching the morning sun gleam on her perfect, cold face.

"Well, Mother, I suppose you'll insist on accompanying Sonya and me into battle tomorrow."

The golem's magenta eyes flared, and another hiss of steam escaped her mouth. She carefully patted his head, then turned toward where Sonya was preparing for the last day of their long march.

53

Sonya still struggled with seeing her mother in...whatever state it was. Her brother said it wasn't actually her anymore, just a memory or wish or something equally difficult to comprehend in any sort of concrete way. Sonya honestly didn't care if it was truly her mother or not. Even if it was only a shadow, she would treat it like her mother. Maybe then she could quiet the seething regret that twisted up her insides. Eventually.

But first that meant growing comfortable with her mother's new form. And that was why she made a point of riding beside her as they embarked on the final stretch to Magna Alto.

The golem plodded tirelessly across the meadow beside Peppercorn with Mordha strapped to her like a backpack.

"So this whole time, you were planning to kill Lady Marzanna?" she asked the warlord, still not quite able to accept the idea. "Is that even possible?"

"When it comes to gods, who can say what is possible and impossible?" asked Mordha in his usual stoic manner, even though he was bobbing ludicrously up and down on her mother's back.

He had a point, though. No one knew what the gods were truly capable of because no one had ever been foolish enough to test them. Mordha's current shape was proof of why it was unwise.

"Does it hurt?" she asked.

"It has never stopped hurting from the moment Bàs turned me into this ghoulish creature. Losing my limbs added little to it. Although I do find my inability to move around on my own frustrating."

"Well, at least you have such a beautiful caretaker, isn't that right, Mother?"

The golem let out a puff of steam, which Sonya decided was agreement.

"Had she not taken me with her, I don't know what would have become of me," said Mordha. "And my people might not have been stopped from destroying the Raízians."

"What about everyone else in Magna Alto?" asked Sonya.

"We could not find them," Mordha said gravely.

"You lost a whole army?"

"So it would seem."

"What could have happened to them?" she asked.

"I have no idea." His scarred face creased for a moment. "Well, I do have one *concern*, I suppose. The Uaine have always dedicated themselves to Bàs, thereby receiving his protection from his sibling, Beatha. But when I opened the door to the Eventide, I broke our allegiance to him, not just for me, but for all our people. Rowena has since renewed that allegiance, but there was a period of time during which the Uaine were no longer under Bàs's protection."

"And you think Beatha or Zivena, or whatever they're called, did something to them during that time?"

"I can think of no other way that an entire army could be obliterated."

They traveled on in silence for a while. Sonya felt some relief that at least Blaine hadn't been among the missing Uaine. It was a terrible thought, she knew, but it was how she felt.

After some time, Mordha asked her, "I am surprised that you are not upset that I planned to kill your goddess."

Sonya thought about it. "Our relationship has changed a lot since the last time I saw you. We have an arrangement of sorts, but I wouldn't say I worship her anymore. In fact, there's probably been a few times I might have considered killing her myself."

She looked at the scarred, limbless Uaine for a moment.

"Although, no offense, I think it would take a lot more than you to do it."

He nodded. "The moment I was in the presence of Beatha, I understood just how foolish I was. Hopefully it won't be the undoing of my people."

"You said Rowena sounded different when you talked to her?"

"When she renewed our allegiance, she made a bargain with Bàs that I do not fully understand. In fact, I fear we may not truly grasp its consequences for some time."

"Did she say how Jorge was doing?"

"She did not."

"Hm."

"Representative Elhuyar is alive and well," said Ambassador Boz as she guided her horse closer. "In fact, according to Onat Duman, he may have even made a personal breakthrough."

"Oh?" asked Sonya.

"Apparently he and Blaine have expressed their feelings toward each other in a very public way."

"Really?"

A strange welter of emotions snaked through Sonya. She was pleased, of course. They'd been pining after each other for so long it had gotten a little ridiculous. And yet, to not be there for it. To not be part of it. Though neither of them were to blame, she couldn't help feeling hurt. And then deeper, there was something else. A sense of…relief? That she didn't have to worry about them any longer. She wasn't sure what that meant.

Sonya realized that Boz was still looking at her carefully, probably waiting to see how she would react, so she could add yet another detail to whatever assessment she was making about this continent for her rulers in Victasha. Sonya understood that was the true cost of their aid. Knowledge. The only consolation was that Sonya and the others had been able to learn things about Victasha as well. Most importantly, their secret communication magic.

Even so, she didn't want to give the ambassador any more than she had to. So she did her best to mask the mess of emotions inside her, and smiled in the old Sonya way.

"That's great!"

"It certainly is," agreed Boz, who didn't seem to entirely buy Sonya's presentation, but wisely chose not to press further.

"Do they have an estimate of when they will reach Magna Alto?" asked Mordha.

"Within two days," said Boz.

"And what of our allies inside Magna Alto?" he asked.

"At last contact, Sezai Bey reported that Vittorio had pulled his remaining forces back to the palace. Queen Galina and the Kantesian hexenmeisters have set up fortifications in case it's a ruse and Vittorio launches a counterattack, but that seems unlikely."

"And there has been no sign of my people?" predicted Mordha.

"Correct."

He nodded gravely.

"Tatiana and Andre are okay?" asked Sonya.

"From Bey's reports, it sounds as though it would take significant force for them not to be," said Boz. "Certainly more than Vittorio has so far shown."

"But now we know for sure that he's serving Zivena," said Sonya. "So there has to be more. He's not just going to hide in the palace and do nothing."

"I agree," said Mordha. "The man is devious, ruthless, and utterly mad. He wouldn't take up such a cautious position unless it was a ruse of some kind."

"Whatever he has in store, it hasn't happened yet," said Boz. "Bey has orders to contact me the moment the situation changes."

"It could be some trap he's planning to spring when we assault the palace," said Sonya.

When the sun began to set, the Herzog of Weide pondered whether to set up camp for the night. They were close enough that if they pressed ahead, they would reach the city shortly after midnight. But they were all weary from another day's march, and Boz's representative hadn't reported any changes, and with the risk of a potential trap laid by Vittorio, he decided it would be best to make camp and join the battle well rested on the following day.

They woke early the next morning, a nervous eagerness buzzing throughout the army. They broke camp in record time and marched with an enthusiasm not seen since the day they first departed Weide. Morning dew still glittered on the grass beneath the gentle Aureumian sun when they came in view of Magna Alto.

Something was very wrong.

It was a sight unlike any Sonya could have imagined. Tens of thousands of people appeared to be funneling in through the main gate and the canal. Only so many could fit through at a time and the rest covered the meadows that surrounded the city, swarming like ants.

"What is going on?" Sebastian asked, his eyes wide. "Ambassador, I thought you said nothing had changed."

Sonya didn't think she'd ever seen Boz look so surprised in her life. "I . . . I don't know. Let me just . . ."

The ambassador closed her eyes, pressed the fingers of her left hand to her forehead, and spoke rapidly in her native tongue. She waited a moment, then her brows furrowed down and she spoke again, sounding almost angry. After waiting another moment, she looked back at them with a haunted expression.

"We've lost contact with our forces inside the city."

54

How could it have all gone wrong so quickly?

Her Majesty Queen Galina Odoyevtseva Prozorova stood on the roof of a building in the broken remains of Magna Alto and looked down at the sea of human-shaped monsters that crowded the streets below.

"What are they?"

"I don't know, Your Majesty," said Andre beside her. "But they stink of magic."

"The same magic as the mushrooms," added Tatiana, who stood nearby.

Galina presumed the monsters and mushrooms must be connected somehow, though she had no idea in what way. But given the dubious nature of goddesses, she wasn't sure if it would have helped if she'd known. Clearly, Vittorio had played his hand, and to devastating effect.

The creatures had appeared inside the building where she had been sleeping as if out of thin air. They staggered about with odd, jerky movements, like puppets on strings. Mushrooms bloomed from their mouths, noses, and ears. Individually they seemed almost mindless, but collectively they appeared guided by a terrible purpose. As clumsy as they were, they easily homed in on any regular person they could find. They were unarmored, but seemed indifferent to injury. They were unarmed, but capable of great strength and speed. In the moment it took Galina and her Rangers to take in the bizarre intruders, one of them grasped poor Sezai Bey by the throat and tore out his windpipe. Galina thought that could not be a coincidence. Whoever was controlling these creatures had figured out how she and her allies were coordinating their attack.

The queen of Izmoroz was unaccustomed to sudden physical danger in her immediate surroundings, so she could only gape in horror as the Victashian clutched at the gushing hole in his throat and toppled forward. In the next moment, Andre unceremoniously hoisted her over his shoulder and carried her up the stairs, with Tatiana defending their rear. Once they reached the upper floor, Galina thought they might try to hold it. The narrow passage would keep the enemy from swarming, and the incline would be a serious disadvantage to the uncoordinated creatures.

But apparently her Rangers did not consider the upper floor sufficiently defensible because Andre did not slow his pace as he moved directly to the window and tore off the shutter. Galina was still puzzling out his intent when he climbed through and began clambering up the side of the building one-handed. Galina, still slung ingloriously over his shoulder like a sack, stared helplessly down his back at the vast open space below them, trying to determine if they would survive a fall. A moment later Tatiana followed behind, her expression tense but blessedly not panicked. That gave the queen some small measure of comfort.

After several harrowing moments, Andre at last reached the roof. Here he finally remembered his manners and placed her gently on the flat, overlapping tiles. She was embarrassed to find that her legs wobbled beneath her, and she might have fallen over if Tatiana hadn't been behind to steady her.

Despite the trauma of being hauled up the outside of a building, Galina was grateful her Rangers had taken this additional step. It seemed few of the creatures had the dexterity to even attempt climbing up after them, so they were far safer. And it allowed Galina to assess just how bad the situation had become.

It only took a moment to understand that it was very bad indeed. As far as she could see, the streets were teeming with the mushroom creatures.

"It looks like the entire population of Aureum down there," she murmured.

"Very close to it," said Tatiana.

The way she said it made Galina pause. She watched the Ranger's large owl eyes shift back and forth across the seething masses below.

"You mean that quite literally, don't you," she said.

"How else would I mean it, Your Majesty?"

The full weight of that settled on her. "By the goddess, would he really do that? Sacrifice his entire nation for victory?"

"So it would seem," said Andre.

"What is the point of saving the empire, if there are none left in it?" she asked.

Neither of them answered, which was just as well.

"Tatiana, can you see any other survivors?"

She nodded. "Others have made it to the rooftops, though none are close enough for us to reach."

"What of the golems?"

Galina crossed over to the other side of the roof, which faced the road leading toward the palace where the machines had been stationed. She saw the golems were still there, stomping on any creatures who approached. But they did not seem inclined to come back into the downtown area to help Galina and her troops.

"What on earth are they waiting for?"

There was a sudden blast of sound behind her, and she turned just in time to see several figures shoot up into the air from one of the rooftops, then drift slowly toward her.

She stared in astonishment as Ernesto Reyes, flanked by several of his Viajero, floated to her rooftop and landed as gracefully as a cat.

The moment his feet touched the roof, he bowed deeply. "How may I be of service, Your Majesty?"

"You do know how to make an entrance, Ernesto," she said.

"Thank you, Your Majesty."

"How do your men fare?"

"Thankfully we all survived the initial attack and made it to the roof."

"Did you see where they came from? How did they bypass our fortifications?"

"As far as I can tell, they were already inside, lurking in cellars and storage closets until somehow signaled to begin their assault."

She shook her head. "Even the townspeople, then."

"Your Majesty?"

"Our suspicion is that Vittorio has sacrificed his entire populace to spring this trap."

Reyes stared at her. "*All* of them?"

"As near as we can tell."

He closed his eyes. "Monstrous."

"That about sums up our opponent," said Galina. "Now, this flying ability of yours. Can you utilize it to reach the hexenmeisters and ask them why the golems are not entering the fray?"

He shook his head. "It requires those of my men who remain back on the other roof."

"That is unfortunate."

"I'm not certain if it would have done much good, anyway," he said. "The Kantesians' grasp of our language seemed tenuous, and I don't know theirs at all. I suppose that translator fellow—"

"I'm afraid he was the first one to fall," Galina said. "I can't help wondering if some intelligence is directing these creatures, and knew him to be a high-value target."

"And now we have no way to get word to our allies?"

"I'm afraid not."

Reyes leaned over the edge of the building and gazed down at the swarms below. While they lacked the dexterity to scale the wall, they seemed to be piling on top of each other, gradually forming a slope that would, after many deaths, reach the top.

"Our allies *are* coming, however," she assured him. "We will simply have to hold out until they arrive, however long it takes." There was no point in pondering what would happen if they couldn't.

He gazed at her with his soulful brown eyes. "Will they be enough?"

"If not even the Wizard of Gogoleth can save us," replied Galina, "then we are beyond saving."

55

The Kantesian cavalry rolled down the sloping meadow like a wave of bristling steel and crashed into the throngs of people surrounding Magna Alto. Under normal circumstances, even the most steadfast of hearts might have broken and run at the sight alone. And even if they'd been able to hold their ground, they would certainly have panicked once their fellows were being trampled and hacked to pieces.

But these people, if they could be called such, seemed not to notice. Furthermore, they appeared to be so strong that if two or three could grab hold of a horse, they were able to pull it down. Then they set about ripping it and the rider apart with chillingly methodical precision, flinging armor and flesh in all directions.

The Herzog of Weide observed the battle with a telescoping glass from his encampment at the top of the hill. He turned to those he had gathered.

"What *are* they?"

"I can feel magic emanating from them," said Sebastian.

"Like the golems?" asked Isobelle.

"A lot more intense than that," said Sebastian. "Yet also far more . . . crude? It's hard to describe. Your enchanting magic, and the Raízian creative magic, have a certain amount of refinement and skill. This feels savage. Wild."

"Goddess magic," Sonya said.

"Yes," said Mordha.

"Wonderful," Weide said bitterly. "*Die Hand Gottes* once more intrudes. My cavalry isn't going to be able to break through alone. I can commit my infantry, but without the golems, we won't last long."

"Are they still inside?" asked Boz.

"Presumably," said Weide. "I gave the hexenmeisters orders that once they had entered the city, they were to hold position until we arrived."

"Surely they would realize that is no longer practical," said Sebastian.

Weide eyed him. "You overestimate the common sense and generosity of hexenmeisters. They will defend themselves, but I doubt the idea of assisting their non-Kantesian allies within those walls will even cross their minds." He held up a rolled parchment with a wax seal. "Someone will have to deliver these new orders."

"I'll do it." Sonya snatched up the parchment and headed for her horse.

"Not alone, you won't," said Sebastian as he hurried after her.

She smirked. "You sure you're up for it, oh mighty wizard?"

"Please. How much of an impact do you really think your little arrows are going to have on those creatures."

"Good point," she admitted. "Okay, you cut a path, and I'll take the orders to the hexenmeisters."

Their mother's golem fell in step beside them.

"It appears we will be accompanying you," Mordha said dryly.

"Will she be safe?" Sonya asked anxiously.

Mordha chuckled. "I lost count of how many imperial soldiers she killed as we were leaving the city. She is like a small army unto herself."

"What about you, though?" said Sonya. "Maybe she should leave you behind?"

"I realize the chance is slim, but if my people are still inside, they will join us immediately when they see me."

"I suspect we'll be able to use all the help we can get," said Sebastian.

"Okay, so it's the four of us!" Sonya grinned, and there was a gleam in her eye that concerned Sebastian.

"Just make sure you don't get so excited that you forget what we're supposed to be doing." He tapped the rolled parchment in her hand.

"I know, I know," she said. "I'm not *that* far gone."

"Good luck to you," called the Herzog of Weide. "Once you're ready, signal me and I will engage my infantry. That should take at least some pressure off you."

"Understood," said Sebastian.

Sonya and Sebastian mounted their horses and guided them down the slope toward the mob of milling creatures that surrounded the city. Their mother's golem easily kept pace with her long, clanking strides.

"I honestly don't know what sort of control I'll be able to get out of this thing," Sebastian admitted as he unfastened the ruby-adorned staff from his saddle.

"How much control do you need?" asked Sonya. "Just make the magic whoosh in front of us to clear the way."

He scowled at her. "*Whoosh?*"

She gave him an innocent look. "Is that not the technical name for it? Then please tell me what is?"

Of course, he didn't have one, so he decided to ignore her. Instead, he looked over at his mother's golem and Mordha. "Are we ready?"

The golem hissed steam.

"I will do my best to keep an eye to our rear," Mordha said calmly.

Sebastian didn't know the Uaine well enough to determine if that was a moment of levity, so he decided not to comment. He turned to face the command tent at the top of the hill and lifted his staff as high as he could.

A deep, sonorous horn sounded. Then a roar slowly rose from the lines of infantry. They began clanging their swords against their breastplates, making a jangling sound that likely would have terrified a normal foe.

The horn sounded again and the infantry charged down the hill. As they did, they divided into two groups. One circled around to the right enemy flank, the other to the left. The creatures shifted in response to this attack and also split in two, opening a gap in the center that led straight to the sundered main gate.

"This might be easier than I thought," said Sonya. "Come on!"

She shook Peppercorn's reins, and he shot forward so quickly that it took Sebastian several moments to catch up. Their mother's golem was right behind them. Perhaps it really would be easy to get through.

But that hope was fleeting. Like water draining into an empty pool, creatures from within the city streamed out through the gate to block their way.

Sonya turned to Sebastian, her eyes sparkling gleefully. "Time to whoosh!"

"You're still the worst!" he shouted over the pounding hooves. Then he lifted his staff and focused his intention on the ruby. It felt different from the diamond. Not as clean, but perhaps more... forceful? Did gems have personalities? He couldn't say, but when he gathered the wind from behind them and sent it forward, even he was surprised by the sheer pressure of the gale that blew the creatures back and slammed them against the outer wall of the city.

And he had to admit, it did sound somewhat like a *whoosh*.

Sonya let out a laugh, and they rode swiftly through the gap and into the city.

But they quickly discovered that the interior was far worse. The streets of Magna Alto were flooded with the creatures. Sebastian couldn't see a single square foot of cobblestone. He cast another blast of air, and a swath of them went flying, but the opening quickly filled back up with others. There seemed to be no end to them.

"Now what?" he asked.

Sonya eyed the seething streets. "I can't see anything from here. Hold this."

She handed Sebastian the reins to her horse, then leapt from her saddle to the windowsill of a nearby bakery. From there she quickly clambered up the side of the building until she was on the roof. She stood on the very edge, perfectly at ease though she was several stories up. Her golden eyes scanned across the building tops, and then she smiled.

"I can see the golems. They're all the way on the other side."

"That's great." Sebastian knocked back another surge of the creatures. "But how do we get to them?"

She was silent for a moment, then she looked down at their mother's golem. "You take care of him." She indicated Sebastian. Then she looked at Sebastian. "And you take care of him." She indicated Peppercorn.

"Sonya..." Sebastian did not like the feral eagerness that now shone on his sister's face. "What are you doing?"

"You just keep whooshing them away, and maybe try to find Queen Kukla. I'm going to deliver the message."

Before Sebastian could respond, she leapt from the rooftop and landed on the head of one of the creatures. Then she began jumping from one to the next, stepping from head to shoulder, sometimes banking off the side of a building as she moved steadily to the other side of the throng. Some tried to reach up and grab her foot, but she readily avoided them, vaulting to her hands and somersaulting to the next one.

Sebastian sniffed. "Show-off."

In truth, he would have loved to sit there and watch his sister work her way across. Her movement was like poetry, and he felt a swell of pride to be the brother of this exceptional woman. But the creatures were already pressing back in on him, and he had to move.

Then the golem gave a hissing groan and began plowing through the masses up the main road.

"I guess we're going that way," he muttered.

His mother's golem waded through the bodies like they were water, but when several got ahold of her, they began to drag her down. He was worried that a raw blast of wind might knock his mother over as well, so he tried to figure out another way to get them off her. Their mouths, ears, and noses were filled with mushrooms, and when he began to stretch forward with his magic, he felt that they were as much mushroom as flesh on the inside.

He didn't know a great deal about fungi, but he was fairly certain they thrived in damp, temperate environments. When he drew out the moisture and warmth from within them, they immediately seized up and dropped off his mother's golem.

He wished this new technique was something he could perform on a larger scale, as it seemed to permanently disable the creatures.

But with the intricacy involved, doing more than one at a time made his ruby vibrate in a worrisome way. The last thing he needed while surrounded by a horde of fungi-controlled people was to have another gem crumble on him. So he alternated between brute winds to keep the bulk of them at bay, and gripping cold for the few who managed to get through to him or his mother.

But where is she going? he wondered.

The golem was moving with clear purpose farther up the road, as if she had a goal in mind. Could it be some memory from her mother's life that drove her? Mordha had said she seemed to recognize him, and that she had gone out of her way to free Ernesto Reyes and his Viajero from the brig before leaving the city. What if she was going to Reyes right now? After all, he could still be in the city, fighting off this horde of abominations on his own.

With new resolve, Sebastian helped his mother clear the way before them, and they made slow but steady progress through the city until they reached a large building in the main town square. The creatures were particularly dense in that area. They piled up on top of each other with the same disconcerting methodicalness with which they had torn apart cavalry, but in this case, they were throwing their own lives away so that those behind them could get a little higher. There was a cruel and effective simplicity to it, and they had nearly reached the top.

On the roof, Sebastian saw their goal. Ernesto Reyes, just as Sebastian had hoped. He danced ferociously, each movement knocking back several creatures. But his face was drenched in sweat, and it was clear he was reaching his limit. A few other Viajero that Sebastian recognized fought by his side, looking exhausted, singing and painting with less precision than he'd ever seen, but with a desperate energy.

Beside them fought two beast-like people that could only be Sonya's fellow Rangers. One had a massive, bear-like build, and each swipe of his clawed hands sent a creature flying into the air. The other had large owl eyes and feathers. The razor-sharp talons on her swift, darting feet tore creatures to sheds, rendering them into useless, quivering hunks that rolled back down the slope.

Sebastian took all of it in as he and his mother forced their way closer. But he was not prepared for what he saw next.

Behind the captain, Viajero, and Rangers was a beautiful warrior queen resplendent in gold and white. Her flaxen hair fluttered in the wind and her eyes were as hard as Kantesian steel as she shouted encouragement to the small band defending the rooftop. She had no weapon, and was easily the smallest and frailest of the bunch, but by sheer force of will, her words seemed enough to fortify even the most exhausted among the combatants. There could never be any doubt that this was the queen of Izmoroz.

"Galina...," whispered Sebastian, feeling his heart wrench within his chest. There were so many conflicting emotions that he could not hope to parse them all. But more than anything, he felt a wild desire to protect her at all costs.

"Mother, keep the ones behind us at bay."

The golem turned her head, then nodded, and shoved a line of creatures out of the way to give him some room.

Sebastian focused on the writhing slope of creatures that was trying to gain purchase on the rooftop. Wind would do no good. And he couldn't use the same precise cold on so many at once. But a blanket of cold....

"All of you, step back!" he shouted to those protecting the edge.

They stared at him in dazed confusion until Galina said something and in unison they moved out of harm's way. Then Sebastian took a deep breath and yanked the heat away from the mob of creatures so forcefully they froze instantly, leaving a grisly hill of ice that led to the rooftop.

"Mother, let's go!"

Sebastian prayed that she was following, but he knew they must hurry because while he had stopped the immediate danger, he had also provided an even more stable way for the creatures to reach the roof.

He urged his horse and Peppercorn up the jagged icy slope. At first, they shied away, but then the Rangers called down to them in Old Izmorozian. Despite the chaos surrounding them, the horses' ears perked up. Maybe it was the commanding tone or some Ranger magic, but he was grateful for it when the horses began dutifully clambering up the hill of frozen human shapes.

Once they had all reached the roof, Sebastian turned and set fire to the entire hill of frozen creatures. Perhaps the red gem had some particular affinity for the element because the inferno erupted like an explosion, knocking Sebastian off his horse.

He felt himself embraced in large, warm arms.

"Ah!" rumbled the voice of the one who had caught him. "This magic lemming smells like *Lisitsa*! She is here at last to join the fun!"

Sebastian looked up at the grinning, fanged face of the bear Ranger.

"Thank you for catching me, but would you mind putting me down?"

The bear Ranger chuckled and deposited him on the rooftop with surprising gentleness.

Then Sebastian turned to Galina. She returned his gaze, her expression unreadable. There was so much he longed to say to her. But he knew in that moment of crisis, there was only one thing he *should* say.

So he took a breath, then dropped to one knee.

"Sebastian Turgenev Portinari at your service, Your Majesty."

56

The sluagh gorta could have run from the Raízian border to Magna Alto without rest, but Jorge knew the living among them would need a break now and then, so he had proposed a signal that could be passed down from one litter to the next until it reached Rowena, who would then halt the undead march.

For the first night and the early part of the following day, the only stops were so that people could relieve themselves. But around midday, Onat Duman suddenly waved his hand with such urgency, Jorge had a feeling it was more than a full bladder.

While the bulk of the Uaine and Raízian forces took the time to stretch their legs, the leaders gathered beside the army of still and patient undead. In addition to Jorge and Duman, there was Rowena, Chief Ruairc, Chief Conaill, and Bhuidseach Sorcha representing Uaine. There was also the Xefe and Lucia representing Raíz. Thankfully, Jorge and Lucia had been able to convince Maria to return to Colmo with the wounded, including El Adiuino, and oversee their care.

Once they had all gathered, Duman relayed the message from Ambassador Boz.

"I don't understand," Jorge said. "Vittorio has his own sluagh gorta now?"

"Similar, but not the same," said the Victashian. "The ambassador's communication was necessarily brief, but she described them as living people who appeared to be under someone else's control. They think it may be caused by some sort of fungus growing from their orifices?"

"What does *that* mean?" Lucia asked, her face twisted with revulsion.

"I'm not entirely clear," admitted Duman. "The ambassador broke the connection before I could ask for further clarification, and I fear the situation is too dire for me to attempt to contact her again so soon."

"Have you ever heard of such a thing?" Jorge asked Rowena.

The necromancer slowly shook her head. Everything she did now was sluggish and dreamy, as though she was only partly paying attention to what was going on around her.

Sorcha muttered something to Conaill and the chief nodded. Both Jorge and Onat looked questioningly to Blaine.

"Er..." Blaine seemed to be weighing how to phrase something that might be a little touchy, or even offensive. "Bhuidseach Sorcha said there are many things happening right now that have never been heard of before."

Sorcha then said something clearly unfriendly to Blaine, but he only shrugged in response. Jorge suspected that the Bhuidseach of Clan Seacál was resentful that her own sluagh gorta had been commandeered by the clearly more powerful Bhuidseach of Clan Dílis.

"And just as troublingly," continued Duman, "the ambassador has lost touch with my counterpart, who had been assisting the Izmorozians."

"Then we have no idea how things are going inside the city?" asked the Xefe.

"Apparently the two Portinari siblings have infiltrated the city in an attempt to rally the forces inside and discover the fate of my counterpart."

"Only two?" Conaill asked.

"Believe me," said Lucia, "Sonya alone is worth many."

"As is Sebastian," said Jorge.

"Regardless," said Duman, "I suggest we continue on as quickly as possible. The speed of our arrival might well decide the fate of the continent."

So they resumed their strange undead locomotion toward the capital. But only a few hours later, the entire undead army came to a halt so sharply, Jorge would have pitched forward off the canvas sheet if Blaine hadn't caught him.

A short way behind them, Jorge heard Rowena muttering something in Uaine. Her voice still had that dreamy, unfocused quality, and Jorge wondered if she was talking to them and forgetting Jorge and Duman didn't speak Uaine, or merely talking to herself.

"She says there's an enemy coming," supplied Blaine.

"An enemy? What sort?"

"She doesn't seem to know, but she can feel a large magic presence heading toward us."

"She can *feel* it? Is that a new ability she has?"

"Apparently," said Blaine.

They waited for several moments, with the sluagh gorta as still and silent as ever, and Rowena muttering in a tone that seemed to be increasingly concerned. Then she gasped and stood awkwardly on her canvas sheet. The distracted look was now gone, replaced by a fury that Jorge had never seen in her. Her pale face was flushed red and her fists were balled up at her side. She was shouting at whatever it was ahead of them, though it was still out of sight.

"What's she saying *now*?" Jorge asked.

Blaine's face was tense with concentration. "I am not sure. She is so angry she doesna' make much sense. Something about someone stealing what is ours? Everything else is mostly curses."

"What on earth could it be?" Jorge strained his vision toward the front of their undead army while Rowena continued to rant.

Finally, another army crested the rise before them. The individuals moved in oddly disjointed ways, as if they were a legion of drunkards. And they wore the wool and fur garb of the Uaine.

Blaine sucked in his breath. "Those are the other clans. Gáire, Fuinseog, and Rincemór."

"Coming to help us?" Jorge asked hopefully.

"I don't think so. Rowena is still saying they've been stolen? Although what that means, and by whom, I do not know."

Jorge called to the furious necromancer across the heads of the undead. "Rowena, can't you tell us what is happening??"

"What is *happening* is that while my people were unknowingly working against Bàs, Beatha decided they were fair game. But I have reconsecrated the Uaine to Death's service, and I have sacrificed far too much to allow even one Uaine soul to remain in Beatha's filthy grasp."

"Then these must be the things Duman was talking about," said Jorge. "Vittorio is controlling all these Uaine?"

"So it seems," Blaine said grimly.

"We need to figure out a way to free them."

"Oh, I know how to free them, Jorge," said Rowena. "Death, which is the final release for us all."

"Wait, Rowena, you're talking about killing three full clans of living Uaine. Surely there is another—"

But Rowena was not interested in discussing the matter, and since she controlled over half the entire army, there was nothing anyone could do to stop her. The sluagh gorta who held the canvas sheets lowered them to the ground. Then as one mass, they charged forward, letting out a bone-chilling scream that reminded Jorge of the first awakening he had witnessed back in Uaine.

As if in response, the enemy army staggered forward as well, although they made no sound, even when the two forces collided.

Jorge worked his way through the abandoned and confused crowds of Uaine and Raízians that surrounded him. He saw Ruairc and Conaill hastily gathering their living warriors together, looking just as surprised and alarmed as he felt.

At last, he spotted Javier and the other guild masters, and hurried over to them.

"Xefe! What should we do?"

The old man looked grim. "Like it or not, we're already committed." Then he raised his voice. "Listen up, all of you! This army is in our way, so we have to push them aside before we can reach Magna Alto and end this war!"

The mercenaries and Viajero began to group up and prepare to enter the fray. They looked tired but resolute. The Viajero in particular seemed uncharacteristically subdued. Perhaps it was because they'd all seen battle now, and knew its true cost.

But as Jorge watched the distant inhuman forces tear each other apart, he wasn't sure he could call this battle. They were not warriors so much as savage beasts who tore at each other with tooth and claw. No glory, no courage, no honor. They attacked mindlessly, without hesitation or mercy. Limbs torn from sockets, eyes gouged, jaws ripped free, innards yanked out. It was easily the most horrific thing he had ever witnessed.

He felt a hand on his shoulder and turned to see Blaine, his face etched in bitter sorrow.

"Now do you see why we were so desperate to be rid of Bàs?"

"Yes, I think I do."

"This is what happens to mortals when gods play war."

57

Galina thought she had been prepared for her reunion with Sebastian, but she had been a fool for believing so. After all, she had spent the majority of their time apart trying not to even think of him. So how could she possibly have been ready?

Although even if she *had* gone through the necessary mental and emotional work to bolster herself, it might have been for naught. Because what she saw before her was not the Sebastian she had turned her back on at Roskosh Manor all those months ago. Gone was the callow, naive, self-centered, and short-tempered youth. In his place was a man heavy with sorrow, and calm in the acceptance of responsibility. He appeared to have aged thirty years since she'd seen him last. It wasn't just the gray hair or lined face. There was a depth in his eyes that was as fascinating as it was heartbreaking. This was a man who had suffered, yet had not let it embitter him. It was this last detail, perhaps more than anything else, that despite her best efforts, won her over. She did not know if she loved him any more than she had when they'd first become betrothed. But by the goddess, it seemed like now she might actually respect him.

And then there was poor Lady Turgenev. If it was even accurate to call the gleaming metallic facsimile by that name. Galina knew that Irina never did anything without good reason, and she shuddered to think what terrible circumstances had led Sebastian's mother to this choice. She recalled a moment, long ago, when she had fleetingly imagined the woman would be the wise and witty mother she'd never had, and she felt a pang of remorse that she had not tried harder to bridge the gap between them. And now it was too late.

But while these inner maelstroms raged through the young queen of Izmoroz, none of it showed on her delicate features. Sebastian had the right of it. This was hardly the fitting time for maudlin tear-streaked reunions. It was the time for action, or death.

"Right," she said crisply. "Can someone tell me what on earth these things are?"

"Servants of Beatha," rumbled a familiar voice behind the golem.

Galina leaned over and saw a limbless, scarred Uaine strapped to her back. "Tighearna Elgin Mordha?"

"The same," said Mordha. "It was Beatha who also rendered me like this."

"Am I meant to know who this Beatha is?" she asked.

"I think we would call her Zivena," said Sebastian.

"Ah." Galina should not have been surprised that all of this was the work of Marzanna's sibling and rival, and yet she still struggled to reconcile the image of the spring goddess she had grown up reading about in poetry, and the author of this hideous display. "And where is the bulk of the Kantesian army?"

"This entire area is swamped with these creatures," said Sebastian. "Getting a large force in here right now would be impossible. But my sister is currently bringing orders to the hexenmeisters with instructions from the Herzog to assist us."

"Yes, I'm not sure how the Kantesians define the word *alliance*, but so far, I am deeply unimpressed."

"They are a...difficult people to fathom at times," said Sebastian. "But I do think it far better to have them as allies than enemies."

"Scant comfort if we're all dead." She leaned over the side and noted that the creatures were starting to pile up again. "How many more times do you think you can incinerate them?"

"As many as it takes, Your Majesty," he said promptly.

She found this new attitude of his deeply pleasing and had to clamp down on those feelings for fear she might smile. "Excellent. And I

THE WIZARD OF EVENTIDE   349

should note that while their progress has been slower, the same thing is happening on the other three sides of the building as well."

Sebastian blanched. "Ah."

"Don't worry, Sebastian," said Reyes. "Give us a little time to recover and my men and I will be able to assist you."

"Thank you, Ernesto. And I'm sure my sister will be here with reinforcements before long."

Galina closed her eyes and sighed. How could it be that after all this time and effort, she was counting on the least reasonable and reliable person in the world to come to her aid? It was downright humbling.

"Do not worry, Your Majesty," said Tatiana, as though intuiting her unspoken concern. "*Lisitsa* has many flaws, but the Lady Marzanna puts great stock in her, and I cannot think that is by accident."

"You may be right, Anya, but I'm not sure I like counting on a death goddess any more than I like counting on a fox-brained archer."

58

"This is amazing! *You* are amazing!"

Sonya shouted from her perch on the back of one of the massive insect-like golems. She knew this was a dire and tragic situation, and she probably shouldn't be so thrilled, but she couldn't help herself. Getting across the sea of Zivena-controlled creatures had been arduous, even for her. And when she reached the spot where the hexenmeisters were keeping the golems, she hadn't been sure how they would react to the orders. After all, they had been successfully keeping the hordes at bay, so why would they want to abandon their highly defensible position to help a bunch of people they didn't care about?

But maybe they did care after all. Or maybe they just didn't question the orders of the Herzog of Weide. Either way, a sour old man took the rolled parchment, broke the seal, and read the orders without a word. Then he spoke briefly to his fellow hexenmeisters and that was it. Within moments the terrifying mechanical giants were wading into the throngs of killer fungus people, crushing several with each step of their massive legs. Every golem had a cockpit of sorts in the abdomen where one of the hexenmeisters sat. They didn't directly operate the golem, of course, but could issue orders into a tube that the golem could hear. At the moment, however, they seemed to just be letting the golems run amok.

Obviously, Sonya couldn't sit idly by, so she clambered up a leg and sat on top of the abdomen directly above the hexenmeister cockpit.

She was tempted to shoot some of the creatures. From this height, and riding something with such a strange lumbering motion, it would be an interesting challenge. And of course, it would make her feel more a part of this triumphant march to aid her allies. But she knew it wouldn't have made much difference, and there was a chance she'd need her arrows for something actually productive later. So instead she cheered on the golems.

"Forward to victory! You are saving the day!"

The hexenmeister, a tired old woman with a streak of black in her gray hair, glared up at Sonya through the slat in the metal hatch.

"Zey do not need or want your encouragement."

Sonya grinned back at her. "You don't know that for certain."

The hexenmeister continued to glare at her, but did not argue.

Sonya began scanning the building tops, looking for allies. With the streets overrun, she assumed most people had moved to higher ground.

Sure enough, a few blocks later she saw a familiar face.

"Dima!"

He and a large group of Izmorozians were on a nearby rooftop, surrounded on all sides by a mass of fungus people who had apparently reached them by climbing up a pile of their own kind. Such was the way of spring, the desperate and voracious spirit that always clawed up from beneath the dead of last year's fall. Life did not succeed because it *valued* each creature. Rather, it was the opposite. Life would discard a thousand so that one, no different from the others, might succeed. To Sonya's mind, not even death was so cruel or unjust.

The golem was about twenty feet higher than the roof of the building, so Sonya leapt down, using the fungus people to cushion her landing. Then she drew her knife and went to work.

They were insensible to pain, and hardly any blood seeped out when she sliced them. But this Kantesian blade was by far the best knife she'd ever had, and with the thrill of the hunt giving her added strength, she lopped off hands with ease, and with precise cuts between vertebrae, even severed some heads. Sonya might not be a Ranger of Marzanna any longer, but she was honest enough with herself to know that this was the work she had been designed for by that Goddess of Death, and she was grateful that she could help these people in their moment of need.

As she continued to cut swaths of carnage into the fungus people on the rooftop, the golem who had dropped her off now cleared out those below with large sweeps of its legs. Sonya wondered if the hexenmeister had ordered it to do that, or if this was in thanks for the praise she'd given it earlier. She might never know the answer, so she decided to believe it was the latter.

With the reinforcements cut off, Sonya made short work of the remaining creatures. Then she waved up to the golem and shouted, "Thank you!"

"*Strannik* Sonya..."

Dima stared at her, looking both grateful and afraid. He had probably turned on her just like everyone else back in Izmoroz. Perhaps he wondered if she held any resentment, and she realized with some surprise she hadn't even thought about that in months. Perhaps because it hadn't really been *her* who'd been betrayed. It had been the previous Sonya.

"I'm not *Strannik* any longer, Dima."

He looked confused. "But your hair..."

She ran her fingers through the white fur on her head. "Yeah, I still make deals with the Lady, but it's strictly business now. I don't serve her or anyone."

"I... did not know that was possible," he admitted.

She shrugged. "I make my own rules, Dimishka. I may not be *Strannik* anymore, but I'm still *Lisitsa*, you know."

He stared at her for a moment, then suddenly burst into laughter and wrapped her up in a big hug like he had long ago when she'd been his *Strannitchka*. She let herself relax into it, savoring the earthy smells of an Izmorozian peasant. She was glad that this Sonya still appreciated such things, and hoped she always would.

He released her after a moment and she looked around at the group of exhausted but determined Izmorozians. These were well-armed and capable men and women who had seen all the horrors this world offered and held firm.

"Looks like Queen Kukla is doing right by you."

Dima gave her a pained look. "Please don't disrespect Her Majesty like that. I happen to be one of her captains."

"Good for you!" She patted his head. "Can you and your people hold out awhile now that we've cleared some away? I want to go see who else needs help."

"Yes, thank you, er... what should I call you now?"

All the Sonyas who had come before, and each one further from the original. Perhaps it was a name that no longer really applied to her. Yet there was one thing that became more true with each "*me.*"

She smiled wide so that her sharp teeth gleamed. "I think the only name that probably still makes sense is *Lisitsa.*"

Then she leapt onto a different golem that was passing by and began scanning for other rooftop allies in need. What a terrible and glorious day it was.

"You are *amazing!*" she told her new golem.

59

Sebastian and his mother's golem took the front line defending the rooftop while Galina's Rangers and Viajero recovered. Using a combination of wind and fire, he managed to keep the majority at bay, and the golem dealt with those who made it through. Sebastian had expected to feel more fatigued, but perhaps the staff that Isobelle had given him truly was shielding him from the worst of it.

Even still, the enemy seemed endless, and he knew he would tire eventually. Every time he knocked back a line of the fungus creatures and saw another immediately take their place, he felt a tiny flutter of despair. How much longer could they hold out? And where the hell was his sister?

Thankfully, he still had some strength left when he finally heard the thunderous clang and shriek of hissing steam. A moment later the golems trundled into view, stomping everything in their path and sending dozens of creatures flying with each step.

Showing her usual flair for the ridiculous, he saw Sonya riding on top of one. Her face was flushed and there was still that concerning wild look in her eye, but she was laughing and cheering as the golem beneath her laid waste to the town.

"She's completely mad," Galina said, sounding both disapproving and awed at the same time.

"Yes, she probably is," said Sebastian. "But how can you not love that smile?"

Galina sighed wearily, then glanced back at her two Rangers. They seemed oblivious to Sonya's dramatic rescue and still focused on pushing back the remaining creatures.

The ghost of a smile tugged at the queen's lips for a moment. "I suppose I have come to appreciate the simple, rough-hewn charms of Rangers."

The moment of warmth took Sebastian by surprise. He wasn't sure he'd ever seen her express such genuine affection before. And to think it was toward the "beast folk" that she used to disparage. It seemed he wasn't the only one who had grown during this time.

Her eyebrow rose. "What is it?"

"I merely bask in the majesty of my queen."

She gazed at him, perhaps deciding whether he was serious. In truth, he didn't know himself. He had never been one to affectionately tease someone before. Well, his sister, but she didn't count.

After a moment, Galina nodded. "As you should."

The golems made short work of the creatures. The scope and extent of destruction was both a relief and deeply troubling. As Sebastian had pointed out to Galina earlier, the Kantesians might have their faults, but he far preferred them as allies rather than enemies.

Once the golems had taken care of the bulk of the enemies inside the walls, they trundled out into the fields surrounding the city to finish off the rest and rejoin their own army.

The few creatures left within Magna Alto were eagerly hunted down by the Izmorozian militia. Sebastian suspected that their previous helplessness had struck a blow to their pride, and now they felt they were redeeming themselves in some way.

When the remaining creatures had all been killed, Galina ordered her militia to begin clearing the streets so that the Kantesian infantry could enter. They tossed the disfigured corpses in great piles along the sides of buildings. They were clearly overjoyed that the harrowing experience was over, and laughed and joked while they set about their grisly task.

Sebastian did not begrudge them their understandable relief. But at the same time, he had only to look carefully at one of the mushroom-choked creatures to recognize that they had once been regular people who had likely never done anything to deserve such a terrible fate.

"It's dreadful, isn't it?"

Galina joined him, accompanied by her Rangers. They stood and watched several burly men haul a small wagon filled with corpses to the center of the square. They deposited the bodies beside a broken statue of Empress Caterina.

"Yes it is," he agreed.

"A nearly inconceivable waste of human life," she said.

He was reminded of why they had gotten along so well in the first place. Despite her keen intellect and sometimes haughty demeanor, at her core she had the empathetic soul of a poet.

"It truly is."

"This isn't over, you know," she said. "There's still Vittorio to deal with, presumably hiding in the palace with the last of his guard. And I can't help but think that viper has some last trick up his sleeve. He strikes me as the sort of man who only becomes more dangerous when cornered."

"But what can he do?" Sebastian nodded toward the gates, where the Kantesian troops were now filing into the city. "Izmoroz might have taken heavy loses, but the Herzog's forces are still largely intact. And there's an alliance of Uaine and Raízians due in the next day or so. Even if Vittorio has filled the entire palace with soldiers, it won't be enough."

"I've had enough experience with meddlesome deities of late to suspect it won't be as simple as who has more combatants," replied Galina.

Sebastian didn't know what to say to that, but for some reason it brought to mind Ambassador Boz's suggestion that he had been granted his power by Mokosh to be peacekeeper between the gods. It had seemed such a daunting idea, but thankfully it didn't appear necessary now.

"Hey, Queen Kukla, congratulations!" Sonya rode toward them astride Peppercorn, with their mother's golem walking beside her.

"Speaking of meddling and unpredictable," Galina muttered. "The fox is here."

"Sorry I couldn't come over sooner," Sonya said cheerfully. "But my *little brother* decided to leave my horse on a *rooftop.*"

"Oh, er, yes...," said Sebastian. "I wasn't sure how to handle that situation, and he doesn't seem to like me very much, so I thought it best to leave to you."

"It's okay." She leaned over and patted the golem's metal arm. "Turns out Mother is strong enough to lift a horse! Pretty impressive, right?"

The golem let out a puff of steam and Sonya laughed as though it had been a particularly witty response. Sebastian and his sister hadn't really talked much about their feelings regarding their mother's golem. Probably because neither of them really knew. He'd been trying not to think of the thing as his mother, as Isobelle suggested. But during the battle, in moments of stress he had called her *Mother* and she had responded. Some of her was in there. How much of his mother did she have to be in order to "count" as the real thing?

Sonya's face suddenly lit up. "Andre! Tatiana! You got younger!"

"Yes, *Lisitsa*," rumbled the big bear Ranger. "And you seem to have found some inner peace."

"Oh yeah, well..." Sonya ran her fingers through her fur, looking a little embarrassed. "In my last life I had a hard time reconciling Sonya and *Lisitsa*, but now I don't really make a distinction anymore."

"This is good," said Tatiana. "Mikhail would be pleased."

Sonya's expression brightened. "You think?" Then she looked suddenly worried. "But you know, I told the Lady I won't serve her anymore. So I'm not really a Ranger now."

The two stared at her for a moment, then Andre laughed.

Sonya scowled. "What's so funny?"

"Did you think the Lady cares about what you said?" asked Tatiana. "I mean...she didn't seem upset. Or even surprised really."

"You are now at one with *Lisitsa*," said Andre. "The Lady need not command you. Your instincts alone will guide you to her will."

Sonya scowled. "Well, we'll see about that, I guess."

Now that Sebastian knew just how cruel the Goddess of Winter was to her followers, he found it even harder to understand why anyone would ever want to serve her. But then again, since he'd been born a wizard, he'd never had to experience true powerlessness. Marcello had once suggested something along those lines.

Marcello...

It struck him like a blow to the gut. Where was Marcello? And

General Barone for that matter? What about the other captains—Branca, Dandolo, even Totti? Had they been sent south to fight the Raízians? If so, had they been taken prisoner? Or did the Aureumians he knew now lie dead on a battlefield? Worse, they could have remained in Magna Alto and been turned into one of the horrible fungus people.

But no, perhaps they were still alive, stationed in the palace as the last line of Vittorio's defense. If so, maybe there was still a chance to help them in some way. At least to take them as prisoners of war, where they would be accorded fair and humane treatment. Maybe he could even beg Galina to grant them amnesty. She was not an unreasonable or vindictive person, after all.

He glanced over at the sharp-eyed queen of Izmoroz and realized he could no longer say that for certain. He would be a fool to think this regal and fierce woman was the same girl he'd courted half a year ago.

They were soon joined in the square by Ferdinand Cohen von Weide, his daughter, her husband, and Ambassador Boz.

"Presumably this is the Herzog?" Galina whispered to Sebastian as they drew near.

"Yes, accompanied by his daughter, Isobelle Cohen von Weide, and her husband, Wilhelm Sachs von Gestade."

"And the Victashian accompanying them is the illustrious Ambassador Ceren Boz?"

"Correct."

The Herzog wasted no time introducing himself to Galina, sweeping forward with a simple but elegant bow.

"Your Majesty, what a pleasure to finally meet you in person. I am grateful to see you are unharmed."

"Likewise, Herzog von Weide," said Galina. "And my well-being is in no small part thanks to your assistance. I hope we can continue to build upon this foundation toward a mutually beneficial future."

The Herzog gave her a brief smile. "I like your ambition, young queen, but first let us see to the matter at hand. Where do we stand?"

"The last resistance in the city proper has been wiped out. All that remains is the palace and whatever forces Vittorio has sequestered himself with there. We have seen nothing of the Uaine, so perhaps they are his last line of defense."

"No, I'm afraid not," said Ambassador Boz.

"*Afraid* not?" asked Mordha from where he was still strapped to the golem.

"It grieves me to tell you this, mighty Tighearna, but I have received word from my representative that Clans Dílis and Seacál are currently locked in battle with the other three clans, who seem to be infected by the same fungus as those we have encountered here."

The Uaine warlord's face did not change. Or at least, Sebastian could detect no shift in the creases of scar tissue. But his harsh voice trembled as he spoke.

"I . . . see."

Three clans of Uaine. That was three-fifths of their entire population already doomed, with more likely to follow. Sebastian found the idea staggering. But then he looked around at the heaps of bodies around him and realized that Aureum might be in far worse shape.

"The cost of this victory comes too high," he said quietly.

"*Victory*, you say, Sebastian? How presumptuous."

They all turned toward this new, and for Sebastian at least, chillingly familiar voice.

Franko Vittorio was nearly unrecognizable. He seemed to have shrunk. Not just in girth, but in stature. His face was gaunt, his hair lank and greasy, and his clothes torn and stained. He leaned upon his crutches and stared at them all with the eyes of a fanatic. He was alone, without even a bodyguard.

"Have you come to surrender, then?" Galina asked, showing no sign of surprise.

"Ah, look at you, such a funny little thing. I would never have guessed that you of all people would become the Adversary's chief handmaiden. Quite impressive."

"I am no servant, but a queen," she said calmly.

"Even queens are servants to gods," said Vittorio. "Regardless, I did not come to surrender. We still have one final battle, after all."

"You are either foolish or mad," said Weide. "Your desperate gambit has already failed. You have no way to defeat us."

"I don't expect *you* to understand, godless one," said Vittorio. "But Sebastian and his horrible sister know as well as I do that with gods, anything can be accomplished. All it takes is the proper sacrifice. Really, it's a tragedy Irina can't warn you as she usually does. I would greatly enjoy seeing her expression of—"

It happened so fast, not even Sonya or the Rangers could react. The golem, who had always seemed so passive and content to let others lead, shot forward in a blur of steel.

Vittorio's head exploded in a pulpy mess as her fist slammed into it. A jet of blood rose from the neck, and the decapitated corpse fell in a heap.

They all stared at the golem for a moment. Her perfect sculpted face was now streaked in gore.

"Well," Weide said brightly. "I suppose that is that."

"No," said Tatiana. "Magic has just been wrought here."

Sebastian felt it as well. The same wild, feral power that had come off the fungus people. Although now it was in the air all around them. Whatever Vittorio had done, he had used himself as the sacrifice to accomplish it.

"Everyone remain calm," said Galina. "Until we know what we're up against, whatever we do might make things worse."

"I agree," said Weide. "A level head will—"

His eyes went wide and his shoulders began to heave. It looked like he was choking, except his mouth was open and appeared empty.

"Father?"

Isobelle grasped his arm. He looked at her as panic spread across his face. Then he shook his head and pushed her away. He staggered back from all of them, clutching at his neck. His whole body convulsed several times, and then he froze, his eyes staring up into the early evening sky.

A moment later, the head of a mushroom emerged from his mouth.

"By the Lady," whispered Galina as she took several steps backward. "Is it *contagious*?"

A moment later, both Isobelle and Wilhelm also began convulsing.

"Isobelle!" Sebastian reached out to her, but Sonya yanked him back.

"Sorry, little brother."

"Surely there's *something* we can do!"

Sonya only shook her head.

Others began to convulse around them as well, although Sebastian noted it wasn't everyone. In fact...

"It's only the Kantesians," he said.

"The godless ones," said Mordha.

"What do you mean?" asked Galina.

"It only seems to affect those not affiliated with Bàs. Neither us nor your Izmorozian warriors are affected."

"But I'm not affiliated with Marzanna," said Sebastian.

"You are the chosen of Mokosh, though," Ambassador Boz pointed out.

"What about your countrymen?" asked Galina. "Shouldn't they have been protected?"

"Vittorio must have infected them right after I broke our pact with Bàs," said the Uaine.

"So I guess *we're* all safe?" asked Sonya.

Galina gave her a withering look. "The entire Kantesian army is transforming into a new horde of fungus creatures, and we're right in the middle of it, so I'd *hardly* say we're safe."

"But it doesn't make any sense," said Sebastian. "Vittorio massacred his own people, and now he's doing the same with another country. He even sacrificed his own life. Why would he do something like this?"

"Because this is not *his* will," said Mordha. "It is the will of the gods."

The Kantesians seemed to have finished their horrible transformations. They stood perfectly still, often in contorted or hunched poses. Some, like the Herzog, had mushrooms in their mouths, while others had them in ears, and some even in their eyes. A large mushroom cap burst through poor beautiful Isobelle's nostril so forcefully, her nose was now only a torn and ragged flap of flesh.

Sonya's golden eyes narrowed as she gazed across the tops of motionless heads. "It's going to be tricky getting out of here, but as long as they don't—"

As if given a silent command, the Kantesians all began moving at the same time, attacking the nearest uninfected person.

"Everyone, fall back to my position!" called Galina. "We stay together!"

Those Izmorozian soldiers who could reach the queen gathered around her, joining the Rangers, the golem, Sonya, and Sebastian in forming a protective circle around Galina and Ambassador Boz.

"Your Majesty," said Andre. "We should find somewhere more defensible."

Galina pointed to the nearest open doorway. "Will that do?"

"It will have to," said Tatiana. "Come, Your Majesty."

The fungus people began their lurching approach as the group retreated to the building and began barricading the door.

"Don't forget the windows," said Galina.

The Izmorozian soldiers began piling furniture in front of the doors, while Sonya and the Rangers set about sealing up the windows.

Sebastian stood there, unsure what to do and afraid of getting in everyone's way.

Then he noticed Ambassador Boz giving him a stern look.

"Don't you think it's time for you to fulfill your purpose?"

"*Me?*"

"You are the creation of the one you call Mokosh, the Damp Mother Earth."

"He is the servant of Danu?" Mordha asked from the golem's back. "Then there may still be some hope."

"What are you both talking about?" demanded Galina.

"Danu is progenitor of Bàs and Beatha," explained Mordha. "If Sebastian's power is derived from Mother Earth, then he may be strong enough to confront the gods directly."

"Come on, Mordha," said Sonya as she lashed a board across one of the windows. "Do you really think Sebastian could defeat a being as powerful as Lady Marzanna?"

"I don't know," admitted Mordha. "But if not, then we are all doomed."

"Well, we have to do *something*," said Galina. "Because they're here!"

The hastily erected barricades shook as the mass of infected Kantesians slammed into them. They were clumsy, but seemed as strong as the previous group. And they had the added advantage of being mostly encased in armor.

"These barricades won't last long," said Sonya as she began firing arrows through the small cracks. The soldiers took up positions near the blocked doors and windows, their faces grim and pinched with exhaustion.

Galina turned to Sebastian. "I'm sorry to ask this of you when there is so much we don't know, but you may well be our last hope."

"Galina, no!" snapped Sonya as she fired another arrow. "You can't order him to fight a *goddess*! Besides, he doesn't even know how to open a portal."

"Actually, I think I might…"

He still recalled that feeling when he'd called upon the power of Mokosh to kill Rykov. The magic had come from somewhere. Or rather, from everywhere, like it had seeped through the cracks of reality. And he'd felt something similar again in his dreams. That strange mud seeping in, almost like a tangible darkness. What if instead it had been Mokosh preparing him for this moment?

He held up his staff and gazed into the seething red ruby for a moment. "Hold them off."

"Sebastian, tell me you're not seriously doing this!" His sister's face was creased into an expression he'd never seen before. Fear.

"I'm sorry, Yasha. I just… don't know what else to do."

He closed his eyes and recalled that heavy, oozing darkness. The Damp Mother Earth who was before all else, and would be long after. The void before creation. It was all around them, seeping in through tiny cracks—or no, more like pores in reality. That was how he'd always drawn his magic without quite realizing it. Could he widen those pores? Or perhaps collect them into a single opening large enough for him to pass through?

He tried, but reality fought back. It did not like its rules broken in such a way. He strained harder, putting all his will into it. The ruby began to vibrate down the shaft of the wooden staff, numbing his hand, but he gripped it tighter and pressed on. Then the staff began to wither, growing desiccated and brittle, so he pulled the ruby free. Now he could feel the unfiltered raw power coursing through him. Slowly, painfully, the minuscule holes in reality began to gather until—

The ruby burst apart in his hand. He cried out, his palm bleeding from the shards that had cut into his skin.

He looked around in a daze, seeing the soldiers still desperately holding the fortifications in place. But it was already buckling, and steel-encased hands groped through, grabbing and tearing the flesh of anyone in reach. How long would they last before they were overwhelmed?

"I'm sorry, everyone...," he said. "The ruby couldn't take the strain. Maybe if I still had that diamond, but..." He shook his head, feeling miserable. "Without a truly powerful gem, I can't do it."

The golem had been pushing up against the largest barricade over the front door. But now it turned toward him. It kept one hand on the door, and with the other opened the front of its chest. Inside was a pulsing magenta gem.

The golem pointed to Sebastian, then gestured to the gem.

He stared at the seething gem, realizing this was her core. The metal encasement was little more than a vehicle for this perfect stone.

"Mother, you...want me to use this? But this is your soul, isn't it? This is all that's left of you. What if it shatters?"

The golem leaned over, grasped his hand, and pressed it on the gem, then slowly nodded.

"Sonya..." He turned to his sister, tears filling his eyes. "She wants me to..."

Sonya snarled as she fired another arrow. She looked like she was about to give an angry retort, but there was a crack of wood, followed by a bark of pain. They all looked to see Andre, who had perhaps been far more exhausted from the previous battles than any of them had realized. The barricade had come loose from the window he'd been guarding, and he clutched at a sword handle that protruded from his stomach. The fungus people might be clumsy, but they could still apparently stab someone as large as him.

"Andre!"

It was Galina, her cool, stoic, queenly visage now crumpled into horror as she tried to go to him. But Tatiana held her back.

The golem squeezed Sebastian's hand on the gem in its chest hard enough to hurt. It was telling him they were out of time. If there was any way he could stop this, he would need her to do it. But if he destroyed what remained of his mother in the process...

"Mother, please, no...."

Sonya let out an animal growl of frustration, shoved back one more creature, then left the front line to join him.

"Fine, do it!" she snarled, a dark fury in her eyes. "But I'm going with you."

"Sonya—"

"Mother!" she shouted over the din. "I swear to you that I won't let him die. No matter what!"

The golem bowed its head and waited.

Tears coursed down Sebastian's cheeks as he once more gathered his will together and focused it on the gem that was his mother's soul.

And it was so easy.

"Oh," he said.

The world felt as malleable as mud to be shaped by his hand. With a single gesture, he opened a rift in the very fabric of reality as effortlessly as one might draw a line in the dirt. It wavered there, impossibly, seeming to draw his vision into itself.

He looked back to his mother and almost fainted with relief that she still seemed to be functioning normally. She gently removed his hand and closed up her chest. She nodded once to him, once to Sonya, then put her full attention on the crumbling barricade.

Sonya and Sebastian turned to the shimmering rift in space and time before them.

"Good luck to the both of you," called Galina, her face still pale, but now set with determination. "We'll buy you as much time as we can."

"Thank you, Your Majesty." Sebastian looked at Sonya. "Well, big sister?"

"Yes, little brother?"

"Shall we go defeat a goddess?"

6I

Jorge watched from the makeshift command tent as the two armies continued to rip each other apart, and he couldn't help wondering: Where was the Raízian God during all of this? Was He yet another aspect of one of these warring gods, like how Marzanna and Bàs were somehow the same? Or was He above them? Yet if He *was* above them, why did he allow this to happen? Did He approve of this horror? Was he an aloof and impartial observer? Or did he weep along with them? Jorge had no answer to any of these questions.

Blaine had joined the fray, leading his warriors into this hideous battle. Lucia had also plunged in, somehow creating yet another new song to confront these fungus monsters. It did not seem as effective as the one she had used on the sluagh gorta in the previous battle, but it at least partly disrupted whatever unifying control held the monsters. Some seemed merely lost, milling about in confusion, while a few even began attacking their own.

Jorge couldn't decide which side was more likely to emerge victorious, if killing one's countrymen could even be called victory. The fungus creatures were strong and merciless, but they lacked the skill of the Uaine warriors they had stolen, and their numbers were no greater than the sluagh gorta.

"I believe the tide is turning in our favor," said the Xefe as he passed the telescoping glass to Jorge.

"It may not be turning fast enough," Onat Duman said. "I am no longer able to contact the ambassador, which means she is likely in such severe danger that she doesn't have the time and concentration to form the connection."

"Or else she's dead," said the Xefe.

Duman looked at him for a moment, then nodded. "Or that. Even if we are able to overcome this enemy, by the time we reach Magna Alto, it may already be too late."

Jorge was about to advise Duman not to underestimate the Portinari siblings, but then he spied something odd in the telescoping glass. One of the Anxeles Escuros was staggering about, clutching at his throat, but he was nowhere near the enemy. It looked like he was choking, but on what?

Then others began to do the same. Not just mercenaries, but Viajero as well.

"What on earth…"

Lucia's song cut off abruptly, and she too began choking on something.

Jorge shoved the glass at Javier. "Something is affecting our people, mercenary and Viajero alike."

Xefe gazed into the glass, then his thick gray brows slowly rose. "My God…I think those creatures are infectious. The Uaine seem fine, but all of ours, to a person, seemed to be—*hughk*."

Jorge stared in horror as the Xefe began to choke. The other guild masters, too. Wherever he looked, Raízians were choking, and then moments later, mushrooms bloomed from them.

"Wh-what do we do?" Duman asked.

The Victashian didn't seem to be infected, but his brown face was etched with fear. Battle had not fazed him, but this, it seemed, had rattled even his courage. The guild masters were all now blooming with mushrooms and began to stagger toward the only two people in the command tent who were not infected.

Jorge grabbed Duman's arm. "We run."

They dodged through the looming crowds of infected, looking for a clearing. But what then? Just before he began choking, the Xefe had said the Uaine seemed unaffected. Jorge hoped that was true, and pulled Duman toward the Uaine command post.

The battlefield was in a different type of chaos than before, with strategic lines collapsing as the Raízians began turning on their Uaine allies. Jorge didn't know why he seemed to be the only one of his countrymen not infected, but he didn't have time to ponder that now. Instead, he and Duman weaved swiftly through the bedlam until they reached the Uaine command, heavily guarded by living Uaine warriors.

"We're not infected! Please let us through!" Jorge shouted as they drew their swords.

He realized belatedly that they probably didn't understand what he was saying, but thankfully Blaine's father saw him and barked an order in Uaine. The warriors quickly stepped aside, then re-formed once Jorge and Duman had passed.

"Chief Ruairc, have you seen Blaine?"

Ruairc might not speak his language, but he clearly understood what Jorge was asking and shook his head.

Jorge nodded gravely in response, then spotted Rowena farther back and hurried over to her.

"Do you know what's going on?"

Her face was tense with concentration, but her voice was distant, as though she was focused on other things, which she most certainly was.

"Beatha's final counterattack, bending anyone not bespoken by Bàs to her will."

"But what about me? And Duman? Neither of us worship Bàs or Marzanna."

"I do not know about the Victashian, but you are beloved of several of Bàs's servants and so are granted his protection."

"That's . . . generous of them."

A smile twitched at Rowena's lips, though her expression did not otherwise change. "Hardly. You have been serving his will without realizing it ever since you joined Sonya. So in a sense you are a servant, even if you did not know it."

"Okay, that's troubling, but I suppose I can hardly complain right now. Is this happening everywhere? Even back in Colmo?"

"I don't think so," said Rowena. "At least, not yet. It seems to spread through tiny spores carried on the wind."

"Then it might reach them eventually?"

"Yes."

"Unless we stop them here."

"I don't know," she admitted.

"How are we doing in that regard? Are we...winning?"

"We may well succeed. But to do so, we will likely have to kill the majority of my countrymen and yours. I do not think you would consider that *winning.*"

62

Galina hated watching her Andrushka continue to fight with a sword in his belly, but what choice did they have? Even mortally wounded and weary beyond measure, he was worth ten normal soldiers. More, even. In his pain and desperation, he fought with an astonishing strength nearly on the same level as the golem. The two of them stood in the doorway, and the oncoming Kantesian army broke upon them like waves onto rock.

Tatiana stayed back with Galina, always the last line of defense for the queen. The rest of the soldiers fought valiantly at the windows, but inevitably some broke through, and if not for the Ranger, Galina and Ambassador Boz would already be dead.

Even so, it wouldn't be long now for any of them. They were all exhausted and wounded, and the infected Kantesians, though clumsy, fought with reckless savagery.

Galina's hope stirred for a brief moment when she spotted Reyes and some of his fellow Raízians at one of the windows. But no. They were not dancing or singing or making their beautiful terrible magic. They had also succumbed to the fungus. Apparently whatever god they worshipped had not protected them.

Although Galina wondered what sort of protection she and her allies truly had. They had not been infected, but poor Andre, who had given multiple lives to Lady Marzanna, would die with all the rest, and what difference did it make in the end? Aureum, Uaine,

Kante, Izmoroz, perhaps even Raíz, now that she had seen they were susceptible to the infection. One way or another, this war was taking a catastrophic toll on all five countries. It was as though Zivena's aim was not merely to defeat her sister, but to wipe out most of humanity in the process.

"Might we retreat to the rooftops again, Your Majesty?" asked Tatiana.

"Can you carry Andre up there?"

"No, Your Majesty."

Galina turned to Irina, who was pushing hard against the Kantesians, allowing a few Izmorozian stragglers who had just arrived through. If the golem could lift a horse, surely she could lift Andre, but right now she was also the linchpin of their defense. To lose her even for a short time might mean losing everything. And abandoning Andre was out of the question.

"We will make our stand here, Tatiana Sova," Galina said.

Tatiana bowed her head. "As you command, Your Majesty."

"All we can do now is pray that Sebastian and his sister are successful in putting a stop to this."

63

The moment they stepped through the portal, Sonya knew exactly where they were. It was not on the banks of a dark river, but the scentless air and meaningless temperature were enough.

"We're in the Eventide," she whispered.

The sky above was not the dark blue of night, but truly black. There was no moon, but perhaps there were stars? Although there were far too many to be the stars she knew, and they seemed to move and shift, more like snow in a blizzard that suddenly formed swirling patterns, then just as quickly dispersed.

The land beneath them was not like snow, however. More like sand, but multicolored. There were dunes of red that shifted to orange, then yellow, or blue that shifted from purple to red. They rolled and undulated beneath their feet in a way that reminded Sonya somewhat of the ocean.

"You...know this place, Yasha?" Sebastian's eyes were wide with wonder.

"Sort of," she admitted. "I've never been to this area specifically, but it's definitely the place I go when I die and meet Lady Marzanna."

"Well that's encouraging," he said. "I suppose."

They stared at the swirling, shifting landscape around them for a few more moments.

Then Sebastian said, "So where do we go?"

"I'm not sure it matters," said Sonya.

"What do you mean?"

"This isn't a normal place."

"Obviously."

"No, I mean it doesn't really work the way our world does. I don't think places here are fixed points, you know?"

"I have no idea what you're talking about," he said.

Sonya wasn't sure she did, either. But she felt the pull of some... instinct? Maybe Andre and Tatiana were right, and *Lisitsa* would guide her. Was that a good thing? She wasn't sure. Would Marzanna have a problem with them confronting Zivena?

Was that really what they were doing? Directly challenging the Goddess of Spring?

Sonya shuddered.

But *Lisitsa* said *yes*.

"You're just going to have to trust me," she told her brother.

She began hiking across the shifting, colored dunes and Sebastian hastily joined her. They walked for a while, and it wasn't that they came to the end of the dunes so much as the dunes transformed around them.

They skirted a fathomless pit that looked something like an inverted mountain. Then they climbed across a tree heavy with overripe, bitter-smelling fruit that seemed to have no roots, but instead branches on either end that stretched off in both directions endlessly. There was a land in which everything was fur, from the coarse yellow grass underfoot to the downy blue sky above. There was a place that oozed green pus from every crack, and a place whose landscape was made of jagged, vibrating teeth. There were places so dark that Sonya and Sebastian had to hold hands to keep from being separated, and places so bright that they were blinded and still had to hold hands as they walked.

Finally, after all the impossible places, they arrived at a simple, snow-covered clearing in a forest. The trees were bare and black, and the sky above was slate gray. Snowflakes drifted lazily from the sunless sky, dancing playfully though there was no wind.

An old felled log stretched across the clearing, and seated on either end of the log were two forms. One was wreathed in darkness, yet gleamed the pure white of bone. The other writhed endlessly and fit-fully within a festering cloud of blood and bile.

"I've...seen this before...," Sonya said.

"Yes, my *Lisitsa*," said the being of dark and gleaming bone in a voice like a storm of razor blades. "In your dreams."

"Lady Marzanna? Is this your real form?"

"Closer than you have ever seen before, my *Lisitsa*, but your eyes cannot behold my true face just yet."

"Then you..." Sebastian turned to the writhing blood-cloud form. "You must be Lady Zivena."

The shape flexed and compressed a few times, almost like the shak-ing shoulders of laughter. In a voice that squelched and burbled like the guts of a great beast, she said, "Have you come to chastise us once again, Armonia?"

"Again?"

"Not you specifically, but our mother's creations are ever the spoil-sport of our games. Although really, what does she expect us to do? Sit and observe for eternity? My sibling and I grow bored. We long for distraction. And what better entertainment can there be than the foibles of humanity?"

"I cannot begin to understand your plight, Lady Zivena," said Sebastian. "But I will not stand idly by as you abuse my friends and family for your own amusement."

The blooming, dripping shape of Zivena leaned forward. "And how will you stop me, little Armonia? You have none of your prede-cessors' gravitas, I must say."

That drew Sebastian up short. He looked down at his empty hands, as though realizing for the first time that he had no gemstone to focus his magic.

"You see?" said Zivena to her sister. "He is but a child, plucked prematurely from the vine."

Sebastian and Sonya stared at each other for a moment. Had they come this far only to realize that they were powerless?

Then Marzanna spoke. "My sibling is only teasing you, little Armonia. This place *is* our mother, and as her servant, you need no trinket to aid you here. You are free to draw upon its power however you wish."

Zivena made a snorting, or perhaps a farting sound. "How tiresome you have become, my dear sibling. Have you lost all sense of play?"

Marzanna ignored her and continued to speak to Sebastian. "Indeed, brother of my beloved *Lisitsa*, you are capable of calling down such furious might that you could quite easily compel my sibling to abandon her present course of action."

Sebastian squared his stance as though preparing for a fight. "Very well. Then I will."

"Yes, you *could*...," Marzanna said in a drawn-out, almost lazy tone. Then she turned back to Sonya. "But, my darling *Lisitsa*, is that enough for you?"

"What do you mean?" asked Sonya.

"Yes, dear sibling," said Zivena, her squelching, burbling form somehow communicating unease. "What *do* you mean?"

Marzanna once again seemed to ignore her sister and remained focused on Sonya. "Surely you realize that while your brother may stop us this time, we will do it again, as we have in the past. The Winter War, and before that the subjugation of the Raízians and the formation of the Aureumian Empire. Those are earlier games you may recognize, and there have been many before that, here and in other lands as well."

"Wait, *you* made those things happen?" Sonya thought of the countless deaths, both direct and indirect, that had come from the Winter War, as well as the suffering her people had endured since. "You commanded me to free my people.... from the hardship that *you* helped create?"

"That is correct."

Marzanna did not look apologetic or regretful. Sonya could only stare at this being to whom she had given so much of herself. Even when she stopped being a Ranger, she had still believed there was some worth in the goddess. That she would ultimately help the world, not be the cause of its suffering. It was a betrayal that cut so deep it stole any response from her lips.

"But Lady Marzanna," pressed Sebastian, "you're suggesting we could finally end this cycle?"

"No, you can't!" Zivena cut in. "This is how the world is and how it must *always* be. If you kill me, there will be an imbalance of power, and Mother will destroy everything."

"True." Marzanna's black eyes bored into Sonya's golden fox eyes. "There cannot be an imbalance, my *Lisitsa*. Do you understand?"

Sonya thought she might understand but . . . no, surely that wasn't what the goddess meant. It was just her anger wishing it were so.

"Incidentally," continued Marzanna, "if you allow your brother to compel my sibling to give up her current goal, he will succeed, but the effort will cost him his life."

"I won't let that happen," said Sonya.

"No?" Marzanna smiled, showing her jagged black teeth. "And what will you do to prevent it?"

"Whatever I must."

"Yasha, what am I missing?" asked Sebastian. "If we can't kill Zivena, then how do we put a stop to this terrible cycle? Can we perhaps *imprison* her?"

"Imprison?" Zivena let out a gurgling laugh. "*Me?* By all means, little Armonia, please try!"

But Marzanna and Sonya were still staring at each other intently, both ignoring their siblings.

"You *do* understand, don't you, *Lisitsa*?" asked Marzanna.

If both goddesses were allowed to live, they would keep wreaking havoc on humanity in their boredom. If one died, then the resulting imbalance would unmake the world. There was really only one other solution.

"That is what you really want?" Sonya asked the Goddess of Winter and Death.

"It is what I have been working toward for centuries."

"I will do it."

"It will cost you."

"How much?"

There was a dreadful eagerness in the Goddess of Winter's expression.

"Everything."

"Yasha, no!" said Sebastian. "I don't know what you're talking about, but don't trust her! Remember all the terrible things she's done to you!"

"I *do* remember, little brother. That's exactly why I have to do this. Don't you remember what you asked me back in Kante? If I would sacrifice myself to solve all the problems of my loved ones?"

"What? No, we were talking about golems! This is different!"

"Except it's not." She bowed her head. "I accept your terms, Lady Marzanna."

"Ah, my *Lisitsa*, were I capable of human emotion, I think at this moment my pride in you would make me weep."

"Sibling, what are you playing at?" Zivena no longer looked amused.

"I have grown so tired," said Marzanna. "And I long for change. The one true change that I cannot bring."

Zivena's writhing form twisted anxiously. "Wh-what change is that?"

"An end to myself."

"You can't!" said Zivena.

"It pains me greatly that you must die as well," said Marzanna. "But as you have pointed out, the only way I can end myself without unmaking the world is to end you as well."

"This whole time..." Zivena's tentacles and entrails emptied themselves of fluids with something between fury and terror. "You have been working toward *this*? Our *mutual destruction*?"

"I am sorry, my dear, beloved sibling. It was the only way I could finally find peace. After countless millennia of meaningless cycles of life and death, I am so very tired."

"No! You can't do it!" Zivena moved swiftly toward her sister, but the space around her seemed to bend so that she never quite reached her.

"I *must* do it. Otherwise I shall go mad, and all of existence will suffer." Marzanna turned back to Sonya. "Now it is finally time. Brace yourself, my child. Birth is never easy."

Sonya felt it deep within. A brutal wrench unlike any she had experienced previously. It started in her chest and radiated outward, twisting, tearing her insides to shreds. She collapsed in the snow, writhing from pain beyond comprehension as grunts and whimpers escaped through her lips.

"Yasha!"

Sebastian dropped down beside her. "I have so much power right now! Tell me how to fix this! Tell me how to save you!"

Sonya's mouth opened, but instead of words, her insides came pouring out in a gush, splashing across the snowy forest floor, where they were quickly soaked up and disappeared. It kept coming out like a stream of vomit until there was nothing left of her but a dried husk.

Sebastian cradled the shrunken and desiccated body of his sister and sobbed. "Yasha...what have you done?"

"How dare you!" Zivena raged as she clawed desperately toward her sister but remained just out of reach. "This isn't fair! I hate you!"

Marzanna nodded sadly. But not regretfully. "As is your right." Then her black eyes fixed on Sonya's shriveled form, and her face became both savage and triumphant.

"I have taken everything from you, my daughter. So now, I *give* you...everything."

Sonya's shriveled body twitched in Sebastian's arms. Then it began to shift and melt, and change. White fur sprouted all over, and her snout grew long. Her legs and torso reshaped, and she grew a tail. She began to grow, so rapidly that Sebastian was forced to release her to avoid being crushed to death by her weight. She grew to the size of a horse, of a whale, of a building, and even larger. She grew until she blotted out the gray sky above.

At last, there was no Sonya. There was only the towering form of the Great Fox Lisitsa. Her slavering jaws opened hungrily as she looked upon the two small goddesses below. One of them laughed, and the other shrieked with fury.

The Great Fox Lisitsa pounced, swallowing both goddesses in one bite.

64

In her heart of hearts, Galina had always been afraid that she was a coward. That beneath all her boldness and clever speech was still a frightened, bookish girl who was terrified of the larger world. It was a fear difficult to disprove, since there had always been an exception to be made. *This time I knew my father would protect me, that time I knew my Rangers would protect me, the other time Sebastian or some other ally was there.* When her resolve did not falter in a seemingly dire situation, she could always point to some external factor that "proved" it wasn't a true test of her mettle.

Not this time. Andre had collapsed. The golem had been swarmed over. After a valiant struggle, Tatiana had been separated from her and dragged to the far side of the room, where she was barely surviving against the hordes that surrounded her.

Now there was nothing and no one to save Galina. And she was pleased to discover that she was not a coward at all. Instead of quaking in fear or futilely trying to escape, she merely gripped the ambassador's hand, and the two women stood side by side, waiting for the end to come.

The creatures drew close, their blank and cloudy eyes showing no humanity, their hands outstretched like clumsy blunted claws. She had seen how they killed when unarmed. She would likely be wrenched apart slowly, painfully. Her fragile body would be torn into pieces just like a real doll, and her brief reign as queen of Izmoroz would end in blood and screams of agony as the mindless and uncaring servants of the Goddess of Spring ended her life.

She did not even close her eyes as they reached for her. And for that she was grateful, because she was able to witness the moment they all froze in place.

A stillness fell over the world, interrupted only by gasps for air and groans of pain from those who had survived the onslaught.

"Ambassador," Galina said in a hushed tone. She didn't know why she spoke so quietly. Perhaps a part of her feared this reprieve might be temporary and a loud sound would end it. "I think...they've done it."

Boz opened her eyes and looked around. "By all the gods...it appears they did..."

The ground beneath their feet began to tremble violently and those infected people who were now frozen in place tipped over like statues. Then came a high-pitched sound somewhere between a scream and a howl.

With sick dread, Galina wondered if they had merely traded one catastrophe for another.

Then the roof was torn from the building and Galina found herself staring up into the golden eyes of a white fox that was even larger than the giant golems. Sitting on the fox's back and clinging for dear life to its fur was Sebastian. When Galina saw him, she understood what had happened, although she could not conceive of how or why.

"Sonya? Is that *you*?"

The fox looked at Galina for a moment, her eyes piercing. Then she lowered her head so that Sebastian could clamber down to the ground.

"Galina!" He hobbled over to her. His time in the underworld had aged him so terribly that his hair was completely gray and his face that of an old man.

"Sebastian, is that really your sister?"

He stopped and looked back at the massive, looming fox. Sorrow was etched deeply into his weathered face.

"In a way."

Irina emerged from beneath a pile of the frozen creatures. She clanked over to stand beneath the towering fox, and a hissing groan of steam escaped her mouth. The two stared at each other for several moments, and Galina could not imagine what either of them might be thinking or feeling, this mother and daughter, two beings who had both left their humanity far behind.

By then Tatiana had freed herself of the frozen creatures that had surrounded her. As soon as she saw the colossal fox, she dropped to one knee and bowed her head.

"All hail the creator and destroyer, generous and hungry, loyal and cruel Lisitsa, trickster goddess of this world."

"A *goddess?*" Galina asked incredulously. "*Sonya?*"

Sebastian still gazed at his sister, his face pinched. "I suppose so."

"Then Zivena..."

"Yasha ate them both," said Sebastian.

"She *ate* the Goddesses of Winter and Spring?"

"Yes."

"Great Goddess Lisitsa...." Andre tried to pull himself up to his knees, but he was too weak and sank back down.

"Andre, don't push yourself!" Galina hurried over to him and took his clawed hand in her slim pale one.

"My queen, it has been a joy to serve you, but I now beg for your release."

She gazed into his dark bear eyes and bit her lip, willing the tears away.

"Yes of course, my Andrushka."

"Thank you, Your Majesty..."

The giant fox leaned in close to them, and a voice that was not so much spoken as it was felt reverberated in Galina's chest.

Peace, Medved. *You have done well. What would you have as your reward?*

"Rest, most radiant goddess. Only to rest at last."

Then sleep, little bear, and dream for all time of the beauty of Izmoroz.

"I thank you, most benevolent and terrible goddess..."

Then the life faded from his eyes and his hand grew slack.

"Oh, Andre..." Galina closed her eyes and felt the tears course down her cheeks whether she willed them or no.

"Yasha," said Sebastian. "What about all these others? Is there anything you can do for them?"

He gestured to the still frozen and infected Kantesians that surrounded them.

I can take the affliction away from them. Some will die, others will survive.

"Better that some truly live again, rather than all of them remain in this wretched state."

If that is your wish, little brother.

The fox lifted her head and opened her cavernous mouth. She inhaled deeply and a greenish-black substance like tar was drawn from the creatures. As it left them, the mushrooms and other visible signs of infection also disappeared. The tar-like substance came swirling from all over the city like streams in the air and gathered into a massive globule that hovered overhead. Then the fox ate it in one bite.

The Great Lisitsa gazed down at them all for a moment. Then, without another word, she disappeared.

65

Jorge? *Jorge?*"

Jorge heard Blaine calling to him and moved toward the sound, weaving through the grotesque forest of immobilized infected people. He had no idea what had happened or what was going on, but he was grateful that Blaine was still alive.

They found each other in a small clearing, surrounded on all sides by the now statue-like abominations. Blaine's strong arms enveloped him, and his kiss, though salty with sweat and bitter with blood, was still somehow just as sweet.

After a few moments, Jorge rested his forehead on the Uaine's shoulder.

"What happened?"

"I do not know," said Blaine, "but I can guess who did it."

Then the ground shook beneath them, followed by a piercing scream-like howl.

Suddenly there was an impossibly large fox looming over them.

There you are.

"S-Sonya?"

Not anymore, my most beloved lemming.

"What did you *do*?"

She ignored his question and instead asked one of her own.

Do you want me to remove the blight from these people? I warn you as I warned my brother, not all of them will survive.

"I hardly call staying like this surviving," said Jorge.

As you wish.

She took a deep breath and somehow drew the infection right out of them and swallowed it up. The forest of people around them crumpled to the ground, some clearly too far gone to survive, but others now gasping for breath as though they had just run an arduous race, which perhaps in a way they had.

"I don't understand, Sonya," said Jorge. "How can you do this? What have you become?"

She opened her mouth and lolled out her tongue so that it almost looked like the fanged smile he knew so well.

I suppose I should figure that out.

Jorge stared at her. Naturally Sonya of all people would become some kind of omnipotent creature and still not have anything that resembled a plan.

Blaine, you must watch over our beloved.

Blaine gripped Jorge's shoulder. "Of course."

Then she cast her eyes across the battlefield to Rowena, who was walking slowly toward them.

And you, seer of the veil and daughter of entropy. Would you have me take this burden that was bestowed upon you by my predecessor?

"A kind offer, but I decline."

So be it.

"Wait, Sonya," said Jorge. "*Predecessor?* Are you a *goddess* now?"

She cocked her immense head to one side playfully.

What is "goddess," I wonder . . .

Then she was gone.

66

Several months later, the allies gathered in the throne room of the still glorious palace in the ruined city of Magna Alto. Perhaps memories of happy days as a young royal guardsman favored by Empress Caterina had lingered in the broken mind of Franko Vittorio and so he had never let the conflict reach its glorious heights. The pinnacle of Aureumian architecture had survived not only the city that surrounded it, but the people who had revered it as well. As far as could be ascertained, not a single citizen of Aureum had survived the war.

The stained glass that once depicted the Aureumian Ascendance had been replaced with a glittering portrait of the Great Fox Goddess Lisitsa, whose golden eyes gazed down inscrutably at the proceedings below. The throne itself had also been removed and replaced with three less ostentatious but far more comfortable chairs.

Queen Galina of Izmoroz sat on one, flanked by Ranger Tatiana Sova on one side and Sebastian the Wizard of Gogoleth on the other. The voyage to the Eventide and the loss of his sister had taken such a toll on Sebastian that he now looked every inch like the wise, aged, and world-weary wizards of legend.

In the second chair sat the Herzog of Weide, who had survived the infection but lost the use of one arm in the process. He would never play the flute again, but claimed he no longer needed such things now that he had finally found a deity worth worshipping. The once god-less Kantesians had become the most devout of Lisitsa's worshippers, though the goddess herself had never expressed any interest in being worshipped.

He was flanked on one side by Herr Gruttman, and on the other side by Isobelle Cohen von Weide. Isobelle wore a gleaming steel prosthetic nose in place of the one she had lost, tied in place with white ribbon. Her husband had been unable to accept her altered appearance and she had allowed him to dissolve their marriage. She had also disavowed her birthright as the next Herzog, and instead pledged her sword to the service of the Great Fox.

In the third chair sat Jorge, youngest son of Arturo Elhuyar and representative of the Great Families of Raíz. It was now well known that Arturo would not live much longer. The oldest son, Hugo, would inherit the family business in its entirety, as Jorge had pledged his life in service to his country and all the Great Families. On one side he was flanked by the renowned Viajero Lucia Velazquez. The infection had damaged her vocal cords so badly that she could only speak in a throaty growl, and would likely never sing again. But it was said that she had discovered a branch of Viajero improvisational magic more powerful than any other and had begun a school to teach the next generation this formidable art. On Jorge's other side stood Blaine Ruairc. Rowena had taken the few remaining Uaine back to their northern lands, but Blaine had stayed behind. He did so in part because he hoped to convince his people not to return to their isolation, but instead to begin trading along the western coast of the continent. Even if they were not technically a part of the Triumvirate, they could still benefit from its success. The other reason he had remained behind, of course, was so that he could marry Jorge.

Standing before these three rulers and their advisers was a great number of people from Izmoroz, Kante, Raíz, and Uaine, as well as representatives from Victasha.

"I call to order the first meeting of the Triumvirate," intoned the Herzog of Weide.

The murmur of voices in the room faded away to silence.

Cohen smiled, and in a less formal tone said, "Now, how shall we begin?"

"I suggest," said Galina, "that we draw up formal documents concerning the division of the land once known as Aureum between our three countries."

"Agreed," said Jorge. "And I suggest that the city of Magna Alto remain a neutral territory jointly ruled by all three of us."

"I am amenable to that," said Cohen, "so long as we finally rename this cursed city to something that doesn't make my blood run cold every time I hear it spoken."

"I feel the same," said Galina. "But what shall we call it?"

"Perhaps Haevanton?" suggested Cohen.

"Is that a Kantesian word?" Galina asked uneasily.

"It's the name of the legendary Kantesian hero who was said to have stolen the ember from the gods that lit the first forges of Kante. I believe the Great Fox Lisitsa would enjoy the symbolism."

"She'd find it amusing at least," conceded Jorge. "She's always been fond of irreverence."

"And troublemakers," said Galina. "Very well. Since you accepted the use of an Izmorozian word as the preferred name for the Great Fox, I suppose we can let you have this one. And just to even things out, Jorge, we should probably use a Raízian word for something that concerns the Triumvirate as well."

"Oh, er…" Jorge glanced at Lucia, who nodded. "I'm still learning it, frankly, but Viajero Lucia and I will confer and get back to you at the next council meeting."

"Very well," said Cohen. "Are there any other motions to include in the council meeting, or are we ready to start carving up the land?"

"If I may, honored Triumvirate," said Ambassador Boz, who stood to one side with the other Victashian representatives.

"Has the time at last come for us to repay Victasha for your aid during the war?" Galina asked dryly.

"In a sense, Your Majesty," said Boz, as ever with an amused twinkle in her eye. "I believe you know of our concerns regarding the distant country of Aukbontar. Since we have been unable to locate the man known as Mosi Aguta, we must assume he is dead. If he was, as we suspect, a spy, his absence likely puts us at odds with his country."

"With respect, Ambassador," said Jorge, "you have not provided any proof that this Aguta was indeed a spy."

"After great deliberation, Their Royal Majesties have permitted me to inform you that they have the gift of prophecy. They have had several visions in which, in the distant future, Aukbontar invades our continent and yours, with such dire consequences that even the terrible events we have recently suffered pale in comparison."

"And how accurate are these prophecies?" asked Cohen.

"They have never once been wrong," said the ambassador.

"Lovely...," said Galina. "So what do you propose?"

"That we form a joint force specifically created to research this Aukbontar, and if possible open a diplomatic channel with them before things escalate."

"I'm sorry, Ambassador," said Cohen. "Are you suggesting we sail across the Tainted Ocean?"

"As far as we have been able to determine, the prevailing currents make that impossible from our end. It appears to be a one-way trip. But with the combined resources of all our nations, I am confident we can find some way to reach Aukbontar."

The three rulers looked skeptically at each other.

"Gentlemen and lady," Boz said in a tone close to chiding. "Together we have slain gods. Surely a mere navigational challenge is not beyond our means."

Cohen sighed. "Very well. We shall discuss the terms of this alliance once we have finished dividing up Aureum."

Sebastian found his mother sitting in the garden. He recalled when she'd been alive that this had been her favorite place within the palace. She and the other expatriates would meet there regularly, gossiping and plotting. He wondered if Aguta had really died, or merely made a hasty escape. Surely a man who had traveled such distances, spy or not, would be quite resourceful and not so easy to kill.

Sebastian stood and admired his mother's new shell for a moment. The old one had been banged up during the final conflict, but the Kantesians had fixed her up nicely. They were still clearly uncomfortable with a human-shaped golem, but in some sense she was the mother of their goddess, so they had made an exception for her. Not only had they taken out the dents, and repaired the scrapes and punctures—they'd also etched some lovely decorative designs so that she looked more like moving sculpture than metal monster.

"Hello, Mother."

He sat down wearily beside her. He did everything wearily these days. He not only looked like an old man, he felt like one as well. Everything hurt, nothing worked quite right anymore, and he was generally grumpy about most things. It had occurred to him recently on his eighteenth birthday that he now looked older than his father had when he'd died, and something about that really bothered him. So he was not merely a grumpy old man, but also a bitter one as well.

Perhaps sensing that he was stewing, his mother reached over and patted him on the head.

He chuckled quietly, then his smile faded. "What are you going to do when I'm gone?"

She removed her hand and looked away from him.

"You could always help Galina in my stead."

A puff of steam was her only response.

"Just promise me you won't end up sitting at the bottom of a lake until you're so corroded you can't move."

She didn't respond. But what response could she really give? So they sat there in silence for a while.

"*There* he is," came Galina's voice.

Sebastian turned to see his wife walking through the gardens with Jorge.

"It's good to see you again, Sebastian," said Jorge.

"Ah, Representative…" Sebastian struggled to rise as his joints protested.

"No, please, don't trouble yourself," Jorge said quickly. "And call me Jorge. I'd hate for Sonya's brother to treat me so formally."

"She never did care much for decorum," agreed Sebastian. "Personally, I always found it rather soothing. The structure and form of it all."

"We've finally finished our deliberations on the new borders, my dear husband," said Galina. "I think it turned out rather well. Did you want to sit in on the signing?"

He gave her a pained look. "Must I, dear wife?"

She sighed. "Of course not. I know it's not...ideal."

"No," he agreed.

There was an awkward moment of silence, mostly because Sebastian didn't have the energy to argue with her on this point any longer. But apparently she did, so she continued.

"As I'm sure you recall, husband, Aureum practically wiped Izmoroz off the map. They were no better."

"True," said Sebastian. "But I thought we were."

"What would you have done, Sebastian?" Jorge asked gently. "Left this whole country a graveyard to a dead nation? This land has the most fertile soil on the continent. The entire Triumvirate will thrive because of it. Isn't that a good thing?"

"I suppose..."

"They had their chance, Sebastian," Galina said far less gently. "They could have created something grand with their empire, and instead they squandered it. We'll do better."

He looked up at her. So confident and sure. Had he ever felt like that? Perhaps once, a long time ago. "I hope you're right."

"Of course, I am. Now, come along, husband. We've got a busy night ahead of us."

"Oh?"

She smiled wickedly and held up a small bottle. "Representative Elhuyar was kind enough to mix a potion to give you a little *pep*, if you know what I mean."

"Oh goddess...," he groaned.

"Come now, I must have an heir. And you do want the Turgenev Portinari line to continue, don't you?"

His mother pushed him to his feet and gave a puff of steam.

"You too?" he asked plaintively. "Fine, fine. I suppose I can hardly turn down a proposition from the most beautiful woman on the continent."

"Only the continent?" Galina asked archly.

"Well, I've never been to another continent, so I can't speak authoritatively on the entire world, but I'd be willing to put a wager on it."

She laughed and put her arm through his, then they walked with Jorge through the gardens.

"Old Sebastian really is my favorite version, you know," she said.

"Even though I'm withered and slow?"

"Don't be boring, husband. You know that's not what matters to me. And besides, I'll still be fairly young when you die, and as the widowed queen, I'll have my choice of all the handsomest young men to take as lovers. I'm sure no one will begrudge me that."

"You are a cruel woman, Galina Odoyevsteva."

"True. But one does not install themselves as queen and gain a third of the continent within a year by being nice."

He sighed. "Also true."

Nine years later, the funeral of Sebastian Turgenev Portinari, Wizard of Gogoleth, was held in Haevanton, as he had requested. But Jorge was saddened to see how few people attended.

Galina was there, of course, dressed in a long black gown with a high stiff collar. Her eight-year-old son, Vladimir Turgenev Prozorova, stood beside her, his eyes rimmed red from crying. Jorge had always wondered how well the elderly Sebastian could perform his fatherly duties, but regardless it was clear that the boy had adored him.

Directly behind Vladimir loomed his nanny and bodyguard, the golem of Irina Turgenev, or Irushka, as she was fondly called by the Izmorozians. To Galina's other side stood Ranger Tatiana Sova.

But those were the only Izmorozians in attendance. Despite being the queen's consort for over ten years, the people of Izmoroz had never truly warmed to Sebastian. And perhaps still feeling the weight of his crimes during the early days of the Goddess War, he had always borne their rudeness without complaint.

Herzog Ferdinand Cohen von Weide II was there, looking thin and pale in his black doublet. Unlike Sebastian, he was truly old, and his health had been failing in recent years. He insisted on standing for the funeral, but his bony hand gripped his daughter's arm, and he leaned heavily on her shoulder.

Isobelle wore full plate armor, her sword at her hip. There had always been an interesting balance of steel and kindness in her eyes, but in recent years the balance had tipped and there was now little difference between the hardness of her blade and the hardness of her expression. A few years ago, it had been discovered that there was a group of Aureumian survivors who had formed some sort of insurgency against the Triumvirate under the leadership of a man named Marcello Oreste. Isobelle had been leading the effort to stamp out this rebellion with such merciless fervor that it made Jorge uncomfortable. But as national representative of Raíz, he had to pick his battles within the Triumvirate carefully, and pleading sympathy for their past oppressors would have been a hard sell. So after expressing some initial concern, Jorge had not pressed the issue further.

Accompanying Ferdinand and Isobelle was Elias Gruttman, lord of Kochstadt and most likely the next Herzog. Jorge didn't know him well, but he seemed an oddly jovial fellow for a Kantesian, and Jorge hoped that the country might soften somewhat under his leadership. Aligning the interests of Izmoroz and Raíz under the Triumvirate had turned out to be not nearly as challenging as Jorge had feared. But the mindset of Kante was so drastically different from that of Raíz, it was always a struggle for the two nations to come to an agreement.

Other than Jorge and Blaine, the only other person in attendance was Ambassador Ceren Boz. Even after a decade, Jorge remained unsure what the true aims of Victasha were, but they seemed utterly convinced that if drastic action was not taken, Aukbontar and its allies would someday descend upon Victasha and the Triumvirate in a wave of cruelty and horror the likes of which had never been seen before. But as far as anyone knew, there had been no further contact from Aukbontar, and the navigational challenges that Boz had so readily dismissed ten years ago remained insurmountable. So they had not yet been able to reach this fabled land and forestall their supposedly dire fate.

The funeral was performed by one of the Great Fox priestesses dressed in their white, fur-lined robes. Jorge still thought the idea of a religion that worshipped Sonya to be odd, especially in a situation like this where most of the people had known her when she was mortal. But when he'd mentioned this to Galina, she'd pointedly asked if he would have preferred they instead use the religion of the dead Goddess of Winter that Sebastian had hated for making his sister suffer. Jorge had admitted that did not sound preferable.

They gathered on a hill outside the city. The service was longer than Sonya would have wanted, filled with platitudes and exonerations that she never would have said. Each year it seemed that the Great Fox religion drifted further and further away from the mindset of the goddess it supposedly worshipped. But Sonya had not been seen since the war ended, so they'd had no guidance from her. Jorge and Blaine had at times tried to gently point out the discrepancies, although the primarily Kantesian adherents made it clear they were not interested in feedback. For better or worse, the religion had taken on a life of its own that had little to do with the smirking, reckless woman Jorge and Blaine loved.

As Jorge watched Sebastian's coffin lower into the ground, he felt a deep, aching sadness. He had not known Sebastian particularly well, but this had been one of the few people who truly knew and loved Sonya. One day, there would be none of them left, and only the religion would remain.

"I had hoped she might come," he murmured.

He felt Blaine's hand on his shoulder.

"Me too."

"Do you think she knows her brother is dead?"

"She's a goddess. She probably knows."

"I suppose," said Jorge. "Does she just...not care anymore?"

"Maybe," said Blaine. "Or maybe now that he's dead, they can finally be together again."

Jorge turned to his husband, tears pressing on his eyes, and he smiled.

"Thank you for that thought."

He didn't know if it was true, but it was the sort of unreasonably optimistic statement that reminded him of the woman who had rescued him from bandits all those years ago. He could see her in his mind, grinning, her long black hair dotted with white snowflakes as she sat upon her beloved Peppercorn and offered him her hand.

He realized there would be no funeral for that woman who had died so many times. So perhaps this was for both of them. Siblings, rivals, and finally, in the end, friends.

EPILOGUE

Sorcha stood in the small, unlit tent and glared at Rowena. She could just barely make out her fellow Bhuidseach's pale features from the wan sunlight that streamed in through the opening in the tent.

"Well?" she demanded.

"Hmm?" Rowena seemed to only now notice her presence, even though Sorcha had been speaking to her for several minutes. Whatever Bàs had turned her into after she had reconsecrated to him had not faded with the god's death. If anything, it had gotten worse. She barely seemed aware of her surroundings, and would go days without speaking to anyone, only to suddenly burst into some nonsensical pronouncement of events that had never happened.

"I *said*," pressed Sorcha, "don't you think it's time we officially joined the Triumvirate as a fourth nation? We're getting left behind the rest of the continent."

Rowena gazed impassively at her. "But then it would no longer be a Triumvirate."

"So it could be a *Quadrumvirate*, or whatever the number four is in their pathetic, mewling language."

"But that will not be," Rowena said.

"And why not?" demanded Sorcha.

Rowena shrugged. "It is not destined to happen."

"I've had about enough of you and your useless visions of the future. What good are they when it's all names and places we've never heard of?"

"They are not intended to be good or bad," said Rowena. "They merely are."

"Here we go," said Sorcha. "Listen, I'm not having this discussion with you again. I'm taking a ship and our best people down to Colmo. Blaine and I will begin negotiations with Jorge for the Uaine to join the Triumvirate as an equal partner. Unlike *you*, Blaine is concerned about the *immediate* future of the Uaine, not some distant unimaginable future."

Rowena nodded. "This is as it must be."

"I didn't *need* your approval," snapped Sorcha.

Sorcha should have evaluated what Rowena said more carefully: that the trip must happen, but the Uaine joining the Triumvirate could not. But in Sorcha's defense, Rowena said a great many things that no matter how much she scrutinized them, never made sense. So she'd more or less given up trying to figure it out by then.

So the last true Bhuidseach gathered the best remaining Uaine warriors. There were so few these days that clan differences had become irrelevant. It turned Sorcha's stomach to see just how small their numbers had become. Bàs had promised Rowena *the Uaine will survive the centuries, perhaps rising to a glory you can scarce imagine.* Could that promise have been voided with his death? Because as far as Sorcha could tell, the Uaine would disappear in a matter of a few generations unless they took drastic action. They had become a broken, godless, and directionless people. She had no one to pray to now, and instead could only *hope* that joining the Triumvirate would rekindle some of her people's lost pride and resolve.

As they sailed south toward Colmo, she spoke to them often and fervently about the glory of the Haevanton Triumvirate, and how it would enable them to achieve might and renown unheard of even in the glory days of the great Tighearna. Her people believed these bold claims and rallied around her, probably because, like her, they had nothing left but this last desperate hope.

One night, their ship was overtaken by a fierce storm similar to the one Sonya had weathered all those years ago. But the Uaine were not as skilled or experienced sailors as the Raízian crew of the *Endless Summer*, and they were swept out into the vast, uncharted waters of the Ocean of Loss, from which none had ever returned.

Most who were swept out into the Ocean of Loss died for lack of fresh water without ever reaching land again. Those few who survived the harrowing journey were usually dashed upon a formidable line of reefs that would one day be called the Breaks.

But just this once, by chance, or fate, or perhaps the will of a certain Great Fox, the ship that carried Sorcha and her fellow Uaine made it past the Breaks and at last found land. It was a small island, seemingly cold and inhospitable. But once they disembarked, they found an oasis of lush vegetation hidden at the center of the island. It thrived because of hot springs that came from deep within the ground.

There were other islands nearby, but those turned out to be harsh, frigid, and without the benefit of hot springs. Still, it was clear to Sorcha that it would be impossible for them to return to their homeland for the foreseeable future, if ever. So she set her people to clearing out the meek, unwarlike inhabitants who lived there, all of whom had the tan complexion and dark hair of Raízians, although with more angular features. And so the lost Uaine made a home for themselves, carving out a living as best they could.

The years went by and Sorcha struggled to find her successor. Perhaps it was the scant ingredients found on the islands, or the fact that Bàs was dead, but the only people who survived being Death Touched were children, and they were driven somewhat mad from the process. Once again, Sorcha feared that this was the end of her people.

Then one day, a small fleet of ships came from the north bearing fierce warriors dressed in black, and hooded sorcerers capable of bending living matter to their will. They looked like the same race of people that had been driven from the islands, although this group was much more formidable. They were not hostile, however. In fact, they were quite curious about Sorcha and her people. They had never seen anyone with such pale complexion, and had never witnessed necromancy. Perhaps it was a combination of these two things that led them to believe the Uaine were supernatural in nature. It was a mistaken impression that Sorcha did not correct.

One of them, a man named Cremalton, offered to form an alliance with the Uaine. There was apparently a vast archipelago to the north that was rich in fertile land and far more agriculturally advanced. He wished to unite those northern islands into a great empire, and asked for Sorcha's help.

Sorcha reasoned that such abundant lands would likely offer the resources her people needed to return to their homeland. Or, perhaps once Cremalton had conquered the lands, she could depose him and take the empire for herself. Either was better than eking out a meager existence in these barren southern isles.

They met on one of the smaller islands, because Sorcha did not want her new allies to know about the hidden oasis of plenty. On that tiny spit of land, she and her Jackal Lords formed a pact with the self-proclaimed Emperor Cremalton, and his two most trusted advisers, Burness Vee and Grandteacher Selk. Theirs was a daring plan that had a low chance of success, but all knew the risks and were desperate enough to take them.

They named the island Bleak Hope in honor of this auspicious occasion.

Centuries later, after that empire had risen, and stagnated, and begun to teeter toward collapse, the Great Fox Goddess Lisitsa oversaw the birth of a girl on the island of Bleak Hope who would change everything. Not just for her own people, but for the world.

ACKNOWLEDGMENTS

The end of a trilogy is always special, but this one perhaps more than most. Those who have read my previous trilogy, The Empire of Storms, know that we have now come full circle back to my beloved hero, Bleak Hope, whose tragic origins inspired me to begin this long and satisfying foray into epic fantasy in the first place. So much has changed since I urgently scrawled that first chapter in a MUJI notebook all those years ago. For the world and for myself.

The Goddess War is, among other things, about the human capacity for transformation, both gradual and sudden. So it seems appropriate to me that the final book of this trilogy should be the last that ever bears the name "Jon Skovron"—a name that was never truly mine, but acted almost as a protective cocoon during my own very slow and meandering transformation. Although if I'm being honest, it feels less like a transformation and more like a long-overdue acceptance of something that had always been there. Regardless, I find a great deal of value in marking out moments in my life that I define as important and worth remembering. The completion of this story is one of them.

Yet of course there were a number of people who helped me to get to this moment. Thanks to Stephanie Perkins for the early encouragement, Devi Pillai for taking a gamble on a YA writer, Brit Hvide for seeing it through, and Angeline Rodriguez for the boundless support and enthusiasm that got me to the end. And of course none of this would ever have happened without my agent, Jill Grinberg, and the entire team at JGLM. They have always been there for me, championing my work through many ups and downs, and my grati-tude to them is more than I could possibly express.

So this chapter in my life comes to a close. But it has turned out to be an unexpectedly long life, and I find that I am nowhere near fin-ished. I do hope, dear reader, that you will join me for whatever the next chapter holds.

J. Kelley Skovron
Thanksgiving Day, 2021

extras

orbit

meet the author

Photo Credit: Ryan Benyi

J. KELLEY SKOVRON is the author of the Empire of Storms and Goddess War trilogies published by Orbit under the name Jon Skovron. They are also the author of a number of young adult and middle grade novels, such as *Misfit* and *The Hacker's Key*, as well as the fantasy noir novel *Gutter Mage* for mature readers written under the name J. S. Kelley. They currently live just outside Washington, DC, with two teenagers, a cat, and a dog, at least one of whom will be leaving for college within the year. Visit Kelley online at kelleyskovron.com or subscribe to their newsletter at bleakhope.com.

Find out more about J. Kelley Skovron and other Orbit authors by registering for the free monthly newsletter at orbitbooks.net.

if you enjoyed
THE WIZARD OF EVENTIDE

look out for

THE BLADED FAITH
Vagrant Gods: Book One

by

David Dalglish

A usurped prince prepares to take up the mantle of a deadly assassin and reclaim his kingdom, his people, and his slain gods, in this epic fantasy from a USA Today bestselling author.

Cyrus was only fourteen years old when his gods were slain, his country invaded, and his parents—the king and queen—beheaded in front of him. Held prisoner in the invader's court for years, Cyrus is suddenly given a chance to escape and claim his revenge when a mysterious group of revolutionaries comes looking for a figurehead. They need a hero to strike fear into the hearts of the Empire and to inspire and unite the people. They need someone to take up the skull mask and swords and to become the legendary "Vagrant"—an unparalleled hero and assassin of otherworldly skill.

But not all is as it seems. Creating the illusion of a hero is the work of many, and Cyrus will soon discover the true price of his vengeance.

Chapter 1

CYRUS

All his life, Cyrus Lythan had been told his parents' armada was the greatest in the world, unmatched by any fleet from the mainland continent of Gadir. It was the pride of his family, the jewel of the island kingdom of Thanet. Standing at the edge of the castle balcony, his hands white-knuckling the balustrade, Cyrus watched their ships burn and knew it for a lie.

"Their surprise will only gain them so much," said Rayan. The older man and dearest family friend stood beside Cyrus as the fires spread across the docks. "Hold faith. Our gods will protect us."

Smoke blotted out the harbor, but along the edges of the billowing black he saw the empire's ships firing flaming spears from ballistae mounted to their decks. Thanet's boats could not counter such power with their meager archers, not even if they had fought on equal numbers. Those numbers, however, were far from equal. Thanet's vaunted armada had counted fifty ships in total, though only thirty had been in the vicinity of Vallessau when two hundred imperial ships emerged from the morning fog, their hulls painted black and their gray sails marked with two red hands clenched in prayer.

"Shouldn't you be down there with the rest of the paladins?" Cyrus asked. "Or are you too old for battle?"

The man's white plate rattled as he crossed his arms. He was a paladin of Lycaena, a holy warrior who'd dedicated his life to one of Thanet's two gods. It was she and Endarius whom the island now relied upon to withstand the coming invasion. The castle was set upon the tallest hill in the city of Vallessau, protected by a wide outer wall that circled the base of its foundational hill. Thanet's soldiers massed along the outer wall, their padded leather armor seeming woefully inadequate. Paladins of the two gods gathered in the courtyard between the outer wall and the castle itself. Despite there being less than sixty, the sight of them gave Cyrus hope. The finely polished weapons of those men and women shone brightly, and the morning light reflected off their armor, be it the gilded chain of Endarius's paladins or the white plate of Lycaena's. As for the god and goddess, they both waited inside the castle.

"You are brave to call me old when you yourself are not yet a man," Rayan said. His skin was as dark as his hair was white, and when he smiled, it stretched his smartly trimmed beard. That smile was both heartfelt and fleeting. "His Highness ordered me to protect you."

Cyrus tried to remain optimistic. He tried to hold faith in the divine beings pledged to protect Thanet. A seemingly endless tide of soldiers disembarking from the ships and marching the main thoroughfare toward the outer castle walls broke that faith.

"Tell me, Rayan, if the walls fall and our gods die, how will you protect me?"

Rayan looked to the distant congregation of his fellow paladins of Lycaena at the outer gate, and his thoughts clearly echoed Cyrus's.

"Poorly," he said. "Stay here, and pray for us all. We will need every bit of help this cruel world can muster."

The paladin exited the balcony. The heavy thud of the shutting door quickened Cyrus's pulse, and he swallowed down his lingering fear. A cowardly part of him shouted to find somewhere in the castle to bury his head and hide. Stubborn pride kept his feet firmly in place. He was the fourteen-year-old Prince of Thanet, and he would bear witness to the fate of his kingdom.

The assault began with the arrival of the ladders, dozens of thick planks of wood with metal hooks bolted onto their tops so they could lock tightly onto the walls. The defenders rushed to shove them off, but the empire's crossbowmen punished them with volley after volley. Swords clashed, and though the empire's losses were heavy, nothing slowed the ascent of the invaders. What started as a few scattered soldiers fighting atop the walls became a mile-long battlefield. It did not take long before the gray tunics overwhelmed the blue tabards of Vallessau.

Next came the battering ram. How the enemy had built it in such short a time baffled Cyrus, but there was no denying its steady hammering on the opposite side of the outer gate. Even the intervals were maddeningly consistent. Every four seconds, the gate would rattle, the wood would crack, and the imperial army grew that much closer to flooding into the courtyard.

"It doesn't matter," Cyrus whispered to himself. "The gods protect us. The gods will save us."

The fight along the walls was growing thicker, with more ladders managing to stay upright with every passing moment.

Cyrus could spare no glance in their direction, for with one last shuddering blast, the battering ram knocked open the outer gate. The invading army flooded through, and should have easily overrun the vastly outnumbered defenders, but at long last, the castle doors opened and Thanet's divine made their presence known.

The goddess Lycaena fluttered above an accompaniment of her priests. Her skin was black as midnight, her eyes brilliant rainbows of ever-shifting color. Long, flowing silk cascaded down from her arms and waist, its hue a brilliant orange that transitioned to yellow, green, and blue depending on the ruffle of the fabric. The dress billowed outward in all directions, and no matter how hard Cyrus looked, he couldn't tell where the fabric ended and the goddess's enormous wings began. She held a rod topped with an enormous ruby in her left hand; in the right, a golden harp whose strings shimmered all colors of the visible spectrum. Cyrus's heart ached at the sight of her. He'd witnessed Lycaena's physical form only a few times in his life, and each left him breathless and in awe.

"Be gone, locusts of a foreign land," Lycaena decreed. She did not shout, nor raise her voice, but all the city heard her words. "We will not break before a wave of hate and steel."

Fire lashed from the ruby atop her rod in a conical torrent that filled the broken gateway. The screams of the dying combined into a singular wail. The other god of Thanet, Endarius the Lion, charged into the ashen heap left in her attack's wake. His fur was gold, his claws obsidian, his mane a brilliant collection of feathers that ran the full gamut of the rainbow. Wings stretched from his back, the feathers there several feet long and shifting from a crimson red along the base to pale white at the tip. Those wings beat with his every stride, adding to his speed and power.

Endarius's paladins joined him in his charge. They did not wield swords and shields like their Lycaenan counterparts, nor did they share their long cloaks of interlocking colors resembling stained glass. Instead their gilded armor bore necklaces of fangs across their arms, and they wielded twin jagged swords to better support their ferocity. They bellowed as they ran, their version of a prayer, and they tore into the ranks of the invaders, the spray of blood and breaking of bones their worship.

In those first few minutes, Cyrus truly believed victory would be theirs. Thanet had never been conquered in all her history. Lycaena and Endarius protected their beloved people. The two divine beings rewarded their faithful subjects with safety and guidance. And as the imperial soldiers rushed through the gate with their swords and spears, the gods filled the courtyard with fire and blood. From such a height, Cyrus could only guess at the identities of the individual defenders, but he swore he saw Rayan fighting alongside his goddess, his sword lit with holy light as he kept his beloved deity safe with his rainbow shield.

You burned our fleets, Cyrus thought, and a vengeful thrill shot through him. *But we'll crush your armies. You'll never return, never, not after this defeat.*

The arrival of the twelve tempered his joy. The men appeared remarkably similar to Thanet's paladins, bearing thick golden platemail and wielding much larger weapons adorned with decorative hilts and handles. Unlike the rest of the imperial army, they did not wear gray tabards but instead colorful tunics and cloaks bearing differing animals. The twelve pushed through the blasted gate, flanked on either side by a contingent of soldiers. They showed no fear of the two divine beings leading the slaughter. They charged into the thick of things without hesitation, their shields held high and their weapons gleaming.

Cyrus knew little of the Everlorn Empire. Journey to the mainland took several months by boat, and its ruling emperor, arrogantly named the God-Incarnate, had issued an embargo upon Thanet lasting centuries. The empire worshiped and acknowledged no gods but their emperor, and claimed faith in him allowed humanity to transcend mortal limits. Seeing those twelve fight, Cyrus understood that belief for the first time in his life. Those twelve...they couldn't be human. Whatever they were, it was monstrous, it was impossible, and it was beyond even what Thanet's paladins could withstand.

God and invader clashed, and somehow these horrifying twelve endured the wrath of the immortal beings. Their armor held against fire and claw. Their weapons punched through armor as if it were glass. Soldiers and paladins from both sides attempted to intervene, but they were flies buzzing about fighting bulls. Each movement, each strike of an invader's sword or swipe of Endarius's paw, claimed the lives of foes with almost incidental ease. The battlefield ascended beyond the mortal, and these elite, these invading monsters, defied all reason as they stood their ground against Thanet's gods.

"No," Cyrus whispered. "It's not possible."

Endarius clenched his teeth about the long blade of one of the invaders, yet could not crunch through the metal. His foe ripped it free, and a crossbow brigade unleashed dozens of bolts to pelt the Lion as he danced away. The arrowheads couldn't find purchase, but they marked little black welts akin to bruises and frayed the edges of Endarius's increasingly ragged wings.

"This isn't right," Cyrus said. The battle had started so grand, yet now the defenders were scattered, the walls overrun, and the paladins struggling to maintain their attacks against wave after wave of soldiers coming through the broken gate. In the center of it all raged gods and the inhuman elite, and the world shook from their wrath. Thanet's troops attempted to seal off the wall entrance and isolate the battle against the gods. It briefly worked, at least until the men and women in red robes took to the front of enemy lines. Their lack of weapons and armor confused Cyrus at first, but then they lifted their hands in prayer. Golden weapons blistering with light burst into existence, hovering in the air and wielded by invisible hands. The weapons tore through the soldiers' ranks, the defense faltered, and Cyrus's last hope withered. What horrid power did these invaders command?

Time lost meaning. Blood flowed, bodies fell, the armies meeting and striking and dying with seemingly nihilistic determination. A spear-wielding member of those elite twelve leaped into the air, a single lunge of his legs carrying him dozens of feet heavenward. Lycaena was not prepared, and when the spear lodged deep into her side, her scream echoed for miles. It was right then, hearing that scream, that Cyrus knew his kingdom was lost.

"How dare you!" Endarius roared. Though one invader smashed a hammer into the Lion's side, and another knocked loose a fang from his jaw, the god cared only for the wound suffered by the Butterfly goddess. Two mighty beats of his wings carried him into the air, where his teeth closed about the elite still clinging to the embedded spear. All three crashed to the ground, but it was the invader who suffered most. Endarius crushed him in his jaws, punching through the man's armor, smashing bones, and spilling blood upon a silver tongue.

A casual flick of Endarius's neck tossed the body aside, but that was merely one of twelve. Eleven more remained, and they closed the space with calm, steady precision. No soldiers attempted to fill the gap, for what battles remained were scattered and chaotic. There was too much blood, too much death, and above it all, like a sick backdrop in the world's cruelest painting, rose the billowing smoke of Thanet's burning fleet.

"Flee from here!" Endarius bellowed as a bleeding Lycaena fluttered higher into the air.

"Only if you come with me," the goddess urged, but the Lion would not be moved. He prepared to pounce and bared his obsidian teeth.

"For the lives of the faithful," Endarius roared. His wings spread wide, unbridled power crackling like lightning across the feathers.

Cyrus dropped to his knees and clutched the side of the balustrade. He could feel it on his skin. He could smell it in the air. The overwhelming danger. The growing fury of a god who could never imagine defeat.

"Strike me with your blades," the Lion mocked the remaining eleven. "Come die as the vermin you are."

They were happy to oblige. The eleven clashed with the god in a coordinated effort, their swords, axes, and spears tearing into his golden flesh. The god could not avoid them, could not win, only buy time for Lycaena's escape. No matter how badly Cyrus pleaded under his breath for the Lion to flee, he would not. Endarius had been, above all, a stubborn god.

A blue-armored elite was the one to strike the killing blow. A spear pierced through Endarius's eye and sank to the hilt. His fur rumbled, his dying roar shook the land, and then the Lion's body split in half. A maelstrom of stars tore free of his body like floodwaters released from a dam. Whatever otherworldly essence comprised the existence of a god burned through the eleven like a swirling, rainbow fire before rolling outward in a great flare of blinding light. Cyrus crouched down and screamed. The death of something so beautiful, so noble and inseparably linked to Thanet's identity, shook him in a way he could not fathom.

At last the noise and light faded from the suddenly quiet battlefield. Two of the eleven elites died from the eruption of divine energy, their armor melted to their bodies as they lay upon the cobblestone path leading from the main gate to the castle entrance. Nothing remained of Endarius's body, for it had dissolved into light and crystal and floated away like scattered dust. Lycaena was long gone, having taken to the skies during the divine explosion. The paladins and priests of both gods likewise fled. A few entered the castle before it locked its gates, while the rest took to the distant portions of the outer wall not yet besieged by the invaders, seeking stairs and ladders that might allow them to escape out into Vallessau.

The soldiers of the Everlorn Empire filled the courtyard to face what was left of Thanet's defenses. Cyrus guessed maybe a dozen archers, and twice that in armed soldiers, remained inside the castle. Opposing thoughts rattled inside his head. What to do. Where to go. None of it seemed to matter. His mind couldn't process the shock. Last night he'd gone to bed having heard only rumors of imperial ships sailing the area. No one had known it was a full-scale invasion. No one had known Thanet's navy would fall in a single afternoon, and the capital along with it.

The nine remaining imperial elites gathered, joined by the men and women in red robes who Cyrus assumed to be some manner of priest. One of the nine trudged to the front and stood before the locked gateway. He showed no fear of an archer's arrow, which wasn't surprising given the enormous gray slab of steel he carried as his shield. His face was hidden underneath a gigantic bull helmet with horns that stretched a full foot to either side of his head. He said something in his imperial tongue, and then one of the priests came forward holding a blue medallion. The gigantic man took it, slipped it over his neck, and then addressed the castle.

"I am Imperator Magus of Eldrid!" the man shouted, and though his lips moved wrong, there was no doubt that he somehow spoke the native Thanese language. "Paragon of Shields, servant of the Uplifted Church, and faithful child of the God-Incarnate. I command this conquest. My word is law, and so shall it be until this island bends its knee and accepts the wisdom of the Everlorn Empire. I say this not out of pride, but so you may understand that none challenge my word. Should I make a promise, I shall keep it, even unto the breaking of the world."

Magus drew a sword from his waist and lifted it high above him. He spoke again, the blue medallion flaring with light at his every word.

"I make you one offer, and it shall not be amended nor changed. Bring me the royal family who call this castle home. Cast them to the dirt at my feet, and I shall spare the lives of every single man, woman, and child within your walls. But if you will not..."

The Imperator lowered his blade.

"Then I shall execute every last one of you, so that only vermin remain to walk your halls."

And with that, silence followed, but that silence was like the held breath between seeing a flash of lightning and feeling its thunder rumble against your bones. Shouts soon erupted within the castle, scattered at first, then numerous. Screams. Steel striking steel.

Mother! Father! Cyrus's parents were both on a lower floor, watching the battle unfold from the castle windows. That their servants and soldiers would so easily turn upon them seemed unthinkable, but the sounds of battle were undeniable. Cyrus turned to the door to the balcony, still slightly ajar from when Rayan left.

"Oh no," he whispered, and then broke into a sprint. The door wasn't lockable, not from the outside, but if he could wedge it closed with something, even brace it with his weight...

The door opened right as he arrived, the wood ramming hard enough into him that he feared it might break his shoulder. Cyrus fell and rolled across the white stone, biting down a cry as his elbow and knees bruised. When he staggered to his feet, he found one of his guard captains, a woman named Nessa, blocking the doorway with her sword and shield drawn.

"I'm sorry, Cyrus," the woman said. "Maybe they'll spare you like they promised."

"You're a traitor."

"You saw it, prince. Endarius is dead. They're killing gods. What hope do we have? Now stand up. I will drag you if I must."

Nessa suddenly jerked forward, her jaw opening and closing in a noiseless death scream. When she collapsed, Rayan stood over her body. Blood soaked his white armor and stained his flowing cloak. His hand outstretched for Cyrus to take.

"Come," Rayan said. "We have little time."

They ran through the hall to the stairs. Cyrus pretended not to see the bodies strewn across the blue carpet. Some were soldiers. Some were servants. The king and queen still lived, yet the people of Thanet were already tearing one another apart. Was this how quickly their nation would fall?

Once at the bottom of the stairs, Rayan guided him through rooms and ducked along slender servant corridors hidden behind curtains. During their flight, treacherous Thanet soldiers ordered them to halt twice, and twice Rayan cut them down with an expert swing of his sword. Cyrus stepped over their bodies without truly seeing them. He felt like a stranger in his own skin. The entire world seemed unreal, a cruel dream no amount of biting his tongue allowed him to awake from.

Within minutes they were running down a lengthy corridor that connected a portion of the western wall to the castle proper. The corridor ran parallel to the courtyard, and at the first door they passed, Cyrus spotted the enormous gathering of soldiers surrounding Magus of Eldrid.

"I had feared the worst," Magus shouted as Cyrus continued. "Come before me, and kneel. I would hear your names."

Cyrus skidded to a halt at the next doorway. He pressed his chest against the cold stone and peered around the edge. It couldn't be. His parents, they were meant to escape like him. They had their own royal guard. Their own protectors. Yet there they stood before the Imperator, flanked on either side by blood-soaked traitors. His father was the first to bow his head and address their conqueror. With each proclamation, the empire's soldiers cheered and clattered their swords against their shields.

"Cleon Lythan," said his father. "King of Thanet."

"Berniss Lythan," said his mother. "Queen of Thanet."

Cyrus's stomach twisted into acidic knots. How could the world turn so dark and cruel within the span of a single day? Magus lifted his shield and slammed it back down hard enough to crack a full foot-deep groove into the stone and wedge his shield permanently upright. With only his sword swinging in his relaxed grip, he approached the pair.

"Cleon and Berniss," he said. "We are not ignorant of your kingdom and its history. Where is your son? The young man by the name of Cyrus?"

"I suspect he fled," Cleon said. The courtyard had grown deathly quiet. "Please, it was not by our order. We don't know where Cyrus has gone."

The Imperator removed his bull helmet. Cyrus had expected more of a monster, but Magus seemed remarkably human, with deeply tanned skin, silver eyes, and a magnificent smile. His long black hair cascaded down either side of his face as he spoke.

"I requested the entire royal line. Was I not clear? Did my word-lace mistranslate?"

"No," Berniss said. "Please, we looked, we did."

The man shook his head.

"Lies, and more lies," he said. "Do you stall for his safety? Feign at ignorance, as if your boy stands a chance of survival once this castle falls?"

Cyrus took a step, one single step out the doorway toward his parents, before Rayan grabbed him by his neck.

"We must escape while there is still time," the paladin whispered. Cyrus resisted his pull to safety. He would watch this. He must.

"I gave my word," Magus continued once it was clear neither would offer up Cyrus's location. "A clear word, and a true promise. Accept this blood as a sacrifice to your memory. May it sear across your conscience in the eternal lands beyond."

Cyrus knew fleeing with Rayan was the wiser decision. He knew it was what his parents wanted. But it seemed so simple to Cyrus, so obvious what the right course of action must be. He turned away from the door, pretending to go with the paladin. The moment Rayan's hand released from his neck, Cyrus shoved the man's chest, separating them. A heartbeat later he was out the door, legs and arms flailing as he willed his body to run faster. The distance between them felt like miles. His voice sounded quiet, insignificant, but he screamed it nonetheless.

"I'm here!" It didn't matter if he put his own life at risk. He wouldn't leave his family behind. He wouldn't let them die for his sake. He ran, crossing the green grass of the courtyard between him and the gathered soldiers. "I'm here, I'm here, I'm—"

Magus swung once for the both of them. His sword passed through blood and bone to halt upon the white brick. Only Cyrus's mother's injuries weren't instantly lethal, for the sword cut across her arm and waist instead of cleaving her in half. Her anguished scream pierced the courtyard. Her pain ripped daggers through Cyrus's horror-locked mind. Magus, however, twirled his sword in his fingers and shook his head with disappointment.

"Why do I bother?" he said as he cut the head from Berniss's shoulders. "It's always easier to rebuild from nothing."

Cyrus couldn't banish the sight. He couldn't stop seeing that killing stroke. His legs weakened, limbs becoming wobbling jelly that could not support him. His whole family, gone. Slain. Bleeding upon the courtyard stones with their blood pooling into the groove Magus had carved with his shield. Crossbow bolts hammered into the men and women who had turned traitor and brought the royal family out in custody. No reward for their betrayal. Only death.

Too late, he thought. Too late, too late, he ran too late, revealed himself too late. A scream ripped out of Cyrus's chest. No words, just a heartbroken protest against the brutality of the day and the terror sweeping through him as the ground seemed to shake at the approach of the Paragon of Shields. Too late, he had gained the attention of the monster from the boats. Too late to save his parents. Too late to mean anything but a cruel death. Cyrus prayed he would meet his father and mother on the rolling green fields of Endarius's paradise. Face wet with tears, he stared up at Magus and slowly climbed to his feet. He would die meeting the gaze of his executioner; this he swore. Not on his knees. Not begging for his life.

The golden-armored paragon grabbed Cyrus by the throat and lifted him into the air. Instinct had Cyrus clutching at the heavy gauntlet. How easily he carried him. As if he were nothing. Just a ghost. Magus, this man, this monster, towered above the other soldiers come to join him. Cyrus stared into the man's silver eyes and promised vengeance, even if it meant coming back as a spirit. Not even the grave would deny him his due.

"Cyrus?" Magus asked him. The necklace at his throat shimmered with pale blue light. "Prince Cyrus Lythan?"

Cyrus sucked in a shallow breath as the gauntlet loosened.

"I am," he said. "Now do it, bastard. I'm not scared."

One of the soldiers beside Magus asked a question in his foreign tongue. Magus thought for a moment and then shook his head. He tossed Cyrus to the stone, dropping him beside the bodies. Cyrus tried not to look. He tried to not let the blood and bone and spilled innards of his beloved parents sear into his memory for the rest of his life, however long or short it might be. He failed.

"Lock him in his room," Magus said. "We have much to do to prepare this wretched island, and too few years to do it. And one thing I've learned is that when it comes to keeping a populace in line, well..."

His giant boot settled atop Cyrus's chest, grinding him into the stone, smearing him upon the blood of his slain parents.

"It never hurts to have a hostage."

if you enjoyed
THE WIZARD OF EVENTIDE

look out for

ENGINES OF EMPIRE
Book One of The Age of Uprising

by

R. S. Ford

The nation of Torwyn is run on the power of industry, and industry is run by the Guilds. Chief among them are the Hawkspurs, whose responsibility it is to keep the gears of the empire turning. That's exactly why matriarch Rosomon Hawkspur sends each of her heirs to the far reaches of the nation.

Conall, the eldest son, is sent to the distant frontier to earn his stripes in the military. It is here that he faces a threat he could never have seen coming: the first rumblings of revolution.

Tyreta's sorcerous connection to pyrestone, the magical resource that fuels the empire's machines, makes her a perfect heir—in theory. While Tyreta hopes that she might shirk her responsibilities during her journey to one of Torwyn's most important pyrestone mines, she instead finds the dark horrors of industry that the empire would prefer to keep hidden.

The youngest, Fulren, is a talented artificer and finds himself acting as a guide to a mysterious foreign emissary. Soon after, he is framed for a crime he never committed. A crime that could start a war.

As each of the Hawkspurs grapples with the many threats that face the nation from within and without, they must finally prove themselves worthy—or their empire will fall apart.

TYRETA

The journey from Wyke to the Anvil was over five hundred miles of undulating land. It would have taken longer than two weeks by wagon, with regular stops and changes of horse. Tyreta Hawkspur would complete the journey in less than three days.

From the viewing deck of the landship she could already see the rising minarets of the Anvil in the distance, growing ever larger as the open fields and rivers glided by. The vessel was elevated on rails, engines growling, the sound bellowing over the wind as it rushed into her face. It was an ingenious feat of engineering. The Hawkspur Guild had established a network of such lines across the length and breadth of Torwyn, on which the long trains of steel and iron snaked. Tyreta was heir to this legacy, one that had seen the Hawkspurs rise from simple couriers to one of the most powerful Guilds in the land. It should have made her proud. All she felt was bored.

"Try to look more enthused. Your uncle will have gone to a great deal of trouble to greet us. I'd rather you didn't look like you've just eaten a bag of lemons when we arrive."

There it was.

Tyreta's mother, Rosomon, stood at the rail beside her. A constant reminder of what Tyreta was to inherit. Of her responsibilities.

"Oh, there's a big smile on the inside, Mother," Tyreta replied. She said it under her breath, but as usual Lady Rosomon's hearing was almost preternatural.

"Well, when we arrive, see if you can conjure one on your face."

Her mother moved away, off to prepare herself to greet the emperor. It wouldn't do for Rosomon Hawkspur to look anything less than resplendent when she was met by her brother, the great Sullivar Archwind.

As she left, Tyreta contorted her face into a twisted semblance of a smile. It was a pointless act of defiance but at least one she could get away with—Rosomon's hearing might have been keen as a bat's, but she certainly didn't have eyes in the back of her head. As her mother left the viewing deck, Tyreta saw she'd not been quite as discreet as she'd anticipated.

Her elder brother Conall was watching her from across the deck, wearing a mocking grin. He was tall, handsome, sharp-witted, impeccably dressed in his blue uniform—all the things an heir to the Hawkspur Guild should be. Conall never put a foot wrong, in contrast to Tyreta's constant missteps. He was the future of their line and a captain in the Talon, the military arm of the Guild. All her life she'd been trying to live up to his example and failing miserably. He was the last person she would want to catch her acting like an infant. Well, if her mother and brother thought her so feckless, maybe she'd demonstrate just how talented she was.

Ignoring her brother's smugness, she moved from the deck and made her way below into the cloying confines of the metal carriage. If the sound was deafening on the viewing deck, it was much worse inside. The roar of the engines resonated throughout the length of the landship, the walls of the carriages trembling with the power of it. Tyreta could feel the energy coursing through the vessel, propelling it along the rails. For everyone else on board, she guessed it was just about bearable. For Tyreta it was a drug to the senses.

They were almost at their destination now, the Anvil no more than a few miles away. Surely this was the time to indulge? If her mother chided her, what was the difference? What was the worst that could happen?

Tyreta made her way forward through the carriages. Past the soldiers of the Talon, busy polishing their hawk helms and ceremonial blades, past the servants and staff, to the engine room, the head of the snake.

The steel door was shut, a wheel at its centre keeping the engine room locked away from the rest of the landship. Tyreta turned the wheel, hearing the clamps unlock, and swung open the door. She was greeted by the growl of the engine and the hum of the power core within, feeling it nourishing her, energising her.

When she entered, the drivers immediately stood to one side and bowed their heads. There were some advantages to being heir to a Guild.

The men were masked to protect them from the smoke and dust of the engine, but Tyreta ignored the cloying atmosphere as she approached the power core. She could feel its hum, a sweet lamenting tune sung only to her. Reaching out, she placed a hand on it, sensing the energy emanating from the pyrestones within—those precious crystals pulsating with life.

This was her gift. As a webwainer she could control the pyrestones, imbuing them with life, and at her touch they responded, glowing hotter, agitated by her presence. The drivers gave one another a worried look, though neither dared offer a word of complaint.

"Is this the fastest this crate can go?" Tyreta shouted above the din.

One of the drivers pulled down his mask. "It is, my lady. Any faster and we risk—"

"I think we can do better," she replied.

She pressed her palm to the core and closed her eyes. A smile crossed her lips as she felt the pyrestones respond to her will, the core growing hotter against her palm. The engine whined in protest as the stones urged the pistons and hydraulics to greater effort.

"My lady, this is against regulations," shouted one of the drivers, but Tyreta ignored him.

The landship began to accelerate. She opened her eyes, seeing through the viewing port that the landscape was beginning to shoot past at an alarming rate. Still she did not yield. Tyreta wanted more.

She pressed the core further, communing with it, talking to it in a silent whisper, urging it to greater and greater effort. This was what her webwainer gift was for, and for too long she had been forbidden to use it. What did her mother know anyway? Lady Rosomon had never experienced the privilege of the webwainer talent. This was Tyreta's right—and besides, what harm could she do?

The landship bucked, the wheels momentarily sliding on the rails. She glanced across the cab, seeing abject terror on the drivers' faces. Before she could release her hand, there was a yell behind her.

"Tyreta!"

She snatched her hand from the core as though she'd been bitten, turning to see her mother's furious face in the doorway. The train immediately slowed, the rattling and bucking relenting as the landship slowed to its former speed.

Lady Rosomon didn't have to say a word. Tyreta removed herself from the engine room, moving back through the carriages and past the chaos she'd caused. Baggage had fallen from the securing rigs, garments and trinkets were scattered about the floor. The Talon soldiers were picking themselves up from where they lay, their arms and armour strewn all about.

Tyreta reached her cabin and closed the door, resting her back against it and breathing heavily. There might be a price to pay for this later. Lady Rosomon had never been a tolerant woman. Whatever that price was, Tyreta thought as a smile played across her lips, it had been worth it.

The rest of the journey was mercifully short and without incident. Tyreta considered it best not to push her luck, and she dressed as one might expect of an heir to the Hawkspur Guild, her blue tunic displaying the winged-talon sigil on her chest. Despite the tailored fit, it still felt as if it were throttling her, but it would be best to endure it for now. At least until her mother had a chance to cool down. As the landship pulled to a stop, Tyreta couldn't keep herself locked away any longer.

Lady Rosomon was waiting for her when she debarked. On her right stood the imposing figure of Starn Rivers, swordwright to the Hawkspur Guild. He was a bull of a man, thick moustache drooping down past his chin. Tyreta had never liked him or the looks he occasionally gave her, and the fact that he barely spoke was a small mercy.

While their cortege was busy unloading the landship and Conall joked with his cronies from the Talon, Rosomon led the group up through the terminal. Once out beyond the great arched entrance, Tyreta could see the city proper.

The Anvil was a testament to the power of the Guilds. Soaring towers clamoured for space, linked by raised walkways. Everything stank of opulence, and even the lowliest of the citizenry were adorned in fine silk and velvet. A thunderous rattle peeled down from overhead as a skycarriage rumbled by on its elevated tracks. Tyreta marvelled at the perfect union of artifice and architecture, conveying people from one side of the city to the other with such automotive efficiency.

It was a short walk to the main promenade, at the end of which stood the magnificent Archwind Palace. The way was lined with statues that crossed the Bridge of Saints, prominent members of the Guilds from the annals of history given pride of place along the Anvil's main thoroughfare. Between those icons stood an honour guard of giant stormhulks, pistons hissing as their vast mechanical frames suddenly stood to attention. Each was piloted by a webwainer—someone who could manipulate pyrestone and instil life in the huge engines. For a moment Tyreta felt a pang of envy—what a privilege to control an invention of such power—but her focus was quickly taken by the palace, rising up in the midst of the city like a vast mountain.

As they crossed the bridge, Tyreta saw that a reception party was already awaiting them. She could make out Sullivar standing front and centre, his red uniform of office pristine, breastplate of brass shining in the sun. Her uncle had recently proclaimed himself emperor of Torwyn—an affectation Tyreta found a little ridiculous. Sullivar might look the part, but it was widely known he fell far short of being the great ruler her grandfather Treon had been.

431

Before they reached the foot of the vast stairway that led up to the palace, Tyreta caught up with her mother.

"Just wanted to say—" she began.

"Not now," Rosomon snapped.

"But I thought I'd—"

Her mother cut her off with a glance, and Tyreta thought it best not to push it, moving back and letting Lady Rosomon lead the way once more. Maybe it would be wise to let her calm down a little more before trying for an apology again.

When they'd almost reached the stairs, Sullivar could hold himself back no longer. He walked down the last few steps, hugging Rosomon to him in a bearlike embrace.

"It's been too long," he said to her.

"Indeed it has," she replied, smiling through the indignity.

"And you brought my niece and nephew," he said, opening his arms to hug Tyreta.

She embraced her uncle, feeling his perfumed beard soft against her cheek. Sullivar squeezed her a little too tightly, crushing her against the cog sigil embossed on his breastplate, but there was little she could do to stop it. Once he'd released her, Conall reached forward to shake Sullivar's hand, but he too was met with a bear hug.

"Lady Oriel," Rosomon said, bowing before Sullivar's wife, who had come to join them. "Or should that be Empress?"

"Nonsense," Oriel replied, taking Rosomon's hand and leading her up the stairs. "We are family. No need for such affectations between us."

They might have been sisters by marriage, but the difference between them was stark. Where Oriel was dazzling in a gown of red and gold, her hair tied up in an intricate bunch fastened with elaborate pins, Rosomon wore a skirt and cloak of plain blue, brown hair falling straight and unadorned about her shoulders.

Tyreta followed them up to the palace, passing the heavily armoured Titanguard who lined their route. Each one was a behemoth, glaive in hand, bulky armour powered by ingenious artifice. She noticed there was no sign of Lancelin Jagdor, swordwright of the Archwind Guild, but then it was best if that man didn't show his face in front of the Hawkspurs. But Lancelin wasn't the only one conspicuous by his absence.

"Where's Fulren?" Tyreta asked.

"Your younger brother wanted to come and greet you," said Sullivar. "But he is busying himself in his workshop. He has almost made a breakthrough with his studies, so I am told."

"He always was dedicated," said Rosomon, glancing momentarily at her daughter.

Tyreta bristled at the insinuation. Her younger brother couldn't even be bothered to come greet them, yet still he was lauded. Once again she was reminded who the favourites were.

"He's been a great asset," said Sullivar. "His skills have improved beyond measure. You should go see him at work, Tyreta," he added.

She was about to protest, but a look from her mother made her realise she should probably do as she was bid. Best not to push things too far, considering she had still to face her punishment for toying with the landship.

As Rosomon and Conall were led away through the palace by Sullivar and Oriel, Tyreta was taken by a sullen-looking footman down into the bowels of the huge building. Here were foundries by the dozen, smelting works, rows of benches upon which artificers worked on minuscule inventions. The farther down she got the more the place stank of industry—oil and rust permeated the air, the heat of the forges making the atmosphere sticky. Tyreta felt the essence of the pyrestones that lay all about, making her tingle right to her fingertips.

The footman led her to the lowest level. A door stood ajar at the end of the corridor, and the servant stopped, beckoning Tyreta inside. She pushed the door open to see a small workshop. It was in disarray, spare parts of machinery lying all about, and in the centre of the room, hunched over a workbench, was her brother Fulren.

"Hello, Tinhead," she said to his back.

"Hello, Ratface," he replied, without turning around.

She walked toward him, picking up some piece of artifice from a bench. It looked intricate, wires and pins protruding from every surface. Tyreta had no idea what it was for.

"Too busy playing with your toys to greet our beloved mother?"

"I've been busy," he said. "I'm sure she'll forgive me."

"For you, Lady Rosomon would forgive anything."

Fulren turned to face her. On his head was strapped a contraption that supported a lens over one eye to magnify his work. He would have looked every inch the artificer—studious, serious—were it not for the fact that he was broad about the shoulders and lean about the waist. A fighter in body, inventor in mind. The perfect combination of skill and intelligence. She couldn't help but resent him for that.

"I'm sure she's forgiven you plenty," he said. "How was the journey?"

"Let's just say it could have gone more smoothly."

Fulren flashed her a toothy grin. "Just can't stay out of trouble, can you, Ratface? You're supposed to be the responsible one."

"I'm older than you. That's pretty much where my responsibility ends."

"Not for long," said Fulren.

And he was right. Though Conall was to inherit their Guild's title and obligations, Rosomon had demanded that

Tyreta also take on the responsibilities of the Hawkspur Guild. Conall would see to military matters, and Tyreta would be in charge of transportation all across Torwyn—by air, land and sea. She would administer trade routes and supply chains and keep her nation moving. It was a daunting prospect, and one she would gladly delay for as long as possible.

"No," Tyreta said. "It won't be long. I'm to travel to the Sundered Isles after the reception. Mother thinks it will build character."

"So soon?" Fulren seemed genuinely concerned. "I won't see much of you, then."

"You'd see more if you came with me. We could do this together. You could take up Father's mantle yourself. You could—"

"We've been over this a thousand times. My place is here." He gestured to the junk that lay strewn all around him. "Uncle Sullivar has granted me an apprenticeship. I am to become a master artificer. It's all been settled."

"So I'm doomed then?"

Fulren laughed at that. "You'll just have to live up to your responsibilities for once. Who knows, maybe you'll like it. You'll get to see the world."

The prospect of that did excite her, but thinking on the burden of controlling an entire Guild only filled her with dread.

"What about you?" she asked. "Are you going to live out your days cooped up in here, playing with your toys?"

"Who knows? Maybe I'll get to see the world too, one day."

Tyreta glanced around the windowless workshop, then shook her head. "Not you. You'll never leave this place."

"Thanks for the vote of confidence." He winked at her. "Anyway, get lost, I'm busy." With that he turned back to his machinery.

"See you at the reception, Tinhead," she replied before she left him to his labour.

The footman was still waiting for her outside, and Tyreta asked to be taken to her chamber. It had been a long journey, even for her.

Obediently the servant led her back up through the vast workshops until they reached ground level. There they took the elevator, steam pumping and gears grinding until it had juddered all the way to the upper levels of the palace. As she followed the open walkway toward her chamber she could see out onto the vast city. Huge stormhulks walked the streets, but they looked tiny from the heady heights of Archwind Palace. Not even the highest spires of Wyke could rival this place for majesty.

When finally she opened the door to her chamber, Tyreta was brought back to earth with a crash. Her mother was waiting patiently inside, her back to the door as she gazed from the window.

Tyreta closed the door, shutting herself in, bracing for what was coming.

"Mother, I—"

"We won't speak of it," Rosomon said.

That was unexpected. Tyreta had prepared herself for a tirade followed by yet another lecture on responsibility and duty to the Guild.

Rosomon turned from the window. Her hands were clasped in front of her, face a mask of calm. She was far from the raging harpy that usually manifested after one of Tyreta's frequent misdemeanours.

"Your first public engagement is coming." She gestured to the bed, where lay a dress in the deep blue of the Hawkspur Guild. "You'll wear that. You'll fix that." Rosomon pointed at

Tyreta's hair, which, as usual, was worn up in a messy knot on top of her head. "And you'll do your best to act in a manner befitting an heir to the Guild of Hawkspur."

Tyreta wasn't sure what was worse—her mother's raging or her clinical orders.

"Of course," she replied. This was no time for defiance.

"And, if you wish, you can wear this."

Rosomon opened up her hand. In her palm was a silver pendant inlaid with a single gem. Tyreta recognised the nightstone immediately. It was the rarest of pyrestones, one that was useless for artifice but valued for its beauty nonetheless.

"Mother, I don't deserve—"

"No, you don't," said Rosomon. "But it was your father's and you should have it."

She took the pendant from her mother's hand. Tyreta had never been one for jewels or trinkets, but the fact that it had been her father's made it more precious than anything she had ever owned. She was about to thank her mother, to tell her she would do better from now on and live up to her father's legacy, but Lady Rosomon was already on her way through the door.

"And don't be late," Rosomon said before closing the door behind her and leaving Tyreta alone.

She held the pendant in her hand for a moment, feeling the nightstone cold against her palm. It could not be imbued with any power, could not be used for any practical purpose, and yet she suddenly felt more connected to it than she had to any pyrestone. She would wear it with pride.

Glancing down at the gaudy blue dress, she realised there was other attire she would just have to get used to.